LORDS
OF
UNCREATION

BY ADRIAN TCHAIKOVSKY

LORDS
OF
UNCREATION

The Final Architecture: Book Three

ADRIAN
TCHAIKOVSKY

orbitbooks.net

Copyright © 2023 by Adrian Czajkowski

Cover design by Steve Stone

Hachette Book Group supports the right to free expression and the value of copyright. The purpose of copyright is to encourage writers and artists to produce the creative works that enrich our culture.

The scanning, uploading, and distribution of this book without permission is a theft of the author's intellectual property. If you would like permission to use material from the book (other than for review purposes), please contact permissions@hbgusa.com. Thank you for your support of the author's rights.

Orbit
Hachette Book Group
1290 Avenue of the Americas
New York, NY 10104
orbitbooks.net

First Edition: May 2023
Simultaneously published in Great Britain by Tor, an imprint of Pan Macmillan

Orbit is an imprint of Hachette Book Group.
The Orbit name and logo are trademarks of Little, Brown Book Group Limited.

The publisher is not responsible for websites (or their content) that are not owned by the publisher.

The Hachette Speakers Bureau provides a wide range of authors for speaking events. To find out more, go to hachettespeakersbureau.com or email HachetteSpeakers@hbgusa.com.

Orbit books may be purchased in bulk for business, educational, or promotional use. For information, please contact your local bookseller or the Hachette Book Group Special Markets Department at special.markets@hbgusa.com.

Library of Congress Control Number: 2022950530

ISBNs: 9780316705929 (hardcover), 9780316705950 (ebook)

Printed in the United States of America

LSC-C

Printing 1, 2023

To John Catling

CONTENTS

THE STORY SO FAR

Key concepts

Unspace: the underlying nothing beneath the universe. Gravitic drives allow ships to enter and travel through unspace, crossing light years of real space in moments. Most journeys are taken along Throughway routes between stars.

The Architects: moon-sized entities that come from unspace to rework inhabited planets into bizarre sculptures. One of their number visited Earth, which began seventy years of fight and flight, a war costing billions of lives. Only contact between the engineered human Intermediaries and the Architects ended the conflict. Now, fifty years later, the Architects have returned.

Originators: on some planets, the ruins of an elder civilization of Originators can be found, still entirely mysterious. Previously Architects appeared to avoid any trace of this ancient culture. More recently they have taken to painstakingly removing such traces from ships and planets they plan to rework.

The Hegemony: an alien empire controlled by the inscrutable Essiel, who have sole access to the technology that allows

Originator artefacts to be moved. They promise their subjects eternal protection from the Architects. However, the newly returned Architects no longer seem to be as in awe of the artefacts as they once were.

Humanity's factions

Following the explosive expansion of refugee humanity in the "Polyaspora," humanity now exists across numerous colonies, from the comfortable settled worlds to the vast numbers of spacers who still live precarious lives between planets. Trade and travel within the Colonial Sphere is greatly helped by the Intermediaries, who are among the few able to navigate unspace without using the Throughways. The Colonies are governed by the Council of Human Interests, familiarly known as Hugh, from the world of Berlenhof.

Humanity stood alongside many others during the first war against the Architects, but its closest allies came from within. These included the Hivers, who are a composite cyborg intelligence, built as tools but now independent. Dr. Parsefer's Parthenon, an artificially created society of women, also formed the front line in the war.

Following the secession of both Hivers and Parthenon, hostile Colonial factions have arisen, including the humanity-first Nativists and the Betrayed, who believe in a conspiracy that has denied humans their pre-eminence in the universe. Various groups within Hugh encourage and draw support from these growing factions, including the dictatorial noble houses of the Magda, one of the Colonies' most influential worlds.

Key characters

The *Vulture God*: a salvage ship. Its crew includes drone specialist **Olli**, lawyer and duellist **Kris**, trade factor **Kittering** and **Idris Telemmier**. Idris is one of the last of the original Intermediaries, who wanted nothing more than to live out his days in peace until an old friend from the war, the Partheni **Solace**, came looking to recruit him for her government.

Havaer Mundy: an agent of Hugh who has variously pursued and associated with the crew of the *Vulture God* as they became entwined with the return of the Architects.

Delegate Trine: a Hiver archaeologist, an old friend of Idris and Solace from the war and an authority on what little is known about the Originators.

Ravin and Piter Uskaro: Magdan nobles linked to Hugh's more xenophobic elements, part of a powerful clique seeking to preserve a hand-picked selection of humanity on ark ships.

The Unspeakable Aklu, the Razor and the Hook: an Essiel gangster from the Hegemony, by turns an enemy and a dubious ally of the *Vulture God* crew. Seems to feel a kinship with Olli, as someone who has not given in to their physical limitations.

The research team at the **Eye**, a rogue scientific venture, led by **Ahab**, an obsessive Naeromathi. Other members include the human **Doctor Shinandri** and the cyborg engineer **Tokamak Jaine**. They work alongside the **Harbinger Ash**, the alien that originally warned Earth about the Architects over a century ago.

Recent events

The return of the Architects has blazed a trail of reworked planets across human space. And beyond. Even the Hegemony has not proven immune to their attentions.

Idris Telemmier's defection to the Parthenon inflamed hostilities between the shipboard warrior women and "Hugh," the Council for Human Interests governing humanity's colonies. Thanks to his assistance, the Parthenon has now been able to develop an early class of Intermediaries of its own, simultaneously a weapon against the Architects and a potential threat to Hugh.

A faction within Hugh, led by the Uskaro family, launched an attack against the Parthenon, seeking to annihilate them in a costly war while safeguarding the fleet of ark ships they had been building, and on which they planned to preserve their own pick of humanity. However, this conspiracy was exposed by Havaer Mundy, working for the disgraced spymaster Chief Laery.

Laery is now spearheading the Cartel, working with the Hiver Assembly in Aggregate, the Hegemonic criminal Aklu and the enigmatic alien Ash the Harbinger in a cross-species coalition. They have recently stepped in to take control of this ark fleet, and to strongarm peace and cooperation between Hugh and the Parthenon, unifying their attempts to defend against the common enemy of the Architects—and, if possible, to strike back against them.

Hopes of bringing the fight to the Architects have been kindled by Idris's experiments with a functioning Originator facility known as the Eye. A maverick research team, led by the Naeromathi Ahab, have been using this installation to track down the origin of the Architects within unspace. With the assistance of Idris, they have discovered what appears to be the Architect nursery and believe that an attack into unspace is possible to end the threat. Idris, however, is sure the Architects are merely the slaves of some other unknown power within unspace, pawns forced to attack worlds against their will. Now the Eye has been brought under the protection of Laery and the others, Idris finds himself at odds with their mission. While trying to protect the very entities that humanity views as the greatest enemy in the universe, he is instead set on locating the true enemy within unspace.

PART 1
ESTOC

1.

Andecka

Andecka Tal Mar: Intermediary in a three-crew ship named the *Skipjack*, currently operating with only two because every resource was stretched right now, especially the human kind. At her back sat the world of Assur. A unique ecosystem; agricultural, scientific and mineral prospects. A population of seventy million, mostly humans but a fair number of Castigar and Hanni as well. And every vessel that could get into orbit currently lifting away as many of them as possible. Just like in the old war historiotypes. Because the old war was back.

In front of her, at a distance of several hundred million kilometres, not even visible to the naked eye, the Architect. It was eating up that distance at a steady pace and Andecka's pilot, Staven, had plotted the elegant curve of its course. This would bring it in to intercept Assur's orbit with pinpoint accuracy, slinging it around the world, and then...

Unmake it. Remake it. Turn the living world into dead art.

Estimates gleaned from Assur's kybernet were that around sixty-seven million people would still be planetside when that happened, best-case scenario.

"Any word on our backup?" Andecka's scars were itching. The ones that ranged like lightning over her scalp, from the surgery. There had only ever been one Intermediary born naturally, and that was Saint Xavienne, who'd been killed right next to Andecka defending Berlenhof. Back then, they'd been in a hell of a bigger ship than the *Skipjack*, a full-on Partheni battle cruiser and it hadn't helped a damn.

Staven just grunted, and when she asked the question again he snapped, "If we'd *had* it, then don't you *think* I'd have *told* you?" in that sarcastic tone he used when he was frightened almost to death.

The help hadn't come. Which was a problem when your whole plan of attack was based on there being someone to play off.

"We'll improvise," Andecka said.

"We're *dead*," Staven decided, though he wasn't turning the *Skipjack* around.

The kybernet's cheery casualty estimate was based on someone actually buying time for the evacuation to happen, and that *someone* apparently meant Andecka Tal Mar. Back in the old war, it had been fleets of warships, drones, every damn thing that was more useful as a momentary distraction than a refugee transport. At least this had changed for the better. Now it meant Intermediaries like Andecka. Because, of all the universe, she could try and talk to the Architect. Contact that vast and alien mind to shriek out, *We're here*, like in that old kids' mediotype story. To give it a moment's pause.

Perhaps even more…except with her one feeble voice she didn't see that happening. Instead, it would get tired of her, and then turn her and Staven and the *Skipjack* into an interesting filigree of molecules, before going on to do the same to the planet.

"Wait, something *big* came through." Staven's voice was briefly on fire with hope, then dropped. "Not them. It's not them."

Andecka fought over her instruments, even as Assur receded behind them. Staven had put them on their intercept course, ready to go shout their infinitesimal complaints in the Architect's crystal ear. "Then who...?" The worst-case scenario was *another Architect*, which had happened a couple of times. Apparently there were some planets the monsters wanted extra-dead. Whatever chance Andecka had against *one*, she wouldn't even be a speedbump for two.

"Transport. Sod me." Staven sounded as if he was having a heart attack already, hyperventilating around the words. "Transport. Castigar."

She dragged the data over to her own screen. Not what she should be focusing on right now but she had to know. "Damn, that's big," she admitted. Not Architect sized, certainly, but she hadn't realized the Castigar were just throwing mega-freighters like that around. She was still linked to the Assur kybernet and hopped into the conversation there, getting a full-on view of the tentacle-fringed mouth that was a Castigar head, each writhing tendril capped with a pearl-like eye and a claw.

"They're saying..." Andecka blinked. "They can take two and a half million people. How can they fit...?"

Staven passed over the ship's specs. She really hadn't appreciated *how* big the freighter was. She'd lived in smaller cities. The human Colonies relied a lot on small transports, a relic of the days when every cubic metre of hold space had been needed to shift a rapidly disintegrating civilization. The Castigar, however, believed in bulk shipping between their worlds, and here was one of their largest vessels, over a human world perhaps for the first time. And it was coming in at the sort of pace that made Andecka hope Castigar gravitic braking was superior to human tech, or else the Architect might not get the chance to rework the planet after all.

The kybernet started hailing them. Because the space to get an extra two and a half million people off-planet was no use unless you had the time to embark them.

"Tell them we'll do what we can, of course," Andecka said. *Where the hell is our backup?* She then took the helm of the ship, just because the illusion of control helped with her own mental prep. Arrowing in towards that distant pinprick of reflected light she could now make out. A monster the size of a moon, and inside it, a mind. Her target.

"Makes you wonder, though," Staven said, breaking into her careful concentration.

"What, Staven? What makes me wonder?"

"I saw the 'type footage from that Hegemony place. Where the Architect got attacked. Two more just jumped in, practically straight into *orbit*. I mean, they can do that. So why all this long *lead*-in?"

"I don't know. Maybe they need some quiet time to *think*?" Andecka hissed at him, but her mindset was well and truly shot now. Because he was right. There was a weird politeness to the way Architects approached their murderous business. They plainly *could* just emerge from unspace right in a planet's gravity well. Even if it was difficult or costly, that was a capability they had. No reason for this slow advance, to give people all this time to get offworld. It was as if they were savouring the terror of their victims, the anticipation of the end. *Or as if they're giving us every chance to escape.*

It was safe to say people's opinions were divided over what the Architects actually wanted. The majority said they were genocidal monsters, and a fair few of a more scientific bent just said they were unknowable and didn't care about people. Then there were the people who actually *knew* because they'd touched the minds of the entities. People like Andecka. People like her semi-mentor, Idris Telemmier, the oldest living Intermediary. The man who'd gone further than anyone, and right now was going further still.

They were slaves, he'd said. Most people—even within the current joint Intermediary effort at the Eye—didn't quite believe him. Andecka did, though. There wasn't much Andecka wouldn't believe, if Idris Telemmier said it. It was a hero worship he was profoundly uncomfortable with, but she'd seen him at work close-up in all his wretched glory. He was the human candle that somehow burned twice as brightly, but never burned out. And burning hurt, she knew that. She'd felt the heat of it, but she reckoned Idris was on fire all the time.

It was at least partly through Idris that she'd been scrambled out here to Assur, arriving *before* the other Intermediary, in time to tell the kybernet to begin its evacuation. That was something else they'd never had in the first war. An early-warning system.

Now if we only had the Hegemony's magic tech that lets them just teleport everyone off a planet. Apparently that was a thing, except the Essiel Hegemony wouldn't even admit to its existence, let alone share it.

Ahead, the Architect was a bright spot the size of a thumbnail now. If she squinted she could make out some detail on the jagged face it presented towards Assur and the system's star.

There's something at home in there, she told herself. *I can reach it*. Without going mad. Without suffering fatal biological feedback. She could slip her Intermediary consciousness into the vast labyrinth of the Architect's inner world until she reached that focal point, where a modified human and an inconceivable giant could sit and talk. Almost. She'd never done it unassisted before. *First time for everything*.

"You'll need to keep us steady." Speaking too fast and jittery. "Keep us wide of whatever it throws—"

"I *know*, I *know*." Staven's voice cattier than ever in his terror.

She focused in towards the reflected light of the Architect, already feeling her mind unpacking, extending into the nameless direction that would bring her into contact with the utterly *alien*.

Feeling the fear reach up from her guts to claw at her mind, and not knowing in that moment whether to fight or embrace it. Neither seemed much use. They were human-level responses and she was going after a profoundly inhuman thing.

And then:

"Contact!" from Staven, as though he was the Intermediary, not her. His next words came out in a confused babble and she had to separate them out in retrospect. "It's them. Thank God. Thank *fuck*. It's them!"

Her own instruments were already dominated by sensor bounce-back from the Architect, but she registered another ship in-system, erupting from unspace between Assur and the Architect. Not another gift from the Castigar. A warship, and a big one.

"How come," Staven complained, "we get this tin can and they get *that?*"

"*Skipjack*, this is the *Gran Brigitte*," came a voice over comms, speaking in clipped Colvul with a Partheni accent. "Situation report."

"You had better have a goddamn *Int* with you," Andecka snapped at them, protocols and rank be damned.

A strained pause, which served to emphasize just how many *Skipjacks* would fit inside the *Gran Brigitte*'s shadow, and then, "*Skipjack*, Cognosciente Intermediary Grave speaking. Is that Andecka I hear?"

"God and his prophet save and protect us, yes it is," Andecka said. Way back before volunteering, she'd been brought up by religious types, and some of that tended to come back when she was under stress. As well as a stab of envy, to be sure. Not only because Grave got a personal war cruiser to gad about in, but also because Andecka's Partheni counterpart didn't have the same lattice of scars and internal trauma to go with her Intermediary abilities. *They cheat*, was the uncharitable assessment of most Colonial Ints, but right now Andecka reckoned help from a cheater was better than no help at all.

She had worked "combined operations" like this three times before. She knew the drill. In the end it didn't actually matter how big a ship, or how many weapons, the Parthenon had brought. The war wasn't being fought with guns, after all. It was Andecka's mind and Cognosciente Grave's mind, and the Architect's mind.

Staven flung the *Skipjack* into a looping course, buying

time without losing speed as the *Gran Brigitte* caught up with them, then matched their pace and trajectory with the larger ship. The Architect had grown from a thumbnail, to a hand, to what it was: a moon-sized monster that screamed out at all Andecka's Intermediary senses. Displacing far more mass than its vast proportions could account for, casting a huge shadow in unspace. Death; destroyer of worlds. Except it wasn't even something as comprehensible as that. Remaker, artist, artisan. The planets they left behind moulded into exacting sculpture. Not all the Intermediary contact in the universe could account for it. If the Architects did what they did because their masters compelled them to, nobody knew why the masters directed it. Why they would want every inhabited planet in the entire universe to become their gallery of twisted exhibits, one by one.

"How much closer?" Staven breathed. The jagged crystal mountain range that was the forward face of the Architect now filled their screens.

Andecka passed the decision tree she'd prepared over to Grave. Within moments the Partheni had modified it, then thrown it back to her again. In the seconds of their approach, this plan went back and forth between them a half-dozen times. It was a procedure hammered out between Ints in the first few combined ops encounters. Because most of the time it took more than one mind to triumph over an Architect. Unless you were lucky, or you were Idris Telemmier.

The last tree Grave sent over was close enough to something Andecka could work with. *Agreed*, she sent back. Every Intermediary was different, and every one had a play they could make and one they couldn't. It was all about fitting the circles together and seeing where the overlap came up.

There'd been lots of talk back at base about training dedicated pairs of Ints who knew how to work together, and probably that'd happen sooner or later. But right now there was too much universe, and too few Ints. So the Colonial Liaison Board had come up with the trees—a mutable plan of attack that each thrown-together pair could customize to fit their strengths.

And then the Architect was there. Not *physically* because that had been a fact for a while. There in her head, almost reaching forwards to meet her, as though it was just as much a part of the game as they were.

Andecka made a sound and felt the pain distantly as she slammed back in her seat, neck whiplashed, joints twisted, tongue bitten. The faintest echo of Staven's cry of concern came through. And then the vast convoluted city of the Architect's mind enveloped her. Its maze of spaces and narrows merely what her Int mind showed her in place of the true alien complexity of it. She remembered her first time, when she'd stood with Telemmier and tried this. He'd almost died, and the others with them really had. She was going somewhere the human mind was not fit for, just as she could never have endured the vacuum of space. And the mind took it out on the body. Her heart, her brain, each part of her, twisting and rupturing to try and escape where she was leading them. All the while she continued to hunt that spark, the soul within the cenotaph which was where she and the Architect could touch.

And she wasn't alone.

The tree was intact. She could feel Grave out there too, making choice after choice, following the plan. As though they were a left and right hand which just about knew what each other was doing. Complementing each other, even though their tickets to this mind-destroying show had come by very different means. They'd carved up Andecka's brain, shot her full of chemicals, implanted cybernetics and killed a hundred of her fellow subjects just to make her what she was. Grave was one of the new class, emerging from the Parthenon without the scars, just a genetic predisposition and a vast hanging garden of tech. For a moment the sheer *envy* Andecka felt almost tore the bond between them apart, but she mastered herself again. *Be bitter on your own time.*

They were closing. Nobody could understand an Architect mind, not truly, but repeated contact and Hiver data analysis had shown common patterns and pathways. Techniques and mental gymnastics that brought the fragile human mind closer and closer to unravelling it, and which informed the nodes and branches of the decision tree they were following. As though they were fencers or game players moving through one particular standard set of openings and responses. The trees worked so well they actually *had* made a game of it. Something the Ints could practise when there weren't Architects around. Andecka had even heard civilians were playing it now, pretending they understood what it was like.

Try playing it during brain surgery in a hurricane, she thought uncharitably.

The Architect was becoming aware of her, trying to shut her out. She wanted Grave to know, and in that instant Grave adjusted her own approach, coming closer to support. Andecka's mind's eye showed her vast white stone slabs crashing down on all sides, entombing her. The temptation was to grow, to match strength for strength, hold the doors open, beat them down. But you could never win doing that.

Whatever strength you had as an Int, be you Idris Telemmier or Saint Xavienne herself, you'd never be stronger than an Architect. So, be swifter, be smaller. Play off your human advantages and make yourself insignificant. A dust mote. A bad dream. She slipped under, between and through the atoms of the Architect's gates, Grave drawn with her, hunting, hunting...

She'd done this before. Four times she'd succeeded at reaching the seat of an Architect's cognition. And twice before she'd failed and a world had died because of it. That was a better hit rate than most.

She had a clearer sense of Grave now, the Partheni woman off in her fancy big ship with all her gleaming new tech. Except the woman herself wasn't shiny or even complete. Wounded, hurting. She had scars too; they were just on the inside. And as they homed in on the Architect, they grew closer, more inside each other, converging as a single blade, prising at the hairline cracks and joins of the Architect's inner mind until—

It had them. They had it. Fingertip touching fingertip. Save that their side of this exchange was all they ever were, and the Architect's was just the least iota of its being. But it was enough.

Why? they asked, and *Please*, they said, then summoned forth the millions on-planet. The people, the biosphere, the life. The sheer irreplaceable variety of forms and species unique to Assur. The individual dreams of its people, the vast majority of whom could never be evacuated in time. All that would be lost.

The Architect—vast, inhuman, twisted—shook them and assaulted their minds with its very being. Not even trying to obliterate them, because if it so much as had an idle thought in that direction they would be dust, atoms, mindless husks in their respective ships. But it wasn't trying, not yet. It might. Sometimes they did. But the Architects were a lot like ancient conceptions of God. Too vast for comprehension, and yet they could note the fall of a sparrow. They were powerful enough to appreciate the universe at every level all the way down to the atomic. And that included, somewhere along the chain, the human.

Andecka and Grave were not warriors, in that moment. They were petitioners. All they had was begging. Their only weapon was empathy. While extreme military resistance had, on two known occasions, resulted in an Architect's physical destruction, empathy had saved more worlds by far.

Its response tore through Andecka, and she had a ghost-sense of her body jerking and flailing in its restraints as Staven administered medical support to keep her heart regular and her blood flowing.

Don't make me, the Architect was saying. The sense came through, no matter how alien the originating intelligence. She didn't know if it, in turn, was begging them, or begging its masters.

Grave set in motion a new assault, regurgitating the information the Assur kybernet had been feeding them. The children's pictures and the demographic information, the plans for new homes and families, the half-created mediotypes, the ecological studies. The weaponized zeitgeist of a world.

It pushed back. Desperation bled through, and she didn't know if it was hers or Grave's or the Architect's. Until it grew and grew and she knew no mere human mind could contain such grief and loss.

It's going to do it anyway, she thought, sensing Grave's kindred conclusion. They had laid out all they had at its feet, and it was very, very sorry for their loss. Thoughts and prayers from the godlike destroyer for the worlds it crushed beneath its crystal feet.

Then.

A moment of brutal disconnection. She was screaming, but that was something her body was doing. For a lost second, her mind was caught between unspace and the real, trapped on the boundary, in imminent danger of ceasing to exist. Grave had her, though. Grave was her beacon, her lifeline, her anchor. She climbed hand over hand up Grave's focus on her, until she was Andecka Tal Mar once more and fully in existence, praying thanks to a god she didn't really believe in. And the Architect...

Was gone. Submerged back into the unspace which had birthed it. Leaving only a bitter understanding. *Pain. Loss. Price.* The nameless things its masters would exact from it, somehow. However that worked. Nobody knew.

She came back into her body amidst a symphony of medical alarms, and it felt like returning home. The awareness she had of Cognosciente Grave faded, dwindling until the woman was no more than a voice on the comms, who had a moment before been somewhere between a sister and a self.

The Assur kybernet—and quite a lot of the rest of the planet—was trying to talk to them. They probably wanted to say thank you, but Andecka was recovering from a serial cardiac arrest right then, with only the ship's medical suite keeping her going, and she wasn't really in the mood for well-wishers.

"What now?" she asked Staven. There would have been a packet ship stop at Assur recently, dropping off the next batch of finger-in-the-air predictions from Foresight at the Eye: the early-warning system they'd never had in the first war, and that had saved so many worlds in this one. But still failed to save so many others. There was sure to be another assignment for her, and precious little time to get there. Andecka knew she wasn't dead enough to be taken out of active rotation yet.

"Good work," she sent to the *Gran Brigitte*. "For a Patho." The jab was practically *de rigueur*.

"Likewise, refugenik," came Grave's instant response. And then, before the *Brigitte*'s commander could clamp down on comms, "But really, sister. A pleasure."

"Three unclaimed," Staven reported. Meaning worlds that were under imminent death sentence and no other Int had flagged as covering them yet. Maybe there would already be someone by the time they arrived, and they'd be able to move on. Or maybe they'd be truly alone for the next encounter, and most likely doomed. They never knew, what with the intermittent nature of communications between stars. "Are you ready for unspace? How much time do you need?"

Unspace. Where the Architects came from. The unreal void beneath the real. Staven could go into suspension for the trip, but Andecka would have to stay awake to pilot them. Awake, but not alone. The other joy of being an Int, above and beyond shredding your mind against the jagged face of the Architects.

"Pick one," she told him. "Let's go."

2.

Kris

Keristina Soolin Almier, lawyer. It might be the end of planetside human civilization but people still needed lawyers. And yes, she'd thrown her lot in with a radical melange of factions who were just about holding the Colonies and the Parthenon hostage, but that just meant the lawyering intensified. It was the great truth of law that the more savage things got, the more you needed a lawyer to dig you out. Right now, with everything crashing down and being rebuilt around her, she was actually doing work far closer to her original skillset than in the previous ten years. Travelling as Idris Telemmier's guardian angel had been civil rights work, and she was rated for that, but she'd trained first with contracts. And contracts were the connective tissue that held the universe together as far as a lawyer was concerned. It wasn't as if the Eye actually had a superfluity of legally trained personnel either. Or, if it did, most of them were part of the Hiver Assembly in Aggregate. The human Colonial parts of the joint venture needed every legal mind they could get right now, and so she had as much work as she wanted.

She and the rest of the legal team had just been on

Berlenhof, wrangling with Hugh and a couple of Hannilambra factors about resources, shipping and supply. Because the Eye was an intensive venture, greedy for power, material and personnel. Nobody liked it, but everyone knew they needed it. For now. Or Kris certainly hoped they did.

Right now, though, having woken from unspace and with news of their success already being sent ahead of them, she was looking forward to time with friends, and not having to wrangle legal arguments in her head for at least a couple of days. She was owed that, she reckoned.

"What the hell am I looking at?" asked one of the others, a fellow Scintilla graduate named Maxin Dreidel. He was new to the venture, taken on for his understanding of Berlenhof jurisprudence. This was his first time off-planet, as far as she could tell, which meant that Estoc was a particularly unfair place to bring him.

It was an isolated system, with only one unspace Throughway discovered going to it. Its original masters, still very present, somewhat resentful but playing along for now, had chosen it for that reason, and one other. There was a sullen clenched fist of a star, shuddering with internal collapse and emitting staggered gravitational waves that racked its one dead ember of a planet. It was in geostationary orbit around this world that the ark-yards had been built, with a vast array of harvesters ready to catch all that free gravitational energy and store it for later use.

That was enough to open any groundbound eye, but as their ship neared—it was a robust old passenger shuttle more than adequate for lawyer transport—the ark-yards themselves demanded everyone's attention. Kris still remembered the first time she'd come here. She'd seen shipyards before, of course, having made that transition from settled to spacer life. Nothing could surprise her any more. And then the *Vulture God* had just kept getting closer, and the yards, and their ships, had kept getting bigger and bigger, even when they'd still been very far away.

It had been a grand and secret project, an incredible venture both in logistics and in clandestine planning. A handful of powerful factions within the Colonies had been engaging in covert talks ever since the first war, as far as Kris could work out. Talking about if the Architects came back. How it simply wasn't practical to protect the Colonies, all those worlds, and the Intermediaries such a fragile, unreliable shield. And so had begun a slow build-up of expertise and materiel aimed towards reconfiguring humanity—or a select percentage of it that could be saved—into a permanently shipbound, nomadic existence. For which they would need ships.

The yards at Estoc were on a grander scale than anything possessed by any species known to humanity. The great warship foundries of the Parthenon had nothing on them. The vast haulers of the Castigar only got so big because the wormlike aliens constructed them segment by segment, and then assembled them in empty space. Perhaps only the Naeromathi had owned something similar once, when they'd begun their own ark-bound existence. If so, it was long lost along with their worlds, no evidence remaining.

To give them credit, the secretive ark cabal had thought big, doing their best to provide living space for as many humans as possible, even if that would still be only a fraction of all the people out there.

And it might still come to that, Kris was well aware. Work on the ark fleet hadn't halted, though it had slowed as resources were diverted to the Eye itself and the vessel that housed it. The jewel in Estoc's crown, which the Eye Cartel had appropriated by force from its original salvagers.

The arks themselves were vast, but human-comprehensible. They were built the same way humans built spaceships, just on a grander scale. As their great curved hulls slid past, one after another, Max Dreidel goggled at them. A score of great bloated ships, five hundred kilometres long, some complete and others just skeletons still under construction. But none of this was what would really blow his mind.

Kris knew salvage, or she thought she did from her years on the *Vulture God*. It was a grimy, uncertain trade; dangerous too. Salvagers had their own stories and culture, working on the liminal edges of human space, out where things had failed and died. And one tale you heard a lot was the Big Score. A particular find that would make or destroy a salvage crew. An alien vessel—meaning not Hanni or Castigar or even Hegemony, but something unheard of, tumbling through the deep void out there. Unknown tech, unfamiliar aesthetic, the work of a culture and a mindset not encountered before. The *Vulture God* had never made such a fabled score, and Kris had never met any salvager who had.

But someone had.

It had been found by the Cartography Corps, she'd been told. Just floating in space in a planetless system where the Throughways petered out. And the Corps was still exploring that system now, because this thing had to have come from *somewhere*. There'd be more Throughways to be found there, people were sure. Perhaps a whole new thriving civilization on the other end of them, or just a field of dead ruins. Either way, it would be the discovery of the century.

Nobody had quite understood the magnitude of the find at first. It had just been pieces. All technically complex, but whatever had come into that distant dying system had died in turn. Broken apart on emerging from unspace, leaving not even a wreck, just a cloud of components held together by their own minuscule gravity and a faint magnetic field. Until, decades later, a diligent science team had uncovered its secret.

They called it the Host. As in, Heavenly. Of course everyone'd assumed it *had* once been a ship, but nobody had realized that it still was, present tense. A ship built by a species which had a spectacularly cavalier approach to things like hull integrity, atmosphere and gravitic forces.

The Eye itself was a great ragged-edged chunk of stone, the only semi-intact Originator facility ever discovered, wrested from the soil of a toxic world and hauled out here to Estoc. It was the centre of the Cartel's efforts to turn the war against the Architects, and if not for the Host, it might only have been a static facility out here in this isolated system, sponging off the vast shipyards for resources and personnel. A base of operations and research facility, nothing more.

Maxin swore, face ashen, as they rounded the bulk of a half-complete ark and he saw the Eye rolling in its socket.

The Host's pieces had been its hull. When the science team had activated them, those hundreds of individual components had generated a gravitic field between them, enclosing a space that could be shaped and expanded just by moving the pieces. And together they formed a ship which existed only for as long as the power lasted. The moment the switch was flipped again, it would become no more than a cloud of floating fragments once more. But, while reality consented to its presence, the Host could enclose a space as big as one of the arks or—once the Cartel had got hold of it—as big as the Eye. They could use it to turn the broken stump of the Originator facility into a mobile fortress. Able to flee, should the Architects ever appear at Estoc. Able, as the more hawkish members of the Cartel insisted, to carry the fight to the enemy.

Except the enemy dwelt in unspace, as far as anyone could decipher. How could you strike back in a place where you weren't real? Apparently even that wasn't a hard limit for the Cartel's ambitions. They were, Idris assured Kris, working on it.

The Host was like a coat of scales, shimmering red-gold in the blazing light of the Estoc rift. Curiously shaped, each scale was without symmetry, yet together they formed an eye-twisting whole. Something about the way the separate components organized themselves was like a paper cut to the human soul. Whichever unknown species had designed it had thought very differently to humans. Even now, the reverse engineering of the ship had turned up no data on the Host-builders. Trine, the Hiver supervising the current phase of investigations, had theorized it might have been an ancient species somehow reaching an advanced spacefaring stage without developing any form of written notation.

"Comms for you, Kris," their pilot said, and Kris linked to her own board. "Idris?"

"You'll be lucky," came a familiar voice, still with her faintly antique Partheni accent. "He's under. Barely comes up for air."

"Solace," Kris identified.

"I need you to talk to him. He's pushing himself too hard." Solace never had been one for small talk.

"Okay, I'll come over to Wellhead after debrief." Kris had one eye on the news, all the word that had reached Estoc while they were in transit. As she and the others had just come from the Colonial hub, most of it was old to her, but a few developments stood out. "I see we managed to keep Assur intact," she noted. "That was good work."

"Yes, but Dos Tiemos has gone," Solace said flatly. Kris couldn't even place the name. Some world she'd never been to and now never would. "As well as two other worlds in Castigar space. Small mining colonies. There's some gravitic maze theory they're using to tweak predicting the Architects' movements somehow. We're negotiating over the maths. All past my competencies." Kris pictured Solace shrugging. "Looking forward to seeing you. Come give Idris and Doc Shin some grief, will you?"

*

Kris hadn't had a chance to see the Eye when it was still planet-bound. For which, to be honest, she was quite thankful. The planet it'd been set into had been so hostile even the actual Originators—whoever they'd been—hadn't been able to go back to dismantle it. Hindered because they were trying to work from the other side, from unspace, according to Idris. But then, of course, Idris had got hold of it and used its Machine's vast gravitic engines to rip the whole thing out of the planet and cast it through unspace into orbit. Where it had ended up an airless piece of maze-wormed rock because, needless to say, its original builders had not designed it for space.

Then the Cartel, that unruly pack of temporary allies, had

hauled it to Estoc and installed it within the shifting scales of the Host, giving it atmosphere, gravity and as much stability as that shifting dream of a shell could ever impart. Kris always felt queasy for at least an hour after going aboard it. The Eye itself was an assembly of spaces and orientations, tunnels and drops and sudden expanses, which no human would ever have designed. And, when you got to one of its ragged, torn-off edges, there were the shimmering plates of the Host, with nothing between them but the void. She preferred ships where flicking the wrong switch wouldn't turn the hull off.

The combination of the Eye and the Host had other advantages, though. Nobody knew who the Originators had been, or who the Host's builders were, but merged together their technology presented a unique opportunity.

The various locations on the Eye had been named by a deranged committee, as far as Kris was concerned. There was Foresight, where a rotating team of Ints used the Eye's machinery to listen out for the movement of the Architects and try to forewarn whichever worlds might be their next targets. There was Dissipation, where a team of highly theoretical physicists and philosophers were supposedly working on anti-Architect weapons. And there was Schema, central command, where everyone who had a say argued about what to do with the technological riches they'd gathered here. There were also various parts of the alien edifice that had been co-opted for mundane needs like sleep and eating and rec. Finally there was the Wellhead, which had become the project's focus, where everyone's understanding of universal physics was put through the wringer.

She had to get someone to lead her there. A taciturn Hiver

instance eventually volunteered, because she'd given her report at Schema and was just cluttering up the place. The four-legged, can-shaped entity could scuttle through the vertically challenging reaches of the Eye far faster than she could follow, and communicated their impatience with her human limitations quite eloquently, despite the lack of any kind of face. It wasn't as if she'd never been here before, but Kris was part of a large minority who were simply unable to learn the layout, or even follow the tacked-on signs that had been put up to at least three conflicting plans. Something about the place offended her internal sense of space and direction, which was usually so reliable.

They came out at the Wellhead unexpectedly through its ceiling, and she had to clamber down a rickety metal ladder to get down. The whole of the Eye was like this: various lesser hands adding their conveniences to the Originator stone—doors, ramps, stairs, ducts and cables and relays. All of it just bolted on with no thought for aesthetics, some of it human scale and some designed for something larger.

The Wellhead itself was practically all bolt-on, a domed bubble nailed to what Kris tentatively thought of as the "underside" of the Eye. Much of it was raw scaffolding. They kept saying they'd enclose it, but every time she came back she could still look straight out at the great sliding pieces of the Host and all that empty vacuum between them. And that was only the second most eye-offending thing about the place.

There were a dozen human and Hiver technicians working there, mostly adding more *stuff*—wires, boxes and ducts, and other things Kris couldn't guess the purpose of. There were now five big column-shaped installations around the circular space, just riveted in without any sense of symmetry. In the centre, of course, was the Well itself, but she was trying not to look at that right now because it was open, and it hurt her mind to perceive it.

Solace hailed her. The Partheni was armoured up, Kris noticed: everything but the helmet and, thankfully, the accelerator gun. She crossed quickly, keeping her back to the Well, and gave the woman a quick hug.

"Trouble with the neighbours?"

Solace shook her head. "Not yet. Soon, I think, but for now they're behaving themselves." The majority of the staff at the Estoc shipyard were still in the employ of the place's original owners, from before the Cartel's intrusion. They weren't friends, particularly the notorious Magdan noble family of Uskaro, but they'd reluctantly knuckled under to the Cartel's vision and threats. Kris, who'd been their prisoner-guest previously, was amazed things hadn't kicked off already. *Six months of this tentative alliance. I wouldn't have put money on it.* It was mostly down to Solace's people, she knew. As long as the Parthenon remained committed to supporting the Eye, and the blow it could conceivably strike against the Architects, then everyone else would likely stay in line.

"Where's...?" Kris started, and Solace nodded in the direction she didn't want to look.

"Doc Shin!" she shouted. "How long?"

Kris spotted the dark, angular man across the space by one of the columns, where he'd possibly been trying to hide from Solace's scrutiny. Doctor Haleon Shinandri scuttled over, seeming to move shiftily sideways, even when he wasn't.

"Nineteen hours now, yes," he said quickly, as though trying to rush the words through a border inspection without being stopped. "It's not a problem. Doesn't have to be a problem, oh my, not at all."

Solace looked as though she wanted to slap him until it became a problem, but she sent Kris a mute look of entreaty.

"Do I have to go talk to the Cartel?" Kris demanded. "Or are you going to haul him out?"

"He doesn't *want* to come out," Shinandri muttered. "Such dedication to the cause, yes indeed. How can I ask him—?"

"You don't *ask* Idris. You just tell him," Kris said, from long experience. "This is why he's spent half his life hiding from responsibility. Because once it gets hold of him he doesn't know how to stop. Pull him out please, Doctor."

Idris

Idris was completely stationary and yet he was falling. In the back of his mind he willed himself to fall faster, just in case he could escape the voices that way.

An uncertain amount of time ago they'd strapped him into the Machine at the heart of the Wellhead, lying on a slab as though he'd arrived early at the morgue, connected to more medical monitors than he knew what to do with. And he wasn't alone. Prepped, briefed, coddled, reassured, asked to share his feelings. A Partheni medical Cognosciente reeled off numbers in flat Parsef. Doctor Shinandri rubbed his hands together and speculated about progress. And Idris tried to block them out because suddenly his solitary vocation had become very crowded.

And there were others. Five more Intermediaries. Three longtime Liaison Board veterans—meaning they'd been at it a third as long as he had—one novice going under for her first time and already panicking fit to give herself an embolism; one of the latest Partheni class, her slab bulked out by the extra tech she needed to follow where Idris led. They were a team now, and entering unspace together.

The thing you couldn't do. Ever.

He had lived his life by this one maxim. When you're in unspace you're by yourself. Nobody else survives the entry. *Everyone* was on their own on the far side of the real/unreal border. Didn't matter if there were others on your ship, at your side, holding your *hand* even. You plunged into unspace alone, until the Presence registered your intrusion and began to hunt you down.

Yet here he was, leading a team there.

It was the engineering of the Eye. Not that this had been its original purpose, as far as Doctor Shinandri guessed. But a lot of very clever people had gone crawling over that engineering, and they'd used it as the foundation of the Wellhead. Doc Shin himself, Ahab the Naeromathi, Harbinger Ash, Delegate Trine, plus any number of genius Colonial, Hiver and Partheni scientists, working themselves half to death until they had something that broke all the forbiddances of unspace. Then they'd put Idris and the other Ints into it and asked them to go hunting.

All very well to have Foresight calling out the next target of an Architect attack, with around a seventy per cent reliability. All very well to have roving Ints doing their best to fend off the monsters when they arrived. But Idris knew full well that the Eye project was full of hawkish types who weren't happy with just a piecemeal defence. It was hardly a long-term solution to the genocide the Architects were enacting.

He was lying on his slab right now. Around him, the cavernous space of the Wellhead echoed to strange sounds. Strained metal, bulkheads under pressure, the deep groans of stress and structural failure, distant as whale song. Sounds of decay, and nobody knew entirely why, but he would put Largesse on it not being anything good.

And the others. He could half see them, like movement in the corner of his eye. Moving about the curved space of the Wellhead, staring out into the bruised grey void of unspace. When he squinted, really hurt his eyes with it, he could bring them into focus. There was the Partheni in her grey uniform, fists clenched and eyes closed as she reached out with her mind. There was the novice from the Board, hugging her knees and rocking. He could go to her, he knew. Comfort her. He hoped someone would, but it wasn't in him. The thought of human contact within unspace was anathema. This was his alone-space, and he'd lived his adult life on that understanding. Hearing their voices was bad enough. Hearing the distorted tones of Doctor Shinandri from up the Well, feeding him data, harvesting what Idris had discovered, freaked him out. It was as though he couldn't be master of his own mind any more.

Plus there was the issue of having to lie about what he was doing. Hoping nobody would work out he was vastly off-mission. Burrowing down through the non-existent layers of unspace, hunting for something very different to his stated objective.

The others were doing the job well enough, and he'd probably only get in the way if he tried to help. They were attempting to map unspace—that region which didn't obey normal spatial laws and didn't actually exist in the same way that regular matter and space did. Blazing a trail through the impossible, they would supposedly bring the fight to the Architects with whatever weapons anyone could come up with. So let someone else have the glory of finding that last elusive waypoint through nothingness that would take them to where the Architects were. Idris, despite it being his job, wanted none of it.

Voices came to him from the real again. Shinandri, Ahab, their engineer Tokamak Jaine. And now it was Trine, the old Hiver. Trine, who knew more about the Originators and their work than anyone else alive. Who'd come to awareness of themself as a mechanical secretary and someone's property during the war. They'd then lived through their artificial species' fight for rights and independence and were now the universe's greatest expert in the subject their original masters had been studying.

"Idris, my dear old fellow researcher, you're off course again." Trine's wry, light voice, that could get scalpel-sharp with sarcasm at a moment's notice. "One might almost think your mind was not on the task at hand."

Nothing could be further from the truth, save that *his* task and *their* task were at variance. "What do you need?"

"I am taking a further reading from the Eye, my human sonar machine, and I need your data. Pulse for me, Idris. Pulse, and show me what echoes back to you from the furthest reaches of nowhere. I rather think I am close to a breakthrough. Or possibly breakdown, if you continue to meander."

So Idris had to drag himself back in line, play well with others for a little while, while Trine experimented. The Hiver had been holed up with Ahab, Ash and Shinandri, Idris knew, and some grand and baffling plan had been hatched between them. A way of utilizing the Eye against the Architects.

When they'd first strapped him into the Machines within the Eye and given him this infinite view into unspace, Idris had been looking for something quite different. And when they'd located that cluster of organization and structure, buried within a non-space where nothing should *be*, he'd thought he'd found it. But it hadn't been the Architects he'd been hunting. Ever since that encounter over Berlenhof, he'd been after the hand that held the whip. The unimaginable entities that had turned the Architects into their personal hammer and chisel with which to resculpt the universe.

Instead they'd found the Architects themselves. Their origin. A knot of information within unspace that was their breeding ground, and which the Eye project was determined to uncreate. That was the target which Trine was working out how to destroy.

Idris was still after bigger game, though, no matter what he told his handlers.

And now—meaning after some measureless additional lapse of time since Trine had spoken to him—those handlers were in his ear again, whispering like demons.

"Idris." Shinandri's hitching voice, always on the verge of veering into a hysterical giggle. "It's time, Idris. You've been under long enough. Come back and we'll see what you have."

But Idris's mind was far away, outside the notional borders of the Wellhead. He was down the Well, deep into unspace, feeling the sluggish shifting of the Presence as it tried to find him. He had no visual reference for it, just a visceral sense of something vast at the heart of all things, uncoiling and expanding out through all the unreal volumes. Extending its blind reach as it quested for him. The Thing Most Feared. The entity that could not be engaged with, without destroying yourself. Except Idris had been dodging it for half a lifetime and he had just a little more dodge left in him. Whatever he sought, whatever it truly was that gave the Architects their orders, it was down there too. Not the Presence itself, but some other denizen of those same depths.

"Idris," from Shinandri again, but Idris was used to ignoring the man. After all, the others were still out there too. Let Doc Shin pick on them.

And then: "Idris!" A new voice. Kris. Back already, apparently. "Idris, we need you to disengage."

But he was getting somewhere, he knew. He fell further, their voices fainter and fainter. He was a diver with a weighted belt, plunging himself into the black abyss. He was the drifting astronaut whose momentum could only carry him away from his ship.

It shifted beneath him, homing in on him. He could feel the space about him becoming complex as the Presence curdled into existence all around. Kris was still speaking in his ear but he made her very far away. He was staring into the void, willing it to stare back into him. *I am coming for you.*

"Idris, I will damn well start pulling these pipes out myself," Kris said, quite clearly, as though she was right beside him.

"Go bug the others," he hissed back, knowing that somehow his voice would be heard by other ears than hers, that he was accelerating his own doom just by speaking. "They've been in as long."

"Three shifts have been and gone, Idris," Kris said reasonably. "Six hours safe limit. You're in the fourth now. You have to come back to us."

"Impossible." But he opened his eyes—the unreal eyes, that looked into the unreal Wellhead—and realized the shifting shadows of his co-workers were *not* the people he thought they were. A completely different set now; new faces, new gestalt identities pressing in on the edges of his mind.

"I—" And the Presence was with him, there in the Wellhead. A seventh where there should only be six. A figure at his back, stalking around the curved space.

Of course it never spoke, everyone knew. But it had spoken to him once before, and now he heard it draw breath.

I was so close! But that was a lie, he knew. Unspace had no markers and he couldn't ever know if he was getting anywhere.

"Idris," said Kris again, and there was a whisper of another voice that got lost in her naming of him. A breath on his neck. Cold lips at his ear.

"All right. Fine." He made it sound petulant and bitter, but when he resurfaced into the real his augmented heart was stuttering and he practically fell into Kris and Solace's arms as he lurched off the slab.

3.

Havaer

"A fresh intrusion," came Colvari's crisp, artificial voice in Havaer's ear.

"At last." They'd been waiting for this for too long. Their little rat had been very careful. The last two incidents of data leakage had been on Havaer's watch, but covered up carefully enough that he'd only discovered them in retrospect. If there hadn't been such a shortage of trained personnel on the team, his boss would likely have fired him. Honestly, *Havaer* would have fired himself. The only mitigating circumstance was that this particular rat was very much at home in the system it was infiltrating. It was one of the covert agent's standard nightmares: taking up residence in somewhere the enemy had previously made itself comfortable. You could never be sure you knew all the back doors and booby traps, no matter how hard you searched.

And here was another little hidden accessway finally betraying itself. Someone was in the Eye system, syphoning off the most recent data. Nominally that data would eventually get shared with the class, Havaer knew. This condition was buried somewhere in the complex web of agreements the Hiver Assembly in Aggregate had drawn up regarding

34

the Eye and its use. However, none of the other partners in this weird-ass relationship trusted the Cartel not to redact it, and Havaer reckoned they were entirely right not to do so.

There was more than just the unspace scrying data—as people had begun to call it, as though the Eye and its bolted-on machinery were the universe's most expensive crystal ball. There was a steady leak about the ark fleet admin, system security, all manner of useful little tips should anyone decide to mount either a mutiny from within or an invasion from without. Neither of which were impossible, given the abilities and predilections of the junior partners.

Havaer's team consisted of three other human agents, a single dissident Hannilambra and an unknown bank of Hivers headed up by his old associate Colvari. Right now the Hivers were doing the hard sums, dismantling the leak's re-routing and masking protocols to work out where the actual intrusion had come from. Somewhere in the ark fleet, a physical person was giving the commands to make this happen, pairing some top-of-the-range hardware with living skill and intuition to keep one step ahead of the hunters.

"It's the Builders," Havaer decided. Almost a relief. The last time they'd tried this, the leak had turned out to be on the Partheni end of things, and that had promised to get a little too shooty for his liking. In the end the spy had given herself up peaceably enough, because the Parthenon was playing a civilized game for now, but next time it could just as easily be a shipload of Myrmidons with accelerator cannons and the whole peace would be in ruins.

Right now, though, whoever was leading them such a merry dance through the virtual architecture of the ark fleet was definitely on their home ground, meaning it was an agent of the Colonial magnates who'd first set up the ark project. Hugh and the Colonies as a whole were taking something of a backseat right now. Havaer had the impression that the speed of events had outstripped their ability to react. There were still a score of committees in session debating how to respond to the disaster before the disaster before the current problem. However, that group of worthies who'd been preparing to abandon planetary life for a ship-bound future—ideally without competition once the Colonial and Partheni fleets had fought each other to mutual destruction—were quite on top of events. They were also profoundly furious that their shipyards at Estoc had been commandeered and their arks sidelined in favour of the Eye project. They were particularly stung about their beautiful alien-tech Host being repurposed as the housing for the Eye itself. It had, after all, been intended as their personal giant space-yacht in the nomadic future of humanity they had envisaged. And, as this latest intrusion evidenced, they could smile and glad-hand in public all they liked, but privately they weren't taking it lying down.

"And traced." Colvari's voice in his ear again, along with coordinates.

"Well, this is needlessly embarrassing," Havaer decided, seeing where they were. "Everyone out of the ship." They were packed into an armed shuttle docked on a scale of the Host, having assumed that the spy would be in their own, probably armed, shuttle elsewhere in the fleet. Instead the Builders were clearly brazen enough to have someone actually within the Eye itself, right there and tapping the network at source.

The Hivers were leaving the physical side of security to

their human counterparts, which Havaer reckoned was a poor precedent to set, given how human–Hiver relations had shifted recently. Since winning its independence after the war, the Hiver Assembly had never flexed its political muscles, no matter all the nightmare scenarios Colonial humanity had envisaged. The fact that each Hiver instance was basically a colony of cyborg bugs in some kind of walking frame hadn't helped, even though that was how people had built them. Then decades had gone by, and the Hivers had hired out their instances, large and small, to humanity, and the whole thing had become an accepted business. Hivers worked and didn't complain, and people forgot that at the heart of their network was a great hive mind that wasn't controlled by humans any more. Until just now, when they'd suddenly declared to both Colonies and Parthenon, *This is how it's going to be.* Havaer had somehow ended up on the Hiver side of that equation, due to his chief being a founder member of the Cartel, but he wasn't entirely happy about it. Put bluntly, he could see how the ark-builders, and a large slice of the rest of humanity, were more than twitchy about the whole deal.

Sure, sure, he decided, *let's stick it to the Architects. Hard to argue with that as an aim. Except what if, when that's done, the Cartel decides there's some other grand project everyone needs to cooperate on, under pain of death?*

He had picked a side, though. And so long as it was the Architects under the notional hammer, he could live with that. There was a point in the theoretical future, though— always assuming events permitted him one—when he would have to take a long, hard look in the mirror.

By the time he'd bundled into the isolated computing node within the scale, the spy was already gone, but Havaer had spread out his team to cover all the regular crawlspaces leading from where they'd been. Each individual scale of the Host was a peculiar construction: a curved shield five hundred metres across, its outer surface was warty with sockets and field generators, while its smooth inner surface was built up with a mess of later additions that let human hands interface with the alien tech and control its field generation. There was a pilot's seat in each, intended for an Intermediary, and there was a cramped network of accessways for maintenance. Each scale was a ship unto itself, or could be the bridge of the wider Host. All very modular, and not remotely how humans would normally go about things, but this had been the place the Builders were going to run their ark empire from. It was intentionally flexible and ready to survive anything.

Their rat had been in the tunnels. They'd tried to get to the pilot's seat next, and Havaer reckoned they probably had override codes that could have torn this entire scale free from the whole, hoping to nip away while everyone else was busy repairing the vessel's field integrity. In most ships that would have just meant restoring gravity, but with the Host the field between the scales was also the hull and so it was a bit more of a priority. However, Havaer had made sure one of his people was in the pilot's seat already—his Hanni, who could skitter at twice the rate of a human down narrow ductways. The rest of his team were closing in, but it seemed the rat wasn't done. They knew the specs better than Havaer. Better, in fact, than the actual specs as set down in the Builders' data. Which was why they emerged fully suited up onto the exterior of the Host, already extending gravitic handles from their shoulders ready to ride the Host's field all the way to some theoretical safe point.

And there they met Havaer. He hadn't known exactly how they might try this trick, but he'd sure as hell guessed there was a way. He had a corkscrew mind, did Havaer, and right now every twist of it was being used, because Chief Laery just didn't have that many faithful agents to call on.

The range to his target was past two hundred metres and the exterior of the Host scale was slightly curved, but he still had a good angle on them, and someone had been fool enough to trust him with an accelerator. Plus this was hard vacuum, where projectile weapons didn't really have a maximum range other than any theoretical limits to the universe at large.

"Lift off and we'll just take over the gravitic fields," he informed the distant figure. He had a magnified view in one corner of his helmet display, and he saw them freeze. They had some sort of small arm holstered at their belt, and if they sprayed some shot in his direction that could be a problem, accuracy be damned.

"Don't," he said, but they went for the gun anyway, and he cursed, lining up his own accelerator, clumsy in his suit. "Look." He even sent them the image from his targeting: their body right in his reticule.

They paused, and for a second he hoped reason might prevail. Then they turned the pistol to point at their own helmet.

"Oh, for—" Havaer thought in a mad instant of shooting the weapon from their hand, but to be honest the reticule image had been mostly scare tactics. He just wasn't a great shot at this range, not even with all the assisted targeting in the world.

Then his target was flailing out of his sight. He'd been zoomed in so far he lost them entirely, and had to come back out to locate them with his eyes the old-fashioned way. His suit telltales informed him of weapons fire, but nothing seemed to be coming his way. A moment later he located his target, not flying as he'd thought, but pinned to the scale's hull. There was a great cloud of particles exploding away in all directions and he guessed this was frozen droplets of blood.

Colvari was there. The Hiver's current frame was just a block with a variety of multipurpose limbs, perfect for scrambling around on or within complex alien machinery. They'd emerged the same way as the spy and jumped them, removing the pistol by the simple expedient of scissoring the relevant hand off at the wrist.

Too late, though. Some of those particles were helmet matter, and some of the blood was cranial. They carried the spy inside as quickly as possible, and did their best with the medical facilities on hand. Havaer was left looking down at one spy who wouldn't be giving up any secrets, though. Save the one patently obvious just from looking at her. Scarring, which he recognized sure enough. Someone had carved up the woman's skull long before the bullet had finished the job. Possibly the thought of blowing her own brains out had held few terrors. Liaison Board Ints had a miserable life, he knew.

If she'd got to the pilot's chair she could have taken the whole scale into unspace and we'd never have caught her. Which meant this was probably a counter-espionage success, but looking down at the corpse Havaer didn't feel particularly triumphant.

Then, of course, he had to go report to Chief Laery. Never a pleasure at the best of times, and he was damn sure *she* wasn't going to count this as much of a win either.

*

Chief Laery had been a department head at the Hugh Intervention Board, an attenuated veteran with the physique of a withered stick, grown brittle and spindly from too long on the zero-gravity listening posts. She'd also been a holy terror to her subordinates, enough so that Havaer couldn't quite work out why, when she'd gone rogue, he'd ended up on her side of the divide. Supporting her against mainstream Mordant House, as the Colonies' security service was informally known. Because at that time the powerful clique who'd been building these ark ships had already secured control over the House's upper echelons.

Perhaps it's just that nobody asked me which side I wanted to be on, he thought dourly.

Laery had been ousted, dispatched for a long-deserved retirement that she hadn't arrived at. Instead she'd continued to run Havaer and a handful of other loyalists as her private spy ring, and made new friends. And now she was on top of the world, or at least balancing precariously on a teetering stack of uncertain allies and unwilling underlings.

He still wasn't sure how she'd done it, but then she'd been in the game a lot longer than he had. She was the human face of the Cartel, even if that face looked like it'd been sucking lemons through a straw. Somehow she'd been on top of the game all the way through. Not the little keyhole view Havaer had been granted of it, but the whole big picture.

She'd reached out to alien powers and mad scientists and even criminals, and she'd built, not an empire, but a capstone that kept the great empires of human space just about under her thumb.

She had the Hivers, and that was most of her leverage. The Hiver Assembly in Aggregate had a perspective untarnished by factional thinking, and wanted to be able to get on with its composite existence. The Architects threatened that, and so the Hivers backed the Cartel and its plans to deal with them once and for all. The rest of her muscle was the Broken Harvest, which was some kind of Hegemonic crime syndicate, except neither of those words had its regular meaning in the Hegemony. Her know-how came from the Eye and from Harbinger Ash. And Havaer was happy to admit that his own know-how stopped at around that point. Ash had been a mystery since the creature first turned up on Earth warning of the Architects. Now, a century on, it was no less opaque. It had only stuck around after Earth's destruction, Havaer reckoned, because the development of Intermediaries could offer a way to strike back. And now the team at the Eye might just find that way. The mad Naeromathi Ahab, the equally mad human Shinandri and the cyborg tech Tokamak Jaine, who actually seemed quite pleasant and sane, even if someone had replaced her torso with machinery at some point in the past. Again, the science was way over his pay grade, but between them and the equally deranged Int Idris Telemmier there was, apparently, a prospect of winning the war.

That was the Cartel. Its muscle and promises had given Laery just enough leverage to stomp over to Estoc and take over the ark fleet's yards and resources, as well as their flagship. It had also given her enough sway to cool the actual full-on shooting war that had just started between Colonies and Parthenon, turning it down to a dull simmer. Nobody was happy, and both sides were pushing and prying wherever they felt they could get away with it. On that basis, Havaer was not short of work. But right now the entire human sphere was pointed in the same direction. If, he thought with a pedantic wrinkle, a sphere could be said to point.

When he next saw Laery with his own eyes, it was as a consequence of the operation he'd just so bloodily rolled up. She had him in to loom and provide first-hand evidence as she confronted the dead Int's spymaster.

This was the Morzarin Ravin Okosh Uskaro, the Uskaro family being a big part of the old Builder clique that the Cartel had displaced. The most mutinous part too, given how much they'd had taken off them in the name of defeating the Architects. Not just the Host and the ark fleet's resources, but the majority of their Ints as well. Because of all things, the strike against the Architects needed Ints. The Eye practically ate and drank them. They were working all over it in shifts, plumbing the depths of the Well, manning Foresight, training in the mental disciplines that would supposedly let them fight the unthinkable. It wasn't just Uskaro's Liaison Board conscripts, of course. The Parthenon had its new class, who were probably also conscripts even though nobody was saying it, and they'd been borrowed for the cause too. The fact that, the last time Havaer had been here, it had been Monitor Superior Tact whom Laery was confronting suggested they weren't exactly delighted with the state of affairs either.

Uskaro was an elegantly dressed old man, hair and moustache silver. He stood with that faux-military straightness the Magdan nobility used when they weren't slouching. The front of his emerald shirt was bright with strips of medals. The effect was slightly buffoonish, and Havaer reckoned that was intentional because Ravin Uskaro was no man's fool. What he was right now, though, was on the back foot.

"Thank you for sparing me the time before your return to Magda, Morzarin," Laery said blandly. "This won't take long."

"I understand your people have murdered one of my Intermediaries." A game try at going on the offensive, Havaer had to give him that.

"Well, I'm glad we're on the same page." Laery leant forwards in her chair, or at least her chair leant forwards for her in a series of slightly jerky motions. Havaer had been on the wrong end of that chair far too many times. The obvious pain she was in only fed Laery, but what also fed her was the discomfort of underlings. The Morzarin was nobody's underling, however. He bore the sight stoically.

"I'm used to your attempts to pry information from our project here," Laery told him summarily. "I consider the time spent in fielding them a reasonable rent paid to you, for the use of your spacious facilities." A nice jab under the man's guard, given what she'd taken from him. "But now you have brought the Ints into this. You took one of a very limited pool of our living weapons and turned her into your spy. Then, when she was apprehended, you gave her orders to kill herself. Thus robbing the human race of an irreplaceable asset. You know exactly how many—how *few*—Intermediaries we have, even with the Liaison Board's leashes. Even with the Parthenon. To waste one for your petty espionage is criminal."

Uskaro set his chin, not backing down. "You think that the Colonies will be your creature forever, in this venture? You think that the whole of your former species will sit by meekly for this treason? You've seen what's being said, back at Hugh. You hold your current place on sufferance. You have stolen from us, and now you keep your secrets from us. The ships and facilities here are not yours, they are ours. The Ints are ours."

The Ints are their own, Havaer thought. It was a legal and moral grey area, though. The original Liaison Board Ints were all turned out under leashed contracts that practically made them property—after all, they'd largely been convicts to start with. The new class of them were mostly volunteers, what with the war back on, and free. And the Cartel had ostensibly freed the leashed Ints too, when they took over at Estoc. Those same Ints would have ended up back as property the moment they left the system, though, meaning they didn't really have a great deal of say about whether they wanted to be part of Laery's grand project or not.

"I know exactly what's being *said* by your allies in Hugh, Morzarin," Laery said flatly. "And we both know they can talk all they like. Hugh is, at best, divided on the subject. Any time that might change, I'm more than happy to send a Hiver Delegate over to present to everyone just how you were planning to run this little ark venture of yours. How you yourself were going to select who got a seat on the boat and who didn't, abandoning most of their worlds to the Architects. And how you sparked off the fight with the Parthenon just to be rid of some rivals. I'm sure you'd respond that you were making hard choices for the good of humanity but I don't think they'd see it the same way."

"Perhaps you don't have your finger on the pulse at Hugh as much as you think," Uskaro growled softly, and he sounded sure enough that Havaer couldn't keep back a shiver.

Laery was unmoved, though. "Well then, it comes back to the same old stick, doesn't it. Even if you somehow get the bulk of Hugh dancing about to your tune, I know plenty of others who'll have something to say if the Colonial Navy turns up here trying to take it all back by main force. We *women* do talk, don't you know."

"You overstep yourself," Uskaro told her in a tight whisper. "You are a bureaucrat with delusions of significance. I look forward to your fall."

Laery gave him a long, level stare and then flicked emaciated fingers to dismiss him. Havaer watched the man go, all the tatters of his noblesse oblige drawn about him like a cloak, and was worried.

Ravin

It would be possible for Ravin Uskaro to spin things for his allies back home, just about. The other Builders, the rest of the Uskaro clan on Magda, the Nativist lobby back in Hugh. Everyone was incensed enough about the Cartel's muscling in and taking over, nobody was happy.

He'd stared down that withered old hag Laery, and wouldn't give her the satisfaction. He'd assured his nephew Piter that everything was going according to plan, that losses were inevitable. There was always a grander plan, behind anything the enemy had uncovered or torn down. Were they not magnates of Magda, most powerful of the Colonies?

Only back aboard his ship, proof against any prying eyes as it prepared to leave Estoc, could he stare at his own reflection and admit that he was stymied. Everything the hateful Laery had said was true. He and the Builders had been outmanoeuvred, their secrets stolen, their work uncovered and now *co-opted* for this ludicrous Eye business. They were going to strike against the Architects, were they? Expend every Int and every chance humanity had on some lunatic scheme? Laery could sneer all she wanted about the arks, and just how skewed that project might have become from its original humanitarian aims. *At least we would preserve something of humanity!* The Architects made planets their sport, but they hadn't gone chasing after the spacebound Naeromathi, or attacked Partheni garden ships. Regular humanity needed to save itself!

And yes, that small slice of humanity left would be governed by men like Ravin Uskaro, but then that was his role. He was born into a governing class, blessed by a superior heredity. It was just the way things were. Ironically, he felt that the most honest amongst his opposite numbers in the Partheni would agree with him on this one point. They were, after all, a eugenics project run out of control. Their founder had picked over and chosen which elements of humanity to include in their genetic makeup, to make her "perfect race." Yet people like Laery couldn't see the *danger* in that!

As long as the Parthenon remained intact and a threat, though, Laery would use them as a stick to beat him with, just as she probably used the Colonial Navy as a stick to threaten them in turn. Such a small woman. Such an insignificant pen-pusher, and yet she'd somehow installed herself at the balance point of the political universe, her finger on the scales. Ravin could swear revenge as much as he liked. Right now he had no way to bring it, except to deploy whatever agents he could and hope that the dribble of information he'd sneaked out from the Eye project would yield something useful.

That was another sobering thing. It was all very well to put on that iron front for Laery, but he *hadn't* given the order for his agent to terminate herself. She'd done that entirely of her own mind. A dead Int helped nobody, and he knew the Liaison Board Ints were problematic. The process that turned them into Intermediaries was mostly fatal, while the survivors emerged damaged. But the ark fleet was profoundly reliant on having that stock of Intermediaries to draw on, without which it was a slave to the Throughways. Vulnerable, and limited.

He would like to think that his agent's final, desperate act was born out of the engrained loyalty and conditioning they'd tried to instil in the leashed Ints. Laery had stripped enough layers from his composure that he could see *escape* there, though.

I'm not a monster, he told his reflection. *It is necessary we do these things. It is necessary that humanity have more Intermediaries, through whatever means. The survival of the species . . .*

When the chime came he expected it to be his crew, telling him they were ready for him to go into suspension for the trip. Instead, it was an external communication. He froze. He'd put himself into isolation so he could work through these dark thoughts and then face the rest of the universe with proper composure. Hence, whoever was contacting him now was making a particular point. *We can circumvent your security.*

Laery, he guessed. The woman couldn't resist rubbing his nose in it. *You can't get your spies past us, but we can get to you.* He wouldn't give her the satisfaction. But then the chime went again, a delicate musical note played by a real metal hammer delicately striking a physical bell, because the Uskaro knew how to appreciate the finer things. He flattened his features to his customary polite disdain and his headware signalled the comms system to open a channel.

He couldn't quite retain control of his features. He knew his eyes widened and his eyebrows twitched. It wasn't Laery. Instead, he stared into an all-too-familiar and yet entirely unexpected face.

4.

Olli

"That," said Olli, "was just about the most fucked-up thing I ever saw."

Kittering, at her back on the swaying howdah they were travelling on, made a brief ticking sound that was probably agreement. His translator was currently trying to wrestle with a new software patch that let him speak to certain local species in their own language about two times out of three. His ability to chat in Colvul had degraded commensurately.

"I mean, is this a regular occurrence, in this gig?" Olli went on. She was strapped into her walking frame, which was clinging to the howdah's soft, organic floor with most of its legs, but she spared one to prod the woman beside her. As always, jabbing a Tothiat felt more like poking a wall than a person. Heremon didn't say anything, and neither did the segmented lobster-thing that ran down her spine and was, apparently, also Heremon. The whole Tothiat entity gave Olli the creeps, but right now she was on a very alien world within a very alien polity, and at least Heremon looked human and could do normal speech and expressions and so on.

She'd half expected to be offered the Tothiat treatment

herself, when they'd come here to the world of Desecrat. She was currently amongst the favourites of an Essiel crime lord and/or fallen angel, depending on exactly how you translated the Hegemonic concepts to a human level. And being a Tothiat was apparently a living hell of constant and formative pain that also made you the next best thing to immortal. Which was what Aklu the Unspeakable, the Razor and the Hook, looked for in its lieutenants. Olli had met three of them so far, two of whom had not (she considered smugly) survived the experience. Admittedly in one case she'd had nothing whatsoever to do with it, but right now she was in a strange and hostile place and she'd take her confidence boosters where she could.

But nobody had offered to graft an alien lobster-wasp onto her to make her immortal, and she wasn't sure whether to be relieved or insulted by that. Given she'd been born without most of the standard human complement of limbs, she also wasn't sure what the symbiont would have made of her. Probably, the thing would have considered the business a bit of a raw deal, she thought sourly. Plus its intrusion would doubtless have robbed her of her knack of getting inside drones and other remotes, which was what actually made her *useful* to anyone. So overall she should come down heavily on the "relieved" side of the equation, but it was still a bit galling not to be asked.

Except Aklu wasn't a creature that took "no" for an answer, when offers were on the table. Aklu was a founding member of the Eye Cartel currently dictating galactic policy, and it had decided Olli was someone it wanted as a travelling companion—or possibly a pet. It was hands down the scariest and most powerful single entity Olli had come across, short of an actual Architect, which made what she'd just seen all the more shocking.

They were coming up to what passed for a spaceport on Desecrat. Basically a great big metal plate and some sort of ungodly-powerful gravitic engine sunk into the earth beneath it. This would then just lift them, and a bubble of convenient atmosphere, all the way up to orbit, where Aklu's ship would be waiting for them. Which meant Olli would have to sort out the logistics of getting down from the thing they were currently riding. It looked something like a jellyfish would if it had grown to the size of an elephant and evolved to walk about on land. The entire creature was rubbery and unpleasant, and the crown-shaped howdah seemed constantly on the point of slipping off it. Here she was in the heart of the Hegemony, the most technologically advanced polity humans had ever met, and apparently they'd developed past the need for efficiency. In fact, taking your own sweet time about everything was absolutely the Hegemony's thing, as far as she could work out, and sometimes that time seemed to be "never."

On all sides of them was a landscape that probably counted as jungle. It looked more like feathers forty feet high in darkly iridescent blues and purples. If she reached a metal leg out to prod them, the individual fronds retreated from her like tubeworms. And there was no actual path—the "forest" really was on all sides. Except some vibration or signal meant this forest was constantly shrinking away from their mount in its direction of travel and then bursting back into place behind them.

"They have engines buried everywhere," Heremon had told her on arrival. "You need a thing, they conjure it up, carry it in, make it happen. Nothing you can see the workings of, though." It was, apparently, how a lot of the Hegemony worked. Sufficiently advanced tech actively trying to look like magic.

The cleared disc of their ride up into orbit was ahead. Olli wondered if their viscous mount would deign to crouch down, or whether she'd have to scale the side of the damn thing or, worst of all, have to ask for assistance. She'd wanted to come in her Scorpion, the Castigar-built engineering frame that was good for everything up to and including full-on war, but apparently that wasn't appropriate. Goddamn Essiel propriety.

"So the chief," she asked Heremon. "It'll be . . . along?"

The Tothiat had said nothing since the ceremony they'd just witnessed. Fair enough. Olli hadn't exactly felt chatty right after. It had been a sight. Still, the woman was taking avoidance of the subject a bit far, and Olli prodded her again, harder this time, enough to make the whole howdah wobble.

Heremon looked at her, and Olli would have welcomed a snarl or a scowl or a harsh word. She knew where she was with that. Instead there were tears in her eyes. Actual human misery. Olli opened her mouth to make some kind of mean capital out of it, then found that she didn't actually hate Heremon that much any more. *I'm getting soft.*

*

The spectacle had taken place in an amphitheatre deep in the jungle: a hollowed-out hemisphere half a kilometre across, walled with stone and hidden engines. Seven Essiel had been waiting there, each on its own hovering couch and attended to by a retinue of red-clad human cultists, as well as skittering little Tymeree and a handful of other species Olli didn't even know the names of. The red, vaguely froglike ones were the Desecrat locals, she understood.

Aklu had arrived with its own entourage, consisting solely of Olli, Kit, Heremon and the golden Hiver frame that acted as its major-domo and translator. It rode in its own couch, which hid the tentacled prosthetic limbs it used to get around when things got nasty. Seeing Aklu get person-ally nasty was a terrifying thing, given how swift and strong that prosthetic frame was, but for Olli, connoisseur of the walking frame, it was also a thrilling sight. The thing was, Aklu was a *scary* son of a bitch. Except here it was leaving the three of them behind to glide forwards alone, to the very centre of this vast stone bowl. It appeared as a long shell standing on its end, like the other Essiel. At the top was its fan of thin arms and eyestalks, at the bottom its serpentine holdfast, which it now uncoiled, relinquishing its grip on the couch so that gravitic fields could lift it into the air. Olli felt a deep squirm of wrongness in her gut at the sight. There was something primal and awe-inspiring, seeing the alien lifted up, its tail describing naked arabesques and its array of limbs unfolded like a fan. The complex tracery of silver across its three-metre-long shell flowed like mercury.

"So what's—" Olli had started, and then columns of liquid had thrust up, surrounding Aklu, forming into hard, trans-lucent engines that reminded her too much of the crystal puppets Architects deployed on the ground when the monsters needed to get their hands dirty. For a moment everything was still, and even she recognized a point in time when her voice and input were not required.

She wasn't sure where the light came from, when it did. Whether the pillars were harvesting the sunlight or generating it themselves, or what. The air around them shivered and lensed, and then there were beams between them, leaping across the space that they enclosed. Meaning they intersected with Aklu. Where they did, they drew on the alien's shell, scoring black lines from which the charr evaporated like dust, leaving new channels. It happened seemingly at random, by accident. As though nobody had checked to see if an enormous alien shellfish was in the way before turning the lasers on. And then Olli could almost see a pattern in it. Each little handspan of line burned in a particular order, joining up erratically, an entire picture written in tiny sections. Or else it was writing, the latest chapter of a long record to be added to all the meandering script already carved into Aklu's shell. She'd thought it was just the shell, at first, but then she'd brought up an image magnifier from her walker and seen that each line burned clear through, smoking into the shuddering grey flesh beneath. It hurt. She could see how much it hurt. Aklu's long holdfast writhed and spasmed, and its arms jerked and shuddered, going into little fits of semaphore. She'd seen an Essiel die before—at Aklu's pleasure, in fact. So she knew how graceful and delicate their pain could appear to human eyes.

"They're torturing the boss," she'd said eventually. "That's the deal, huh?" "The boss" was her best human approximation of where she stood with Aklu now, and nobody had tried to correct her.

"The brief and abstract record of the Hook," intoned the Hiver in their musical voice. "Its crimes and failures inscribed up to date, the chronicle of all its deviations."

She'd assumed all that silver lacework already webbing Aklu's shell was just surface decoration. But no, the mercury sat in channels cut clear through to the inside, so that she wasn't sure how her boss even stayed together, save by constant application of a personal gravitic field.

Why did Aklu, the rebel angel, placidly return and submit to whatever the hell this even *was*? It was a criminal, wasn't it? A rogue element? And yet also, somehow, the whipping boy for its whole culture. With the Essiel, even rebellion was enacted according to specific rules and rituals.

I am involved in something crazy. I need to get out. But, weirdly, the whole hours-long process seemed to bind her more closely to the monstrous creature. She was inner circle now. To see this atrocity was, apparently, a great honour. And Aklu was *her* monster. She wanted to storm over and shout at the other Essiel, break their stuff and make a nuisance of herself. But she wasn't important enough to be a nuisance and their stuff was some liquid tech you couldn't break. She still felt indignant rage at what they were doing to her boss, though. In that instant she understood that *boss* wasn't just lip service. Something about the Razor and the Hook's life in defiance of the Hegemony spoke to the rebel inside her that had never agreed to live within her inbuilt limitations.

Then it was time to leave, go back to that part of the universe she at least halfway understood. Aklu and the major-domo would be back on the *Almighty Scythe of*

Morning shortly, she was told, after they'd filled in all that new carving with quicksilver. Another instalment of crimes written there for every other Essiel to see.

*

The jellyfish-octopus-elephant thing she was on now compressed itself down to about a half-metre in height, meaning she could step daintily down to the lifter plate without any difficulty at all. Even the monsters were all mod cons in Hegemonic space.

"Considerable gladness in leaving," Kittering announced as they touched down on the metal. Olli could only agree.

The plate began its smooth ascent, just a big disc of metal flying off to orbit without any visible assistance whatsoever. Olli came from a culture where it was practically a point of pride to have all your wiring and pipes exposed to view, so you could more easily fix the problems you just knew were going to spring up. The Hegemony gave her the creeps, frankly. And that wasn't even the maddest thing about this business. For her money, the absolute intergalactic lunacy prize went to the fact that, as they ascended, there was literally nothing else but that jungle, with its unseen froglike denizens. Apart from the faint suggestion of the amphitheatre off in the distance, half hidden in feathery trees like a ruined temple, there was nothing more on the entire planet. Desecrat had a single purpose within the Essiel Hegemony. It was where they brought their wayward sons to punish them. Other than that, the frogs were left to get on with whatever the fuck they actually spent their time on. An entire world, just to rap the notional knuckles of Aklu and its fellow fallen.

Or maybe the prize went to Aklu, because it kept coming back to have those non-existent knuckles rapped. But it sure as hell wasn't Olli's place to say anything. She'd just sit here in her walking frame, borne skyward by tech she—the technician—couldn't even understand, and think about how she'd somehow ended up a part of all this crazy.

*

Back on Aklu's ship, she went first to the lower dock levels, to make sure her *Vulture God* hadn't been disassembled by one of its goons. Aklu had good technicians, but they were also criminals, and she didn't want to find out at an inconvenient moment that her personal getaway had been stripped and sold for parts. The ship bays of the *Almighty Scythe of Morning* didn't have the same raucous, echoing workplace air she was used to. They were part temple, part zoo. When she'd finished running diagnostic checks on the *Vulture*, and got back into her Scorpion, she went to take a look at the latter end of the scale. Because she liked that. It was calming. She got on with the monsters better than the people around here, although some of the monsters were people too.

They had one regular Ogdru to manage the others who served as the *Scythe*'s battery of navigators. The Hegemony didn't have human Intermediaries yet—although with the franchise being expanded to the bloody Parthenon, it was probably only a matter of time. Instead, when the Divine Essiel wanted to travel through unspace away from the Throughways, they used these beasties. Regular Ogdru, as far as Olli understood, were a peaceable aquatic species, about twice human size and kind of scary-looking, but philosophical and very slow to anger. Back in the evolutionary day, however, they'd been the top predator in their ancient oceans, and every so often an Ogdru pup was born who channelled their inner monster a bit too well. The hunting instincts and general lack of manners were paired with a suite of spatial senses that opened the doors of unspace to them without all the angst and hand-wringing that Olli's friend Idris was so prone to. On the other hand, Idris was at least theoretically more biddable than a mature hunting Ogdru.

Aklu kept three on hand, two huge adults that were a good fifteen metres long and scared the crap out of Olli whenever she went near their tanks, and Junior. Junior was already bigger than her, almost the size of a regular Ogdru save that the feral kind grew way larger. When she approached its tank—which was to say a great orb of water held together by a gravitic field—it eeled its way over and brushed against the side, so she could extend one of the Scorpion's limbs and scratch its rock-hard scales. The front end of an Ogdru was basically a four-way jaw fringed with a band of sensory tendrils. The back end of them was muscular coiling tentacles. One of the adults could have got a good hold on the *Vulture God* and crushed its hull, she reckoned, should such an unfortunate encounter ever occur. But Junior was frisky and playful, like the universe's most murderous squid-puppy. She liked Junior, and Junior had taken a shine to her. Probably because she could scratch the monster with an arm that didn't register as edible.

She was glad to be back aboard, and within arm's reach of her own ship. The Hegemony freaked her out. Aklu freaked her out. And as soon as the suitably chastised crime boss was back aboard, they'd be measuring the Throughways back to the fringes of Colonial space and Estoc. This should theoretically have made her feel better, except Olli found, sitting there and feeding Junior torso-sized chunks of unidentifiable meat, that the prospect made her uneasy. Things had spiralled way out of her control or even understanding back there. Her old pals were all involved in something that seemed just as mad as the ritual she'd recently watched on Desecrat. Everyone was suddenly friends with people who were not, Olli was damn sure, *her* friends. Being here surrounded by thugs and cultists was almost normal in comparison. And sure, she'd seemed the logical pick to be human liaison to this aberrant branch of the Cartel, but right now she wasn't sure who she was supposed to report on, or to whom.

She brought up the Scorpion's internal slate to see what reports she'd received. That was a thing now: paperwork, albeit sans paper. And it was a burden of her own making, for sure. Someone had been fool enough to make her the favourite of a crime lord, and that meant that, when the Scorpion went and loomed over one of Aklu's people and Olli asked nicely, things happened. It wasn't exactly power. She wasn't someone like Heremon, whose mere word could have people tortured or killed just because she was having a bad day. And, Olli was forced to admit, she herself had a sufficient number of bad days that it was probably just as well. But if she asked for a little info, an eye on the multifarious dealings of the Broken Harvest, then she got it, no questions asked. Along with the killers, thieves and smugglers, Aklu employed a lot of clerks and accountants and the like. Which meant a whole lot of information went through its organization, and Olli had been spooning it out for her own personal use.

It was probably going to get her into trouble when someone joined the dots. Or else this was just one other thing that would have been problematic anywhere else, but they did things differently in the Hegemony and so nobody cared. Olli had been collecting news, however. Of ships where they weren't supposed to be. Most of the Harvest's business involved ships where they weren't supposed to be anyway, and she reckoned she was seeing a pattern in what *else* they saw out there too.

Not Architects. That was above her pay grade. Not an alien menace like the Naeromathi either. Nothing so grand. Olli was more worried about what their ostensible *allies* were doing. She was still pondering this as she put herself into suspension, ready for their journey and dropping out of the real.

*

Her unease only grew when they woke her up at Estoc. They'd dog-legged it across unspace from system to system, using the Ogdru to pull them out at each Throughway terminus well away from any planet. They were criminals, after all. Neither the Hegemony nor the Colonies were exactly pleased to see them. Even though Aklu was a part of this Cartel at the Eye who were calling the shots, stopping to answer questions and demand, *Don't you know who I am?* every time they emerged was just an exercise in time-wasting.

So she'd been in suspension a good while, and woke up

to find the whole Parthenon Navy cruising around the ship-yards at Estoc as if they owned the place.

Well, okay, three ships. But they were big ones. And supposedly their presence was all about shift changes for the Partheni Ints who were helping out at the Eye. The Partheni liked to keep their new human weapons well protected, after all. Which was fooling nobody, honestly. It wasn't as though having a big ship could save you from an Architect, but it would let you go toe to toe with other humans. They were doing it because they'd be going for the Colonies the moment Cartel HQ gave the universe the all-clear.

Some of Olli's best friends were Pathos. Or, maybe not quite that. One person she got on with all right was Partheni, though Olli liked to think that Solace had been out of the nest long enough that she'd started to pick up a few Colonial ways and pull that stick at least halfway out of her ass. But the rest of them . . . It truly freaked Olli out the way everyone was treating the Parthenon as their best mate just because it was playing nicely with the anti-Architect offensive. The woman who'd designed its culture and genomes from the ground up had possessed a particular vision for the future of the human race, and Olli was damn sure that a fuck-up like her wasn't a part of it. Solace could talk forever about how that wasn't the path they'd chosen to take, but Olli was confident *someone* in Patho high command had a seven-point genocide plan tacked up on their wall. And, just as with those bastard ark men, once you've made the plan, and you've got the wealth or power to make it happen, nature takes its course, doesn't it?

*

Once she'd boarded the Eye, they gathered the whole gang together for once. Kris reconfigured the refectory there to put a chain of tables together, and they actually ended up eating a proper Colonial-style found-family meal. Meaning the horrible prefab food from the printers they'd bolted onto the alien stone walls, but that was home cooking to Olli. She and Kit were there, and Kris. Olli wanted to talk to Kris, like the old times, just bitch and complain and exasperate her. Except Kris was sitting next to Solace and the pair of them were chattering away like they were new Best Friends Forever. Sure, they'd been left with only their own company since Idris had been down the Well and Olli had been off on her cultural exchange trip in the Hegemony. But still, it was galling that Kris wasn't just putting that down now Olli was back and making herself available to be bitched at.

They had Trine there too, the Hiver unit with the holographic face who'd been a big-shot Originator scholar since the war, supposedly. Trine sat on Olli's other side and talked, and at least they were engaging enough, even though they only really talked about themself. Their phantom face twinkled and smiled, and the battery of arms set into their cylindrical body tore apart every morsel placed in front of them and fed it to the colony of cyborg roaches that lived inside them. Olli was fine with that, because Hivers were good people as far as she was concerned. So she listened to Trine distantly while Kris and Solace got in each other's way over some anecdote. She wondered if the pair of them were sleeping together yet. Because everyone knew how the Partheni were in that department, and Kris wasn't exactly shy. Olli scowled down at her food.

At the other end of the table, past Trine, there was the

creepy science guy, Shinandri, picking at his food and occasionally uttering a shrill titter at the Hiver's wit. Across from him was Tokamak Jaine, the Eye's chief technician, who was a proper Colonial tech in Olli's exacting book. The way she'd rigged the facility up for human occupation, by just nailing every damn thing they might need to the wall, no frills, no fuss, was the sort of practical thinking Olli admired. So she and Kit talked tech with Jaine across the table, and that at least felt normal and reasonable. More than normal, if Olli was honest with herself. What with how weird everyone else had got, sometimes it felt like Jaine was the only human being around here that Olli could actually understand.

Past Kit, after a pointed gap, there was Idris, slumped on the far side of the table like he'd turned up early for his own funeral. They'd finally coaxed his mind out of the Well and his body out of the machinery that Jaine and Shinandri had developed. He looked miserable, but that was just Idris-standard as far as Olli was concerned. Eventually he met her gaze and mustered a wan smile, and she wanted to take him by the skinny arm—the single natural arm he still had, rather than the mechanical replacement for the one he'd lost—and get him alone to talk. Not like the old days, because Idris had never been a talker, but about the old days, and how things weren't the same. They'd been crew on a tramp salvager. A good one, true, because they'd had Idris and could do the deep void work nobody else was able to, but still just crew. A little tin-can family, just like most spacers ended up in. The two of them, plus Kris and Kit. Captain Rollo: dead. Barney: dead. The Hiver Medvig: also dead. Spacers died and life went on, but it felt to Olli that life had taken a sharp turn and she hadn't been consulted. *I've just spent way too much time as an Essiel's pet because it felt more like home than being with my actual friends.*

The conversation lulled and there was her chance to say, "This isn't what I signed up for. I'm not happy with it. Can we just not?" Except they were doing Important Things here. They were saving the universe from the Architects. Where exactly did the personal preferences of one Olian Timo figure in all that? Besides, Olian Timo bitched and complained, but she didn't get *upset*. She was *tough* and *ornery* and didn't feel abandoned by her friends or get depressed because life had moved on. That was for people like Idris. Olli was the person who was always there to clean up the mess, not the one breaking into bits.

So the moment passed and she insulted Trine instead, which the Hiver was more than able to riposte to. Then she and Kit broke out a little Landstep board and she lost some money to him, and they both went on to rook the crap out of Shinandri and Jaine in a two vs. two, which was fine. But Solace and Kris's laughter grated away at the back of her mind, and she looked forwards at how things might go once they'd actually accomplished what they were trying to do here. She didn't see everyone coming back to the *Vulture God* and resuming a life of itinerant salvaging. They'd be big shots with big prospects, unlike her. Or else there'd be a war on and they'd be choosing sides. Olli knew which damn side she was on, and she wasn't sure it'd be the same as Kris's. It certainly wouldn't be the same as Solace's.

Fucking Parthenon. She made some brusque, Olli-esque excuse and then had her walking frame tap off out of the refectory. She was going to play with Junior again, and plot the downfall of her enemies.

65

5.

Olli

"Your face," Olli said derisively. "Almost like the universe doesn't revolve round you after all. Which it does, in case you didn't notice. Or this bit of it here, anyway."

Idris wouldn't even look at her. It was the day after the big meal. Nobody was letting him play with the cool Machines owing to how much he'd overdone it. Instead, someone had sat him down with a bowl of tofusoya in front of him, although he wasn't actually eating it. Olli cast a look around in case Solace or one of her sisters was in earshot, and then flicked the facing chair out of the way so she could take its place with her walker frame.

"Idris," she prompted, and then used one of the frame's rubber leg tips to jab his shin.

"Hi, Olli. Yes. Idris. It's me," he mumbled. One hand found the spoon and separated out a scoop of food, then didn't seem to know what to do with it.

"Fuck me, they said you'd been frying your brain but I didn't realize you'd turned the heat up so high." Olli shook her head disgustedly. "You need to go for a good lie-down and stare at the ceiling for twelve hours or something." One of the many screwed-up things about Idris was that he hadn't slept for longer than Olli had been alive. Or aged, apparently. They'd done a real number on him when they made him an Int.

At last Idris looked directly at her, and Olli had to brace herself against the withering distances buried in his gaze.

"They won't let me back down the Well until I rest," he said, voice shivering. His organic hand was jumping and fidgeting on the table. The mechanical prosthesis that was his left hand held the spoon completely still. "But I can't rest. I need to go back down the Well."

"There's a whole list of things you need, and 'help' is at the top of it," Olli grumbled. "Listen—"

"I'm so close." He was very quiet, but somehow he cut her off anyway.

"To the Architects? Their nest or whatever-the-fuck?"

"To *them*."

For a moment she'd forgotten what he meant but then it came back to her. The supposed masters he'd been going on about since Berlenhof. As far as Olli was concerned, just kicking the Architects themselves was absolutely fine, but she'd heard Idris going on about it enough that she knew better than to argue the point.

"Look," she tried. "You've been pushing yourself, right? You need a break, but like you say, you can't just put your head down. You need a change of scenery, is what."

Idris looked at her bleakly. "Olli—"

"Hear me out. You need a break. I need a navigator. To go do a bit of scouting around the local area. Security check, see, right? We all need a hobby." She was talking too fast, and he was in way too deep with Solace and the Parthenon for her actually to tell him *why*. She'd need hard evidence for that, and to get hard evidence she needed him. His senses and his ability to take the *Vulture God* anywhere. "How's about it? Come on a little skip around on the *God*. Be like old times. Get your mind settled. Into unspace the old-fashioned way, none of this strapping you into a fucking torture lab like I've seen over at the Wellhead."

"Olli, you don't understand. I've got to get back."

"Look, a change of perspective could help, right? You see unspace from outside again, maybe it'll shake something loose."

"It's not the same. As being *inside*. As diving deep." His voice hit a vein of something haunting, mournful. Enough to make her shudder. Whatever Idris was on, it was eating him alive. "The Well goes all the way down, Olli," he told her. "If I can just keep climbing. If I can do it without being *found*. We never knew how it worked, until the Eye. How unspace is structured. It may not be real, but it still has structure. Just like an idea can have a shape. Simply an idea, but the whole universe we know is stretched over it, like a skin. And it's small, Olli. So small, compared to the real. But at the heart of everything, everywhere, all the time, all at the same time. And at the heart of it..." A broken bit of laughter escaped him, alarmingly similar to one of Doc Shinandri's giggles. "Those old stories about the underworld. There's a monster. You ever read that? A monster to get past, before you can cross over fully. There's a monster in unspace, Olli, and I think there's something *behind* it."

"Or just...there," Olli countered. "I mean, why does it have to be things behind things behind things? Why not just the monster at the centre of everything? Given how fucked the universe is, that would actually make sense, you know?"

But Idris was shaking his head violently. "No, I can *feel* them there. I just need to get past *it* and...talk to them. Explain. Like it was with the Architects. Tell them we're here. Tell them they're killing us and then...then it goes away. Then I can stop."

"So what I'm getting here is that you're not coming with me on the *God*," Olli summarized, because if he could be a monomaniac, so could she. Idris just blinked at her, as though she'd started squeaking and stridulating like a Hanni, and she gave up.

"Nothing doing," she sent to Kit. "He's making no goddamn sense again."

"Little clarity attaches to your own purposes either," Kittering returned shortly. She'd told him she wanted to take the *God* out on her own recognizance but no more than that. And now she was faced with being limited to the Throughways, because it wasn't as if anyone else was going to lend her an Int, one of the galaxy's most in-demand resources right now.

Unless...

"Kit, I'm shuttling back to the *Scythe*. I'll see you there."

*

"It's like this," Olli said, and then had to think about just how it was. Or how it would come across best to Kit, anyway. She was in her Scorpion now, because she preferred that, and on the *Almighty Scythe of Morning* it didn't raise many eyebrows. She'd collected Kittering from the *Vulture God* and they were in the Hegemonic ship's aquarium, as she thought of it, with the Ogdru tanks floating like worlds on either side of them.

"Tell me what it is like," Kittering prompted. His immobile eyes were fixed on her, his body very still and his shield arms planted on the ground with the vague air of a human leaning on their elbows. His mouthparts fidgeted and twined about each other, and she'd known him long enough to read suspicion there.

"All right then," she said. "So what you don't know is, I've been doing a bit of digging while we've been off on Harvest biz. Been playing spies. Keeping track of the opposition."

"The Parthenon," Kittering supplied helpfully. "This is known."

"No, listen. I'm trying to tell you what you *don't* know. Because I've been...wait..." Olli leant forwards in the Scorpion's capsule. "What *do* you know?"

"Information has been accumulating on Partheni ship sightings, as reported by various agents associated with the Broken Harvest and those they deal with," Kit explained. "Your source 'Hexapos' is myself, drawing upon trading contacts to broaden your pool of data."

"The fuck?" Olli demanded, finding her thunder so thoroughly stolen. "Why didn't you say anything?"

"The presumption of clandestine activity precluded it," Kit said, and then clarified: "I thought you were being secret."

"I *was* being secret," Olli burst out, loud enough that her voice made ripples in the suspended bodies of water. "But listen, I thought you... You know, I thought you liked Solace."

"Also you," Kit noted.

"I...I don't *not* like Solace. I mean, for a Patho she's okay. But she's...She's all chain of command. If that Monitor Tact told her to jump, she wouldn't sit about arguing, right? And...I don't reckon she asks questions, because she knows she wouldn't like the answers. It's just...I don't trust the Parthenon. I mean, I don't trust Hugh either, but it's...Ah, fuck. I didn't realize you knew. I feel really fucking stupid now."

"Pleasure can still be experienced in your wishing to tell me, even if the knowledge was already present," Kittering told her brightly. "Are we done here?"

"Yes. No. Look, I...Have you got a slate handy?"

He produced one from behind his shield arms and held it attentively, and she pitched over her carefully curated data. A complex tangle of connections like a conspiracy theorist's pinboard, showing all manner of sightings of Partheni vessels. Or possible sightings. Or rumours of where they'd been.

"It looks like they're planning something," she explained, as Kit studied the data. "I think they've been shifting ships into position to go after Hugh, or the Cartel, or...just *something*. I can listen to Solace all day about how they aren't like that, or they aren't like that any more, or...just... Then every time we're at the Eye there's another three warships and it's all 'Oh, we're just loading and offloading Ints, honest,' but one day it'll be...I mean, the Eye, the arks, all of that just sitting there with fuck-all protection. So maybe they want revenge for that garden ship of theirs that got trashed, or to take out the ark fleet so those Hugh elites can't get away, or to capture the Eye for themselves or... *something.*"

Kit stared at her, mouthparts still fidgeting, as her words trailed off. Olli grimaced with frustration, snapping the claws of the Scorpion and lashing its tail.

"You don't believe me, do you?" she finished. "It all sounds crazy talk."

71

"Belief is only partially the issue," Kittering said. "You are not credible to me. I am not infallible to me. You are distressed by the possibility. What proposal is being made?"

"Are you humouring me?" Olli growled. "Is that it? Letting me chase shadows for a bit, get it out of my system?"

The rapid flicking of his mandibles eloquently conveyed exasperation, as his translator said, "You will get no better than this. You would prefer I not humour you? I am being a friend. No charge."

It was absolutely in her nature to kick against that and go on the attack, make it all about him and her, but she bit down on it because he was offering quite the olive branch right now. He was agreeing to go along with her paranoia, for old times' sake. It was, as he said, all she was going to get.

"Well then, fine," she said. "In that case, help me shift this big glob of water and get it hooked up to the *God*'s nav console."

"Clarification needed?!" The exclamation and question were right there in his translator's delivery.

"Idris won't play ball," Olli told him. "But we'll get nowhere if we just piss about on the Throughways like regular traffic. Parthenon has Ints now. They're not going to be sitting around the regular spacer haunts with all their ships and soldiers. We need to go wide. And so we're going to borrow Junior."

*

In retrospect, Olli wondered if part of her had anticipated the plan would crash to a halt at the first hurdle. After all, she was only taking a priceless asset out of the hands of a godlike and criminally insane alien, by walking into the centre of its power, surrounded by the murderous cultists who obeyed its every whim. Not something to be done lightly, she'd have thought. Except she'd never pushed the boundaries of her nebulous influence with Aklu the Unspeakable before, and now she found they were considerably further out than she'd imagined. Presumably the aforementioned criminal insanity of their chief meant that when one of Aklu's favourites turned up and started taking important stuff, nobody dared raise objections for fear of being summarily eviscerated or something. It would probably have been different if she'd run into Heremon or the Hiver major-domo, or some other leading light. As it was, she just found the controls for the gravitic generators that maintained Junior's spherical tank, worked out how to unlock them from the *Scythe*'s structure and then basically led the juvenile sea monster back to the *Vulture God* as though she had it on a string. There was a three-metre disc below the tank and a counterpart above, and between them they produced the sort of ironclad gravity field that would make a Colonial engineer weep. It occurred to Olli even then that her betrayal of the Broken Harvest was going to be two-fold, because aside from stealing a priceless navigator, these generators alone were the liquid Hegemonic tech that no other species could replicate. If she decided to make a run for it and sell her ill-gotten gains to Hugh or the Hanni or something, then she would probably become very rich and then very dead in that order. *Life goals...*

Junior and its tank filled a big chunk of the *Vulture*'s drone bay, the only space big enough to fit it. She'd even had to take out her own control pod, which ordinarily was where she spent most of her time on board. Except of course the old *God* was running on a skeleton crew these days, what with Idris, Kris and—she grudgingly included—Solace having so many *better* things to do. So she'd be up in command with Kit and give over her old stamping grounds to Junior.

It was just as well she'd made relationship inroads with the immature specimen, she decided. If she'd tried to kidnap one of the big ones then she'd have had to put the ship in the tank rather than the tank in the ship.

"Right, then," she announced, when she'd got herself settled there in her walking frame, because the Scorpion didn't fit well. "I've got a plan. A search plan." Space was, as the saying went, very big. But even Intermediaries didn't just turn up in the void between stars much. Especially if they were, say, part of a fleet that was going to muster together. You needed landmarks to navigate by, meaning known systems. But if you were an Int, those systems didn't need Throughways. And distance was still a thing, as Olli understood it. Parts of the universe which were further away meant more time to travel. So she'd been studying star maps. Not the Throughway network plans that looked like a cross between a planetary transport system and a bowl of ramen, but honest old-fashioned 3D volumes of space, showing the arrangement of stars therein. Starting with Estoc in the centre and then working outwards. Because maybe, somewhere out there, she'd find traces of ships where there shouldn't be any. Drive signatures, waste products, debris. Suggestions that someone with ready access to Ints—the Parthenon, let's just say, hypothetically—was shifting a big old fleet of warships around in preparation for taking control of the Eye. Olli may not have understood much of what was going on at Estoc, but she did understand that the Eye was one hundred per cent the biggest prize in the galaxy right now. And all those snippets and sightings, that insidious trickle of reports she'd scavenged from the Harvest's sources of information, contributed to her suspicions that the perfect genetic exemplars of the Parthenon were not going to be happy to share that prize for much longer. Clandestinely, silently, the warrior angels were on the move.

"Junior, you're linked in?" When she'd ensconced the Ogdru in the drone bay, its generators had seemed to be making connections to the *God*'s systems—a little too readily for comfort, to be honest. She knew Junior couldn't understand her or reply, though, because the feral Ogdru weren't actually sentient like that. Smart animals, basically. Smart and vicious, but that was how Olli liked them.

She fed her wild-goose-chase coordinates into the *God*'s system and waited to see what sort of response she got. The possibility that some essential software incompatibility would scotch the entire mission seemed fairly high.

"Junior?" Her voice would come through in the drone bay and she knew the liquid surface of the tank conducted sounds inwards. Ogdru certainly used sound and hearing as part of their mundane sensory suite. "You ready to go hunting? Just give the word, flap a flipper or something." She had an eye on the bay, seeing the tentacled shape circle round and round its little globe of sea.

"No system activity is detected," Kittering noted mournfully.

"Yeah," Olli agreed. "Hey, Junior. Let's go here." Flagging up her first search point in the *God*'s navigational systems. A location off the Throughway grid, where she could never get the ship to by herself. *I am going to have to kidnap Idris, aren't I?* For a moment her mind became entirely occupied with the image of a trail of cake crumbs or something, leading Idris unwittingly into the *Vulture God*, where she could shut the door on him and remind him who his actual friends were. She almost missed it when Kit said, "Drive activity registering—"

They bullied their way into unspace as though ramming the boundary. It wasn't anything like the way Idris did it, not even when he'd been stutter-jumping them through the battlefield off Berlenhof that one time. Junior just took control of the *God*'s gravitic drives and made the ship an extension of its body. And because Junior was at heart a brutal ambush predator, given to sudden open-mawed rushes, they tore brutally into the interstice between the real and unreal, and Olli was abruptly reeling, alone in the *God*'s command bay. As alone as any human had ever been, the only real thing in the whole universe. So alone that she was in danger of going out the other side and meeting something she really didn't want to.

She fought the walker out to where the suspension beds were, knowing that, in his own universe, Kit would be skittering down to the Hanni-adapted couch in his own quarters. Getting her truncated body out of the walker and into the bed was a further challenge, and all the while the hairs on the back of her neck were telling her that something was paying attention. It had noticed poor Olian Timo struggling with her biological limitations, and that was like blood in the water. Then she collapsed into the suspension bed, that part of it she even filled, and used her implants to set it to wake her the moment they came out of unspace. She mentally flicked the final switch to put herself under. By that time her eyes were closed because she didn't want to look through the bed's clear cover and see the something looking back at her.

And then the bed was waking her again and she was instantly up and flailing, aware that if her hunch paid off this first time, she was by no means ready to exploit it. She linked into the ship's sensors and systems. Demanding reports.

Nothing.

They had come back to the real far closer to the star than a regular navigator would have liked, but presumably the Ogdru didn't care about that so much, just as they didn't seem to care about the whole horrors-of-unspace thing that so oppressed the human mind. The advantages of being a dumb brute. There were three planets in-system, one rock and two big balls of gas way out. Olli ran all the scans she'd prepared, to uncover the footprints of the encroaching Partheni fleet. But nothing.

This was just the first step, though, and she had a whole board of possibilities. Even narrowed down to the volumes within striking distance of Estoc, space was very big.

She liaised briefly with Kit, and then flagged up the next pin in her board. Didn't even get out of bed this time, and made sure she was headed into suspension even as Junior took hold of their drives again.

By the ninth exit into the real she had a system going. She'd always known it would be a long haul, after all. She woke, checked the readings, then had the *God* potter about a bit. She'd seen big red stars and blue-white stars, yellow friendly stars and one sullen ancient ember that barely qualified for the name. There had been planets that were rocks, and some that were balls of ice, and one that had been hosting a thriving biosphere of eye-offending green. Maybe there were even creatures down there who might look up at the sky and speculate about life elsewhere, but since this whole system was cut off from the Throughways, and Olli didn't have the time to go say "Hi," nobody would ever know.

She had a lot of other destinations on the itinerary, after all.

*

Idris and the other Ints might always complain about the toll of spending too much time awake in unspace, but by the twenty-eighth wake-up call Olli was starting to think they had it easy compared to bouncing in and out of suspension like a rubber ball. Junior was apparently more than happy to romp around like a half-trained puppy, while they'd still discovered precisely nothing. Oh, a barrel-full of data she could probably sell to the Cartography Corps, but not what she'd been so sure they'd find. No fingerprints of a stealthy Partheni noose drawing tight about Estoc in the silent void where regular traffic didn't go. She was frustratingly aware this didn't mean they *weren't* out there, with so much of the universe to hide in, even within an easy step. But having spent so long working out the optimal way ships could sneak up on the Eye project, she'd just been so *certain* she'd catch them red-handed. It had all been a pipe dream born of her own suspicion, though, and a need to feel as though she was *doing* something.

"Kit, I've made a mistake," she admitted. She was out of the bed now, her search paused. Back in the walker and tottering over to command.

"This was the expected revelation," Kittering said over ship's comms. More mobile than she was, he was already at his board when she got there.

"Didn't believe me from the start, right?"

"That is correct."

"Going to say 'I told you so'?"

"On the basis that no such words were said, it would be inaccurate. Consider yourself indulged. Do you feel better?"

Olli shot the Hanni a narrow look. "Humouring me still?"

"As a friend."

Who knew what "friend" really meant to Kit? But Hanni and humans saw eye to eye well enough, so she reckoned it was a concept the species had in common. She preferred to believe that, anyway.

"I've been a dumbass," she admitted.

"No arguments here."

"Fuck it," she decided. "Let's go home and see how much trouble we're in with Aklu." And then Junior took control of the ship.

She hadn't designed the interface that way, but apparently the Hegemonic tech could effortlessly get past the locks and bars she'd placed on it. She'd been exercising Junior well enough up until this moment so the Ogdru hadn't had any objections but, now they'd stopped chasing around, her rambunctious pet was *bored*.

"No, wait—" Olli managed before the *Vulture God* plunged back into unspace.

She'd only got her walker halfway back to the suspension

79

beds when they were out again, and she managed a half-sentence of profanity and garbled injunctions to Junior before the Ogdru thrust them back out of the real once more. Alone again, Olli had a moment's panic, feeling that invisible Presence still with them from last time, rather than resetting back to square one like it should have done. She almost fell out of her frame, then had its metal legs pelting for the beds again. They were out into the real even as she got there, shouting at Junior and hearing Kit shouting at her. Then under again. Fighting with her implants and the ship's systems. Trying to override Junior's access, and yet terrified that if she did so when they were in unspace, they might never come out. Springing into the real, getting ship sensor readouts and knowing they were some place completely off her search grid, she realized Junior wasn't even continuing her hunt, just dashing about the universe at random, completely off the leash. Because it was a half-grown alien sea monster with an Intermediary's grasp of unspace, and she'd been treating it like a pet.

When they plunged back into unspace the next time she didn't want to go into suspension, because by then she could absolutely sense *it* aboard the ship. That mythical *it* Idris used to talk about. It was there, right outside in the central corridor. And if she went under, *it* would still be there, and would come to stand over her pod and stare down at her helpless form and...

Out into the real, a jarring, tumbling exit. She was pleading with Junior now, just bawling into the comms. *No more! Not again, please!*

And then Kit was saying, "Hailing is occurring."

"What?" she demanded.

"Correcting. Orders to prepare for boarding. We are targeted!"

Olli scrabbled for the sensors, then saw what was out there.

They were in a system known only by a number in the Colonial database. The Cartography Corps had never even gone there. An angry orange star was surrounded by a ring of dust and rocks, wide spaced, that had either never become planets or had ceased being planets a long time ago.

And they had come out right up close to the Partheni fleet. It was here. Junior hadn't just been rushing about like a dog with attention-span problems. It had grasped what she was after and had been hunting for her. Only doing it properly, casting through the void for a scent. Because hunting was what the feral Ogdru understood. One of them had tracked the *God* through unspace before, which wasn't supposed to be possible by Colonial understanding. The Ogdru experienced the unreal at a deeper level even than human Ints, if only they could communicate their experiences.

Now Junior had found their quarry. A whole fleet: four big warships and their swarm of attendant vessels. Just lurking out here beyond the Throughways, exactly as Olli had imagined. Except she'd also imagined spotting them from a hell of a longer way out than this, and they were already pinning the *God* down with their targeting, demanding to know who she was. Demanding her surrender so they could get a squad of Myrmidons aboard. Olli had no illusions how that would go.

"Get us home!" she shouted, trying to put together instructions in a way that Junior would understand. Right then the Partheni lost patience with them and started shooting.

Kit had already thrown up the best of their gravitational

shielding, and perhaps the Partheni hadn't expected a shoddy little tug to be packing quite that much punch, because the first scatter of accelerator shot diffracted away from them in a rainbow of frustrated targeting.

"Go!" Olli was shouting at Junior, sending every conceivable signal to the Ogdru tank. Cameras from the drone bay just showed their impromptu navigator turning somersaults in its tank, seemingly very pleased with itself. *I got you here!* Junior seemed to be saying. *Aren't I clever?*

"Go! Home! Back to Aklu! Goddamn it, *home!*" Olli shouted, pointlessly. If Junior wasn't receiving her electronic signals then it certainly wasn't hearing her meagre human voice. By the next chain of shot the Partheni gunners had compensated and it carved into them.

They seemed to be aiming to cripple, so they could unshell the *God* of its contents and find out just who knew what. It was slipshod spacer engineering that saved the day, as no part of the old salvager's innards was entirely where it was supposed to be—everything inside it had been re-routed a dozen times since its original construction. Olli saw a scatter of damage notifications, but the vital systems the Pathos had been aiming for survived. Still, the board lit up red and the ship gave a convincing impression of being about to give up the ghost.

Junior got the meaning of *that*, ramming them back into unspace so hard that Olli bit her tongue.

They travelled for longer this time, with the Presence already on board. Prowling between her and the suspension beds now, the cunning bastard. She couldn't let herself go under anyway, because she didn't know what might be waiting when they emerged into the real. So Olli closed her eyes and cut off her own access to the ship's systems. And she fought herself over her own attempts to re-establish it. Because her one backhanded advantage right now was that her ability to kill herself would be limited if she couldn't use the ship as a suicide method.

After far too long, they were back in the real and every muscle her body possessed ached from being clenched and strained, and she swore never to rag on Idris again.

"Kit?" she asked, because first things first.

But Kit had made it to his pod and apparently slept out the whole thing. He was only just waking up out of a doubt-less delightful sleep.

She put out feelers to ship sensors. They were...well, nowhere, really. Literally. Not even a star. They'd needed to escape, and so Junior had taken them off into the deepest nowhere there was. For a moment Olli felt an almost existential dread, knowing herself in the void between stars in a way she had never truly been before.

Then she remembered exactly what they'd been fleeing *from*. Because the next order of business was to get the word out. Let everyone know the Partheni were the treacherous bitches she'd always known they were. Oh, sure, probably there were plenty of good reasons they'd have a whole secret *fleet* out in the trackless spaces near Estoc. She'd look forward to hearing Solace trying to justify that one.

Actually, she wouldn't. She realized she really didn't want to face up to Solace, because she was absolutely sure that, whatever the Partheni were about, they wouldn't have told their oh-so-trusting daughter about it. In truth, telling Solace was going to hurt. Olli was surprised by how much she didn't want to have to do it. But what she *did* have to do was tell *someone*.

"Tell Aklu," she decided. "Get us back to Estoc and Aklu'll sort it out." Or she hoped the Essiel would. Although it was hard to know what the Razor and the Hook would actually do about any given thing. It didn't react to events like a human would. "Tell that spindly bitch Laery," Olli next considered, finally coaxing the *God* into revealing to her where they were. Nowhere near Estoc, apparently, because Junior really had taken them into the weeds. But not just out and away from everything. Back towards Olli's regular haunts, in fact. Hiding from the Parthenon by tucking up into the skirts of the Colonies. By her reckoning, she could get to a number of human worlds in a short hop from here. And a short hop was all she'd trust the ship with, right now. If she'd properly digested these damage reports then she might just have died of fright during that extended fall through unspace. The *God* was limping, and a whole bank of the red on her board pertained to unspace travel.

Laery, she echoed. She didn't know Laery. Havaer knew Laery, but then she didn't *trust* Havaer. Laery had been quick enough to skip out on Hugh and start shaking hands with all sorts of other critters, some of whom didn't even *have* hands. Who knew what sly agreements she might come to with the Parthenon.

Telling Laery sounded like a recipe for old Olli, Kit and the *Vulture God* to get disappeared without anyone ever finding out what'd happened to them. Sure enough Laery had buried some bodies in her time.

And Aklu had one ship. It was a good ship, sure. It was Hegemonic. Could he take on an entire Parthenon fleet with it, though? How much did she want to bet on it? And what if Aklu just...didn't care? Parthenon, Colonies, they were all just *humans*, right. Not even good, red robe-wearing Hegemonic cultist humans. What if she went to Aklu and the Razor declined to get its hooks into the situation?

There was a Parthenon fleet, and it was probably going to make Estoc a one hundred per cent Partheni concern, which could be used against the Colonies the moment the Architects were whipped back—or even sooner than that. Or maybe they'd skip Estoc and appear over Berlenhof, armed with their bright spanking-new class of Intermediaries reclaimed from anti-Architect duty at the Eye. Because Idris, the dumb sap, had thought they could be trusted and had given them the universe.

"No," she said. Kit cocked his eyes at her.

"I like it even less than you, but I think we have to go legit, Kit," she almost spat. All her life she'd been a spacer, proudly independent of any kind of external control and speaking of the Colonies and their government in tones of utter disrespect and distaste. An impediment to be avoided, rather than any kind of benefit or shield against the universe. But right now, if she wanted to throw a big enough stumbling block under the inexorable wheels of the Parthenon advance, there was only one place she could go.

They'd do only short hops through unspace on the way back to Estoc. It was all that she'd trust the *God* to pull off, right now. She could practically draw a dotted line, leaning on the Throughways wherever possible. And if she squinted a bit, she could twist that line of hops so it'd pass through a whole sequence of systems with a Colonial Navy presence.

She was going to rat out the Parthenon's angels to the government, and what a sour taste *that* left in the mouth.

6.

Ravin

"The identification is certain?" Ravin Uskaro prompted. "It's the *Vulture God?*"

On his screen—the ornate-framed mirror in his quarters —his nephew Piter nodded. The boy was grinning, which could be a good sign or a bad one. Ravin's nephew and heir-apparent was, despite his best efforts to educate the boy, still a loose cannon. That sharp grin could indicate a triumph for the family or some self-destructive piece of spite that Ravin would have to spend money and time smoothing over.

"They've been sighted three times now," Piter reported. "Coming out of unspace close to naval installations, broadcasting this incoherent rant and then dropping away again."

Ravin studied the data, already overlaid with a Throughway map. It didn't take much to see that the *God* was making its way back to Estoc. Exactly *why* they'd strayed so far from their usual haunts was anybody's guess.

"And damaged, you say?" he queried.

"That's the consensus," Piter confirmed. "Someone shot them up a treat."

Ravin had seen far too much of the *Vulture God* crew six months ago. Their lawyer, Almier, had almost killed Piter, and that murderous cripple of an engineer had fought her way onto his ship. They were not, fair to say, his favourite itinerant vagabonds in the galaxy. He played through the messages that the *God* had been sending, which were expletive-laden enough to suggest that it was the murderous cripple at the helm right now.

A warning, he considered. *About the Parthenon*. And right now the navy wasn't taking it seriously, because the *Vulture God* was not a credible source. But Piter had been out liaising with Ravin's partisans within the service, and they, good little soldiers, had decided the family needed to know.

A few simple algorithms let him predict the *God*'s course. If they were trying to draw a line from where they were to Estoc, especially through systems where the Colonial Navy had a presence, it was easy enough to second-guess them.

"Piter," he said, "inform our friends that we have passed the message on to the relevant parties, and they shouldn't worry themselves about it. Doubtless it's just those reprobates on the *God* pulling everyone's noses, the way they do, but just in case, we'll look into it. Remind them of our family's turbulent history with the Parthenon. Who better to see if there's any substance to this, after all?"

He took some time to think, after that. He was on the very brink of a lot of things, right then. A throw of the dice that would risk all to gain all. Could he afford to ignore the *Vulture God* charging around with this bizarre and alarming warning?

He wouldn't be the man he was if he had left things to chance.

He sent the projection for the ship's next real space coordinates to Piter, as well as to the naval vessels he'd cut out of the regular chain of command. Those led by captains whose Nativist sympathies were strong enough, or who were Magdans first and Colonials second, or in one case where the captain was also a niece of his. A specially picked detachment, separated out from all the forces he'd been able to pull together for his upcoming, desperate bid to regain leverage in the universe.

And all of it leant heavily on that single meeting he'd had just days before. That unexpected face who'd appeared on his comms screen, breaking through his isolation security to make a very interesting proposal. After Laery had chewed him out and sent him off to Magda with a dead Int on his conscience.

Olli

When they lurched out of unspace this time, the navy was waiting for them. For a moment Olli just stared, as though the Colonial military had taken up witchcraft or something. A moment later common sense pointed out that she and Kit hadn't exactly been subtle about the line they'd stitched between unspace and the real.

"Well I guess someone was listening after all," she admitted, eyeing the little naval blockade. It hadn't been clear before that anybody had actually taken any notice of them. Now they had, she wasn't sure how she felt about it.

However she felt, it was put into serious context when the hail came through.

"*Vulture God*, this is the Colonial Navy vessel *Retarius*. We understand you've got something to tell us."

Olli stared—not at the board or at Kit, but at something inside her own head. Bad memories, fighting memories. Because she knew the voice.

Kit was plucking at the rim of her walker frame, obviously wanting to get the hell out of there. She could see his point. It wasn't hard to recognize the smug, self-satisfied tones of the Boyarin Piter Uskaro.

"What the *fuck*," she asked, "do *you* want?"

If he took offence at her lack of respect for feudal privilege, it didn't come over in his voice. "What's this about the Parthenon?"

"Have they hit Estoc yet?" Olli burst out before she could stop herself. Kit was actively pinching at her now, and she shook him off irritably.

"Hit Estoc?" Piter was probably aiming at baffled, although the closest he could come was derisive. "Whatever do you mean?" A sigh. "Look, Timo, isn't it? If you have some warning about the Partheni, then let's talk. They're no friends of ours, after all."

Olli blinked. The drone bay cameras showed Junior circling in his tank uncertainly.

"We're not getting any closer," she told Piter. "You get on a shuttle and come over, then we'll talk."

"Unsatisfactory feelings are present," Kit said primly. Olli grimaced at him.

"It's not ideal, I get that," she said. "But look. We go tell Aklu, we don't know what the clam bastard'll do. And the *Scythe*'s a nice toy, but will it stand against all those Partheni ships?"

Kit made a little screechy sound with his mouthparts that didn't translate.

"Look," Olli said again, aware that her need to keep talking about it spoke volumes about her own deep reservations, "I know we've fucked with these boys before now. They're shits. They'd grab Idris if we had him. But if we can play one set of shits off against another for the greater good, shouldn't we do that? And they're Colonies, right? They're humans."

"Humanity is one attribute they have." Kittering wasn't looking at her, his shell tilted over his own board. "Also possessed by Solace."

A shuttle had indeed departed the *Retarius*, heading out for them. Olli carefully jockeyed the *God* so that the shuttle's trajectory would complicate any offensive moves from the warship.

"What're you saying?" she demanded of Kit. "We go and hug it out with her and she'll somehow find the balls to make her side stand down? I like Solace, Kit. But she's not her people. Can't trust them. Too many of them look at us and think we're obsolete. Yesterday's mediotypes. And the Uskaros are greedy bastards, sure, but they're not going to go all genocide any time soon. Maybe he and the Pathos can blow each other the fuck up and make the universe a better place."

"A lack of conviction emerges," Kittering told her.

"You've got something to say, say it."

For a moment it was just her glowering at him, and his little crown of eyes turned resolutely away from her. But then he shifted on his stool, a little dance of jointed legs so that he was facing her square on, shield arms raised. It was a punchy stance for a Hanni, someone in a fight or an argument. He was angry, she realized. Or whatever Hanni got instead of angry.

90

"This is too far," Kit told her. "These are unreliable business partners." Or that was how his translator spat it out, but she reckoned it was Serious Bad Words in the original Hanni. "Past dealings grant no confidence. All past social contracts with Solace have been fulfilled beyond expectations. These arrangements would not be approved by Kris or Idris. Or Rollo."

Olli opened her mouth to say something she'd regret, about Rollo being dead and all. Except the mad venture which had killed him had been one Solace signed up for when she needn't have. And Olli was absolutely aware she could twist that into *Without her he'd still be alive*, but she wasn't *that* dishonest with herself.

"You don't get it," she muttered, surly. "You . . . It's humans. Humans and Pathos. Or regular humans and Parthenon humans, if you want. But . . . it's like if there were other Hanni out there who might come in any moment, edge you out of all the good deals, take all the stuff for their hatchlings and leave you with nothing. You get me?"

"Your half-hearted attempts to understand my life cycle aside," Kit said acidly, "this is not appropriate behaviour. Of which you are aware."

"You don't get to say what I'm aware of." She watched the shuttle draw closer.

"You receive the benefit of the doubt regarding my estimation of your ethical character."

Olli drew breath for another angry answer. Something that would escalate matters, turn everything back on Kit, and pick some other fight just so she didn't have to deal with this one. Perhaps call him a crab bastard and sling a few Hanni profiteer stereotypes his way to avoid the real issues. But she stopped. Ripped off the conversational scab so that only the raw truth was left. The thing that scared her most.

"We can't just let the Parthenon walk in," she said. "We need these fuckers to deal with their fuckers. It's just... zero-sum fuckery. Or something. You wouldn't understand, Kit. It's war. Hanni don't do war."

"Wars were done by Hanni," Kit told her. "They are not known to you. We got better. Why do you think we like games so much?"

Olli digested this, wondering if she was actually any the wiser, and accepted that what Kit was saying just echoed the little voice inside her which had been trying to get her attention for a while now. "Right," she agreed. "Okay then." The shuttle was close, hailing, telling them to maintain their position. Instead, she started letting the *God* drift further out, breaking from the rendezvous point the shuttle was aiming for.

A battery of cautions instantly came their way, from the shuttle and *Retarius* both. Telling them to power down, hold their place. To prepare to be boarded. That last command was the final straw for Olli. Abruptly the shuttle wasn't just a safe delegation, it was packed out with navy troops or Magdan Voyenni house guard.

"Junior, go. Now. Go now. Get us the fuck out of here!"

The first volley of accelerator shot was already on its way, picked up by their instruments only moments before impact. A hail of projectiles shredded the volume of space they were in and enough of it tore into the *God* that Olli's entire board lit up red, again, and then just died. There were alarms and then half of these stopped, for the bad reasons rather than everything miraculously fixing itself. They were losing atmosphere, and she couldn't adjust the gravitic envelope to hold it all in because Kit was using everything they had to fend off the next salvo.

What? The Uskaro hate me this much? And yes, of course they did. She had trashed their nice yacht last time, and they were never to be trusted. She shouldn't be surprised. But she'd also taken them for bigger-picture boys, especially in light of the information she'd just passed on to them.

Kit's efforts with the shield saved them from the next burst. The *God* was tumbling wildly, some of its reaction drives firing, even those she didn't want to, while others were unresponsive. The brachator drives that should have been yanking them left and right against the gravitational microstructure of space were doing *something,* but whatever it was, neither she nor Kit had any input. The *God* was a loose cannon, and right now that meant, between the shielding and their wild gyre of a course, the second volley hadn't torn them any new holes. But that was a strictly temporary state of affairs.

"Gravitic ring full power! What are you doing?" Kit demanded. Abruptly they had no shields and all the ship's available energy was being funnelled into the main drives.

"It's not me," Olli said, and obviously it wasn't Kit either, which only meant bad things. Most likely that a catastrophic failure of the drives was imminent. The engines themselves didn't actually have that much *bang* to them, but the potential energy in the space–unspace boundary had *bang* to spare. And if the drives tore that up and then lost control of it, they'd make a very pretty firework for Ravin Uskaro to enjoy, leaving behind less than would fill one of the man's fancy wineglasses.

Her screen filled with characters. They were Colvul characters, because the *God* ran a Colonial computer system, but whatever thoughts they might be expressing came out as untranslated garbage. She had a weird feeling from it, though. Like it was something panicking, screaming, trying to get away.

She had no eyes on the drone bay, not with all the damage they'd taken. But that area obviously retained its connections to the rest of the ship because Junior had just taken the helm. Junior might be a predator, but every predator knew when it was outmatched. Their pet monster was trying to run and Olli had no idea if the *God* was intact enough to survive the transit.

But it wasn't as though they'd last long staying here either.

She craned over to look at Kit, about to give him whatever warning she could, and then the *Vulture God* tore out of the real and away, shedding pieces of itself and gouting atmosphere.

Ravin

The Morzarin Ravin Uskaro watched the ragged hulk of the *Vulture God* tear into unspace. The captain of the *Retarius* reported promptly that the salvage vessel had a seventy per cent chance of not surviving re-entry from the real, based on damage estimates. Ravin's bleak personal prediction was that he hadn't seen the last of the pestilential ship. Olian Timo was harder to get rid of than a venereal disease working for the Hugh tax office.

But she wouldn't be charging about blurting her idiot warnings, anyway. Not for a while. Which left the board clear for Ravin to make his move. Along with his new allies.

That surprise contact, after his dressing-down by Laery. The unexpected face seen in his personal viewscreen. The last face in the universe he'd have expected to see, in any of its incarnations. His enemy, and yet...

A physical meeting had seemed absurd under the circumstances. If it hadn't been for the nature of their mutual opposition, doubtless they could have dealt with everything remotely, over properly coded transmissions. Except their enemies included a Colonial spymaster, the Parthenon and, worst of all, the Hivers. Nobody really knew how far the Hivers had dug into human affairs. They'd been everyone's best friends and most convenient tools for decades.

The fact that Ravin was up against both his own people and the Parthenon made any meeting through subordinates problematic too. So it was that he'd gone out to the secret rendezvous in the newly refitted *Raptorid*, purged of anything even resembling Hiver tech. He and his nephew Piter, his catspaw and co-conspirator since the boy had reached majority. Plus a handful of his personal staff, men whose families had been vines clinging to the Uskaro name for generations, and his Voyenni house guard, who would die for him without hesitating or asking questions.

It might well have been a trap, but since the cursed Cartel had taken over, Ravin had felt himself in a trap anyway. All the ark-builders' planning was exposed and ruined by Laery's damned people. No chance of gently, covertly shepherding the appropriate parts of humanity into a new mobile dawn. A galaxy-striding civilization, living with all the comforts and luxuries of home. And, had their plans come to fruition, they'd not even have had the threat of the Parthenon coming after them. But it was all in ruins now. All those resources stolen and committed to the will-o-the-wisp idea of going to fight the Architects *in unspace*. A doomed venture, but apparently Laery was more than willing to spend the future of her species on it.

You drove me to this, he'd decided gloomily, as the *Raptorid* emerged from unspace, closing in on their meeting point. His leashed Int navigator was the only individual on board not sworn to him by blood or generations of service, but there was more in her head than just the Liaison Board's surgery. She knew full well she was his property. He'd broken her and made her his creature, and that would have to suffice.

"Are they there?" he asked Piter. The young Boyarin leant over the bridge displays, frowning. Out there was a single blue-white star, the bright point his Int had steered towards. One ice ball of a planet orbited it, at the very edge of the star's gravitic reach. A dead system, of no use or interest to anyone, and without any unspace Throughway their instruments could detect. As anonymous a place as any for a clandestine meeting, or an ambush.

"One ship, Uncle," Piter reported. "A warship, though. One of their big ones. Beacon identifies it as the *Skathi*. They're hailing us." He swallowed. "We can still leave."

There was a tremor in Piter's voice, and Ravin felt just the same quaver within him, but he snapped, "Cowardice? Is that what the Uskaro name has come to? Respond appropriately. We are here as equals. Behave like it."

Piter cast him a wild look, and a moment later he said in a small voice, "They invite us to dock."

The die is cast, Ravin decided. Laery had taken too much from him to be borne. He had lost face with the family, with his ark-builder peers and with humanity at large. The Nativist faction was bucking under his hand right now—they said he'd knuckled under, that he wasn't the champion of the human race they'd thought. Another few months and he'd have lost them entirely to some opportunistic demagogue. And when you lost a hold on *that* particular serpent, you could expect to feel its fangs soon enough. They were always after someone to blame for their misfortunes.

Before this unexpected contact, he'd been a blind man in a maze. Now he'd been promised a way out and he would lunge for it, come what may.

The *Skathi* was everything he would have imagined. A great segmented tapering length, its fore muscular and brutish, bulked out by a gravitic drive and its main weapon batteries. A Partheni warship, top of the line. Even if he'd turned up in the most powerful cruiser he could borrow from the Colonial Navy, he wouldn't have rated his chances toe to toe. And so here he was, in an armed yacht, just clipping along into the warship's shadow. Showing no fear. He'd be damned if he'd give them the satisfaction.

There were Myrmidons in full armour waiting for him when he and Piter disembarked. He brought half a dozen armed Voyenni with him and nobody objected. The lack of protest was a pointed insult that he could only let slide.

After a short walk past far too many staring women with the same face, he ended up in a small stateroom. Possibly this was just economy of space aboard a ship. Or else this sort of room normally saw the kind of discussions where one person asked the questions and the other got beaten into answering them.

A single woman was waiting for him. Compact and lean, like all the Partheni; a touch of silver in her hair and a few lines on her otherwise standard-issue face. Her uniform marked her as an Exemplar. Captain of this ship and its associated support vessels. Not quite a grand magnate of the Parthenon, but then these were unprecedented times. You never knew who might seize the day and rise to pre-eminence.

"Morzarin Ravin Okosh Uskaro," she named him, speaking Colvul with a twist of accent.

"Exemplar Mercy," he responded with a nod of precisely calibrated respect. Partheni naming conventions had always seemed like a joke to him. He had no idea why their founder, Doctor Parsefer, had decided to use descriptors, nor why they always went by the translated meaning when dealing with outsiders, rather than keeping the original Parsef word and making it sound like an actual *name*. All those virtues they garlanded themselves with and then waved in your face. And he had a feeling that, of all the Partheni, Exemplar Mercy was amongst the worst named.

She had a smile on her face, and he didn't like it. Perhaps neither of them had come out of the Cartel's rise with unhurt feelings, but she surely hadn't lost like Ravin had. That smile said she knew it, and was enjoying seeing him laid low, even while she graciously reached a hand down.

So: "Let's assume we have exchanged the appropriate pleasantries," Ravin told her. "We have enquired after one another's family, made all necessary small talk about our homes and gardens and the spotless uniforms of one another's servants. However, you saw fit to contact me. So, perhaps you might explain what subjects of substance we have to speak about?"

A minute nod from the Exemplar. "I contacted you because you do not appear to be satisfied with current arrangements at Estoc and within the Colonies."

"I cannot imagine why you think such a thing," Ravin said blandly. "Surely the salvation of the universe from the threat of the Architects is in everybody's interests."

"You do not believe this will be accomplished," Mercy said. "And, before you give me any more stock denials, neither do I. I have had access to limited data from the project, as have you, no doubt. There are too many unknowns to be gambling so much on it. It's a pipe dream born of those who would burn all of humanity for even a chance at harming the Architects. Ash, this Naeromathi, Telemmier the Intermediary. None of them a rational mind."

She sat at last, and he did likewise, Piter still at his shoulder. Lowering herself into the chair had been a stop-and-start movement for Mercy. Old wounds, he guessed, and wondered whether they came from service against Architects or against humans.

"You've said nothing so far that I'd disagree with," he allowed. "And you're aware of what I've lost. I'm sure you revel in it, if you think of it at all. But I had a future for humanity and they've taken it from me. And, most likely, signed the eventual death warrant for my species."

"I am very aware that the future you had for humanity did not include us," Mercy said pleasantly.

Piter and the Voyenni were wire-taut, staring at the Myrmidons, weapons ready. Ravin sensed imminent violence boiling just beyond the walls of the room, ready to descend on them. If the shooting started, it was probable nobody would get out of the room alive. He made himself radiate calm, even smiled pleasantly at the woman across from him.

"I deny nothing," he said. "Your spies have had enough time to join the dots. Your people have lived as a spacebound force for a long time, and we have too much history. You would always have been a threat to us, and there would always have been a voice amongst the Parthenon saying, *Hunt them down.* A voice like yours, perhaps."

"A voice exactly like mine." Her soldiers were right on the edge too, but she matched him smile for smile. "When you orchestrated your attack on the *Ceres*, I was the first to argue for all-out war, no prisoners, no restraint." A wider smile. "No mercy."

"Then the Cartel emerged, and I lost my arks and my future," Ravin pointed out. "You lost nothing but your war. Which was only postponed. So, it seems to me you have come through this very well in comparison. Why, then, are we having this pleasant talk?"

"Morzarin Uskaro, I am a realist, above all," she told him. "I won't say I don't find the idea of refugium humanity offensive in principle, but I don't feel it necessary to beggar ourselves just to have my war. Because we have other options now, if we can extricate ourselves from you."

Ravin stared at her for a long time, turning the cogs of his mind until something clicked. "I understand."

"Do you?"

"Something has changed for your people, since the *Ceres.*" Half a year, but so much had happened. "Only because of Telemmier." He felt he was owed that small jab, reminding her that her great leap forwards was only as a result of a Colonial turncoat. Nothing the Parthenon could have accomplished on its own.

"It's a big universe, Morzarin," she agreed, hiding any irritation well. "Or it is when you have Intermediaries to pilot your ships. That was your plan for the arks, and that can still happen. And now we have our own Ints, we can take ourselves wherever we want. Except for one thing."

"History."

"There are still those amongst my people who are mired in the past," she agreed, "tethered to the Colonies, seeing themselves as the defenders of our disadvantaged siblings. Too many memories of the first war. Of how we spilled *our* blood to save *your* lives. As if that is something to celebrate. We need to cut ourselves away from you once and for all. To admit that, if being like you is to be human, then we are not merely *human*. We have our own destiny, and you cannot expect us to be your shield. But for now, our Intermediaries are all committed to the Eye project, or to saving your worlds. They work alongside the Ints the Cartel stole from you. So neither you nor I have what we want. When one of my subordinates is *summoned* to stand before them, they tell me, *You cannot fight us and the Colonies.* And I am sure they tell you, *You cannot fight us and the Parthenon,* am I correct?"

"You are. And I see that you are proposing a third logical step in that syllogism," Ravin noted. His heart, he was almost embarrassed to discover, was racing.

They cannot stand against us both.

It wouldn't be all of the Colonies by any means, just whatever force the Uskaro family could muster, aided by the fact that the whole of the Estoc yards had been theirs once, as had all the workers spread across the ark fleet. And it wouldn't be all the Parthenon, either. Probably just a minority faction. But Ravin knew how a minority could look like a majority if it acted decisively enough.

"I'm guessing," he said, "you already have forces in place.

101

And that, if I refused you now, I'd not leave this ship and you'd make your play anyway, without inside aid."

"These are all reasonable guesses," Mercy admitted.

"I'm not refusing you," Ravin told her flatly. "So, let us talk details of what I can do for you, and what you can do for me, and how we part ways amicably afterwards."

7.

Idris

"Idris." Andecka Tal Mar's voice, sounding from right by his ear and very far away. "Idris. Menheer Telemmier, you are too far."

He tried to tune her out. To get so far he couldn't hear her. She was right there in the corner of his eye, or at least the ghosting shadow of her. Intruding on the solitude of unspace. Linked by the machinery.

The others were further off. Except they were all with him, in the Wellhead, almost within arm's reach. When he was under, the limited footprint of the Wellhead became mutable, though. He could travel away from them without their spatial relationships changing at all, falling down a decline in that *other* direction. Receding; waving; just a dot now, too far for them to haul him back hand over hand, yanking on his oxygen line to drag him back from the depths. He was far and going further. Let Andecka hail him like the buzzing spectre of a fly in his ear. Let the voices of the Well crew echo tinnily down to him from up in the real. Shinandri's high laugh and Jaine's careful numbers and the rest. Let them. He was going away. He was hunting his own prey. He was—

"Menheer Telemmier," again in his head. "We need your

103

assistance, please." Tugging on that connection between them that was common humanity, however thinly stretched he felt it. Until he came back to them, shrank the dimensions of the Wellhead Machine room as he perceived it. Repacked all the notional space that had unrolled between them like an infinite carpet.

"I was close," he muttered, peevish as a schoolboy.

"Menheer, you were too deep." Andecka Tal Mar, the volunteer, the committed. A woman who'd put herself forward for the barbarity of the Liaison Board because she'd been convinced humanity would need her. And been right. She was the best of her class because she wasn't a convict conscript. Bore her scars with pride.

"This structure here." One of the Partheni, her face and shadow shimmering briefly in Idris's mind's eye. Hooking at his attention as she highlighted part of the complex information construct that was the Architect nursery. While he'd been off on a frolic of his own, they'd all been doing their jobs, of course. Solving the equation. Unpacking the unthinkably dense knot of information that constituted *Where Architects Came From*. Working out how it might be vulnerable to attack. Feeding data up the Well to Shinandri and Ahab and the rest, so they could apply the half-understood engines of the Eye to it.

And so he weighed in with his little insight, which they always seemed to want, but which felt so meagre. Because they were the new class, and they listened in the briefings. They knew all the numbers and the jargon, the technical language they were all making up as they went along, because nobody had ever done this before. They approached it as if it was a science, where you could put logic in and get understanding out. But he hadn't learned the trade like that. He'd just *done*. There hadn't been anybody to teach him, save Saint Xavienne, the one and only natural Int. She'd just been born that way, and had understood it as little as he had. They'd learned together, but at the same time they'd each learned alone. None of this gregarious comparing notes business.

So he chipped in until he felt they were satisfied they'd had some genuine Telemmier input, about as efficacious as him rubbing the equations for luck, and then he was sneaking off again. Putting distance between them even though they were all in the same boat. Falling.

As though his corner of the Wellhead Machine was extending down and away. Dragged into an impossibly attenuated spike as he pulled against the gravity of the Eye and the Well and all the rest of it. The perceived walls around him revealed as tissue-thin, mere illusion. Wallpaper over the infinite horrors of unspace. Closing his eyes, and his mind's eye, until he could reach out beyond all that flummery to the reality—the *un*reality.

He felt *it* stir immediately. That was the way of it these days. Not even a grace period to let him catch his breath. He was the fly now, in the ear of the kraken.

He remembered how it had been back in the day. All those Intermediary Program psychs telling everyone there wasn't a Presence. Just the human brain reacting to the problematic emptiness of unspace. Mindfulness and mental exercises would rid them of the fear of it. Still the party line at the Liaison Board, as far as he was aware. Except he and every other Int knew it wasn't so.

It uncoiled. Vast, sightless, lazy. Its unreal tentacles reaching up through the lightless abyss to touch him. If it caught him, would it just be in *his* head, or would he act as a conduit that brought the monster into their midst? His solo exploration a profoundly reckless and selfish act?

Falling further. Picturing himself: a single suited figure receding into the darkness of an ocean chasm. Into the dark. Into the monster-haunted depths. Gone beyond the reach of the sun. Brushed by the touch of leviathan but twisting aside from it.

"Idris." Faint in his mind. Andecka again, having noticed him gone. *Leave me alone!* Blotting her out. Cutting the cord, or trying to. Let them worry away at the data like rats. Again, he wanted no part of it.

No part of saving the species? Was that his own mind, adopting the voice and mannerisms of the alien Harbinger Ash? Or had they actually brought Ash to the Wellhead to reason with him?

"I have no objection to saving the species," he told nothing and no one, as he hung in the void. "I have an objection to exterminating another species to do it."

Are the Architects even a species, though? Ash's maddeningly reasonable voice. *Or just constructs doing the will of their masters? Or even just some randomly occurring aberration arising out of the structure of unspace? Who are you to judge what the universe should and should not include?*

"Go try that logic on the Hivers and see what they say," Idris suggested. The part of his mind severed from the conversation was still feeling out the nothingness below him. He felt himself in the very shadow of the Presence, sneaking past the limitless expanse of its leathery flank. And beyond it, beneath it...

The abyss gazed back at him.

A moment of infinite clarity came. The helplessly descending diver's lamp illuminating the seabed. The ruins. Atlantis.

That was his mind's translation of what his Intermediary senses were reporting. A lightless, sunken structure. A broken shell, unthinkably ancient. Weed-wreathed. Roof cracked open by the pressure and the flood. And within...

Staring back at him. Startled, even. *Who dares intrude...?*

Then gone. The vastly unravelled distance snapped back. Partly from his own shock. Partly from the shouting of the others. Andecka, Shinandri, too many voices. And lost in them all was the mocking whisper that might be Ash and might be that other thing which borrowed Ash's voice.

Or might just be his own diseased brain going sour and curdled at being cut off from the real for too long. Plunged into depths and pressures not good for human consciousness. Not even for his, the second child of the Intermediary Program, as close to an unspace native as any human had ever become.

He exploded back to them, swinging like a drunk thrown out of a bar. "I had it! I don't, don't *care* about your calculations. I've got, I haven't—no *insights* for you. You think my perspective's worth anything more than—" Furious, incoherent, flinching away from them even as he rounded on them. Aware he'd been away, under, gone too long. That they'd been trying to reach him for ever. That if they hadn't dragged him back then, there might not have been anything *to* drag back. Or else, what got hauled up into the sunlight might not have been *him*.

Andecka's voice came through, cutting down his protestations. "Idris, we're under attack."

107

Solace

She'd grown complacent. There had been a time—chasing after Idris, fighting the Uskaros and the Broken Harvest, embedded in the *Vulture God*'s crew—when she'd felt like the fulcrum of the future. Tarekuma, Arc Pallator and Criccieth's Hell; brutal worlds and brutal actions.

Then the Cartel had stepped out of the shadows and seized the helm. Moved the Eye here to Estoc. Taken over. The long-awaited Partheni Intermediary Program had turned out its first class of Ints, with all the mechanical assistance that wouldn't have been possible without both Idris's help and the Eye to crib from. The "thin steel line" against the Architects had started saving worlds, or at least buying time for evacuation in a way that wasn't just throwing people and ships to their doom, the way the last war had gone. As Foresight had begun feeling out the tides of unspace so the movement of the Architects could be predicted, she'd been able to relax. Just kicking her heels on the Host, nursemaiding Idris alongside Kris. The three of them an unlikely triangular cog in a bigger machine where she didn't have to turn the crank by hand. Which was how things should be, as far as she was concerned. That was the heart of the Parthenon way: being part of something grander than yourself. Even seconded on clandestine work for the Aspirat intelligence service, she knew she was a part of a wider team. Giving of yourself for your sisters, but always having them there for you. The future of the human race was heavy, but that was why you split the burden over as many shoulders as possible.

Idris being down the Well—as seemed to be the case more often than not these days—she was in the canteen with Kris and Trine. "Canteen" was probably more than the place deserved. An awkwardly angled chamber within the Eye, formed from three uneven corners of Originator stone, walled off with great ugly metal plates by the installation's first, inhuman, intruder, and then with human-scale additions bolted on. All that spacer aesthetic, heedless about how it looked just so long as it worked and you could get at all the ducts and wiring easily.

Trine was holding forth about their most recent discoveries. Focusing less on the technical details, which neither Kris nor Solace understood, and more on the fact that it was Trine who'd made them. On the Eye, Trine was finally getting the credit they felt they deserved. Or at least some of it. There probably wasn't enough credit in the universe to actually reach Trine's self-determined desserts.

The voice that crackled in on her personal comms channel was half lost in corrupted signal. Staccato instants of half-familiar tones sliced and spread thin. "Executor Solace —please, Idris—betrayed—being silenced—have to—" And nothing. She was on her feet, chair kicked back, Kris and Trine's projected face staring at her as the Hiver's tirade stuttered to a halt. Waving down their questions, accessing every channel she could. Pulling rank with her Executor status and what little Aspirat cred she could muster. Trying to identify the voice in retrospect, because the channel had come without ID.

Cognosciente Grave? One of the Partheni Ints, the first, in fact. One of Idris's protégées. Solace was sure of it. She reached out to the woman. Was she even still in-system? Yes, there was her name on the roster of those being rotated out of the "thin steel line" and into the diving rota at the Well.

She signalled, but got nothing. Tried again, aware that just about everyone in the canteen was staring at her now. Trine extended one metal arm to pluck at her sleeve and get her to sit back down, but she twitched away from them.

Not just a lack of response. Her channel was down, as well as the whole Partheni network. She couldn't reach anybody.

She ran from the canteen without explanation, aware that events had already overtaken her. She needed armour, a weapon. Barging through a room of off-duty technicians and a handful of hollow-eyed Ints, she saw a pair of Myrmidons at the far end looking equally thrown. They spotted her and started to run over, seeking orders she didn't have. As they were halfway to her, the next development washed over the room. She saw the ripple of it pass across everyone. Haphazardly placed screens lit up with the news. Individual comms channels, private chat networks. The same word getting through to them all. Ships were entering the system, tearing out of unspace too close to the Estoc yards. Two big warships and a half-dozen mid-sized combat vessels. Some of them Colonial Navy, some of them painted up in the complex livery of Magdan Boyar families.

Betrayed. Grave's word. Except did this even count as a betrayal? Was Solace remotely surprised?

"Gear up," she told the two Myrmidons. "Enlist everyone you run into. The Cognoscientes will be working on comms." How the Colonials had hacked *that*, she didn't know. Complacent, all of them. There had always been a war on but she'd forgotten, and so had the others. *Forgot to watch our backs.*

She gauged the forces out there as best she could, with

her rough and ready understanding of Colonial capabilities. A strong force, but not overwhelming. There was a Hiver factory that would be weaponizing its units even now. And there was the *Almighty Scythe of Morning*, which she reckoned would be able to live up to the hyperbole of its name.

But it would be tight. Time to muster the home-front troops and prepare to receive boarders. Because the Colonies weren't about to just destroy their precious Host.

With no one else taking charge, she ended up using the general in-Eye comms. It wasn't as though she'd be spreading any more panic than was already running riot. Giving muster points for every Myrmidon who heard her. *Arm and ready.* Ensuring there were Partheni hands controlling the gravity and the atmosphere. Instructing civilians to keep their heads down and get out of the way. And all the while wondering why the hell Monitor Tact wasn't doing all this herself, what with her being the ranking Partheni on board.

There were thirteen Myrmidons, fully kitted out and ready, when she reached the nearest muster point. By then there were around a million comms requests waiting for her, as just about everyone *except* her troops tried to ask her what was going on. She banished the lot of them, even the calls from Kris and Trine. It was time to be a soldier again. Time to buy time, if nothing else. The Host's displays showed her that some of the Magdan ships were already moving in to take possession. Except that was a hard thing to do with a "ship" as weird as the Host. It was, quite literally, all over the place. Any attacks would have to fight for each individual platelet of it, and then fight through the nightmare labyrinth of the Eye. And Solace would make their lives difficult every step of the way.

Then a new raft of ships arrived. Except she knew these —well, their shapes and their specs. The *Medusa*, the *Queen of Aragon*, the *Skathi* and all their attendant fleet. A ragged cheer went up from her Myrmidons, and though it was a breach of discipline she joined right in. Whatever scheme the Colonials had cooked up, her people had been ready for it. Now the noble Uskaros and their navy allies were going to get their asses royally kicked.

Comms cleared immediately, as though a switch had been flicked, and Solace reported her disposition and readiness the moment she felt the change, like a release of pressure in her ear. One line to Tact, one to the newly arrived ships.

The immediate response came from the Exemplar of the *Skathi*: "Received and understood. Stand down and await further instructions."

Solace frowned inside the little world of her armoured helm. "Repeat? I said we are ready to repel boarders." Seeing that the Uskaro vessels weren't slowing or peeling off.

"Do not engage. Stand down and offer no resistance." It was a shocking enough order that she double- and triple-checked the credentials of the transmission. "Shuttles will be dispatched to repatriate you to the fleet when occasion permits."

Solace had the sense of each of her cohorts staring at her, waiting to see if the chain of command would change those orders as they passed through her particular link of it. But the broadcast had been on open Partheni channels. It was unthinkable she do anything other than confirm what came from above to those below. That was how it worked. Cog in a greater machine. Many shoulders to bear the burden. Suddenly Solace wasn't remotely as happy with the thought.

She tried for Tact again, but there was nothing, not even an echo. Her own personal chain of command had been decapitated.

She called up a screen inside her helm and watched the ships nearing, orienting themselves to dock. Gripping her useless accelerator, she tried to work out what had just happened to the universe.

Ravin

Piter had begged for command of the yacht *Raptorid*, which to Ravin's mind showed a lack of ambition, but he could hardly begrudge the boy the "honour." The yacht's captain had strict instructions to keep the vessel out of danger. Ravin was all for tempering the scions of his family in war, but not in any way that would genuinely endanger them. The difference between a respectable duelling scar on the cheek and a back-alley knife in the kidneys.

He himself had taken the bridge of the vessel named the *Grand Nikolas*, which had been navy once, mustered out somewhat before it had reached obsolescence after a little family finagling with the brass, and then refitted for modern combat. Not something that would last long if it went toe to toe with the navy's latest or anything from the Parthenon, but the best iron fist in which Ravin could hide his velvet glove.

And there was the yawning moment when it looked as though he might need to take the *Grand Nikolas* out of Estoc as precipitately as he'd arrived. His fleet was cruising in towards the Host and the shipyards, all those ark ships begging to be reclaimed by their true master. But with no sign of his allies, and challenges already coming his way from the Cartel's administrators. Not that he couldn't take the Host with what he had, because he'd brought a lot and the turncoat Colonial and Partheni forces there didn't have *that* much punch. He was more worried about the Hiver factory out there, which had been under contract to him and his peers before becoming part of the Cartel. It seemed the main Hiver Assembly had decided it should have a vote in galactic politics now, after decades of machine work and obedience. And, yes, the nest of bugs had won some sort of political *independence*, but Ravin had always felt this was on the strict assumption they wouldn't do anything untoward with it.

And out there beyond the Hive factory was the real threat. Ravin reckoned his forces could deal with the Hivers, left to their own devices, but he didn't even *know* the capabilities of the *Almighty Scythe of Morning*. He'd had a close call with the Hegemony half a year ago, enough to reaffirm that the state's legendary inertia didn't mean technological stagnation. Before going head-on with Aklu the Unspeakable, he'd want half the Colonial Navy, and not to care much how many of them survived.

The *Scythe* was still idling, though, and possibly Aklu simply didn't interpret the sudden appearance of Ravin's force as an attack. Who knew what the Essiel thought, save that they thought very highly of themselves. Ravin liaised briefly with his subordinate captains. They were all older navy men, out of retirement or near to going into it, many of whom could remember when Hivers were property. They were Colonial patriots, Nativists. Men who remembered military service as glorious because they'd not personally been there when the

Architects had arrived. Men who felt betrayed by the Partheni secession, and by the general tide of history. Men who had enough ambition to be useful but not so much initiative that they might ask the wrong questions or prove dangerous. He confirmed their orders, assured them that allies were on their way, then sent them off towards the Hiver factory to teach the cyborg intelligences what happened to appliances which got uppity. A word to the captain of the *Grand Nikolas* had the vessel and its escorts arrowing in towards the Host. All according to plan, save the plan had envisaged backup. And now the *Scythe* had changed its heading, sluggishly accelerating, turning its broad face in towards Estoc's solitary world and mortal concerns. It was a nasty piece of work, that ship. Made like a stylized sun, some quirk of iconography where human and Essiel imaginations met. A rayed shape like a spiked disc, built around a central hub of crewspace and deceptively slight gravitic engines. The Hegemony could pack a lot of power into very little room, and their liquid tech probably meant that every system could be repurposed as anything else, if need be.

"Hold our course," he told the *Nikolas*'s captain, voice admirably steady at the man's look. Watching the *Scythe* glide in-system like a curious shark.

Then every bridge alarm went off at once as the cavalry —odious but necessary—arrived. A great fist of Partheni ships, jumping close in-system with their new Int navigators. Hadn't that been the nightmare of every Colonial strategist since the secession? And here was Ravin virtually cheering them on. *The universe has gone mad.* But that madness had begun with the reworking of Earth over a century before. This was just the next logical stage. The point when humanity finally let go of the deadweight, the next step in the species' social evolution. Life in space, not on the illusory stability of a planet. The Parthenon and the ark-builders had come to the same conclusion, in the end. Ravin would be one of the lords of a nomadic fiefdom, and humanity's future would be preserved, no matter what the Architects did.

Exemplar Mercy appeared on his display, her stern, sour visage. "My agents within the shipyard have neutralized the dissidents within my own people, and all others are being ordered to stand by. Do not engage and you will meet no opposition aboard your target, Morzarin."

"Confirmed and likewise." He had plenty of loyalists amongst the work crews and technical staff of the yards and they would all be playing their part. Laery hadn't been in a position to replace everyone, after all. She'd kicked out the senior administration when she took over, but Ravin and his peers had hand-picked all the staff at Estoc. Laery didn't understand the whole system of deep-ground feudal obligation that Magda practised. She was a bureaucrat, not a true leader.

"We are moving to engage the Essiel," Exemplar Mercy informed him crisply, and Ravin nodded. His own navy vessels were already burning up the outer fringe of the Hiver defenders—a swarm of construction frames flooding out of the factory's ports to meet detonations and massed accelerator fire. And the *Scythe* hadn't slowed. Nothing in its bearing suggested the arrival of a Partheni fleet had changed the odds in the slightest. Ravin licked suddenly dry lips. *What if it's right?*

But he'd come too far for fear, now. Without the ark fleet and the yards at Estoc, all his plans were dust. He would commit everything, and if necessary he would pay anything. It was the future of his family and his species. How could he give anything less?

Havaer

Within seconds of Ravin Uskaro's little fleet entering the system, Havaer Mundy received one word on his encrypted channel.

Silence.

He didn't allow himself to think about it until he was already under way He'd been on one of the Host's scales, checking for hardwired comms taps the old-fashioned way. Just routine anti-intrusion work because Chief Laery had been feeling out a possible security breach. Then the jolt of surprise came from everyone around him—tech crew, a couple of Intermediaries—when the ships turned up. Followed by: *Silence.*

He'd been on his feet, casually walking away. Avoiding notice as best he could, easy enough because everyone had other priorities at that moment. He headed to the emergency lockers which the ark-builders had installed within the scales' odd geometric spaces.

He suited up, still moving as casually as if he was off to grab a cup of kaffe, not making eye contact with anyone. *Silence* was the worst case. It meant no further orders should be expected in the near future. It meant trust nobody and go dark. Each individual scale was frankly too small to hide on, so it also meant a trip over to the Eye, and he didn't have a ship.

He used his overrides to get through the airlock without triggering any alarms, fretting out the half-minute he was trapped in the little box of a room as the atmosphere cycled. Then he was out, standing on the ruby-coloured hull of the scale, looking up/down at the great ragged eyesore of the Eye.

Having originally been buried in the crust of a particularly nasty planet, it was now a hideous broken mass of dark stone, loosely surrounded by the curved shields of the Host's scales. It constantly looked as though it was about to fall on him.

He checked his pack. It had reaction jets and a fuel store if things got desperate, but at the moment the Eye and the Host together had a gravitic field he could ride using the pack's stubby handles. He used his overrides to link to the Eye's systems and got himself cruising across the void, up/down from the scale's underside towards the raw-edged exterior of the Eye. He was in near vacuum now, but as he got closer to the rock the air would thicken, held in place by the gradient of the gravitic field. He'd start to hit turbulence and actual micro-weather events, and have to take an active hand in the steering. Right now he could just glide, though, which meant he'd also be able to see what was going on.

Silence meant he was on his own. Could he reach out to his own contacts? A judgement call, and he made it. Because the general channels showed him exactly where those ships were headed, and though he couldn't necessarily rely on human help, the Hivers weren't going to have turned on him.

He pinged the channel he shared with Colvari. Staccato bursts of contact, re-routed, encrypted. He didn't even know if anyone was looking for him. Most likely Havaer Mundy was the last thing on anyone's mind, friend or foe. *Silence, though. Silence* meant you couldn't be too careful.

What can you tell me? to Colvari, wherever the Hiver even was. With any luck not on the Hiver factory, given what was going down.

He could feel the Eye's thickening atmosphere pressing on the suit by the time the response came, Colvari establishing a bounced link under cover of the constant traffic that regulated the scales' positions relative to one another. Compressed volleys of data, encoded for him using the private protocols the pair of them had agreed on and shared with nobody else. Just like when Havaer and the Hiver had been unravelling the files which exposed the ark-builders' plan out over Arc Pallator.

It was nice, Havaer thought faintly, *to be out in the open for a while.* But apparently it was back to the shadows for him. Possibly forever. *Silence.*

Once he'd decoded the first images, he just stared at them on his helmet's display, falling upwards towards the Eye.

They were from the Hiver factory itself. He sincerely hoped Colvari was just passing them on, rather than being their start point, because they showed the handful of navy vessels there taking the satellite apart. The Hivers were fighting back, that much he saw. Individual construction frames wheeled in a great cloud about the factory, casting themselves into the withering storm of the defensive fire the navy accelerators were putting out. Each one would have within it a Hiver colony, a seething knot of cybernetic insects that, between them, generated a conscious artificial mind. And they were being flayed. The navy ships had clearly come equipped specifically for this fight, decked out with batteries of fast-tracking accelerators. Where the Hivers made it through, they got to work on those ships. All their tools of construction now used for deconstruction, tearing at every vulnerable point they could reach. Hacking at the hardened systems of the attacking vessels. Trying to suborn them, overload reactors, foul atmospheres, cripple the gravitic drives. But there would be navy troopers swarming the outside of their ships like ants, hunting down every frame that made it through the fire. Havaer didn't give them much of a chance.

When it was clear phase one was dead in space, the factory started up phase two. Using its own gravitic drives to accelerate untenanted frames and parts, and just any piece of junk really, it reconfigured itself into a makeshift railgun and just blasted mass at the enemy. The first onslaught caught the navy by surprise and Havaer saw one of the attacking ships fold around a barrage of super-accelerated machinery. A vent of frozen atmosphere, a flare of instantly extinguished flames and then a shudder as the big ship's drives detonated. The rest of the fleet quickly readjusted shielding then, though, shouldering through the sudden storm of projectiles. Fingers on the scales of the gravitic gradient, so that space sloped away from them on all sides and the hail of missiles spun harmlessly away, into the void, without ever deviating from their straight-line courses.

End of transmission.

Havaer adjusted his angle of approach, and then received a brief scatter of images from a different perspective, enough to suggest Colvari wasn't on the doomed factory. The Partheni had arrived, but Havaer had already gathered this was bad news from other channels. Now he saw their trio of big ships unloading at the *Almighty Scythe of Morning*. A blizzard of accelerator shot rushed invisibly across the kilometres of intervening space and then...Havaer blinked. The gravitic drive of the *Scythe* had taken the barrage and effortlessly folded the contours of space around it, gathering every pellet with the care of a god counting sparrows. Lighting them up so that a sudden wheeling constellation flared before the great rayed disc of the Hegemony ship. Then it cast them, burning, into the void in every direction, with a gesture of sheer divine contempt. He'd never seen anything like it. Half that storm of stolen shot went right back at the Partheni. Colvari's data registered the *Queen of Aragon* and *Skathi* were taking damage. The *Scythe* sailed blithely on, sedate as a pleasure cruiser and priming who knew what Essiel weapons...

Then that transmission cut too, even as he touched down on the stony surface of the Eye, and he saw Chief Laery in the next one. Standing in her office, stick-thin frame hanging awkwardly in the spindly exoskeleton she wore beneath her clothes. Four Voyenni were shouldering their way in, guns levelled, demanding she get down on the ground. Demanding she drop the weapons she didn't have. The camera position was behind her, so he couldn't see her face when she spread her hands arthritically. *Me, an old woman? What trouble am I going to give you?* They hadn't just gunned her down, at least. This was a civilized coup, so long as you weren't a Hiver or a Hegemonic.

The Voyenni were big men, kitted out with accelerators and combat armour in Uskaro green and gold. They surrounded Laery, gun barrels right in the woman's face, still demanding she get down. Havaer was on the exterior of the Eye by then, labouring under the gravity, pushing through the atmosphere, which was shockingly restrictive after his long free ride. There was a raw-edged opening a hundred metres away, and he called up maps of the labyrinthine interior, working out how he could get to his chief. But knowing it was too late.

The view switched. Laery was now being escorted out into one of the awkward spaces within the Eye, making a big show of how frail she was: her small steps, her careful motions. And the Eye was a terrible place for access. Weird-angled Originator spaces cut up by great metal slabs of Naeromathi ironwork, then pierced by ladders and crawl-spaces and walkways installed by the humans Ahab had brought in. He could read the frustration and impatience in the Voyenni as they tried to get Laery through a hatch. So brittle they could hardly lay hands on her without breaking her twig-thin limbs.

She struck just as she cleared the hatch, as Havaer's perspective shifted to the suit camera of one of the Voyenni. Colvari was fighting their own information war, he knew, infiltrating the enemy systems.

Two of the Voyenni were below Laery, one reaching up to pull her off the ladder. Another two were above, one partway through the hatch when it slammed explosively shut and cut the man in half.

Laery just collapsed, a bundle of bones at the feet of the men below. They were still reacting to the hatch when the anti-fire system went off, flooding the chamber with flame-retardant powder that was sucked out a moment later. Of course the Voyenni were suited up and Laery hadn't been, but still, when replacement air flooded in, one of the men at the ladder's base was down. Havaer had no idea what had happened to him, but his gun was gone and so was Laery.

He almost signalled her then, but *Silence* meant silence. He held a channel open, and hoped she'd call him when she knew where they could rendezvous. For now he got himself inside, lowering his body until *down* sorted itself out and the shaft he'd been about to tumble down became a crooked corridor with an unnerving, stomach-twisting slope. And that was about the best you could expect from Originator spaces. They hadn't been intended for humans to crawl about in.

Another momentary jitter of data. For a second he was trying to decode it into images, but then he registered the origin: not Colvari, Laery. A random scatter of data that he could sieve coordinates out of. She was on the move and he'd need to chart his own course to intercept her.

He didn't even have a gun. Not long ago it hadn't seemed necessary.

His map of the Eye interior gave him a madman's obstacle course of ladders and hatches, drops and crawl-ways that could take him to her. He'd be quicker without the suit, but right now he didn't trust the atmosphere, and the next development could see him back on the outside and making a break for it. He had to labour on and hope he didn't meet any narrow gaps the flight pack wouldn't fit through.

He couldn't even confirm to Laery that he was on his way. Comms within the Eye was a tricky proposition even without the hostile takeover. The Originator material itself was basically impenetrable. You were relying on the haphazard skeleton of links Tokamak Jaine had installed, and whatever additions Laery's own techs had added. And as those techs might well be Uskaro's too, anything Havaer sent out was encoded and masked and bounced around so that nobody would be tracking it back to him any time soon. He continued to move, winding his way like a grub in an apple. Just one tiny human being in the stone organs of this great dead relic.

He hailed Colvari as best he could, getting a mere rattle of data in return: Radio Free Colvari was alive, relocating, somewhere else within the tangle of the Eye. And who else could Havaer call, honestly? Kris Almier maybe, because she of all people wouldn't be welcoming the Uskaro family with open arms. Solace? Not now there were Partheni vessels slugging it out with Aklu. Telemmier? Hard enough getting through to the man when you were standing right next to him under ideal conditions, let alone now. Havaer just put his head down and pressed on, waiting for Colvari or Laery to signal him.

Then he was two rooms away from the rendezvous point and the next hatch wouldn't open. He tried his overrides, but he was locked out now. Someone else had muscled in on the system and cut it off by brute force. Crouched in his encumbering suit, his breath loud in his ears, Havaer fumbled out a toolkit and started to work on the panel. Jaine's human-level furnishings were spacer standard, meaning they were designed for someone to crank them by hand in an emergency. He reckoned this wasn't the emergency she'd been thinking about, but it counted in his book.

Halfway through the job, Colvari re-established a video link. A Voyenni suit bodycam again, because that was the only transmission being allowed through.

They'd caught up with Laery.

She was against a hatch, and from the look of it, it could be the same one Havaer was struggling with. She had her stolen accelerator braced against the knob of her shoulder —not that the weapons had a recoil, but it helped to aim. Two skeletal struts had hinged up from her exoskeleton to further steady the weapon, another little trick nobody knew she had. From his point of view, Havaer could see at least half a dozen Voyenni in the cover of slanted stone bulkheads jutting from the ceiling. One put his head up and Laery fired, accelerator pellets striking sparks from the dark material and ricocheting about the room.

He doubled his attempts to get into the hatch's workings, ripping off his gloves so he could work faster. No technician, but he came from a culture where everyone learned the basics because it had been life or death a generation before.

Laery's stance changed. That little stick figure straightened, as though finally acknowledging the presence of her firing squad. From close to the bodycam, Havaer heard a voice call, "You've given us a remarkable run, for someone of your vintage, but this is as far as you go." Ravin Uskaro himself, doubtless safely in cover but come to see the end of his fox-hunt in person. "I'll give you to the count of three to get rid of that toy and surrender. We both want what's best for humanity, Laery. I respect that. I hope you can, too."

Laery's head cocked, thinking it over. Havaer's hands worked. He was trying to signal her now, *Silence* be damned. *I'm right here. Just stall them.* But there was no way through. Uskaro had locked comms down. Havaer couldn't even send a signal through the workings of the door.

Her gun drooped, and then, just as the first two incautious Voyenni were coming out of cover, she brought it up and emptied it in their direction, chewing chips from the stone, carving up the unwary vanguard, with the resulting back and forth of bounding shot turning another three into jerking bloody puppets. The man wearing the bodycam hurled himself back, making Havaer's view arc across the stone angles of the ceiling. Then there was a high singing whine of an accelerator closer to hand, returning fire.

The barrage put three holes in the hatch he was working on and came within a finger's width of doing the same to his skull. He fell back, tools scattering, seeing the craze of cracks across his helmet face-plate from where one shot had lightly glanced against the exterior.

The bodycam point of view stabilized: Voyenni emerging cautiously, guns levelled. A weird, brittle tangle of nothing very much was at the base of the punctured hatch. Hardly enough material there to be a whole human body, surely. Just a doll, a model, a bad simulacrum of a human form. Bare bones.

His point of view advanced until the Voyenni stopped in a wary, almost respectful, ring around the body of Chief Laery. Her torso was carved up, a Rorschach spray of blood wet across the black stone like an art installation. Probably only a handful of shots, but the shock would have done for her almost instantly.

The Morzarin Ravin Uskaro stepped to the fore, bold now the guns had gone away. Havaer saw his aristocratic profile as the bodycam tilted towards its master.

"Such a waste." Though Ravin didn't sound exactly unhappy about it. Havaer couldn't imagine he'd have kept Laery around for long. Too dangerous a mind to hold onto. The Magdan noble took another step in, bending over the corpse as if to reassure himself she really was dead.

Laery lunged for him and Havaer almost screamed at the shock. It wasn't a human motion. He saw her tired old joints split with the force of it. The hand that closed around Ravin's throat was all brittle bones and atrophy, but it was backed by an exoskeleton following its owner's final instructions. The view danced and swung as Ravin staggered back, the featherweight corpse clinging to him, its mechanized grip digging into his flesh. One of the Voyenni smashed a gun-butt against Laery's dead arm and just snapped it off at the elbow, but the hand continued its inexorable quest for closure. Havaer silently cheered it on.

But they finally managed to prise it away, leaving Ravin sitting, gasping, blood pooling about his collar from the claw-marks Laery had posthumously gifted him. He'd live, the bastard, and Laery was already dead. But Havaer vowed to return the favour, first chance he got.

He and Colvari were on their own now, and there were a whole host of Laery's people he needed to look after. The fight between the Partheni and the *Scythe* continued, and that could still tilt in his favour. Laery might be dead, but until he joined her, there was work to do.

8.

Olli

They came out into the real and the last red lights on Olli's board guttered and died. She waited for the emergency lamps to flicker on, but one of those red indicators had apparently been telling her about the death of that system, too.

"Kit?" she asked.

A leaden grey glow slowly built from nearby. The screens built into Kit's shield arms and back, the ones he used for paid advertising, were now repurposed as feeble lamps.

"Attempts at damage diagnostics are being hampered by damage to the damage diagnostic systems," came the clipped voice of his translator. "We have very limited power."

"I see that," Olli agreed soberly. She couldn't get the internal cameras working, so in the end she trekked down to the drone bay using her walker—which had a long battery life, but not unlimited. Junior's big sphere of water was still a big sphere of water, and hadn't become a splat all over the floor, or a ball of ice. That was something. It was just about one of the only things she had, because everything else was coming up flat nothing.

But she was a spacer. She was a scion of folk who had lived on the expanding edge of the Architect-driven Polyaspora, back during the war. She could fix things. She could bootstrap.

She transferred herself into the Scorpion. It had less internal power, but it made her feel better and had a lot of inbuilt tools. Then she set about seeing what could be fixed.

*

Comms between the bowels of the ship and command had been easy enough. That let her talk to Kit, at least. After some tinkering and swearing and hitting things with a claw, she got emergency lighting on as well, though it was dimmer than she liked and she suspected the power cells it relied on were bleeding out even now.

No heating, though. No power. The reactor had taken some direct hits and just vented out into space, an option preferable to venting into the crew areas, admittedly. For most ships that would have been it. Time for the distress call. Except Junior had flung them right into the middle of nowhere, and a distress call would take several centuries to arrive anywhere useful. The deep-space salvage ship *Vulture God* had, as its final action, turned itself into a piece of deep-space salvage. And Olli was very aware of how long most of those floated around before anyone found them. For ever, in most cases.

The Scorpion's internal heater was working overtime to keep her just very, very cold rather than dead. She saw that Kit had screwed with the efficiency of his screens until they were glowing a cheery red and keeping him active. Apparently Hanni could also selectively shut down organs and limb segments in sub-zero conditions, so score one for non-human biology. None of that was a long-term solution, of course.

And she had a long-term solution. It was sitting right here in front of her. A new reactor. Or, well, "new" was an interesting word to apply to a conflation of old pieces of junk, but it was there. She'd cobbled it together from all the pieces that Kris constantly told her to throw out, and which she'd stubbornly kept, because you never knew.

Well, she had never known, and nor did Kris, but now she did. Specifically, that it wasn't enough.

Olli was the exemplar of the spacer adage "make do and mend." Kit was also a good hand—or clutch of mouthparts —with Colonial tech by now. They had worked with a feverish haste, each pumped up on species-appropriate stimulants because going to sleep on a dying ship was a good recipe for not waking up. And in the back of Olli's mind was a clock counting down. The Partheni were making a move, and that Uskaro bastard was doing the same. She couldn't be sure whether it was the same move, or if the pair of them were about to slug it out and wreck everything in the Estoc system in the process. However it was going down, it was her *friends* in the middle of it, and here she was, lost in the trackless void, on a dead ship.

She had that corpse of a ship on the slab, with the replacement heart right here. Her ludicrous cobbled-together piece-of-shit reactor. And it wouldn't react. Nothing would come of nothing, and nothing was all she had.

As she'd been building it, she'd dreamt of showing it to Jaine. Joking about it. *Yep, we rescued you with this.* Imagining the cyborg laughing at her engineering. The thought *hurt.* Kris, Solace, Idris, yes, but right then Olli wanted to see

Tokamak Jaine more than anyone. The feeling surprised her, like a knife in the kidneys when you didn't even know you were in a fight.

But she wouldn't be seeing Jaine, because she couldn't jump-start the reactor. Just that jolt it needed, to trigger the reaction and snowball into a force that would let Junior take them back into unspace, to vanish into oblivion or come out in Estoc. Everything else was fixed, secured, jury-rigged just enough for that desperate leap. Everything except the actual burst of power that would breathe life into the reactor so it could breathe life into everything else. The one technicality that stood between the *Vulture God* being a spaceship and becoming a piece of debris lost in the vastness of the universe.

"Kit," she said at last. "I can't do it. There is nowhere on this ship that has the power to get this thing going." She'd factored in the Scorpion and her walker, the emergency power, even Kit's own screens. She could drain every erg of fizz they had on board and it wouldn't get them over the threshold. "Fuck me, I'm sorry, Kit. I really screwed up. I've made so many bad decisions."

"Query, how is Junior?"

Olli frowned, but Kit was community-minded, and Junior was one of the crew, sure enough. She pivoted the Scorpion to look behind her. The big swirling sphere of water was still there. Junior hung inside it, pointed towards her, probably hungry and trying to remember if she was a snack or not.

"Junior's fine." It was another thing to whip herself over. One more creature she'd screwed over, on this idiot quest of hers.

"Why?" Kit asked.

Olli frowned. "Why what?"

"Drone bay ambient temperature is what?" Kit's translator had been getting more and more terse.

"It's..." She checked the Scorpion's instruments. "Fuck. Twenty-nine below out there. And falling."

"Similar recording here," Kit confirmed. "Query *why* Junior is fine therefore."

Olli turned fully around and stared at the Ogdru in its watery world. Watery. Unfrozen. And fine. It was Hegemonic tech, but Hegemonic tech still needed *power*. The tank had been drawing from the *God*'s supply. She'd be damned if she'd accept that their sufficiently advanced technology actually *was* magic.

"So where...?" She took a reading, yanking the meter back before Junior could destructively investigate it. Water temperature inside the sphere was a couple of degrees above. Positively balmy. And yet Junior wasn't drawing power from the ship any more, for the perfectly sensible reason that there was nothing to draw. So...

"Kit..." Olli was reconfiguring her instruments, not just the Scorpion's but all of the toolkit she had that still worked. For a moment lights flickered weakly about the drone bay as she let her frame's batteries drain out into the ship's wider systems.

Her eyes went as wide as an owl's.

"Kit, Junior's... generating power."

"Biological?" Kit quizzed.

"No, it's not... I'm not sure I believe what I'm seeing. Junior's interacting with unspace."

"That is why we brought it on board?"

"Yeah, but for *navigation*. Inside unspace. If I'm reading this nonsense right, Junior's interacting with the unspace boundary from *this* side. Just...making friction. Keeping the bath warm."

There was a long pause that hung between the two of them, and although Kit wasn't human, Olli reckoned he was feeling the same reluctance she was about saying it out loud. Voicing that faint hope they'd both just conceived.

Junior was generating power, through a means entirely outside Olli's technical understanding. But once it entered into real space, it was apparently mundane enough to use as a water heater. And maybe, just maybe, there was a deep enough well of it to get the reactor going.

Kris

Getting Idris out of the Eye's machinery was a whole military campaign in itself. Hard enough even in peacetime and now apparently they were being invaded. She had to explain everything to him three times while he visibly pieced his mind together. Little clickety spasms kept running through his artificial hand, out of sync with the shivering of the rest of him. One of his eyes kept half-closing lazily, then jerking too wide. She would have been worried about him giving himself brain damage, but that was basically Ints in general and Idris in particular.

"They can't do this now," he managed, when she'd finally got through to him that there were not one but two hostile armed fleets in-system. Both of them inexplicably ignoring their lifelong avowed enemies to go after the shipyard's own defences.

"This is exactly what I was attempting to communicate,"

133

Shinandri agreed, with tart outrage. The remaining complement of the Wellhead had gathered around the now-emptied
Machines, nervously awaiting developments. Getting word
from anywhere else in the Eye was patchy, and from the
actual *outside* even worse. There seemed to be multiple
ongoing attempts to interfere with comms. Kris sat and
hugged the twitching Idris, the centre of a ring of confused-
looking Liaison Board Ints such as Andecka Tal Mar. Shinandri
was hunched on one of the Machines, half in the hose-
bedecked encounter suit he used to dive in with the
Intermediaries. He couldn't experience unspace first-hand
like they could, but he was able to glean data from their
neurometrics, Kris understood. He'd been down with them
when the fighting had kicked off, and now he was hugging
his knees and scowling, as though the whole business was
aimed at him personally. Jaine, by contrast, had just sat down
with her tools and taken a panel off, using the emergency
as an unscheduled maintenance break.

There was a clatter from outside and everyone jolted, but
it turned out to be just Trine again. The Hiver had got fed
up of waiting and gone off, as they'd said, to give someone
a piece of their mind. At people's hopeful look, their illumin-
ated face burlesqued a frown. "I have been unable to find
anyone of use, my fellow inmates," they announced. "The
sole individuals locatable anywhere near this facility were
some of the original technical staff, who were profoundly
disrespectful to my person and species. I am beginning to
think all is not well." They were clowning, Kris saw.
Grandstanding a little, to raise morale generally or perhaps
just for themself. "I take it our glorious leaders have not
emerged with a battle standard and an army?"

Kris shook her head, glancing at the irregular-shaped iron-plate door that led to the next chamber. This was still part of the Wellhead, and there was another Machine there, but it wasn't built for humans. It was Ahab's lair, the main driving force which had transformed the Originator site into the Eye in the first place. And, because Ahab was a leading light in the Cartel, it was where two of their other leaders had gone. None of them had come out yet and Kris dearly hoped some kind of plan was emerging, because right now nobody was telling them anything.

Then Idris finally woke up enough to ask, "Where are the others?"

Kris exchanged an awkward look with Jaine. "They... The Partheni just up and left, Idris."

"What now?"

"Their Ints, they just... they all got a call, and then they left. Not happy about it, but I think they got orders. Those are their ships out there, after all. Among others." She grimaced. "We've lost them."

"Solace—"

"I've tried to call Solace. I can't get through."

"But we have to." Idris jumped up, then sat right back beside her, blinking rapidly. "Trine—"

"I detected not a trace of even one Partheni on my travels," the Hiver confirmed. "Evacuated, the lot of them. I, too, would very much like to have an open channel to our old compadre Myrmidon Executor Solace right now, if only to give her some select words about her choice of loyalties."

"Working on it," Jaine said. Everyone stared at her and she arched her eyebrows at them. "What do you think I've been doing? I'm trying to get around this mess of comms embargoes they've saddled us with. Just hold your flaps, will you?" Her head snapped back to the knot of wiring she'd been eviscerating. "Wait, hold on. Something incoming."

A voice sounded from the emergency speakers riveted into the ceiling. Kris was already forming the word "Fuck" after a few seconds because, despite the static and distortion, she knew it well.

"Attention all crew aboard the installation known as the Eye," announced the Morzarin Ravin Uskaro. "Know that the facility at Estoc has now been returned to the control of its rightful owners. All personnel are instructed to remain where they are until liberating forces give them further instructions. You will not be harmed unless you offer resistance to our troops, or refuse to obey instructions given to you." There was probably more, but Jaine made a little sound of triumph and Ravin's voice cut off abruptly.

"Got a channel," she announced. "Dumbass son of a bitch just about handed it to me with his public service announcement shit. Don't have long. Who do we want?"

"Solace. Partheni channel." There was possibly a better use of the window but Kris was with Idris and Trine on this one. They *really* needed to know what was going on with the Parthenon.

"Gotcha," Jaine said. "Imagine some music or something. Doot-de-doot-de-doo and... You're ready? Speak now or forever you know what."

"Solace?" Kris asked, and Trine spoke over her with, "Myrmidon Executor, old comrade in arms, I hope you have some explanations," because with them, why use one word when a dozen would do? Idris said nothing, just stared hollowly.

"Kris?" Solace's voice, faint, but also low like the woman didn't want to be overhead.

"What's going on, Solace?" Kris asked evenly.

"I don't know, Kris, but—we've all been stood down. Orders at the Fleet Exemplar level. There are Voyenni all over the Eye now. We're just watching them walk past. I don't understand." Solace's voice, shaking slightly. "I shouldn't even be on comms right now. I'm...sorry, Kris. Trine. All of you."

Then she was gone, and Jaine cursed, going back to working on the panel.

"Well, this is plainly unsatisfactory," Trine observed. "I shall file a complaint." The hollow bowl of their face then tilted, cued by some sound Kris hadn't heard. A moment later they had visitors, just about the last person she wanted to see plus enough of his bully boys to keep everyone there in line. Ravin Uskaro himself, come to take possession of the Wellhead. It struck her that, yes, the Estoc shipyards, the half-built arks and the Host had all been in the hands of him and his allies before the Cartel moved in. The Eye, though, was a bonus. An alien treasure hauled through unspace and dropped into his lap. What he'd do with it, she had no idea, but he needed to understand it was a unique and priceless prize.

The look he turned on them was avuncular, proprietary. After all, over half the Ints gathered there had been his family's property before, under their leash contracts. Now they were his again, and he'd finally added Idris Telemmier to his collection.

He'd been having a mixed day, she could see. He'd turned up in full regalia, a Magdan dress uniform with a battery of medals he'd presumably been born to. There was a serious medical casing keeping his neck stiff, though, enough that he'd have difficulty looking left any time soon. Someone had got close enough to sour his triumph.

Trine strode forwards. Kris lunged to snag their casing but they were too fast for her. The armoured Voyenni all had their accelerators levelled, a second's work to chew up the Hiver and all their long academic career, but Trine didn't seem to register the threat. Instead, they drew themself up to their full height—six inches over Ravin once they'd completely straightened their birdlike legs.

"I lodge a formal protest," they announced grandly, their multitool rack of jointed arms splaying in annoyance. "I am a Delegate of the Hiver Assembly in Aggregate. I demand to be accorded the proper diplomatic benefits and repatriated with my embassy. This conduct is unacceptable."

Kris waited for Ravin's temper to flare, but apparently whatever tribulations he'd endured were very much in the past because he regarded the Hiver with only mild contempt.

"Delegate," he said with mock respect. "May I show you something, before you present me with your itemized grievances? A little update of news, as you may be slightly behind on recent developments?"

One of his people then zipped open a filmy screen. Everyone craned to see what it might be. They'd been mostly cut off since the Colonial ships hit system.

She recognized the Hiver factory. Even in that first image it was holed and battered. Parts of it vented flaming atmosphere, the fires guttering into the void. Its angle to the world below seemed terribly wrong, and Kris understood that it was falling. Dropping into the planet's gravity well, so that its underside had already started to glow with atmospheric friction.

She flicked a glance to Trine's face. It was entirely unten-anted, frozen in the diplomatic outrage they'd been broadcasting a moment before.

They watched the Hiver factory die, falling into the world, blazing like a star. Burning, yet still with enough mass to impact like a meteor on the lifeless crust below. Countless Hiver instances winked out, a repository of minds cracked open. A war crime.

"You were saying, Delegate?" Ravin asked pleasantly. "Only, you may wish to reassess the importance of your diplomatic credentials. As well as your request to be returned to your embassy, such as it now is." He gave a nod that obviously sent a jab of pain through him, and one of his Voyenni stepped forwards. Without ceremony, the man took out a baton and smashed Trine across the barrel torso, then swept the Hiver's legs out, obviously intending to topple them to the floor. Trine ended up in a weird crouch instead, utterly inhuman, caught on their fan of arms and one foot.

"You are an acknowledged expert on the Originator tech-nology we are surrounded by," Ravin informed them. "On this basis I will retain your services as a data store and ana-lytical engine. But do not confuse the matter. You are not a Delegate. You are not, as far as I am concerned, a *person*. You will not presume to act like one. My technical staff will come and remove you to your new place of work shortly."

Kris waited for the sharp rejoinder that would probably get Trine's limbs torn off, but the Hiver reoriented themself and then just sank down onto their haunches, knees as high as their head. Their face flicked to a neutral, inoffensive expres-sion and they retracted their arms. She remembered that Trine was *old*, possibly the oldest continuous instantiation of any Hiver personality anywhere. They had been property when they'd first *become*. They'd lived to see their people given rights as sentient beings. For all their bluster and bombast, they *remembered* and knew when not to push their luck.

Some message obviously reached Ravin, because he stiffened and stepped away, and the Voyenni formed a guard around him. A moment later, Kris heard marching feet and then a squad of Partheni Myrmidons entered. Short and compact women, faceless in that infamous grey battle armour. The Voyenni bristled and tried to loom, but the women plainly didn't rate them as much of a threat. Although if a fight kicked off between them here at the Wellhead, there would be enough shot flying around that just about everyone there would catch some.

Half the squad stayed facing off against the Voyenni, evidence that whatever unholy alliance was in place wasn't exactly cast iron. The rest stomped up to the big door that led to Ahab's quarters, and waited.

Kris found she was holding her breath. Were the Cartel's leadership about to explode out of there, guns blazing? It didn't seem their style, but she was off all maps right now, as far as knowing where she stood.

The door finally ground open with an ear-offending whine. Kris saw Jaine's head twitch and could almost hear the woman thinking, *Been meaning to get round to that.*

Out walked a single woman. Monitor Superior Tact, formerly known to Kris as Solace's boss. She regarded the Myrmidons without expression.

Tell them to fight, Kris urged her mentally. *Turn it around! Do your goddamn spy stuff. Do something!*

But Tact just stared for a moment, not even acknowledging

Ravin and his people. Then she stepped forwards and the Myrmidons surrounded her, very clearly a prisoner escort and not an honour guard. They proceeded to march her out of the Wellhead, and that was that.

"Fuck," Kris said, too loud. She hadn't realized how much of her hopes she'd pinned on that going very differently.

Ravin chuckled indulgently and got as far as, "Now then, Mesdam Almier, you shouldn't—" before Ahab exploded out of the next room, its bulk barely fitting through the door.

Ahab was the only Naeromathi Kris had ever seen close up. What the species had looked like originally was unknown, given the Architects had destroyed the worlds they'd evolved on and just about everything else of their species, save the predatory ark fleets they roamed the universe in. They'd been aquatic, people thought. Usually you saw them in tanks and globes, dimly glimpsed, long-necked monsters.

Ahab had adapted. Its hide was scarred with hideous implants, most of its head a battery of artificial senses and possibly weapons. Its bulk sat lopsided on a six-legged walking frame, constantly on the point of toppling over yet as agile as spiders when it needed to be, and now it was advancing on Ravin's people at a rate of knots. And shouting. Ahab had the only Naeromathi–Colvul translator anyone had ever come across. It always shouted.

"Why has the work stopped?" it demanded. "This interruption must cease!"

Shinandri and Jaine, Ahab's old confederates, were on their feet and trying to intercept it. All the Voyenni had their accelerators levelled. The room was one twitchy finger away from becoming a massacre.

"Ahab, calm!" Shinandri's high voice cried, and "Boss, you can't!" from Jaine.

"Our victory is close!" Ahab howled. "The maiden voyage must not be prevented!" Kris had no idea what *that* even meant, because the precise details of what they were doing with the Eye were frankly beyond her. Ahab had obviously registered the guns, though. It loomed and thrashed its neck back and forth, but halted its headlong rush. Ravin stared at the Naeromathi in fascinated horror. Possibly he was considering how it would look stuffed and mounted in one of his grand houses back on Magda.

"Is this thing of value?" he asked.

A metal growling rattled from within Ahab's implants, but Shinandri stepped between it and the Voyenni, arms outstretched. "Your lordship, Menheer Boyarin, however the appropriate address goes. I cannot know what your plans are for any of us, or for all we've built here, but *please*. We are engaged in valuable study, irreplaceable additions to the store of sentient knowledge. An exploration of unspace without parallel anywhere in the universe. A means, I might even dare say, of striking against the Architects themselves. Of becoming masters of those volumes that extend into the nighted depths beneath us, yes indeed, even there! I implore you, do not cast such things away. And know that Ahab, standing at my back." In fact the Naeromath's blunt, ravaged head was hanging over and ahead of him. "This is the chief mind behind all of this. I am myself a scientist of no small note, but nothing of this could have been achieved without Ahab's genius."

Ravin's face was unreadable. Kris judged him entirely capable of just cancelling the whole Eye project with extreme prejudice right then, having Shinandri and Ahab gunned down and thinking no more about it. But he was no fool, and who knew to what use he could put the Originator tech in the future.

"Keep it on a leash," he informed Shinandri. And then some other call plainly came in to grab his attention. "When we have finished securing the system, you'll all be taken to your proper places," he told his prisoners. And then he was gone, leaving a half-dozen Voyenni to watch over them and make sure nobody got any ideas.

Olli

They arrived in time for the end.

Olli was braced for trouble when they emerged into the Estoc system, and trouble there was. But it was of such a scale that nobody noticed the arrival of the *Vulture God*.

The Partheni fleet that Junior had previously tracked down was already there and in action. There was some other business going on as well, with Uskaro's mob all over the Host and the ark fleet, but it was the Parthenon that had Olli's attention. It were going toe to toe with Aklu the Unspeakable.

The disc of the *Almighty Scythe of Morning* was spinning on its axis like a slow buzzsaw blade. Three big Partheni cruisers were throwing a ridiculous amount of shot at it—so much that she could almost see the *Scythe*'s gravitic shields with the naked eye. Instead of just warping space to curve the accelerator fire away, the Hegemonic ship was forming vortices and bowls with the basic fabric of space. Juggling the structure of the universe to catch and gather the enemy shot, before casting it back at them in great shotgun storms spanning tens of cubic kilometres of space. The *Scythe* had its own accelerators too. The weapons opened like pores, like eyes, emerging from the faceted hull to blink and glare and then close in sleep. Olli saw one of the Partheni vessels —the *Medusa*, its ident said—abruptly lurch sideways as one barrage struck home, its rear segments crumpling as it shunted the energy back down its length. And it wasn't just the big guns. There were a score of smaller vessels braving the busy space between the cruisers and the *Scythe*, including a numberless swarm of the little Zero Point fighters the Partheni deployed to distract Architects. The *God*'s instruments weren't equal to tracking all the moving parts of the battle, but she could see brief bursts of fire and data as the *Scythe* filled nearby space with crystalline chaff, shredding any ship that got too close.

For a moment she thought it was that simple. The unassailable might of the Hegemony would prevail, as it always had. Even against the very best that human engineering could throw at it. And for once it was okay, because she was now inexplicably on the side of the Divine Essiel. Or one of them, at least.

But then Kittering flagged up a whole spectrum of warnings and fractures across the *Scythe*'s radial hull. Olli was used to human ships, after all. The *Scythe* had been built to an alien design aesthetic. Not a Hanni aesthetic, for that matter, but apparently Kit had been paying more attention when they'd seen Hegemony and human go at each other over Arc Pallator that one time. The Partheni possibly didn't realize either, but the *Scythe* had taken heavy damage. Some of those regular geometric lines she could see weren't a design choice, but fractures in the hull. The Parthenon had taken its losses, but it seemed it was winning.

The three cruisers moved in, and Olli's board lit up as their mass looms discharged, clenching space around the *Scythe*. She saw the rays of that artificial sun warp and deform under the force of this. In the past she'd witnessed regular vessels pulverized by that sort of treatment—it was a weapon inspired by the Architects, and the crystalline structure of the *Architects* had been cracked by it too, for that matter. Yet the *Scythe*'s jagged rays sprang back. Twisted, tattered at the edges but gamely trying to return to their original shape and orientation.

"Comms established. Hail from the *Scythe* incoming," Kittering announced.

"Timo. You steal any weapons when you took our Ogdru?" It was Heremon, Aklu's lieutenant. Sangfroid incarnate, even though her transmission shuddered with static in time to the bombardment the *Scythe* was receiving.

"Nope," Olli said. "Incoming, though. Situation?"

A pause, and somehow this told Olli how bad things were. Just that space of dead air while Heremon tried to find words, someone who'd never been short of them before.

"How's the boss?" Olli asked, because right then she needed to hear someone talking to her. Even if it was an immortal half-human gangster. "Come on, I brought your squid back. Tell me what I can do."

"The Razor and the Hook has received a slight to their honour," Heremon said tightly, whatever the fuck *that* even meant. A human translation of an Essiel's mood, except Heremon wasn't even all that human. Then a blast of data came through that Kit fielded and translated. Damage reports. Most of it was still a long way from any tech specs Olli recognized but the overall message was clear.

The mass looms spoke again. Closer now, the *God* caught the outer ripple of them and Olli heard tortured bulkheads singing out in sympathy. The *Scythe*...

For a moment she thought it had just gone. Her screens fuzzed with a storm of data suggesting the Hegemonic ship had come apart, fragmented into a billion pieces. But then it was back again, seemingly whole, except there was something dreadfully wrong with it that the instruments could detect but not analyse.

"Can you reach us?" Heremon was asking.

"Not with the mass looms," Olli said tightly. Kittering was swearing. It was a Hannilambran obscenity, which his translator wouldn't parse, but she recognized it and he was keeping up a constant tirade of incredulous profanity. He'd processed what they'd just seen better than her, and it had scared the crap out of him.

"Eat this, you fuckers," said Heremon, entirely calmly. Not, thankfully, directed at the *God*.

Kittering sent a swathe of maths over to her board, trying to describe what had just happened. It bounced off Olli the first time but then she got it, and joined him in the swearing. The mass looms had shattered the *Scythe*, or rather the *Scythe* had allowed itself to be shattered. It really had broken apart, the rigid structure splintering into pieces still held in loose association by its field. The liquid tech the Hegemony used couldn't just be broken apart by gravitic torsion, though. So the entire ship had been put through the shredder and simultaneously rebuilt itself to ride out the colossal disruption of the mass looms. Olli didn't know where that left any of the actual physical *people* on board. And yes, Heremon was still speaking, but then Heremon could survive just about anything.

Then the *Scythe* retaliated. Getting close enough to use their mass looms had put the Partheni in reach of Aklu's own big guns.

There was no beam, no missile. The *God's* sensors just about blacked out for a moment around the Partheni *Queen of Aragon*, even as it fired up its mass loom again. The gravitic signature of the cruiser became momentarily the shadow of something vastly larger.

The impression, to a fallible human mind, was that something had risen up impossibly *beneath* the ship—meaning out of the underlying structure of the universe, out of unspace. As though a gaping maw was drawing all of space down into itself. Monsters and nightmares. Rationally, sensibly, Olli understood that what the *Scythe* had really done was put a delicate remote finger on the scales of the Partheni ship's own mass loom as it tried to fire, inverting the fields the weapon generated and centring them on the *Queen* itself.

In the space of three-quarters of a second, the *Queen of Aragon* became a spiralling streamer of metal and organic material a thousand kilometres long, twisted into a complex arabesque that Olli preferred to think read *Fuck you* in Essiel.

After that, the remaining cruisers put more distance between themselves and their enemy, out of the effective range of gravitic-field weaponry like the mass looms and whatever the hell Aklu had just unleashed. Accelerator cannon had a theoretical range limited only by the curvature of the universe, though, so they still poured that on, and the *Scythe's* shields fielded less and less of the incoming storm.

"Coming in now," Olli sent to Heremon, and danced the cumbrous old *Vulture God* closer, keeping the *Scythe*'s hull and shielding between them and the death the Partheni were filling space with.

The rear dock she chose took them to the aquarium where the Ogdru were kept. She had vague thoughts of repatriating Junior with its parents or pod-mates or however it worked. But that wasn't going to happen, she quickly realized. Things were worse on board the *Almighty Scythe of Morning* than she'd ever dreamt.

Kit stayed on the *God*, as Olli ventured out in the Scorpion. Not that even *that* battle-tested frame would survive the sort of existential-level problems the *Scythe* was suffering.

Whatever they'd done to survive the mass loom barrage, it hadn't entirely worked. When the *Scythe* had pulled its pieces back together, nothing had quite fitted where it should. Every surface Olli could see was jagged with discontinuities. There were spiralling fractal patterns of bristling edges across each wall. Everything was crooked. The very ground beneath the Scorpion's feet was rough and fuzzy with molecular-level mismatches. She could feel the whole ship around her vibrating with a terrible *wrongness*, as if only its master's fierce concentration was preventing it just flying apart.

The Ogdru were dead. The machinery of their tanks had failed, the discs tilted, half-swallowed by floor and ceiling. Long spines and spindles of ice jutted at random all around her, slowly melting. The navigators themselves were great blubbery masses of tentacles collapsed under their own bodyweight.

The remains of one of Aklu's crew was there, half in a wall, and she hoped it had been quick.

"I'm here," she said to Heremon. "I'm right here. I'm coming. Where the fuck am I going?"

Her only reply was a beacon, and she followed it through a ship that had become a nightmare version of the one she remembered. Every pearlescent corridor was jagged and broken, sudden dead ends of wall where doors should be, abrupt windows gaping nakedly onto empty void. And the dead. She didn't see a single living crewmember. And yet the ship fought on all around her. She could feel it rock with each fresh accelerator salvo, and the fact that it hadn't just disintegrated under the bombardment told her *something* was still doing its job.

Finally she reached the throne room. Or the crumpled, non-Euclidean space the battle had left of it. And there, in its centre, was Aklu.

Courtesy of Aklu, Olli had once seen far too much of the inner workings of an Essiel, and she'd been worried she'd get a refresher course in the Unspeakable itself.

It wasn't that bad, though. The a-grav couch Aklu usually sat in hadn't survived the fight. What remained was a tilted mess of sheared components, with the Essiel hanging at an unlikely angle, still attached to it, and still alive. Beside and partly beneath it was the golden frame of Aklu's Hiver major-domo, which had always been its mouthpiece. They weren't saying anything right now, although the open birdcage of their torso was seething with insect activity. Still theoretically alive then, too. And there was Heremon.

She had suffered the same fate as the crewman in the aquarium. A leg, a hip and part of her abdomen and ribcage were merged with the rippled pearl of the floor. Her back and the Tothir symbiont she carried on it were clear, though, so of course she was very much alive. And very much in incredible pain, to judge from her rigid face. Olli considered that calm voice over the comms and shuddered.

"What can I do?" she demanded, because the whole disaster seemed over her pay grade.

"Cutting torch," Heremon got out. "You have one?" Still that dreadfully even tone.

"I got all sorts on this frame." Olli turned to Aklu's broken couch. "You need me to free up the boss? His feet still work?" Because of course she knew Aklu's secret, the bizarre stigma of its alienation from its own species.

"Yes, but first me," Heremon told her.

"You what?" Around them the ship shuddered again and she felt a terrible grinding sound—not part against part, but molecule against molecule, only temporarily united and eager to be free.

"Got you, you fuckers," Heremon remarked conversationally. An excited Kit on comms in Olli's ear reported that the *Medusa* had just taken a massive accelerator hit, more than even Partheni segmentation could soak up. It was only the *Skathi* left in the fight now.

Looking around her, Olli reckoned that would be enough.

"Me first, if you please," through Heremon's clenched teeth.

Olli noticed there was a hand cutter lying within reach of the Tothiat. She did the maths.

"You...?"

"Couldn't," Heremon said. "Tried. Hurt too much and I keep *growing back*. Fucking metabolism."

"Yeah, yeah, immortal and invulnerable, poor you." But Olli felt profoundly sick. Heremon couldn't free herself from the hull because she regenerated faster than she could sear

150

away at her own flesh. Olli, on the other hand, had better tools and probably owed Heremon some hurt. She prided herself on being a bastard, after all. Why shrink from torturing a gangster or two?

Except it was the hardest thing she'd ever done. Even with Heremon holding completely still and not even screaming much—a perfect patient who did everything the doctor ordered. And even with the Scorpion's life support filtering out the scent of burned flesh. She had to work fast because the mindless tendrils of the Tothir were constantly trying to reattach to the lost body buried in the wall.

At last she got Heremon free, hauling what was left of her away to stop any questing reattachment. She then turned her attention to the broken couch where Aklu had been patiently waiting, and stood over the Essiel in her brutal multi-legged frame. Aklu's own artificial limbs were trapped in the cage of that crushed seat, and she realized that if she wanted, she could rid the universe of a monstrous gangster right here, right now. Aklu's arms flickered and rumbling groans issued from its shell, but there was no silver-tongued Hiver to translate, and the awful majesty of the Essiel had fallen away from it.

It didn't matter. She just got to work with the cutter and carved away the couch's dead systems, slice after slice, like a cancer surgeon, except she felt almost as if she was destroying the body so that the infection might be free. Once she'd done enough, Aklu opened out from the jagged ruin of the couch like a poisonous flower. Its holdfast writhed and buried itself in the midst of a great knot of segmented tentacles, erupting from an impossibly small space and knocking Olli back on the Scorpion's metal ass. For a moment

Aklu towered over her like a cyberneticist's worst nightmare, before it sank down fluidly to less monstrous proportions.

"We need to go," Heremon said. She'd crawled over and now had the Hiver's bug-crazy torso cradled in her arms. Without needing to be asked, Olli stalked over and picked her up.

"You going to regrow those bits?" she asked. Where Heremon's body ended, the Tothir fibres were coiling about one another in an anxious, undirected way.

"No fucking idea," Heremon said softly. "Never been like this before. How's your ship?"

"Kit, how's our ship?" Olli passed on.

"Very desirous of having you back on it," Kit told her shortly.

Suddenly an almost organic spasm went through the *Scythe*. Olli felt as though each part of the ground beneath her was filing for trial separation.

"Coming back with friends," she told him, getting under way with Aklu undulating along in her wake. "And then we're getting the fuck out of this system."

PART 2
ESTOC, OCCUPIED

9.

Ravin

Eventually, all was quiet, calm and within his control.

The medical dressing about his throat was a prickly reminder that he'd underestimated the opposition, even at the very brink of triumph. Ravin could, after all, have stayed back on a ship while his Voyenni took care of matters. There was a certain noblesse oblige to the business, though. There would have been precious little *satisfaction* in merely being brought the news and a drone recording of Laery's arrest or death. She had *taken* from him. Stolen the fruits of a decade's careful scheming for her ludicrous project. And now she was dead. He'd rather she was alive to be turned to his purposes, but dead would do. A dangerous character, had been Adela Laery. Perhaps best that she'd refused to be taken.

With the Host and the Eye in hand, he'd retreated to his flagship, the *Grand Nikolas*. It had stayed clear of the fighting with the Hivers and so was free of the untidiness of repair that would disturb Ravin's equilibrium. Under ideal circumstances he'd be looking to the Host itself as a base, but of course his fragmented alien vessel currently held the ragged length of rock that was the Eye.

Decisions, decisions... He could fire the damn thing into

the sun if he wanted, of course, and reclaim the Host for its original purposes. Leaning back in his chair, hearing the bustle of his servants about his quarters, he called up the plans. A whole distributed ship, without hull, just rooms and connections in space, all held in place by the Host's gravitic field. An open-plan ark, where the masters of the fleet could look out over the cosmos that they had taken possession of. Some of the other builders had blanched at the thought of all that abyss on display, worrying that it might have a similar effect on the human mind as going into unspace. Ravin had sneered at them. Small minds for small worlds, not fit to inherit the universe.

The Eye fascinated him, though. Powerful, unique, what wasn't to like? And yet the purpose it had been put to by that clique of science-minded freaks seemed entirely too much like navel-gazing. No harm, certainly, having a reliable advance warning for an Architect attack *here* and *now*. But to try and feel out the whole inhabited universe was absurd and wasteful. To try and plumb unspace to go *look* for Architects was the height of foolishness. If this Eye was basically an engine that could read and affect unspace, then it had other uses, however. And if the mad Naeromathi thought it could be a weapon against the Architects, then it could be a weapon against anything. The Hegemony, the Parthenon, alien races not yet discovered. This was potential enough to keep it and its attendant menagerie around for now. Perhaps to be transferred to a less prestigious housing in due course.

Of course he'd need to get all those Ints off it. He'd planned his strike—with the aid of the plentiful fifth columnists left over from the original ark project—so that the vast majority of the Cartel's stolen Intermediaries would be on the Host. Now they were his again, as they should be. And they were needed to serve humanity—*his* humanity. The people he'd stock the arks with, to embark on the next phase of the species' evolution. He'd hoped reclaiming his tame navigators would be as simple as clicking his fingers and sending the relevant commands. The Cartel had been busy, though. A handful had come meekly at his call but the majority had already had their conditioning blunted, their implants removed. Ravin was currently assembling a packet ship to take his will and words into the wider universe and included in the dispatches was a call to the Liaison Board. He'd require a full medical team to re-domesticate the Intermediaries, returning them to the pliable and reliable state he needed. Thankfully the Magdan nobility, and the Uskaros in particular, had long been generous donors to the Board, and most of the directors were in Ravin's shadow one way or another. He'd have all the resources he needed from that direction. They would set up a mass conversion clinic at his request, and tighten up the mental shackles where necessary.

Then there was Idris Telemmier. Sitting in his stateroom, Ravin called up the files on the man—the impossibly long history. A first-generation Int somehow still hale and well —or well enough. Young, even, despite being far older than Ravin in mere years. Arguably the greatest success of the old wartime Intermediary Program. The man Ravin's nephew Piter had stumbled upon and taken for a Liaison Board deserter. Also the man who'd cost Ravin too many good Voyenni on Arc Pallator and Criccieth's Hell. And here he was, bundled up as a bonus with the rest of them. Too dangerous, right now, to give a helm and a navigator's board to, but that would change. Telemmier's broken little mind could be chained just like anyone's, with the right psych programming and punitive implants. He would be the jewel in the ark fleet's nomadic crown. And, as he apparently didn't *age*, he might serve many generations of the family as they roved from system to system, masters of all they surveyed through the transparent walls of the Host...

A chime informed him that Piter was outside, and he signalled to let the boy in. His nephew had acquitted himself tolerably in the destruction of the factory. Smaller family ships were now having some fun hunting down the last active Hiver frames in-system, picking them off for target practice, but that was something that didn't need aristocratic oversight.

"Uncle, a new Partheni ship just dropped out of unspace," Piter informed him, with a faintly peevish edge to his voice, as though it was Ravin's fault, or such developments should be cleared with Piter first. *Give the boy one fighting command and he's getting ideas above his station.*

"Hence my sending for you. A unified family front." This was where things might become tricky. The Partheni had taken rather gratifying losses in their fight with Aklu. Ravin could even spare a fond thought for the late Unspeakable for putting up such a spirited defence. *Two full Partheni cruisers scrapped! What a windfall!* If the Essiel had just caved or run, Ravin would be looking at a full four-warship fleet across the negotiating table, far more force than he could match. Right now, with the *Scythe* finally shattered to fragments, Exemplar Mercy had only her own battered *Skathi* and this newcomer, the *Medea*. Still not a fight Ravin was particularly keen to get into, but one where he reckoned he had the edge if the Partheni were foolish enough to bring it.

"We're about to test the honour of our allies," he told Piter. "Mouth shut and face composed."

The boy looked mulish but nodded, and then Ravin confirmed his readiness to Mercy's channel.

She appeared on his display with a stern officer on either side, the same sort of show of strength he and Piter were making with their uniforms and medals.

"Congratulations on your victory over the Hegemonics, Exemplar," Ravin told her with crisp jollity. In amongst those words were all the barbs he could possibly wish concerning her losses, diplomatically irreproachable and yet she'd know exactly how he meant it. None of that showed on her face, of course, but then who knew how much the Partheni really retained of human feelings?

"Likewise yours over the Assembly," she noted. "One hopes you were not relying on their services elsewhere. They may take this as a breach of contract."

He took that for a joke and chuckled dutifully. "The days of humanity being reliant on the manufacturing capability of cockroaches are over, thankfully." There would probably be a hundred diplomatic attachés desperately trying to put distance between Hugh and the ark-builder clique right now, given that they really *had* been reliant on the Hivers, but Ravin and his peers had severed those ties already. Just one more way to keep ahead of the competition... "I see you're moving shuttles into the Host."

In fact, his own ships were watching very carefully. And the Voyenni forces within the Eye and the various Host shards were on high alert in case there should be a force of Myrmidons about to disembark. The structure of the Host made it a hard thing to capture unless you already had agents on the inside, though. If the Partheni were going to betray him *that* way, they'd be disappointed.

"We will reclaim our people aboard my *Skathi*." Mercy sounded tired. "We are to reunite with the rest of the fleet and plan our next move, now that we have extricated our assets from this unnecessary venture." She said all this with a straight face, and Ravin nodded smoothly. Between them was a gulf of knowledge—what he knew and what she knew he knew. Because getting a handle on what a united Parthenon was doing had always been next to impossible. Obtaining information about a fractured Parthenon, which was all but engaged in a civil war, was another matter entirely. Plenty of third-party brokers had interesting intel for sale right about now. Parthenon ships in odd places, damaged, offloading mutineers, fighting each other. Mercy had made her move, but Ravin felt she didn't have the majority with her just yet.

What she did have, now the shuttles had docked, was the Partheni Intermediaries. Of course Ravin would have welcomed being able to keep them, but *that* had never been on the table. He and Mercy both knew that they might just be setting the stage for some future conflict, when the nomadic fleets of Partheni and Colonial humanity met around some unthinkably distant star. He'd far rather none of this had been necessary—that he'd provoked the Partheni into a mutually disarming war against the Colonies and never lost hold of the Estoc shipyards and arks in the first place. But the Cartel had muscled in on his business, and so he'd been forced into this unsavoury alliance.

So let Mercy fight her sisters, or else just take her secessionists and navigate across the galaxy, outside the

Throughways. It was a big universe. More likely that the two itinerant branches of humanity would never meet.

There were no marauding Myrmidons on the shuttles. The hitch in their alliance came from elsewhere. "The *Medea* will remain in-system," Exemplar Mercy explained to him.

"Will it, now?" Ravin asked. "And why would it need to?"

Mercy's look at him was one of cold loathing. "Because I have matters to attend to elsewhere, and while I am sure you also have business requiring your attention, I do not wish to find Colonial ships appearing to interfere in Partheni matters. The *Medea* will provide you with some much-needed security and fighting strength should the Hivers or the Hegemony take offence over what has happened here, Morzarin. And it will service a sequence of packet ships that will bring me word of your efforts here. Confirming to me that you have returned to your intended business with these arks and your hand-picked human future. As opposed to taking any other action that we might both regret."

"I could of course give you all assurances that none of this is necessary," Ravin said lazily, "but if this gives you peace of mind, then by all means, I extend a formal invitation to the *Medea* to remain in-system, as a token of our ongoing alliance." No love lost in the smile he gave her, and none taken from it either. "Any addition to your force here might be taken amiss by my own ships, however. My crews are fired up from their victory. I'd hate for them to mistake some act of yours as a fresh commencement of hostilities."

Mercy nodded. "We understand each other, Morzarin."

After that onerous business was done with, he nodded to Piter. "Time to attend to the home front. Round up the Ints for transport and processing. And I suppose we need a spokesman for that science team of theirs."

"The lead scientist is...eccentric," Piter recalled with a curl of the lip.

Ravin nodded. "Not him. Leave him to his toys. And not the Naeromathi, obviously. Has there been any word of the Harbinger?" All reports placed the alien, Ash, on board the Eye when it was taken, except nobody had laid eyes on the distinctive creature. It had a long history of appearing and disappearing by mysterious means that Ravin hadn't particularly believed in, but now he was starting to wonder...

"No, Uncle," Piter confirmed. "But I know just the person."

It was, perhaps, the perfect choice, and so Ravin sent the boy off to do the honours, and then composed the last of his messages to go out on the packet ship. Word for the rest of the ark-builders, informing them that their assets had been reclaimed and the project could move into its next phase. And, tacitly, making it plain that Ravin and the Uskaro family now controlled a great deal more of everything that mattered than they had before.

Kris

Given her previous history with the Uskaro family, Kris had expected worse. Confined to quarters seemed mild, considering. And yes, "quarters" on the Eye wasn't exactly the lap of luxury: a corner of stone walled off with a jigsaw of iron plates and then fitted with makeshift conveniences wherever Jaine could get the wiring in. Kris could fold out a bed, relieve herself and argue with the printer, which was being uncooperative. But no comms, no media. The door wasn't locked because Jaine could never be bothered to fit any, but there was a Voyenni guard outside; so much for easy escapes.

She'd complained about the printer to the guard, who had roundly ignored her. She was therefore, and unadvisedly, trying to fix it herself. Kris had never quite partaken of that spacer life which maintained everyone needed to carry a toolkit and know what to do with it. She'd been born to a mining family, true—but, by the time she'd come along, the Iron Guilds had made sure the mining wealth stuck around, rather than being exported with the products of their labour. Hence she'd never exactly had to go dirty her hands with the robots, and had then gone to quite a prestigious academy to study law. Aboard the *Vulture God*, and much to Olli's derision, she'd generally hidden behind her education as a way of shirking routine maintenance. Now, she supposed, she was paying for it.

She hoped Olli was all right. She'd heard no word from her. No word from any of them. Once they'd led her away from Idris and the others in the Eye, the Uskaros might have had the lot of them shot for all she knew. Except if shootings were being handed out, she reckoned she'd be top of the list. Her continued semi-comfortable existence was theoretical proof that everyone else was at least still alive.

There had been a toolkit stowed under the printer, because Jaine had priorities. After her attempts to get something to eat had resulted in a congealed, plasticky mess, Kris tried to tune into her inner spacer and fix the damn thing with the aid of a glitchy diagnostic application.

Abruptly, and without her asking it to, it began to make something. She recoiled, in case the something turned out to be poisonous or explosive. What actually appeared was a frill of gluey strands that spelled out her name.

She stared at them. She'd possibly mishandled the fix-it job so badly she'd just made a printer sentient.

Or else, as a moment's sober reflection suggested, someone was contacting her via the only channel they had.

She glanced at the door, but it was firmly shut. There could be a camera in here but, if so, it was very well hidden. Certainly not the sort of thing Jaine would have bothered with.

Caution reigned. Instead of trying to talk to the thing, she entered characters via the diagnostic program. *Colvari?* The Hiver, Havaer Mundy's friend, had helped her through a printer once before.

The machine groaned and produced what looked like a fraying paper plate. Except her fingers found raised ridges on the underside. Faint words in the whorled surface that told her: *Yes. Limited time. All Hivers being hunted now. Hiding. Ask.*

She resisted the urge to type consolation. Not a moment for civilized niceties. *Who's free?* she typed one-handed, feeding the plate into the printer's recycling slot as she did so.

The reply came along the edge of a malformed fork. *Havaer. Handful other Hivers. Aklu Laery gone. Others alive. Ints being moved. Ask.*

She froze for a moment as too many queries fought for the privilege. What was most important to her, right now? *What's the plan?*

Wait, said the corrugated edge of a half-melted glass, in letters she could barely make out. *Assessing situation.* But by then she'd caught up with the previous message and was frantically tapping in her question without needing the prompt.

What about Vult God? Hadn't Olli been with Aklu?

Reported destroyed. Unconfirmed, came Colvari's response, confettied into the edge of a sheet of paper. Kris clutched it so hard she ripped it into pieces.

But Olli was a survivor. Of all the people she knew, Olli was a survivor. And Kittering was as sharp as they came. They'd have found a way out, cut and run. They weren't the types for dumbass heroics. Although she rather thought Olli was, deep inside where she'd never admit it.

Then boots came stamping up to her door and the guard snapped to attention. She let the recycler suck up the scraps of paper and typed: *Must go good luck.*

It was Piter Uskaro who graced the awkward angles of her quarters. He'd come with two Voyenni, which was slightly gratifying. He looked as though he'd rather knife her than be polite, but presumably his uncle was still holding his leash. They'd not exactly got on well, the last half-dozen times they'd met. It had started with her thwarting him with a legal technicality and ended with her cutting his throat. She'd had him fixed up before he could bleed out, but she didn't reckon that would count for much with him.

He had a little speech lined up, she could see. Some gloating he'd saved for an audience of one, about how it had all turned up Uskaro after all. How she should just have let him take Idris that first time. And she was getting ready to go up to him and ask, "How's the throat?" or break into his monologue, or spit in his face and stamp on his foot. Be her naturally sunny self and get in the face of the powerful, just like she'd so enjoyed doing in a hundred courts on stations and planets across the Colonial Sphere. Then the two Voyenni shifted outwards slightly: big men in bottle-green uniforms, fists balled, faces devoid of any human connection. Bred and trained for obedience and brutality on a world where people knew their place or got stamped on until they learned it. And they'd brought that world here to her. She didn't even have a knife this time because the damn printer hadn't obliged her.

So she let Piter give his spiel, suffered through it, letting the actual details just slough off her shoulders. Not rising to it left him flat at the end, a comedian whose audience wasn't in the mood. So all he could growl into the silence was, "My uncle requests the pleasure of your presence." Trying to make the words drip venom but denied any satisfaction from her stony expression.

*

They shipped her out from the Host to a big Colonial vessel matching its drift. Kris had a brief view of it through the shuttle's screens, seeing a last-generation general-purpose military vessel. Not the navy's fresh-off-the-line but seemingly the best hand-me-down that the Uskaros could commandeer for private use. It was certainly all military discipline inside, as they marched her at that just-too-quick-for-comfort pace through blue-painted corridors to where the Morzarin awaited her. He had a stateroom decked out with plenty of military and heraldic nonsense, as she'd expect. The Magdan Boyars liked their pomp and circumstance. The man himself was sitting back in a big chair behind a fancy desk, covered in medals he'd probably earned by acts of heroic privilege. They liked playing soldier too, the Uskaros. In other circumstances she'd have made fun of them for it, but right now they'd actually won the battle so she wasn't feeling particularly funny.

A Voyenni shoved a chair forwards for her: carved wood with a padded seat and back. The sort of planet-craft luxury that spacers would scoff at. Kris felt she was letting the side down when she sat on it. But then she wasn't really a spacer, as Olli never tired of reminding her, and she could appreciate a comfy chair, frankly. When another thug poured her some wine in a delicate glass, she decided that there was no mileage in just being stubborn about the whole thing.

"Morzarin," she addressed him, summoning her sangfroid. "Here to look after your investments?"

She tensed for the blow, for the wine to be snatched from her hand, the comfy chair yanked from under her. None of that happened. Instead Ravin Uskaro was watching her carefully.

"You have been quite the thorn in the side of my family, Mesdam Almier," he said. "Not as the representative of any wider concern, not as someone's advocate, but you yourself, the individual. That's quite an achievement for an itinerant notary."

She saluted him mutely with the glass and then sipped at the contents, which were really rather good.

"Piter wanted to have you thrown to the men. Or to space. Or some other piece of theatre," Ravin noted without changing his tone.

"Well, in that case." Kris necked the rest of the wine so as to make reclaiming it from her at least somewhat harder. The corner of Ravin's mouth twitched very slightly.

"I told my nephew that we are civilized people. And that you are an educated woman who understands Colonial ways.

Not some barbaric spacer. You are someone familiar with contracts, agreements and service. And having a place in a larger plan. If the history of your antagonism towards my family shows anything about you, it is that you are a resourceful woman."

She let the sentence hang there, unacknowledged. Ravin tilted his head.

"You are waiting for the threat now?"

She shrugged. "There's a threat-shaped absence in this conversation, Morzarin. But you can spare me the details. I've seen your men on the Eye and I've seen your ship out here. Let's assume I'm more than aware that you have the capacity to follow through with any threat you feel like making. What I'm waiting for is the offer. Looking at what you've just done, I don't imagine you have some legal bother you're worried about and need my help with."

Ravin drained his own wine and laughed drily. "I have inherited a curious piece of business with this facility. Staffed by quite the freakshow, in fact. I've seen the files on all of them. *They* do not impress me as reasonable, civilized people who understand Colonial ways. While they plainly represent an opportunity, they are just as plainly profoundly difficult to handle. And so I am looking for a handler."

"You want me to be your go-between?"

"Mesdam Almier, you are someone I can talk to, and someone known to the menagerie over there. You are also someone persuasive enough to overcome their unhelpful personalities and get me results. How can I use this in my projects? How can their insane dreams become my opportunities? You are by no means my only option, but you are the most likely to get something out of them. Something that means I don't end up shooting the entire circus into the sun. Because if it will not serve me, I have no use for it, and nor do I wish anyone else to have it." His voice had become very hard by the end. "You understand me?"

"You want me to be your collaborator."

"I invite you to consider the alternatives. Do you not want to be there, to soften the blow, sugar the pill? Or would you rather it was my people giving the ultimatum?"

"What about my friends?"

Ravin blinked. For a moment he had no idea who she meant.

"Your former vessel," he said at last, after a long moment when he wasn't going to tell her anything, "is believed lost. Although the wreckage of the Hegemonic vessel is not cooperative to study or salvage. The cost of war, Mesdam Almier."

"And Solace? What have you done with her?"

A curl of the lip. "Haven't you heard? The Partheni are my allies now. They want nothing to do with this charade. Your precious Solace marched obediently off the Host and rejoined her sisters. They're far away now, and good riddance." Kris reckoned it was more complex and less final than that, but the words still hit her hard.

"And Idris?"

Ravin looked at her as though she was an idiot. "The Intermediaries have been taken aboard my *Grand Nikolas* for debriefing. Idris Telemmier will have another chance to be a hero of humanity, Mesdam Almier. After appropriate retraining, he will be the star navigator in the human race's next great adventure."

"Your arks."

"We are the future," Ravin told her, almost gently. "From the moment the Architect wrecked the world of our birth, this was always going to be the future. The Partheni knew it. The Naeromathi knew it. There's no other way to share a universe with the Architects than to sever yourself from planetary life and take to the stars. The stars that are our inheritance, Mesdam Almier."

"We are holding off the Architects right now," Kris told him. "For the first time, we can see them coming, and we can get our Ints there to deflect them. That's progress. That's turning the tide of the war."

"It's a desperate rearguard action, no more," Ravin replied. "It's time to take what we value in humanity and move it beyond the reach of our enemies." He leant across the table a little, medals scraping against each other. "I would like to value you, Mesdam Almier. You are a woman of great capability. Prove yourself useful and become a part of this grand venture. And, in doing so, make me see the value in those misbegotten creatures on the Eye, so they too may be saved. You have it in your hands to improve their lot, to become someone of influence here. You are a negotiator, a compromiser by trade. You are already thinking of ways this arrangement could work to your advantage, and the benefit of those you care about. Believe me, I wouldn't be giving this speech to Olian Timo or to the late Captain Rostand. But you..."

"I get it." She cut him off, and sensed the slight tensing of the Voyenni, reading there just how any freedom would taste. "Well then, Morzarin: show me the contract. Let me see what I'm signing." She was thinking about Colvari, Havaer, the last of the resistance, hidden somewhere in the Eye's structure. Thinking about how much of herself she'd pawn and how much good she could do with it.

10.

Olli

"Try that," Olli prompted, and Kit leant in again, delicate tools juggling in his mouthparts. There was a flash and a flare of electrical connections, and she waited for a voice, a sound, anything. The faint rattle and scrabble that had been their constant companion since they started this venture was the only thing that came through.

This wasn't essential repair work, or something she'd ever been called on to do before. The *Vulture God* had enough green lights on the board now that she could let the ship coast for a bit. Out here in open space, beyond the Throughways where nobody was ever going to stumble upon them. Instead, she was trying to restore speech to Aklu's ruined major-domo.

She couldn't say that being in the deep void without Idris on board didn't give her the creeping horrors. They were entirely reliant on Junior to get them back to... anywhere, really. If the Ogdru became stubborn, or its tank failed, or it just upped and died like a goldfish, then the lot of them were screwed. It would be a thousand years of regular space travel before they got anywhere with flashy amenities like planets and suns. Maybe Aklu could last that long but, frankly, the *Vulture God* wouldn't, let alone the rest of its crew. And somehow when she'd *borrowed* the immature monster she hadn't even considered the possibility. It had all seemed like such a grand adventure.

But right now, she had a range of creeping horrors to choose from, and the one that loomed largest in her mind was looming largest inside the *Vulture God* as well. She'd had brushes with that illusory Presence within unspace from time to time, and it had been nasty, but this was worse. A live Essiel was filling every part of the drone bay of the *Vulture God* that wasn't occupied by Junior's tank. Aklu the Unspeakable, the Razor and the Hook, angry and restless and equipped with a nightmare of tentacles for a walking frame. Last she'd seen, Aklu was clinging to what the *God's* gravity plane reckoned was the ceiling, but which the Essiel's own personal generators had decided was the floor. Meaning that when Olli got too close, her inner ear had screamed at her that she was falling in multiple directions at once. The apex of Aklu's long shell was almost at foot level, its nest of spindly limbs splayed like a spidery hand. The whole business of it looked *wrong*—the shifted gravity, the grotesquery of the mobile Essiel, and the mere, inexplicable *awe* the species carried with them, utterly at odds with their actual appearance. Aklu was very agitated and very vocal, enough that its rumblings carried clearly all the way through the *Vulture's* hull. There was no escaping them anywhere on board. And nobody could understand them, except that the Essiel was pretty damn insistent about *something*.

So it came down to this sad, battered cage of cockroaches she was trying to fix. Olli didn't even know if there was enough of the Hiver's actual living structure to do them any good. Probably some of the bugs had fallen out when the thing had been mauled by... by the *Scythe*'s own defences, she guessed. She wondered if it had been working as intended or if some Broken Harvest tech had become sloppy.

The open cage, its golden finish scratched and mottled, seethed with insect activity. Working on the connections between bug and housing required Olli to go wrist deep into this busy hive and navigate by touch. Of course the arms she was using were the mechanical limbs of the Scorpion, and she could fine-tune her haptics to blot out the worst of the scurry and skitter. *Screw you, people with actual hands.* The thought raised a smile, which was something she'd been short of recently.

She was linked to the cage's diagnostics, which were blithely insisting everything was fine. On another screen of the Scorpion's display she was streaming data from Kittering, because they were trying to link the Hiver, through the *Vulture God*, to Kit's translation software. Which meant she was effectively dealing with the product of three separate species' operating systems. Given how engineering and coding standards varied even across human work, it was making her want to tear the galaxy a new asshole about now.

"Okay, this should work," she insisted. It didn't. She swore at Kittering and the *Vulture God*, and the entire wartime industry that had resulted in the creation of the Hivers. Then a loud buzzing issued from somewhere, and some diligent chicanery traced it to the Hiver's limbless torso. It wasn't words, though, and it wasn't helpful.

Around that time, Heremon arrived, and she wasn't helpful either. She hadn't healed the missing pieces she'd left embedded in the *Scythe*'s hull, nor had her boosted body stopped trying to reconnect with them. The result wasn't pretty. In fact, it was organically unpleasant enough that Olli was glad the Scorpion was hermetically sealed.

Heremon had borrowed Olli's walking frame, the little six-legged scuttler she went to civilized places in. Olli was going to have to disinfect it with extreme prejudice before trusting her body to it again, because who knew what jokes the leftover bits of Tothir might play on unsuspecting human flesh? Heremon's one remaining leg was bunched up, knee to chin, because of course the frame was designed for someone without much in the way of legs at all. She was canted at about thirty degrees, one hand gripping the frame to keep herself steady. She hadn't really got to grips with the neural link that operated the thing either, so her progress was an angry series of lunges, bouncing off walls and skidding to abrupt halts. She looked furious, and in enormous pain.

The Tothir part of her had extended a webwork of pinkish-grey tendrils across the walker, fouling one of the legs and further impeding her progress. It bubbled and shifted as Olli watched, reaching out into the air and then shrinking back. It was, she was absolutely sure, still looking for the missing parts of her they'd cut away. If they could have gone back to the wreck of the *Scythe*, she had no doubt those severed portions of Heremon would still be alive, set into the hull. If they sat Heremon where she'd been, she'd reconnect with them and bond herself to the dead ship. The Tothiat part of her didn't understand the concept of permanent loss.

"Anything?" Heremon spat.

Olli gave her a look that mutely asked if Heremon could hear her having a cogent discussion with a Hiver and, if not, then what the fuck did she think?

"Move them in with Aklu," Heremon told her. "They need our master's voice."

"Let's get them actually hearing and talking first. No need to complicate matters," Olli said. "'Sides, not as if we can exactly ignore the fucking divine pronouncements right now."

"Need to *see*." Heremon waved her free hand about, a distant echo of the gestural part of the Essiel language, except she didn't have anywhere near enough joints to make it work.

"Look, I get that everyone's a damn critic, but could you just— Kit, now. Try now." Compensating for some peculiarities in the Hanni virtual architecture she'd been ignoring, in case that was the problem.

The buzzing was, for a moment, loud enough to drown out even Aklu's wordless complaints, and she saw at least one of the *God's* speakers blow, but then, from the bowels of the ship, came a voice:

"Engaging diagnostics; what is lost in functionality is wisdom gained. Percentage mind recovered: eighty-three." All a bit uncanny valley because the voice was Kit's, the exact tones his own translator lent him.

"Right, great," Olli said, feeling a rather childish streak of pride that she'd pulled the trick off only after Heremon had arrived to see it. "You hear me? You—you have a name, actually?" Because they'd only been Aklu's mouthpiece before.

"Conditions of the contract under which we were instantiated state we may not know ourselves but as our master's voice," said the faux-Kittering tones grandly, as though the revelation was a badge of honour.

"Yeah, but..." Olli stole a glance at Heremon and reckoned she could take the Tothiat in her current state, if this was about to get heretical. "I mean, you're...also *you*. You want to walk away from—okay, get *carried* away from—the old deal, you just say. I mean, nobody's a slave on my ship."

Heremon raised a smirk at that, and the disembodied voice of the major-domo said, "We have no needs that do not amplify and echo the Unspeakable's desires. We must be brought before the Razor's gaze to take such benison or penalty as Aklu shall decree."

Olli shared a sidelong look with Kit, or as much of one as a human and a Hanni could reasonably share. "Right then," she decided unhappily, picking up the cage of skittering bugs and dumping it in Heremon's slanted lap. "You still there? Nothing shaken loose?"

"Connection with your systems is confirmed. We have no defects neither have we time. Take us to Aklu."

"Got no thanks either," Olli muttered, but the three of them went back down the ship's central corridor to the drone bay. The four of them, she supposed, but it had been hard to think of the truncated torso as a sentient thing before they started speaking. And now they were speaking, they seemed to be trying to erase their own identity.

She had to pause before stepping across the threshold. Which rankled, because this was the drone bay, her personal kingdom since she'd joined the *Vulture God*'s crew. But she could barely fit in it now. Not with the great watery sphere containing the Ogdru. Nor with the forest of segmented tentacles clinging to the upper half of the chamber like alien ivy, and that blade-like shell jutting down at an angle.

Heremon tried to move the walker past her, to deliver the major-domo. After banging angrily against the Scorpion and swearing at Olli, she devolved the task to Kittering, who was small enough to squeak through.

Aklu changed its angle and began gesticulating furiously at the battered cage, groaning and roaring loudly enough to shake every panel and bolt in the ship. This would be a one-way discussion, Olli realized. Until the major-domo got a body back, it couldn't talk *to* its master or translate for anyone else. It was literally just a mouthpiece. And that mouthpiece had something to say.

"The operation of celestial spheres and proper functioning of thrones and powers demands that this affront be recognized. Set the usurpers 'fore the searing eye of regal judgement, that they may be judged. Unto the Seat of Record shall we pass, not squirming through the wormlike ways but fast and fierce that we may draw the Final Blade and be requited."

Olli's eyebrows went somewhere above her hairline. "Huh. Right. Good luck with that," she said, in the safe knowledge that any irreverence wasn't getting to Aklu any time soon. "I guess we're all very annoyed with what happened. I mean, I got friends back there, sure. I want to go kick some Patho *and* Magdan ass. Anything it said mean we get to go do that?"

"Coordinates have been received," Kittering remarked.

"Say what?"

"Within the *Vulture God*'s systems have arrived navigational coordinates," Kit said. Despite the identical voice, the rhythm of his speech told her instantly who was talking.

"Okay, so it wants to go somewhere. Let me guess, Hegemony."

Kittering made a little up-and-down stridulation she was familiar with as something like a shrug. "The location is unknown to us. Not a recognized Hegemonic system. Extreme size and cultural obfuscation are both Hegemonic traits, however." And of course, the actual geographic proximity of star to star was nothing to do with the borders of galactic polities. If you plotted Hanni, Castigar, Colonial and Hegemony systems in the actual three-dimensional universe, they were weirdly tangled, interleaved and overlapping. The Throughways were the important thing: the connective tissue of the universe, sitting beneath the real in unspace. Your neighbour was who you could get to without needing a specialist navigator, not whose star was the fewest light years away from you.

But this place, this location Aklu had picked out, was well beyond any part of the Throughway network Olli had ever plumbed. Somewhere that the regular Colonial gazetteers didn't even include. So, clearly Hegemony, and some part that human traders and diplomats had never been allowed to visit before.

"Got a name, this place?"

"The Seat of Record," said the Hiver and Kittering at the same time, a weird synchronicity of the same voice stepping on itself.

Olli glanced at Heremon. "Mean something to you? Ever been there?"

"No," the Tothiat said. Her eyes were very wide. "Heard of it. One of the...When the Essiel say 'Seat' they mean something to rule from, to command from. Somewhere the Hegemony is run from. There's a Seat of Introspection, and a Seat of Distinction, and some others I could never get a good Colvul translation of. It's a place we don't go. Because we're the shadow to the Essiel sun."

"Well, I guess we're going there now. They'll give us a fleet or something? To go slap the bad guys?" While the political ramifications of actually invading the Colonial Sphere with a Hegemonic war fleet, and kicking off the biggest non-Architect war in the history of space travel, should perhaps have daunted her, it also sounded extremely satisfying right now, on a personal level.

"I think...they can do anything there. If they want to," Heremon said quietly. Olli knew that she was six parts gangster to four parts fanatical cultist, and at this moment the godly bits were in the ascendant. Or maybe she'd left one or two parts of her gangster self stuck in the hull of the *Scythe*. "A lot of the Hegemony, the power and the tech, gets portioned out so the people only have as much as they need, as much as the Essiel need them to have. Things are more stable that way. It's all about equilibrium, right? The Seats are where..."

"Where the good stuff is."

"Where everything is."

"They got a new leg there for you?" Olli needled, but the jibe failed utterly.

"They can mend me," Heremon said. She picked at the writhing growth that was twisting from her hip and Olli shuddered.

"Yeah, you need to get that seen to. Unsightly blemish doesn't cover it. Kit—"

"Departure has been readied," the Hanni confirmed. "Currently all efforts are in restraining our navigator."

Junior was circling its tank restlessly, flurries of tentacles and fins pushing it faster and faster.

"Let's get the beds ready, then," Olli agreed, and then cocked an eye up at Aklu. "We...haven't got anything for an Essiel, you realize. And this looks like a long haul through unspace."

179

"It is the penance of the fallen god to stare into the void and there to strive with all the horrors of the vasty deep," came Kit's voice and the Hiver's words. Whether Aklu actually did have some way of hearing and understanding her after all, or it was just coincidence, she didn't know, but it spooked her.

"The Unspeakable has never—" Heremon started, but Olli waved the explanation away with one of the Scorpion's arms.

"I got it," she said shortly. "As for me, I *do*. And you better too. Don't need you getting any more mad."

*

Of course Junior was just a dumb beast. It didn't realize it was guiding a ship through unspace, just that it had been given coordinates like a scent, something it could hunt down as though it were in its ancestral seas. But when the *God* emerged into the real and woke Olli, they'd come out way further from the system's sun than she'd expected, compared to the Ogdru's previous preferences. As though it was respectful. Or scared.

She took a look at what was out there and decided she was scared too.

The Seat of Record, or whatever the Essiel called the actual system where it was located, had no planets. It had probably once possessed them. Or otherwise someone had imported a crapton of mass from elsewhere, and to Olli's Colonial mind that seemed impractical. But she was getting a crash course in what "practical" actually meant if you were the Divine Essiel, and it was expanding her horizons more than she was comfortable with.

As everyone else woke—and the unsleeping Aklu continued

to brood within the drone bay—she set the *God* arrowing in-system towards the single largest artificial structure she'd ever seen. Or anyone had ever seen. Except this was the Hegemony so probably there was a Seat of Bigness or something else out there that was twice the size.

They'd built a ring around the star. Olli was vaguely aware that there were human theories about colossal astro-engineering—Dyson spheres, ringworlds and the like. Nobody had ever built anything on that kind of scale, though. Neither the tech nor the need had existed. She had no idea about what needs drove the Essiel, but right here was proof of concept for the tech. A ring all the way around the star, fifty thousand klicks wide on average, but with irregular, fractal-looking edges. Was it still being constructed? Her mind kept picking at the frayed-looking shape and finding patterns there. Perhaps this was how it was meant to look. She could see a vast swarm of little vessels or construction remotes fizzing around the ring's edge and pondered whether they were just maintenance. Or maybe constant re-edification of the thing was a religious duty for some weird Hegemonic sect. The inner edge, as far as the *God*'s sensor suite could tell her, was made of some impossible substance that was taking in the star's radiance and giving out absolutely nothing. The outer edge was actually a bit chilly by human standards, wrapped in an atmosphere of hydrogen, helium and some kind of complex organic molecules she didn't want to be inhaling any time soon. She had no idea where all the solar energy was going, or how the thermodynamics of it worked, or what it was for. Except as a substrate to build things on, because there was a dotted string of enormous cathedral-like warts all the way around the ring, each one the centre of a complex interchange of ships. There were orbitals hanging over the ring too, she saw as they drew closer. They seemed to be linked to the buildings below by a conduit, by which loads were being carried up and down. An elevator, except there was no cable, just pure gravitic force.

Kittering had joined her by then. The Hanni was crouching on his stool, almost frantically trying to get a handle on what they were seeing and how any of it worked. One of his jittery messages to her board set out an idea of scale. The cathedral-looking structures reached fifty kilometres and there were more from the pearl-sheened ring surface. Some of the orbitals were the size of small continents. Everything was bigger than it had any right to be, but then it was a ring around a star, and even though they were a long way out, they could still see details on it.

Olli didn't like feeling humbled. She resented the implication that there were things in the universe she couldn't just throw her weight and her Scorpion at, and make them get out of her way. But right then she confessed herself beat and settled in for a good long spell of humility.

"An absence of Throughways," Kittering noted. Which suggested that an Int or a feral Ogdru, or similar, was the only way to reach this particular jewel of the Hegemony. This in itself was insane. Except Kittering topped that by commenting that he'd heard the Essiel could turn Throughways on and off to secure and isolate their most precious systems. Of course that was impossible, but Olli wasn't entirely sure she'd been using the word correctly in her life to date.

Since Heremon hadn't deigned to join them, Olli stalked

off to kick the Tothiat awake. She got to the woman's suspension couch and recoiled with a curse. Things had gone badly wrong there. The Tothir part of her hadn't gone peaceably to sleep like it was supposed to but had continued trying to heal and reattach.

The inside of Heremon's pod was webbed by a fungal-looking mesh of branching tendrils, and Olli could barely see past it to the woman's body within. The pod's readouts seemed to think nothing was wrong, but they also thought the thing was empty. Whatever was going on with Heremon's biochemistry, it wasn't meshing at all with a system designed for a human. Olli then went to get the Hiver's torso, which entailed going into the rather cluttered drone bay.

Aklu loomed over her, already gesticulating and blarting as she entered.

"The Razor and the Hook has tasked us with petitions to the Seat," the Hiver told her without ceremony. "Bring us therefore where we might cast our words into the fire."

"Sure, right," Olli said. "Heremon's gone wrong. She's all screwed up." The central corridor that took her from drone bay to command went past the suspension beds, so she could demonstrate the problem to the Hiver.

The busy nest of cyborg bugs seethed and then informed her, "All things can be made right, in proper form. Communications, promptly, if you will."

She wasn't privy to the conversation the major-domo had with Godlike Docking Control or whatever the hell they actually had there, but it resulted in an approach vector and a warning not to deviate from it. Not a straight line, of course. Nothing so human or practical. A path that took them over three of the colossal orbitals, pausing each time to receive some ritual curse or benediction, or tick a box in some cryptic treasure hunt. Olli resigned herself to slouching in her Scorpion and letting Kit fly them back and forth in what seemed to be meaningless errands. Except, just for a moment, the *God*'s sensors picked up a grid of energy—not exactly all around them, but bleeding out of unspace. A vast and complex labyrinth of fields, existing for a fraction of a second as some part of the ring tapped into it. Perhaps the invisible section of the iceberg that was the Seat of Record, the scaffolding which held it all up. She then thought about the path they'd been brought in on, and just what might have befallen them if she'd decided to cut a straight course through it all. This was the problem with the goddamn Essiel: it all seemed like pseudo-religious nonsense until they actually started doing miracles.

Their eventual dock was at the centre of an amphitheatre-like bowl on one of the orbitals, large enough to have fitted most of the Partheni fleet with room to spare. Like most Essiel construction, it was all shiny, mother-of-pearl smoothness, geometric patterns of triangles and other polygons repeated to infinity up the curve of the bowl and beyond. She had to stop looking at it eventually, because if she stared too long into those patterns she could feel the Meaning of the Universe trying to intrude into her mind. In Olli's book, going space-out crazy because of the fundamental nature of things was Idris's bag and he was welcome to it.

Some things turned up and took Heremon away, suspension couch and all. They were as big as Olli in the Scorpion, armoured in segmented encounter suits. Their two arms were enormous, their six legs absurdly spindly and stilt-like. They glided across the surface of the orbital with the languorous ease of water creatures, buoyed up by personal gravitic fields. Olli had no idea what they were, but then the Hegemony was very big and the Essiel had a lot of subject species.

After that, a human came to talk to them. A woman, wearing the fanciest red and purple cult robes Olli had ever seen, as well as a starched and gilded collar extending almost six inches higher than the wispy white hair of her head.

"She going to be all right?" Olli asked. "Heremon?" Not that she cared, obviously. Except she did, despite herself.

"It's a long time since I saw a Tothiat in that condition," the old hierograve said. "But yes, we can save them."

Her name was Gethiel. She was the only human being resident in the entire Seat of Record. She couldn't explain why the honour had fallen to her, save that the summons had come and you didn't say no to the Divine Essiel. She took Olli and Kit down into the body of the orbital, where in pearl-encased halls she treated them to a meal she actually cooked herself—Hanni and human cuisine, with an assortment of Hegemonic odds and ends thrown in. She had a little all-u-cook unit there that was exactly like one Olli's family had owned, way back. Real old Polyaspora tech, just sitting in that perfect Essiel place. Gethiel bustled about that crappy old spacer appliance, cooking the home-grown way while preparing the food on invisible surfaces with tools formed momentarily from the installation's universal gravitic fields. By then the culture shock was setting in and Olli wanted to be far, far away from all this mind-wrenching nonsense, but that wasn't an option. So it was a very meek and subdued Olian Timo who sat and ate a good meal, with Kittering by her side, seemingly affected in just the same way.

11.

Solace

They took her aboard the *Skathi* first. They treated her with
a distant respect. They acknowledged her rank. They
answered none of her questions. She filed a formal request
to speak with the ship's Exemplar. It was taken under consideration. She filed a formal request to report to her direct
commander, Monitor Superior Tact. It was taken under
consideration. Neither of these things occurred and, not
that Solace was exactly sanguine about any of it, it was this
pointed omission that sent her unease into actual fear. It
was the Parthenon and things didn't work like that. The
hierarchy respected its every level and component. That was
what bound the sisterhood together, as much as their
training and the inheritance Doctor Parsefer had designed
for them. They weren't like the Magdan Voyenni or some
other Colonial thugs' club, where the new recruits were
beaten, brutalized and isolated until they clung to the jack-
boot that stomped on them as though it was their mother's
teat. The Colonial military was always characterized that
way in Parthenon circles. Those below forbidden to question,
denied succour, treated like dirt until they could be hammered
into the shape their masters preferred. But the Parthenon

was different. The Parthenon inspired loyalty, rather than simply demanding it.

Except Solace had been loyal to the Parthenon every waking day of her long life, and now they were telling her that her requests were "under consideration." Not a yes, but not even the basic decency of telling her "no." Which meant they felt they couldn't trust her.

On board the *Skathi* she was kept apart from the other Partheni who'd been assigned to the Eye. She saw no familiar faces. Then they put her into suspension for unspace transit and she found herself wondering when and where she'd wake up. Or even if.

She did, though, and found they were somewhere else. The Cognoscientes she asked claimed not to know what system. One went as far as to say that, what with the new Int navigators, it was hard to keep track. A nervous little laugh. And then a scowl from a nearby Executor sent the woman scurrying away. Then Solace had an escort taking her off the ship, shuttling over to something bigger. A garden ship—not the *Ceres* she'd last been stationed on. That had been wrecked by the Colonials, hadn't it? A victim of Ravin Uskaro and his friends starting fires in the hope that everyone else would burn to death and leave them custody of the ashes. This one was the *Ishtar*, she was eventually told. She'd never been aboard it before, but she knew of it. It wasn't as though the Parthenon had many such vessels, after all.

She was held for a brief time in one of the green spaces, a great open park ringed with sports courts and running tracks. They let her watch the young trainees at play, the children out from their lessons. As though they were trying to remind her what it was to be Partheni. As though she *needed* reminding. There were always a handful of Myrmidons close by, not exactly guarding her but very much ready to stop her just lamming off on her own. Which she had no intention of doing, being the loyal Partheni citizen that she was. She just wanted to know what was going on, and nobody would tell her.

And she wanted to know about the rest, of course. What had happened at Estoc? How had things gone so catastrophically *wrong*? Perhaps that was another reason she was being shown all this *life*, this regular garden-ship routine, of fond memory. Shown that, no, nothing was *wrong*. She must be mistaken. Maybe she needed to re-examine those memories of hers.

Once, a group of young women paused as they passed her —she was sitting on a plain bench, feeling a hundred years old, which wasn't much short of the truth. She realized she knew them vaguely. They'd been on the *Ceres* too. Her escort tensed a little as they called out her name and came over, but apparently it wasn't martial law just yet. Nobody was looking over their shoulder for the Aspirat agents. It really was just life as it had been. So Solace and her sisters, off-duty soldiers all, shared talk of how it had been when the *Ceres* was hit. Their shock and incomprehension at why the Colonies would do such a thing. They seemed to think that whatever had gone down at Estoc was retaliation for that, even though the Colonial Navy had been just about the only force there that the Parthenon *hadn't* been fighting. Solace thought about standing up and telling them how it had actually been, and how little sense any of it made, but felt the weight of her escort at her back, and said nothing. Pleasantries and solidarity, that was the limit of the chain they had her on.

Then a new escort turned up and she was decanted into their care. And still, no manacles, no guns, just polite, stern-faced women treating her as though she was not quite one of them any more.

"Where now?" she felt that she could ask, and the head of the new escort, a fellow Executor, said, "Debrief." That should have meant Monitor Tact, of course, but it wouldn't. Sure enough, she wasn't taken to a command hub, where she'd expect to give her report. Instead they headed to the lightless decks below the gardens, where the technical facilities were, and the Cognoscientes scurried like moles.

And there was a familiar face.

Cognosciente Superior Felicity had also been on the *Ceres*. She'd headed up the Parthenon's Intermediary Program, working with Idris to isolate a genetic strain within the pruned Partheni genome that was sensitive to the tides of unspace. After that had come the invention of all the supporting machinery their Ints needed, of course. Necessary both because the Partheni inclination to such sensitivity was limited even at its utmost, and because they preferred to avoid all the surgical barbarity the Colonial methods relied on. Felicity had been a key player at every stage, the great scientific hero of the Parthenon. She'd given them their best weapon against the Architects. Doctor Parsefer would have been proud.

Except, as she was led in to stand to attention before Felicity, Solace couldn't help recalling that the reason the Colonials had been so jealous of their Ints was that the navigators were also the Colonies' one great advantage over the militarily superior Parthenon. And so a patriotic Partheni scientist might also have been working towards that end, as she turned out the first Intermediary sorority.

189

"Myrmidon Executor Solace," Felicity greeted her. "No need for the attention. We're all friends here, I'm sure."

Solace relaxed outwardly, not inwardly. She'd been brought into a small room with a complex chair. There was a reaching hand of sensors ready to connect to the head of whoever was to sit there, and restraints on the arms in case the subject wasn't sitting there voluntarily. At the back of the room she heard a low hum as one of Felicity's underlings started up a shaver.

"You're seconded to the Aspirat, so I imagine you know what this is," Felicity said pleasantly.

Solace did. She'd never had to use it herself, never even seen it employed. It was a relic of earlier times, that's what they'd always told her. When the Parthenon had creaked under the stress of conflicting opinions. When the Aspirat had needed to turn its vigilance inwards.

"Mother, if I can ask, what's this about?" Her voice neutral, almost disinterested.

"We are living through complicated times," Felicity told her regretfully. "There is a school of thought currently in the ascendant that holds we've allowed ourselves to become too ...entangled with other cultures. That the true strength of the Parthenon is being eroded by contact with...caustic ideas, let us say."

"I haven't heard such thoughts expressed, Mother," Solace said carefully.

"Your missions have placed you into considerable contact with those other cultures. Of course this is no fault of your own. You've only done what the Parthenon has asked of you."

"My orders came from Monitor Superior Tact and the Aspirat," Solace noted. Tact outranked Felicity, and the Aspirat outranked whatever technical branch was in charge in this benighted place. Neither barb seemed to strike home.

"There is a school of thought," Felicity said, again in that passive voice, as though such things were entirely beneath her, "which feels that returning operatives who have been working alongside foreigners—who have, perhaps, been forced to eat with them, sleep alongside them, parrot their foolishness, speak their languages—are at risk of becoming contaminated. Losing their clarity of vision. Hence the chair. If you would be seated and bow your head."

Solace stared at her. "I am suspected of disloyalty?" she asked, adding a "Mother" that came unhurried and pointedly late.

"If you would?" Felicity asked brightly, and Solace's Myrmidon escort remained present. It wasn't as if making a scene here would actually help. And so she sat, bowed her head, letting the itchy field of the shaver buzz her to the scalp so they could attach the sensors. This wasn't necessary. She'd seen the meshes they'd used during the Int program, so fine as to be lost in a trainee's hair. The chair was old tech, from a cruder age, but of course that wasn't it either. She understood. When she left this room, whatever the verdict, her bare head would mark her to her peers. *Here is someone who was suspect.* A trial period when everyone would look askance at her, and nobody would be her friend or want to be seen talking to her. A punishment for her past associations, even in a best-case scenario. And she had a feeling there wasn't much "best-case" coming her way today.

"I'd bet Mordant House would love to have something like this, that worked on Colonials," Felicity said happily as she checked the connections. "Of course, they never will. Their very best efforts are ludicrously inaccurate, always have been. That's what comes of permitting rampant genetic variance. Everyone's brain works differently, and then where are you? Of course, *we*..." Solace felt a faint tingle as the sensors activated and Felicity's screens built a picture of her mind. A good Partheni mind, built within the careful parameters Doctor Parsefer had designed. Its pathways well-trodden enough that it could be reliably *read*. Just a little. Just enough.

"You are, of course, a loyal soldier of the Parthenon," Felicity told her. "I will not need to secure you." Through the gaps between the words Solace was acutely aware of the Myrmidons of her escort, who could wrestle her into those restraints should her loyalty be found wanting.

"I am loyal," she confirmed, and Felicity looked at a little battery of telltales connected to the chair and nodded happily.

"We have our first positive," she confirmed. "You are, or believe yourself to be, loyal to the Parthenon, as you see it."

"Mother," Solace said. "May we conclude this as efficiently as possible? I'm keen to return to active duty. Please ask your questions."

"I don't have questions, Executor," Felicity told her. "That was the original procedure with the chair, but it's not necessary. I'm going to talk, instead. All you have to do is listen. And, as you yourself doubtless have many questions about what happened at Estoc, I'm going to talk about that. Two birds with one stone, is the phrase, I think? You see, Executor, the Parthenon is going through a period of transition, focused on our relations with outside cultures. There is a concern that your attitudes may have been contaminated by those of the refugia." The old slur word for the Colonies, the idea of a bucket of genetic offcuts, where out-evolved species clung on, shielded from the harsh realities of the universe. A word that Tact had always been adamant those under her command should never use.

"As you are aware, and thanks in no small part to my work, the Parthenon now has access to enhanced navigators," Felicity added.

"Intermediaries," Solace said automatically, then clamped her jaw shut because it wasn't her place to speak. In her mind, though, was the thought, *Thanks in no small part to Idris. Where would you have been without him?* That thought would show in her telltales, no doubt, which Felicity was glancing at even now. But the Cognosciente just went on, quite pleasantly.

"That's the Colonial term, of course. Because of their original wartime purpose. A bridge between humanity and the Architects, after the freak success of Xavienne Torino. But the Parthenon has no need of such a bridge. We have no need to interact with the Architects at all. We have been fleet-bound since before the death of Earth."

Solace said nothing. Her mind said, to the chair, *We fight the Architects. It's what we do. I fought them in the first war before you were even* born. *That's what our Intermediaries are for. That's why Idris gave them to us.*

Another sidelong look at the monitors, as Felicity said, "This navigational capability opens a lot of doors for us, Executor. Bold new options. The universe just got a lot bigger! We can go anywhere. We don't have to share a limited network of Throughways with the others—the Hanni, the Castigar. The Colonies. We can just *go.* We can find some-where entirely unconnected to any of them and perfect Doctor Parsefer's dream in peace."

More silence from Solace, meaning, *But we have a duty.*

"There are those who have argued we should maintain the course we have taken in the past," Felicity went on. "The refugeniks have always been happy to use us as their shield, after all. And, once they've felt themselves safe, they've been more than happy to demonize us, to attack our interests, keep their secrets. You know they hate us, but that doesn't mean they don't want us to die for them when they're in danger. Hence there are those amongst our leadership who have questioned the necessity of coming to their aid, as we always seem to end up doing." Another wry little smile from Felicity, as if they were just two women discussing some common lover's foibles. "As we've always been shackled to them by history, and by the limited scope of the Throughways, that's what we've always ended up doing. Like some mistreated but loyal pet of theirs." A theatrical roll of the eyes. "But now we don't have to. That's the conclusion that Fleet Exemplar Mercy and our current leadership has come to. We don't have to be there for them, after all. They're on their own, and at last we can be truly on our own too."

"This is the War Party," Solace said, out of turn and insubordinate, but for the moment to hell with that. The War Party, the bad old days clique who'd talked of subjugating the Colonies for the Parthenon's safety. They'd been assassinated for it, all those firebrand leaders. Back from the brink of madness just in time.

"Oh, but it isn't, though," Felicity said. "Hardly at all. The War Party wanted, well, war. Our current leadership wants literally the opposite. No war against the Colonies, no war in their defence. Leave the ungrateful refugeniks to their own devices at last. We don't owe them anything. Least of all the shed blood of our sisters. And now, Executor, let's see how you've done."

She made a show of bending over the telltales but the Myrmidons were already moving in, cued by some signal Solace hadn't caught.

"I am disappointed, but perhaps not surprised," Felicity told her mildly. "You've spent a long time amongst them, and it's easy to forget your age. So many of you old guard are still mired in how it was in the old days, before the secession. I've been monitoring your emotional responses, and I'm afraid I can't give you a clean bill of health just yet. Your loyalty remains in question."

Solace stood, and Felicity skittered back a step as the Myrmidons lurched forwards. She was still, though. She'd asserted her independence as far as she usefully could. No point throwing a punch and making things worse. "So what now?" she asked.

"You'll be held," Felicity told her. Through the hairline crack in her composure, Solace saw a real loathing. A woman who'd jumped ship to the new order of things, and must hate everyone who wouldn't make the same leap, to stop being drowned in cognitive dissonance. "Re-educated, if it's judged worthwhile. Otherwise... The new Parthenon must be lean, Executor. I'm sure you understand. There's no room for those not entirely committed to the cause. It's a bold, exciting new era for us all. Or those of us who can adapt to it." And that plastic smile came back on her face as Solace was led out.

Ravin

They'd come with three Intermediaries. Not the leashed Liaison Board thralls which, as Telemmier had always predicted, were next to useless for turning Architects. Three volunteers from the new class. Survivors of both the surgery and the indoctrination. People Ravin felt he could count on. They were already on their way to meet the Architect that had come to Lassacar, forewarned by the Eye's systems. Ravin himself was here to oversee the evacuation.

There would come a time when this would no longer be a part of human life. The arks would be complete and this desperate scrambling to escape would be behind them. For now, though, Lassacar was a populous world with a strong scientific community and a Nativist base, elements that humanity needed to rescue.

Lassacar wasn't Berlenhof or Magda, but it had been colonized for a long time, with the first settlers down even before the end of Earth. There were seven large metropoli spread across its continents, along with countless smaller settlements. These included major universities, manufacturing hubs, mediotype streamers whose content went out on packet ships across the Colonial Sphere. Plenty to save, therefore. And so he'd come here and, with a few words, taken command of the evacuation effort. He was, after all, high in the ranks of the Nativist movement, much of which was funded and encouraged—tacitly or overtly—by the Magdan aristocracy. There were enough sympathizers within the admin staff of the Lassacar orbitals to ensure Ravin was calling the shots within minutes of leaving unspace.

The passenger transports were already lining up at the

elevator terminals or in geostationary orbit over the major spaceports, ready to receive shuttles. The important work was happening on the surface, though. A whole network of Nativist supporters was down there, after all: thousands of willing recruits ready to put his plan into action. Which wasn't the orderly evacuation plan the Lassacar kybernet had drawn up, shovelling people into ships in order to get the most bodies off the ground in the time available. That wasn't optimal, in Ravin's book. He—and therefore the best interests of humanity—had priorities to do with quality, more than just quantity. There were scores of allies, supporters, investors, and their friends, family and staff, people who'd given up their time, Largesse and influence for Ravin's cause. People whose minds or voices, or friends, he would need going forwards. There were at least thirty colonized worlds for which the ark-builders had drawn up a wish list of people who *must* be saved and brought to Estoc, to be a part of the species' future. Lassacar was on that list and so this was going to be something of a test case for how the future would go. Tomorrow it might *be* Magda or Berlenhof, after all.

Right now he was liaising with a Nativist leader named Randall Sleit. Sleit was not the sort of person Ravin would have been seen in public with. A man who'd been in and out of various institutions for various crimes, some of which were for the cause and some of which were purely personal. Whose heavy boots had broken more than one Hanni carapace, and who'd rammed a few pan-species advocates up against a wall, as well as beaten up a journalist or two. Useful, therefore, and not overly worried about formalities. A man who recognized that the universe had changed and that old restrictions didn't apply any more. And a figure who had plenty of followers, who were even now pushing their way into public buildings and private homes. They were grabbing the people Ravin intended to save and hustling them to the spaceports and elevators. Then marching into the departure lounges with guns, kicking out all the useless morass of people who'd drawn the lucky numbers to get off-planet, making space for the *valuable* sort of émigrés whose names were on Ravin's list. Some of them understood what was happening, that their loyalty and support had bought them a place on the last boat out of hell. Others, picked for their talents, had no idea why they were getting bumped up the list, but precious few of them argued about it.

The Lassacar administration fought amongst itself, wrangled, sent urgent memos. The security forces already leant heavily towards the humanity-first creed, and plenty of their top commissioners and officers were on Ravin's little list. So they stood by and let men like Sleit do their work, or else rolled up their sleeves and helped.

Out in the cold expanse of space, the three Intermediaries met the Architect and set about delaying it, fighting their rearguard action. One failed almost instantly. Ravin winced, hearing the report from the vessel's captain that the Int had gone into immediate seizure and cardiac arrest. The other two held on, trying to slow the Architect just long enough. All the while Ravin received Sleit's reports, one name after another ticked off the list. Shuttles dispatched and elevator cars ascending. The passenger liners taking on their select cargo.

Back at Estoc, the work on the arks was progressing again at last. The shipyards had mostly languished while the Cartel had held the place. They'd only cared about their ridiculous unspace fishing expedition. But Ravin was trying to save the *species*, after all. Doubtless Shinandri, Laery and the rest would have spouted nonsense about saving *everybody*, but Ravin saw more clearly. You couldn't save *everybody*. And that presupposed that *everybody* was worth saving.

The efforts on the ground weren't as efficient as he'd have liked, but the two remaining Ints were at least slowing the Architect's progress. He watched the numbers calmly. Instead of an influx of random people just vomiting out of the gravity well onto the ships, his selection were being saved and the thought gave him a warm glow of satisfaction. How could he be criticized, when he was *saving* people? What more virtuous end was there? They were the worthy ones. People who would enrich the future of humanity, not simply take up space in it. And if that meant the elevator cars and the shuttles were taking off half full, because Sleit's people couldn't gather the chosen quickly enough, then it still meant people *saved*. Every name ticked off the list was a victory against the forces of universal destruction and entropy.

Another warning came from his Ints. They were losing their influence over the Architect and it was resuming its determined approach. An apology: *We couldn't turn it back.* But Ravin hadn't needed them to turn it back, just to delay it a little longer.

He sent orders down to Sleit and the others. *Pick up the pace. Use whatever means.* Sleit was a good man for means. They all were. There would be a time, later, when the fate of humanity was determined by the elegant and the educated, people of proper breeding and social graces. But sometimes you needed a thug to do a thug's job. Across every city of Lassacar, the authorities stepped back—those who hadn't already been sent upwell as part of Ravin's list—and let Sleit's brand of anarchy loose. Men with guns, with military-surplus vehicles and body armour, just tearing through every street in every town, grabbing their targets and getting them to the evacuation points; throwing out, beating or just shooting those who tried to insist that, no, they had a ticket. They had a seat. They should be saved. It was hard, Ravin knew. It was nothing to be proud of, that he was having to resort to tactics such as this. A period of history that, once it was safely in the past, could be shrouded in obscurity. The new generations growing up on the ark ships wouldn't need to learn about what had been done to ensure their survival.

The liners were barely half full by the time the Architect was looming in the skies over Lassacar, the last shuttles docking, the elevators stilled. Down below, the spaceports and transit hubs were hopelessly choked with the detritus of humanity, all those people clawing for a place on the lifeboat who just hadn't been useful enough, or hadn't known the right people or been born to the right stratum of society. In an ideal universe, yes, perhaps more could have been saved, but these were times of crisis and Ravin was a man fit for difficult decisions. A leader. A *hero*, as far as the history books would relate. He'd stand at the shoulders of the historians to make sure they got it right.

There were a thousand thousand comms calls fighting to be heard, from all those towns and cities. Amongst them was the final communication from Randall Sleit saying he was in position and ready for the shuttle to come pick him and his faithful up.

"We should be going," Ravin decided, and sent the appropriate commands to his captain. The liners, with their select cargo, cut ties to their elevator cables and orbits, and began drifting away. There were still a thousand small ships, private enterprises, trying to lift people off, but between the Architect's presence and the damage done to the infrastructure by men like Sleit, Ravin wasn't sure what they could accomplish in the little time remaining.

12.

Idris

He was on one of the mostly complete arks, but Idris didn't know which one. The quarters here were cramped: little windowless rooms with a bunk and basic facilities, disconnected comms and a blank wall screen. The doors were clear plastic, zero privacy. He could look across the narrow corridor, crane left and right, and see into three other identical rooms. Each one had an Intermediary as its sole occupant. This was where they'd taken all of them, ready for processing.

Amongst the many competing demands for his bitterness, a small voice suggested that even Ravin Uskaro wouldn't intentionally build a prison ark, and so these bleak little rooms couldn't actually have been intended for cells. They were to be residences aboard humanity's bold nomadic future. Not for men like the Morzarin Ravin Uskaro, God forbid, but for the people who repaired his cleaning robots or hand-polished his expensive shoes.

If he closed his eyes, he reckoned he could feel the Eye out there. That jagged chunk of planet he'd ripped from the surface of Criccieth's Hell and hurled into space, surrounded by the distributed hull of the Host. Still out there and not being used for its proper purpose. It was probably his imagination, but he'd convinced himself that his Int senses now tethered him to that place. He'd been in its Machines for longer than anyone, after all. He'd dived deeper into unspace than anyone. And he'd *seen* it. The shape of it. Just as he'd found the Architect nursery for Ahab before. With the Eye's unique perspective, he had given shape to the formless, a concrete topology to the imaginary.

It's there, I know it is. Deep, deep down in a place where directions were arbitrary. Or…not entirely. There was one inalienable axis in unspace, and it was *down* or just *away* from the real. And it was an axis with a far pole. You could only go so far *down* that inexorable gradient. Until you reached…

Them…

The sound of feet and wheels outside broke his reverie. The doctors were coming. It sounded like several of them this time, not just a single medic doing the rounds. They weren't going door to door, either. They came straight for him. One had a familiar face but he knew they would all be Liaison Board people. Two men and a woman in pale grey smocks, and a wheeled trolley pottering along after them. He stared at it, because it was a core-world thing and he'd been living as a spacer for a long time. Spacers didn't like wheels much. On board a ship, where any moment someone might need to restart the gravity, jointed legs would always be more useful on a machine, so it could climb and scramble and kick off from surfaces. You had to take a lot of civilized things for granted before wheels were the answer.

They had a couple of big and probably not medically trained men standing behind them too. They weren't in military uniform, just more of the bland grey, but Idris reckoned the borders between "orderly" and "security" were fairly fluid right now.

"Menheer Telemmier," said one of the doctors he hadn't seen before, as they unlocked his clear door and slid it into the wall. "It's an honour."

Idris sat back on his bed and stared.

They muscled in, the lot of them and their trolley. One of the two orderlies began connecting him up to the machine, giving it a line to his neural activity.

"I'm Doctor Frye," said the lead doctor. The woman was Doctor Mirabilis and the other man was Doctor Elis, to whom Idris said, "I know you. I saved your world," just to lampshade the general excess of ingratitude he felt was hanging in the air. This was the doctor who'd tended to him over Berlenhof, after he'd scraped his brain raw trying to escape Aklu the Unspeakable. And right before the Architect had arrived to turn the Colonies' most prominent world into murderous art. But apparently staving off the apocalypse didn't count for much these days. Elis didn't look even slightly abashed.

"Menheer Telemmier," Frye said crisply. He was lean and neat and expensive-looking, doubtless very senior in the Liaison Board hierarchy. "May I enquire, firstly, into your general health? To establish a baseline. Your prosthesis is satisfactory?"

Idris looked at the mechanical forearm and hand. It still didn't feel particularly part of him. He was clumsy with it, even on simple tasks. But then his entire life had been focused on the inside of his head and the inner workings of the universe. There wasn't much that required manual dexterity. He shrugged.

Frye had a single lens over one eye, flickering with data as he ran down his checklist. "And otherwise? Eating well? Sleeping well?"

Idris laughed without humour. Apparently the good doctor hadn't read his case notes. Mirabilis leant in and murmured something and Frye said, "Ah," with the air of a man ticking another virtual box. "You present us with a problem, Menheer."

"Good."

A very slight exasperation, plucking at the corners of the doctor's eyes and mouth. "Under normal circumstances I would have preferred to offer you a position on the staff of the Board, given your long experience in the field. Your assistance in aiding and counselling the other Intermediaries would, I'm sure, be invaluable. And this may still be the case, depending on retained functionality. However..." His eye flicked up and down as he scrolled through the records the lens showed him. "You appear to be a maximum-security case." He regarded Idris dubiously: this skinny little starveling, surely far too frail and callow to have anything to do with the long war record attached to his name. "Given refinements to the procedure, I'm hopeful you'll still be in a position to assist in all appropriate ways after the leashing adjustments, but it's not guaranteed. The procedure is designed with the priority of leaving navigational faculties undamaged above all."

Idris stood suddenly. In the second's surprise this won him, his idea was to lunge forwards and get his metal hand around Frye's throat, then crush the life out of the man before anyone could do anything. An entirely warranted response. What actually happened was that one of the orderlies pushed him right back down again, a single hand to the chest imparting a momentum Idris had no way of countering. He'd probably have missed Frye anyway with the clumsy prosthetic and not actually have given the man much more than a few bruises.

I need to go back into the Machine, he wanted to yell at them. Meaning the Eye. Meaning falling into the lightless reaches of unspace, confirming his discovery. Exploding human knowledge of the structure of the universe. Finding the true enemy. But they wanted to put him in a different machine —cut him and condition him and implant things into his skull until he would be their tame shepherd, taking this ark fleet of sheep from place to place for the greater glory of men like Ravin Uskaro. Betray and abandon all the worlds of humanity, all the worlds of every sentient species. Become just one more sled-dog hauling the future of humanity through the wastes, for ever and for ever.

"I saved your world," he said again. "If I'd realized you didn't want to keep it, I wouldn't have bothered."

"Unfortunately," said Frye in that bright, brittle voice of his, "your loyalty evaluation does not suggest that you'll continue to put humanity's best interests at heart. You are obsessive, paranoid and delusional. All of which are common Int traits, of course."

"Did I not save your world, then? Because I thought that was a matter of serious public record. Or am I deluded?"

Frye smiled. Idris, who'd faced Architects on several occasions, trembled before that smile. It was a bland, keen thing. It could make all his achievements and accomplishments delusions. It could see Ravin's mad ark fleet as the future, and cast anyone who wouldn't skin their own grandmother for it as a species traitor. It was a smile that could beam down on lesser people as they were tortured and carved into compliant, useful navigators for a fleet that would go from nowhere to nowhere forever. Or at least until something broke down that couldn't be fixed.

*

After they'd gone, he said, "You can come out now." He wasn't sure how he knew, but there was definitely something in his Int sensorium that registered a presence where there shouldn't have been one.

Ash, of course. Harbinger Ash, in those robes that were the only things making the alien look even approximately human. Ash, standing just past Idris's line of sight, where Frye and the rest of the medical team would have been able to see it. Except they hadn't. Ash came and went and nobody knew how.

"They must be hunting you all over," Idris said. He saw the Ints in the rooms across the way staring. At least that confirmed Ash was there physically, not just in his head. "You must be giving them the screaming jitters, not knowing where you've got to."

"You're welcome," Ash remarked drily, that too-human voice echoing from its trunk of a torso.

"You've got to get me out of here," Idris said. "Look, you know I'm not one for begging favours, but they are going to cut me up. Cut us all up. The old intobotomy. Brain-chains again, Ash. And we just got through freeing all these people *from* that. I bet the science has advanced so the procedure isn't as reversible these days."

Ash regarded him, the knot of alien organs within its hood tilted in consideration.

"You need me," Idris told it.

"*You* need you," Ash said thoughtfully. "I needed you, but that was when you and I were on the same trajectory."

"What?"

"Are you still true to the cause, Idris?"

Idris waited for the flare of anger. It didn't come and he knew why. "You don't know everything," he told Ash stubbornly. "And you're wrong. You and Ahab. Narrow-minded. There's another way."

"Is there." Intoned in such a way that he couldn't tell if it was a question.

"We don't have to butcher their children. I mean, if one of the options on the table is 'butcher their children' then there really should be another way, don't you think?"

"It's not butchery. They're not children. These are human thoughts."

"I'm a human. Still. I'm still human. I can't help it. You want to go where the Architects come from and make there be no more Architects. Genocide."

"They want to go to where you come from, and where everyone comes from, and make there be no more everyone," Ash pointed out. "Does 'genocide' even cover that?"

"But they don't. They don't *want* it. They're forced to it. And I can reach their masters."

"Can you." Again that unclear inflection.

Idris drew himself up to his full height, for whatever that was worth. "I've seen it. The deep structure of unspace. Because there is one. Everyone thinks it's so unreal that nothing exists there, but being hunted by the goddamn Ogdru taught me that can't be true. And everyone thinks, because it's nothing, then the only way you can navigate is via points in the real. Creeping along the very outside edge, the shallow surface. That's where the Throughways are, holding everything in place like rods and elastic. That's where we go. Except there are depths, away from the real. And there's more than that."

Ash's non-head tilted further, as if to say, *Go on.*

"There's a centre to it," Idris said. "It's a fight to get even close. And...*It*, the thing, the Presence, is there—not at the heart of things, but circling around it, like a guard dog. And at the core, that's where *they* are. I know it. The grit in the oyster."

"You'd challenge an entity that literally exists at the centre of the universe?" Ash asked him.

"I mean, not by choice," Idris said. "But if the other option is butcher children, then sure."

"You're wrong," Ash said sadly, but just this once Idris wasn't putting up with its act.

"Am I? So tell me how you know. Where did you get your doctorate of everything? You're one of the Originators? You poured concrete for the first Throughways? You used to go wrangle Architects before you had a crisis of conscience? Because you've always said you're just one more alien victim, last of your kind, come to warn us all of the oncoming storm. Just another refugee, like Ahab. So tell me now, if you have definitive knowledge of how things are. If you've known all along, then I don't see how being needlessly cryptic has actually *helped*."

Ash stared at him for a long time. There was no body language to read there, no affront, no sagging resignation. The loosely human shape was nothing but pareidolia, the human mind seeing human things where there were none.

"Go on." Idris felt his heart stuttering, on the brink of some true revelation. "Tell me. What are you? You come and go, skip through unspace without a ship. You're the grand Int of all Ints. So how? Where does it come from, Ash?"

Ash seemed to diminish, shrinking within the robe. "Nothing, Idris. No more than I've always said. The last survivor of a dead species. A survival that was pure chance rather than from any great significance I hold. Less even than Ahab. Just some sad vagabond alien that wants to thwart the Architects any way that I can. Does that help you, Idris? Does that gladden your heart?"

"Then help me. Free me. Free all of us. Spirit us away. You need us, and you need us *free*. Because with brain-chains on, we're useless. The Architects won't listen. And you heard what the docs said, I'm sure. They preserve navigation at all costs. Doesn't mean they preserve our ability to *fight*. You let them put some more staples in our heads, you can't know we'll be any use to you after. Help us."

"And then you'll destroy the Architect nursery?" Ash asked sceptically.

"No. I'll do what I think is right. But what better option have you got? Up sticks and go to the next civilization along, hope they'll make better Ints than we have?"

Ash shivered, a fluid all-body motion as inhuman as anything Idris had ever seen, and then just left, shuffling away and fading out of Idris's sight. A moment of misdirection when it somehow had Idris looking away, and then it had exited, like an unprepossessing stage magician. Except it did actual magic.

In its wake it left no answers.

Olli

Just as they finished eating their dinner, the major-domo joined them. The battered torso was all she recognized. The Hegemonics had given the thing five legs and crowned them with a webbed fan of arms so they could properly wave back when Aklu wanted to speak with them. There was no head yet, but then that was probably less important to Essiel.

"You got yours then," Olli noted. Since Hivers could consume organic material, and because spacers had proper manners, she shuffled over to make space for them at the mat they were eating off.

"You are required." They'd restored the major-domo's bell-like voice. "The Razor and the Hook makes preparation for the trials to come. And, as you have partaken of its road, you're sent for, to receive a moment's grace."

"That mean pay?" Olli asked them. "'Grace' means I'm getting backpay for hauling your asses all the way out here?" She reckoned basic gratitude was on the long list of all the things the Essiel didn't really do.

"Remuneration no, but yet more precious: an audience with the Unspeakable," the Hiver informed her.

Olli looked uncertainly at Gethiel—an acquaintance of moments but surely the old woman understood these things. The hierograve smiled sympathetically.

"All I know, Mesdam Timo, is that you don't say no to them. They always know best."

"Do they, though?" Olli asked. "I mean, best for *who*, exactly?"

"Ah, well," agreed Gethiel, which wasn't particularly useful. She was right, though. It wasn't as though Olli could just sit tight and pretend the Scorpion's audio was out.

As well as providing the major-domo's new limbs, they'd found a new floaty couch for Aklu. It wasn't as grand as the absurd thrones she'd seen before. It was barely a couch, in fact. A long, spiralling rod like a unicorn horn, hanging in the air within its invisible fields. Aklu's trunk-like holdfast was twisted around it, and its shell was canted at a slight angle. The overall effect was uncomfortable. Olli was put in mind of sackcloth and ashes, a public display of the Unspeakable's outcast status.

She'd have been in Aklu's shadow still, physically and spiritually, save that the chamber they were in was a circular shaft that went up for what looked to be around a kilometre, with nothing but open void at the far end. Its curved walls were set with incomprehensible tableaus, or hieroglyphs, or histories, or maybe they were really racy Essiel pornography for all Olli could make of them. The scale dwarfed Aklu, shrinking the Razor and the Hook until it was barely more than human by comparison.

"Hi, chief," Olli said awkwardly. Some part of her hadn't stopped shaking since they saw the Seat of Record. Culture shock, in a way she'd thought she was immune to, well-travelled spacer that she was. Too much, too alien, too fast.

Aklu's arms fanned out and flickered through a series of patterns. The major-domo translated, "O least regarded of the Razor's brood, O speaker of the curses, She who Scowls, who brooks no barrier 'twixt her and her desires, and she for whom mere nature can't suffice."

"Sarcasm," Olli identified. "Right?"

"The Razor and the Hook wishes to hear what your petitions are."

The Scorpion's four feet shuffled awkwardly as Olli's eyes

roamed about, seeking anything familiar to fix on. She reckoned asking them to repeat the Essiel's commands wouldn't wash. "I mean, petitions, what we want, right? We could do with some fixing up on the *God*. I'd ask for some of that fancy liquid tech 'cept I'd be fucked if it broke down later 'cos I sure as hell wouldn't be able to fix it. Don't imagine you can just turn it off and on again. Not without getting wet feet." She was aware she was rambling, and steered her mouth back on track. "I mean, if you're asking what I *want*, then there's a whole bunch of friends we left behind when I jumped you out of Estoc. Kris and that useless bastard Idris. Solace, I guess. And I was kind of getting on pretty well with that Jaine, from the Eye crew. Got to admire a woman who can fix up a reactor with two bits of string and a point forty-nine staple. So...I mean, I don't know if you've washed your...okay, not hands, your...things... washed your things of that whole business, or if you were maybe thinking of going back and kicking some ass? Or whatever the expression is for kicking with you guys. Look, Hiver, however you want to be called, I pulled you out of the fire on the *Scythe*. You make all this shit sound golden for the big guy, right? Tell it if it wants to go back and give the Partheni and the Uskaros a big old Essiel slap then I'm all for that, so long as my friends don't get caught in the shockwave. You got that?"

The Hiver had been semaphoring to Aklu throughout, and she had to trust her meaning was getting through in a way that wouldn't cause offence, or make her seem like an idiot. Then Aklu started waving back and groaning like pipes about to rupture, to which the major-domo said, "The Razor and the Hook appreciates your burning for revenge. Let it be known the insults levied at the smallest part of the Hegemony must yet be answered. So it is we have come here to have our grievances set down in record."

"Right," Olli said uncertainly. "Vengeance by passive-aggressive bureaucracy. That's how things work round here. Okay then. I don't see how that'll help Kris and the others, but—" and then the major-domo added, with a definite hard edge to its crystal voice: "We shall smite them all."

"Bureaucracy with extreme prejudice, right." Olli looked from faceless Hiver to faceless Essiel, bitterly missing even the slightest recognizable body language or expression to give her context. "But my friends will be okay, right? No smiting them. Freeing and rescuing, preferably?"

"An ending as befits the Razor's wrath," the major-domo informed her.

"Yes, *right*," Olli pressed, desperately. "Look, I don't know if I've got any credit with the Bank of Aklu right now, but tell it—*ask* it super-nicely—can it please maybe save my friends? Can we have a thousand big lads with guns, and a fleet fit to fuck up the Partheni, and maybe let me lead the boarding party or something? Because this all sounds a bit collateral damage to me."

"The rest we leave to vagaries of fate. Do not lose hope. Those whom the Hook held close are not without resource."

She wondered what weird-ass alien concept had eventually ended up as *hope* on the near end of that chain of translation. *Those whom the Hook held close*, though...that must mean the Cartel. The other bigwigs who'd come together to take over at Estoc and instal the Eye there. So maybe they were already on the case, and somehow word had got to Aklu here, though Olli couldn't see how. Or maybe it was just a general assessment of their resourcefulness, and Aklu was only hoping too.

"Okay then," she said. "Well, you just let me know what me and Kit and the *Vulture* can do. We're all in, I reckon. So long as we get our pals back. And poke the bad guys in the eye, ideally. I mean, we're on the same side, right, the same wavelength?"

Aklu regarded her for long enough that she started running internal diagnostics on the Scorpion just to keep her nerves down, but then it waved again and the Hiver said, "Ask."

"What?" The one-word utterance threw her.

"You wish to understand? Then you must ask. It is permitted."

"I…" There was too much she didn't understand and didn't know, and so in the end, instead of the mysteries of the universe, she went with, "Why? I mean, we had our scrap on Tarekuma, you guys and us. You were doing crimes there. That's fine. I'm okay with crimes. I'm not the filth. But then …Then you become part of this crazy galactic conspiracy, with the Patho Aspirat, that Mordant House woman and the Naeromathi, as well as *Ash*, actual Harbinger Ash. So why you?"

Aklu tilted precariously down towards her, eyestalks crooking in to examine her from all sides. Its gestures to the major-domo seemed different, subdued even.

"Because it's wrong to strive against the way the universe is made. The Essiel do not prey upon the lesser, nor rebel against the great. They know their place, as masters of those things they hold to, and that act on their behalf. When comes the fire, the tide, the storm, they have their shells. That is the way. Except there's no perfection in this world, hence there must be exception made. Hence those who cannot live within their bounds are yet made use of. If railing against fate is wrong, let us do wrong. Let us do all the acts unspeakable. Break all the laws. Fight that which must be borne. Be wicked, know no grace. Refuse all walls. And so, though we be cursed, reviled, denied, so we yet serve the way that we have left behind. When comes the threat the shell cannot resist, there shall it find us, waiting."

Olli digested that, not sure if she actually understood, or if she'd just painted a human-scale narrative over all those words. *Be wicked, know no grace. Because sometimes even the Hegemony needs a bastard to fuck things up for them.*

Then a newcomer joined them, another human, she thought. A young man with a hollow face and some serious, unreconstructed burn-scarring across it. She noticed a green-blue segmented lobster down his back. Not a human, then. Another Tothiat.

Except there was something, when he spoke. A weirdly familiar inflection to the words. "Tell the Unspeakable it's time," to the major-domo, no introduction or formality. "They say they're ready."

"And you are?" Olli demanded.

"Olli, it's me," the man said. "Ahremon."

"I don't know any..." Olli let the words tail off. She didn't know that face. She *did* know the lobster. She'd seen a few and they all had different markings, distinct as fingerprints. "Heremon? Wait—"

"Ahremon," the Tothiat corrected her.

Somehow this hit far harder than Olli was expecting. "That's how it goes, is it? Too damaged so you just cut her loose and got a new host?"

Ahremon looked at her, and at least here was a face Olli could read. A little sad, a little contemptuous, a little humour. Heremon's kind of expressions, but on someone else's features. "You of all people can't point fingers about fixing up some new legs."

"It's not the same!" Olli snapped, outraged. "She was—"

"Me," Ahremon said. "There was no *she*. There was only *me*."

"The Tothir."

"No, *me*. Where the human and the Tothir meet. And this is still me."

"But you're not Heremon."

"Not that, either."

"I'm not going to understand this, am I?" she decided.

The snide smile that came to his face was exactly Heremon's. "No, and we have to go. The Unspeakable is to be judged."

Olli blinked. "Judged? I thought we were here to gear up and get an army or something."

Ahremon shrugged. "The Unspeakable has dared come before the Seat of Records to present grievances against those who have wronged the Hegemonic way. There will be a reckoning and a punishment." Again that familiar intonation, the smile Olli half-recognized. "This is the Devil turning up at Heaven with a list of complaints. How did you think it was going to go?"

13.

Solace

They held her on the *Skathi* at first. She was placed in an awkward, artificial sorority: thirty women of different years, divisions and experience, nothing in common save that they were all apparently of suspect loyalties. There were armed Myrmidons close enough to listen in at all times. Instead of the easy camaraderie that was Partheni home life to Solace, she felt a fraught sense of inquisition. Nobody talked about what had happened at Estoc, about the apparent coup that had taken place within the Parthenon. Solace was burning with questions. She didn't know if Mercy had merely a handful of ships and the Intermediaries, and was on the run from a still-righteous majority, or if she represented the new status quo. In which case Solace was basically a dinosaur: a relic of times past and soon to become extinct. They had no outside comms channels, no news. And they didn't trust one another. Yes, perhaps if Solace had stood up and called for her fellow inmates to rally to her banner, they might have been able to force their way out, gather momentum, pick up all those who'd been keeping their head down and take the ship, restoring the proper order of things... or else everyone would have denounced her to help their own personal case. Desperate flag-waving from the similarly suspect, all of whom wanted nothing more than to be back *within* rather than *without*. And so she said nothing, and none of the others said anything either. Which meant that, functionally, women like Mercy and Felicity had won.

Groups of the suspect were constantly being taken off for assessment, then brought back. They didn't discuss what further procedures they'd undergone and Solace was never taken out again. Occasionally a group of Myrmidons would escort people away and not bring them back. At first Solace feared the worst, until she guessed that those were the lucky ones, whose loyalties had been confirmed under later testing. They'd most probably been restored to active duty in service of the new Parthenon that Exemplar Mercy was building. Then she wondered if that wasn't actually the worst after all.

Her own absence from any of these re-tested groups was noted. The other suspect inmates began to keep their distance. Solace was irretrievably contaminated, too far down the disloyalty spectrum to be re-educated or given another chance.

Then they did come for her, and that was worse. A larger escort, a sterner Myrmidon Executor in charge. Solace and about half of the rest were gathered up and marched out to a docking bay. Just a big empty hangar open to space, save for the intervention of the ship's gravitic field graciously holding the air in. Solace stood there, wearing nothing but light fatigues along with all of the other prisoners—forty-seven of them by her count. And there were the Myrmidons in their sealed combat armour. How easy just to breach that gravitic seal, flush the hangar and send them all into space, while their guards remained inviolate in their hermetic suits, their boots clamping them to the deck. She also understood that she was *meant* to think this, that the very scenario was set up to intimidate her and her compatriots. That didn't mean it wasn't working.

Another escort marched in, faceless within their helms. Solace had worn that armour with pride most of her life— far longer than the majority of these women had been alive. She'd only ever seen the uniform as a symbol of hope, strength and pride. And now she was on the wrong side of it and wondering if this was how the Colonials felt, when they looked on the might of the Partheni Myrmidons. *We are terrifying.*

The new arrivals had a single prisoner whom Solace recognized with a jolt. Monitor Superior Tact. Her old commander looked dishevelled, as though she'd not slept since before the attack on Estoc. She was trooped up to the subdued mob of prisoners and unceremoniously pushed into their midst. She ended up next to Solace, as though it was the mere Brownian motion of crowds that had put her there. *And what are the odds of that?*

The tiniest flame of hope in Solace's breast, as she murmured, "Prêt à combattre, Mother."

Tact didn't look at her or register her presence. She really did look rough, gaunt and grey and *old* in a way she'd never seemed before. All her stern authority stripped from her.

"No combat for you, not just yet, Executor." Solace hardly saw her lips move, and had to fight to stop herself leaning in too obviously to catch the words.

"Tell me there's a plan, Mother."

The slightest flick of Tact's eyes towards her. "You're being moved to a ship designated as a penitent hulk. The *Angel Alecto*. You know it?"

Solace kept her face devoid of expression. "That's a fighting ship."

"Well, Mercy's fleet is short of large non-fighting ships right now. What can she do? She needs somewhere to isolate those whose loyalty falls short of her standards. Such as you and me."

Solace considered this, and just what might conveniently happen to such a ship. Partheni naval history wasn't exactly peppered with catastrophic systems failure, but there was room for a sudden spike if Mercy wanted rid of some unwanted sisters without actually lining everyone up and shooting them. How many ships did she have, and could she afford to sacrifice one to clear all those inconvenient pieces off the game board?

"You want me to take the ship?"

Tact chuckled hollowly. "Just you? I can't fault your confidence, Executor. I want you to be ready. I am pulling what strings they've left attached to me. While I still can. Until an opportunity opens up...no heroics, Solace. I don't want you getting yourself killed. When the time comes, you'll know it. Est-ce compris?"

"Compris, Mother. But..." *You'll be there, won't you?* Something suddenly changed: the Myrmidons who'd brought Tact in were muscling forwards to drag her right back out again, separating her roughly from the others, marching her away. Solace had been a soldier long enough to read body language through all that armour. She recognized a squad chastised and could almost hear the superior shouting at them over their comms, *Why did you take her to the rest of the*

221

prisoners? Imagining a trail of orders abruptly gone without a trace, a sequence of events masterminded somehow by Tact and her remaining sympathizers.

And then there was a shuttle arriving, gliding into the pressurized hangar from the void of space with barely a shudder. Solace and the rest were marched into it, and out there, just a point of light, was the *Angel Alecto*, designated resting place for those who had displeased the new rulers of the Parthenon.

*

They'd stripped out the central section of the *Angel Alecto*. Solace had expected a network of walls and small public spaces, the residential decks for off-duty crew where each shift could take over from the last as they traded posts. Instead, there was just one big open area, like a hollow abscess at the heart of the ship. They had Myrmidons on watch, both on the ground and on a balcony level. And they had precisely delineated groups of prisoners, each within an area marked out on the deck with projected lines of light. "Classes," the guards called them. There were almost three hundred women there, even before Solace's half-hundred joined them. Enough that there wasn't much capacity for more, given each "class" was ordered to stay in the centre of its marked area, and not talk to their neighbours. Solace looked over the little camps of quiet, wary women and fought down her despair. At least within the camps there was a low whisper of conversation. And at least her disarmed sisters were orderly and calm, sitting in their ranks. Prêt à combattre. Or she hoped so. Because at that moment the whole weight of the universe seemed to be on her shoulders. *I have to save the Parthenon. I have to save Idris. I have to save everything from the Architects.* Surely Tact intended her to spark a revolution here, to take over the *Angel Alecto*, turn its guns on the rest of the fleet...? Perhaps there were other penitent hulks too. With Mercy's coup just a tiny clique of officers desperate to stop their enemies realizing how little of a mandate they truly had. Perhaps... The despair rose again, welling up in her. What if it was Solace who just didn't understand how the universe worked? That in fact these dispirited dissidents were *it*, and the bulk of the Parthenon agreed with what Felicity had set out: leave the refugia to their fate. Abandon ancestral humanity, which had never cared for them anyway. Partheni for the Parthenon, living in open space with no need of neighbours.

Going slowly insane, spiralling inwards into our own traditions. Don't tell me that was the future Doctor Parsefer envisaged, that splendid isolation. What are we, without a universe to fight for?

And yet she couldn't know. She'd always assumed the thoughts in her head were mirrored in those of her sisters, but now she felt a chasm had opened up. All those women who wore a close cousin to her face might be strangers under the skin.

More prisoners came in. A cause for hope, because it meant she had more allies? A cause for despair, because here they all were under guard, taken without a fight because those who had come for them were their sisters. As she watched the numbers mount, and the great hold of the *Alecto* become more crowded, she started to worry. The prisoner-to-guard ratio was rising sharply, and while that had its advantages, Exemplar Mercy wouldn't have overlooked the maths either.

Why concentrate your enemies within a single fragile hull unless you knew something was going to happen to it...?

I have to do something first. It's just me.

No. Tact has a plan. Tact gave you orders.

Tact failed. A brutal understanding. *She didn't see this coming. She couldn't stop it. She failed.*

Solace looked around, hunched in, murmuring, "Myrmidon Executor Solace," to her closest fellows. A few other names and ranks were exchanged, and she ascertained she was the ranking officer there. Half the rest were Cognoscientes—technicians and specialists with no more than basic combat training. They listened when she spoke, though. *We have to act, and hope the others will follow our lead.* Thinking of a room full of unarmed and expendable women rushing guards with accelerators. *Suicide.* And yet she couldn't just sit and watch Mercy's people suck the life out of the Parthenon, rob it of its virtues and steal it away.

Then one of her fellows plucked at her sleeve. Another group of inmates was arriving, just a handful of them, but these were different. There was a certain common look to them, beyond even the Partheni genetic kinship. A gaunt and haunted expression. Solace recognized many of them from the Eye. Idris's students. Intermediaries, under guard. Of course they'd all been exposed to plenty of contact with outsiders. They'd been working alongside the new crop of Colonial volunteers to stave off the Architects as and when Foresight had picked up a new intrusion. So these were the Ints who hadn't passed Felicity's tests? Solace wondered how good those tests even were, given they were reliant on the exacting parameters of the standard Partheni brain. Had Felicity relied on less certain methods, or...?

She saw it then, and felt a dagger-thrust of betrayal. Overseeing the imprisoned Ints was someone she knew. Grave, the very first of the Partheni Intermediaries. Solace remembered her practically worshipping Idris, seemingly so eager to be a part of the new future the Eye was making possible. Except there she was in uniform and armed, consigning her Int sisters to the last of the holding areas. They had been her sorority, of course, and she'd know them. Shared quarters and conversations with them. She'd know exactly who could be counted on to stand by Mercy and the coup. And here were the rest, those who believed too strongly in that *other* Parthenon, the one Solace felt slipping through her fingers. Mercy must have agonized, she thought darkly, about what to do with Intermediaries she couldn't rely on. Such a valuable resource, after all. Surely she would want to hold onto them in the hope they'd come round. But apparently the new order didn't have room for dissent, even amongst its most irreplaceable personnel.

Solace, far from irreplaceable, understood that her own possible futures had narrowed to two close options: charge the guns of the guards, sans armour, sans weapons, or wait until she and all these other unreliables could be disposed of quietly, with plausible deniability, not even a footnote in the new-written histories of the Parthenon.

Grave

Cognosciente Intermediary Grave felt the eyes of her compatriots on her back all the way to the shuttle, for all she'd left them in the *Angel Alecto*'s new hold with the rest of the prisoners. Her fellow Ints, graduates of the same program, but who'd been more clearly marked by their association with the Colonials, or more outspoken in their loyalty to Telemmier. Women who'd taken a stand, or else who just hadn't dissembled well enough. And who were now, based on their current location, on the wrong side of history. They stayed, and Grave walked away, back to the shuttle, back to the *Skathi* to be a part of the future.

She'd gone before Felicity and the rest of the Aspirat team who'd backed Fleet Exemplar Mercy. The interrogation hadn't been soft because she was an Int. It had been worse, in fact. Felicity's machines were perfectly calibrated for the Partheni brain structure, which varied so little from one to another. Except Ints didn't have that brain structure any more. Their training and modifications made them difficult to read, so Felicity had pushed extra hard, recording every biometric, analysing Grave's breathing, heartbeat and facial expressions. And she'd still not been sure, in the end. But the reborn Parthenon needed its Intermediaries, of all things, and so she drew the line. Grave and most of the others ended up on the "loyal" side of things. Only a handful were too unregenerate to be trusted. The thought made her proud. Becoming an Int had been long, hard work, but that test, proving herself, had been the hardest.

There was a squad of other Ints gathered in the hangar, all part of the grand reorganization Mercy was implementing across the fleet. Crew taken off ships, reassigned. Loyal officers replacing those of more doubtful inclination on some ships. In other cases, whole crews were gutted and taken to hulks like the *Alecto*, out of the way, conveniently in one place in case drastic measures were required. But they were all sisters, Grave knew. Mercy was a hard woman but, given time, Felicity and her team would chip away at the psychology of the prisoners, bring back into the fold those who could be turned. In the end, there would doubtless be a core who were beyond recovery, but Mercy would be aiming for a minimum of permanent losses. They would be starting anew, after all. Every woman was valuable.

She watched her remaining sister Intermediaries being dispatched to their ships, ensuring every vessel in the fleet would have a pilot. There would need to be more Ints soon, in Mercy's plan. So Felicity would gather the single gene-line that permitted it, and most likely those who had previously not volunteered their services would find themselves without the option this time round. Grave understood the harsh mathematics of becoming deep space nomads. She knew the choices Mercy would be making.

She met the gaze of her fellows as they marched smartly off to their new assignments, the ships they'd be shepherding through unspace, starting from now.

To Grave fell the honour of piloting the *Skathi* itself, or at least she was one-third of the flagship's Int team. They'd be taking the navigation in shifts, to remain fresh for action. Mercy was paranoid about the possibility of Colonial warships coming after them, let alone the unknowable resources of the Hegemony. Grave had tried to explain the impossibility of tracking through unspace. Except anecdotal evidence suggested the Essiel had navigator aliens who could pull it off, and who knew what tricks the Colonials had, with their decades-long Int Program?

The *Skathi*'s bridge was a long wedge of a room with a circular display projected into its heart, so that every woman of the crew had head-up access to all the primary readouts, as well as the role-specific display on their board.

Grave's heart sank—slightly but perceptibly—when she saw that Mercy was entertaining a guest. She'd hoped not to be witness to this particular scene. Former Monitor Superior Tact was there, under guard in prisoner fatigues, and Mercy was already beckoning Grave over.

"Cognosciente Intermediary," the Fleet Exemplar greeted her. "Excellent timing. Perhaps you'd tell our guest your most recent assignment."

Grave felt Tact's iron gaze on her and shuffled, fighting back the instant stab of conflict inside her so that nothing showed on her face. She took refuge in a soldier's attentive stance, staring straight forward as she'd seen the Myrmidons do, meeting no gazes. "I was tasked with assisting Cognosciente Superior Felicity in identifying those of my division whose loyalties could not be guaranteed sufficient to place them in control of unspace navigation of a fleet vessel, Mother," she confirmed. "I am just returned from delivering them to the penitent vessel *Angel Alecto*."

"The vessel which holds the rest of your dissidents," Mercy finished, smiling almost fondly at Tact. "Those whom you somehow corrupted to the extent that they could not be relied on to support their sisters and their state."

"You are not the Parthenon, Mercy," Tact said simply. "This isn't exactly our entire assembled strength."

"Ah, but our Intermediaries are limited, are they not? We are planning widespread breeding of the appropriate gene-line, but until then, we have as many ships as we can move. Those who have refused our call can remain with the refugia and share their fate. But we'll survive. The true Parthenon, faithful to the intent of our founder." Tact and Mercy had a moment of crackling tension between them. "It must rankle that Grave and the others came over to us so readily."

Tact's face admitted to no such emotion, or any at all. Denied the satisfaction, Mercy looked to Grave. "Perhaps you'd like to explain yourself, Cognosciente Intermediary?"

Grave felt another spike of anxiety, fighting to keep her own countenance professional. "When I asked to combat the Architects alongside the Colonial Ints, that was my duty to the Parthenon. Now I am asked to pilot our fleet into the wider universe. That is also my duty to the Parthenon, Mother."

Perhaps Mercy had been hoping for more vitriol. She looked a little sour at the impersonal declaration but swallowed it.

"I'm surprised you've not packed me off to the *Alecto* myself," Tact observed. "Or am I here as a trophy?"

"You're here because I respect your intelligence, Tact," Mercy told her. "Far too much to place you in the midst of those who might follow you. Dealing with an insurrection wouldn't tax my forces, but it would cost the lives of too many sisters who might yet be redeemed. Friends close and enemies closer, isn't that the saying?"

"I've heard it," Tact confirmed, not looking at Grave. "This is it then, is it? You're taking the heart of our strength away from the rest of humanity, just when they need us most?"

"We are not placed in the universe to serve their needs," Mercy said, pitching her voice up to carry across the bridge. "Our founder did not engender us to serve the refugeniks. We are sufficient unto ourselves. It's time we grew up and severed ties with them. We owe them no more than we'd owe an ape. Save that apes are already extinct, and the refugeniks have that fate yet to come."

"Refugeniks," Tact said, so quietly Grave had to strain to hear. "You use that word as a slur, I understand that. The refugia—the genetic reservoir left over from a previous age. The species driven to the fringes by their own superior offspring. Easy to see it as a pejorative."

This put Mercy off her rhetoric, frowning. "How can it be anything but that?"

"When Doctor Parsefer coined the phrase for baseline humanity, she meant it as more than a dismissal. The refugia are where variation survives. Variation that the future might need. Without them, what are we? A hollow shell. We only ever had meaning in relation to the rest of humanity, whether we were for them or against them. They balanced us, and shaped us. And without them, on our own in the void, we will collapse inwards. We'll have no heart. We need them, even if it's just because we need someone to distinguish ourselves from. Your plan will destroy the Parthenon more surely than losing a war to the Colonies would."

"It saddens me that you, who have served your people so well, could believe such a thing." There was no room for doubt in Mercy's voice. "Do you know what some of my staff said I should do with you, as the ringleader of any potential opposition? That I should secure you somewhere and leave you awake when we entered unspace. Chained to the mast before the sirens, like the old stories, hmm? But I hold out hope that you will come to serve the new Parthenon. That Felicity can find the correct penitential regimen to rehabilitate even you. I won't let her give up on you, Tact." A smile that could carve hull metal. "So it's time for you to go into suspension. You'll wake into a very different world."

After that it was just the considerable logistical puzzle of putting an entire warship's crew into suspension, ready for an unspace voyage. An effort being replicated across Mercy's fleet, with every vessel reporting in turn. Grave wasn't sure how the penitent ships were dealing with the problem. She had to take on faith Mercy's stated desire to reclaim as many of their sisters as she could, rather than simply disposing of all her problems in transit.

She liaised with the other two Ints on the *Skathi*. She would take the second shift, being woken to take her place as the ship's guide through unspace, within the cerebral engine that permitted her to act as a true Intermediary, and without all that carving and cutting the Colonials relied on. She thought of Idris Telemmier then, whose strident campaigning and tireless work with Felicity's people had spared them that. She hoped he was well, though that seemed unlikely, given whose hands were now at his throat.

Before she went under, she had a final fight with her conscience, about what she was about to do. The fear of it, the terrible cost. Mercy's words, and Tact's, wrestling in her head, trading knife-blows as though they were fighting over her soul. Except Doctor Parsefer hadn't believed in souls, arch-rationalist as she had been. That was for the more backward of the Colonials, like Andecka Tal Mar, who'd been Grave's comrade in arms such a short time ago.

Feeling sick and guilty, Grave finally retired to her suspension bed, knowing that the world she would wake into would be very different, as Mercy had said.

14.

Kris

Ahab wanted to get in the Machine. The Naeromathi-sized one that it had designed, and Jaine had built, when the Eye was still planet-bound on Criccieth's Hell.

The guards stationed on the Eye obviously had orders that nobody was supposed to be using any of the installations there, other than for Foresight. They probably thought Ahab could take the whole assembly into unspace or something, and weren't about to give him the chance. To be wholly honest, Kris wasn't one hundred per cent sure that wasn't the case. Her understanding of the business was that Ahab wasn't an Int-style navigator, and that the primary purpose of the Machine was to look into the unreal, not actually travel to it. Except Idris had used the human-scale machinery to tear the whole installation into orbit, so who actually knew?

Anyway, this had resulted in a stand-off between Voyenni and Naeromath that she saw was on the very knife-edge of violence as she came running in, with Jaine at her heels. And Ahab was *big*. She'd seen images of extinct Earth animals, elephants or dinosaurs or something. Ahab was on that kind of scale, built like an eel on steroids bulked out further by all its cybernetics. Of course none of the Eye crew was supposed to be armed but Ahab might have a whole built-in arsenal.

The Voyenni, for their part, were big men in combat armour with accelerators and very little imagination. Just as scary as Ahab, in Kris's book. Doctor Shinandri, gangling and giggling and waving his arms, was standing right between them in imminent danger of being killed by either side, even as Kris ran in.

She'd been asleep. This was all taking place in the middle of the night by her clock, but the Naeromathi didn't seem to work to any regular schedule. She chalked this up as just one more grievance she had against the universe.

The Voyenni had gone from ordering the Naeromath away, to shouting for both it and the doctor to get on the ground or be shot. Kris didn't know if Ahab *could* even get on the ground. Quite possibly its six-legged prosthetic didn't bend that way. She was damn sure the accelerator shot would carve it up, though. Big didn't mean invulnerable. And Doc Shinandri wouldn't exactly slow the shot much by standing in the way.

She was about to just start shouting along with everyone else, except they were all a good deal louder than she was, and nobody had noticed when she swept into the room. For a moment she paused. Then Tokamak Jaine caught up with her and did something to the lights in the Machine bay, making everything suddenly blindingly bright.

One of the Voyenni unloaded a dozen pellets through the nearest wall, and Kris decided she'd be having words with Jaine about precisely what de-escalation meant at some later point, but the end result was that both sides backed off, blinking. Or, in the case of Ahab, sweeping its metal-sheathed head about on the end of its serpentine neck. Kris wasn't entirely sure how visual the Naeromathi were, naturally, but there were certainly lenses set into that skewed steel hood.

"You talk to Ahab," she told Jaine. The mechanic was one of the few humans the alien would listen to. She herself approached the Voyenni, whom she'd made her problem.

Their leader loomed over her. They liked that, getting in your space. She stood her ground, though, so he ended up virtually ramming her chin with his armoured chest. Then he couldn't actually look at her, due to the design of their helmets not quite giving them the freedom of neck move-ment. She eyeballed the man's chin until he hauled the helm off for a proper glowering.

"I'm well aware your orders are to keep the science team alive," she told him.

"Tell it to go back in its tank, its cage, whatever it has," the Voyenni spat, in a strong Magdan accent. "It is not to come here. *Those* are our orders. If it does not know its place, I will seek better orders. If *it* cannot be damaged, perhaps there is some other that can be whipped in its place."

They'd do it too. With relish even. Everyone had heard stories of how the Boyarin families kept order on Magda. But if she flinched now there'd be no way to wrest any leverage back. So she just stood there, facing him down as though he was a judge or an opposing advocate, or they were knives-out at the duelling piste.

"There are nine new holes in the wall, thanks to one of your people's lax trigger discipline." She didn't actually know how many holes there were but putting a number out there made her seem extra-competent. "Could have been me, and probably nobody would have shed a tear. Could have been the doc there, in which case what does your boss do to you exactly? When his star scientist can't make his unique alien machine go?"

No admission of fault showed in the Voyenni's face. No immediate comeback either. Their brute impassivity game was strong, but she reckoned she'd scored a point.

Ahab chose that moment to bellow, "The work is unfinished! Time! They have stolen it from me!" But it wasn't a full-on roar, just a complaint to Jaine.

"Foresight's still going," came Jaine's reply. "They're still tracking the Architects." Because of course that was information the Uskaros had a use for.

"That is not the work!" Ahab shouted, and abruptly its leathery, preservative-stinking neck was swaying over Kris's head, yearning towards its Machine. "The vessel is prepared! Let us plot our course! Let us depart! Where is my vengeance? Where is the retribution of the universe?" An awful, lost litany of thwarted desire.

"Can you not let it do *something*?" Jaine asked, and here was Shinandri fluttering towards them again, waving his hands and probably about to get shot out of pure annoyance.

"There's no harm in it. Ahab's only interested in stopping the Architects," Kris said, though she knew it wouldn't work. "Don't you want that? What if Magda's next on their list? It could be. We could get the word from Foresight any moment." The words bounced off the man's closed features without leaving a mark. Of course if Foresight reported that any worlds near to Ravin Uskaro's heart were under threat, then all free Ints would be deployed to fend them off. No expense spared for things they actually cared about, and the rest of the galaxy could go hang. And, for this man, if his master told him to stand by and watch worlds get snuffed out one by one, that's what he'd do.

"I'll talk to the Morzarin." She turned round now. Not the crew's advocate to the Uskaros, but the Uskaros' turncoat handling the crew. "I'll explain. I'll get him to open the Machine up again, so Ahab can continue its work. I will." Facing them down and knowing that, in their eyes, she was shifting from an *us* into a *them*.

In that unwelcome moment, Trine bustled in, utterly oblivious, and declared, "My esteemed colleagues and fellow prisoners in durance vile, you are all invited to a diplomatic soiree in my cell, effective immediately!"

This served to take the heat off Kris at least and focus all attention on the Hiver. They spread the fan of jointed arms that reached from their chest cavity, beaming at all concerned. "You and you, and you and you," they declared, picking out Kris and the Eye crew. "Not you, though. You aren't invited." A stern glower at the Voyenni. Trine's face was a projection onto the concave inner surface of their spoon-shaped head, which gave the illusion that they were always looking straight at any observer. Their ebullient cheer only made the effect creepier.

"Trine, this isn't the time," Kris told them.

"Inconceivable. I am pulling rank, my diplomatic inferior. This is very much the time. I mean, what exactly were you going to accomplish? You'll talk to the Morzarin. I'm sure he'll be enthralled by your legal arguments. Until such enthralment has been effected, what exactly is there left to accomplish? Come to my quarters. I have printed off superior wine and nibbles."

Kris felt equal parts frustration and resignation. The Hiver was as annoying as ever, but mostly because they were right. Jaine had calmed Ahab, and possibly the Naeromathi genuinely believed Kris would be able to wheedle some concession from Ravin Uskaro, though she wouldn't put money on it herself. She filed a request to speak with the man, knowing he'd insist she shuttled over to the *Grand Nikolas* rather than just talk over comms. Knowing she'd end up coming back with his words in her mouth to cram into the ears of her fellows, thus widening the divide between her and them. And knowing she was doing a lawyer's work. She'd represented plenty of objectionable clients before, but this was different. She'd sold a part of herself, agreeing to be Ravin's pawn. She could tell herself it would be worse without her, over and over, and probably that was true. But it didn't make her feel any less wretched and dirty.

In Trine's quarters there was indeed wine and a selection of finger food, all of which tasted gritty and powdery—the wine included—because the Eye only had what printers Jaine had been able to instal, and it wasn't exactly embassy standard. However, what Trine's soiree also had was Harbinger Ash.

Kris stopped dead in the doorway so that Shinandri ended up barging her into the room. The alien was just standing there in the middle, apropos of nothing. It even had a printed cup entwined in the tendrils of the "hand" that was at one terminus of its branching trunk.

"What's this?" she asked Trine.

The Hiver was actually handing out cups as though the whole business really was a party. "Apparently it's time," they explained.

"What's time? Time for what?" Kris looked from them to Ash.

The alien adjusted the position of its head in a way that utterly belied its pretence at a human shape. "You want the Eye," it said. "Take it."

"Yes!" Ahab boomed instantly and Kris shot Jaine a desperate look.

"Nobody can overhear us," Ash said with utter certainty. "Not now, for these moments. You know me by reputation, Keristina Soolin Almier. What do they call me?"

"Harbinger," she said unwillingly.

"So hear me now. This is your one and only chance to retake the Eye. To retake the Host entire. Other than the force stationed to keep watch on you, the ship is under-manned, lacking pilots. You must take it, have it ready to leave Estoc, and you must begin the moment this conversation ends."

"Wait, wait," Kris told it. "Let's bring things back to the 'force.' There's a whole bunch of house guard with guns. There's only a handful of us, without guns. Plus we can't take the Host anywhere. We don't have Ints. We don't have Idris. We don't...have anything, basically. Name a thing, we don't have it."

"Agent Havaer Mundy and Asset Colvari have been tasked with freeing the Intermediaries aboard Unnamed Ark Nine," Ash told them. "However, even if they are successful, they need somewhere to take them. They need to come to the Host."

"Yes!" Ahab declared again, and Kris wasn't exactly sure how that "no overhearing" thing was working, given the Naeromath was shouting at the top of its artificial voice.

"No, listen," Kris insisted. "We've got nothing. What do you imagine we can do here?" But Ahab just thundered out of the room, metal legs clattering. Heading for the Machine again, no doubt. Off to get itself shot.

"Jaine!" Kris said, but the mechanic had a wall panel open and was briskly hauling out handfuls of wiring and components. "What are you doing?"

The woman just grunted, and it was up to Doctor Shinandri to say, "My colleague's actions are mutely communicating that we *do* have something, the very least fingertip of a something, that we can deploy. And, if this is the time, then there isn't any better."

"You've ... got something?" Kris asked. "You've been working on something? Behind my *back*?"

"There were certain questions raised of where precisely your loyalties might lie," the doctor said, somehow apologetic while also tittering as though it was hilarious. "We knew matters would have to be taken into our own hands at some point, though. And it's not much. Smoke and mirrors, based on our superior knowledge of what is, in our minds, very much our territory, oh my, yes. Emergency use only, but apparently this is sufficiently emergencious."

"Trine, did you ... ?"

"All a complete revelation to myself, my fellow in exclusion," the Hiver said.

"Okay, so can someone actually tell me what the plan is *now*, or am I still on the watch list?" Kris demanded, and then added, "Where the crap did Ash go?" Because the alien absolutely had not walked out past her, but it somehow wasn't in the room any more either.

At that moment all the lights died, then flicked back on

distinctly different, a weird greenish tint to them. It wasn't the lights that had changed, though, Kris realized. It was the air. It was the Eye. Whatever Jaine had just done had activated the ancient structure, or some part of the cobbled-together tech seeded through it.

"Right." The mechanic stood up. She had something in her hands, retrieved from within the wall. It was blocky and made out of brightly coloured plastics, like a child's toy. It was, Kris was absolutely sure, a weapon. A moment later, Trine stepped forwards and proffered her a knife they'd apparently been hiding within their body cavity, amongst the bustle of their insect hive. She was weirdly touched that they'd thought about her.

She took it. The comforting weight and balance told her it was proper duelling standard, exactly her tool of choice. Not much use against a bunch of thugs with accelerators, but what could you do?

"Let's go take our stuff back," said Jaine, and marched out of the door.

Ravin

The Liaison Board doctors were making their report to him, seven of them led by Doctor Frye, each face projected before Ravin in a little constellation of pompous solemnity. Every speaker cycled to the fore to trot out their particular conclusions, and then shrank back into insignificance when they were done. It was all a precisely calibrated little circus but Doctor Frye was a good administrator.

"It's remarkable how much of our work they managed to

undo in six months," Frye noted, after Doctor Mirabilis had given her report on the state of the conditioning. Liaison Board Ints, being a valuable commodity, were hedged around with as many protections as possible. Not just the legal indentures of their leash contracts but plenty inside the head too. In a few cases there were some fairly brutal implants, but that ran the risk of interfering with the delicate Intermediary mods themselves. A lot of it came down to equally brutal psychological conditioning, building in fear, obedience and dependence. After all, nobody wanted a rogue Int dragging valuable cargo off into the depths of the void, never to be seen again.

Except apparently Laery and her Cartel hadn't been bothered. They'd just been desperate to undo all that good work, and Mordant House was more than capable of it. Of course, they hadn't been after commercial navigators, and slaved Ints were no use to them. Idris Telemmier had done a lot of annoying things in his life, but announcing that leashed Ints wouldn't be listened to by Architects was right at the top of the list. And Ravin didn't even know if it was true. Everyone just seemed to have taken it for granted.

"We have run test-case scenarios on the neural architecture of the broken Ints," Doctor Elis explained, now it was his turn. "We've full confidence we can bring them all to heel, re-establish the programming, get them all properly leashed again. And the upside is that, in the six months they've been out of our custody, they've learned additional unspace manipulation skills and become familiar with the Host's systems. In fact I'm surprised at just how much emphasis was placed on that part of their training. They obviously had big plans for the vessel."

"Yes," Ravin agreed. Normally he wasn't this casual with his subordinates but he was feeling benevolent right now, having won. "There was some mad plan to use it to carry their piece of Originator rock into unspace, to where the Architects come from. Which would have resulted in the loss of not one but two priceless and unique things. Now, tell me about Telemmier." The elusive first-class Int, one of only three still alive, and the other two embedded so deep within Hugh he'd never get his hands on them.

"He'll be a more difficult project, to be sure." Doctor Frye's head swam to the fore. "But I've been reviewing his neuro-graph readings. His length of service has resulted in a more densely convoluted structure in the pertinent sections of the brain than I've seen. It may not be possible to retain one hundred per cent of his cerebral functioning and also guar-antee his cooperation, but—"

"His cooperation is paramount," Ravin said flatly. "I don't care if he can play the violin or not."

"Of course, Your Elegance," Frye acknowledged. Then, past and through the doctor's face, Ravin saw one of the ship's crew waiting to report to him. Meaning, given his standing orders, that something critical had happened.

"Meeting adjourned. Results next time," he told the assem-bled doctors, dismissing their images. "Report." Already thinking, *Is it the Partheni?*

"Morzarin. Communications with the Host have been disrupted."

The bridge data was waiting on his personal display, springing into being in the air where the doctors' faces had been.

Readings were confusing, said the technical analysis of his

sensor crew. Something had activated within the Eye, though, and now nobody could get hold of anybody aboard it or on the Host. Something Originator, therefore, because his people could make nothing of it.

As well as a small crew of his people on the Eye, there was that freakshow of mad scientists, who had presumably chosen this moment to make their stand. He wondered idly if Almier had joined them, or if she was still trying to argue Ravin's case, because it was their best chance of not being killed out of hand. Which was true.

But he was losing patience with them. Yes, they were a five-ring circus with the very best clowns in the business, but you could tire of that kind of thing. And possessing the Eye was a very pleasant bonus to his plans for an unspace-striding humanity. But a bonus was all it was. The ark fleet had been conceived and mostly built before anybody had ever heard of the damned thing.

He summoned Piter. His nephew turned up in his shirt sleeves, still dragging a jacket on.

"You're to take a combat shuttle over to the Eye," Ravin told him shortly. "Combat-ready Voyenni, a full detachment. Ensure we have control over there, re-establish it if not. Try not to kill anyone useful unless it's absolutely necessary. Keep Shinandri. Keep the Naeromathi, unless the thing won't be controlled. The mechanic is more expendable, or use her for leverage."

"And Almier?"

Ravin spared the lawyer a moment's thought. "Use her or kill her. I leave it to your discretion." Not that Piter had much of that, and he had scores to settle with the woman. Ravin reflected that he'd probably just signed Keristina Soolin

Almier's death warrant, but then sometimes there were costs to maintaining noblesse oblige.

When Piter had gone, he sat back and played through the most recent messages the packet ship had delivered from his fellow conspirators. The other ark-builders had mostly accepted the new status quo that placed Ravin firmly at the top of their little fraternity. The more Nativist expressed concerns about working with the Parthenon, which was fair enough since Ravin shared those concerns. Others were just asking when they could start populating the arks, as the Architects weren't showing any signs of slowing down.

Another priority message jumped to the top of the queue, displacing all those withered old men. Ravin's heart clenched briefly as he saw it. *Here we go.* The Exemplar of the *Medea* was signalling him at last. *Demands, ultimatums, some unwelcome change in our relationship.* He reckoned he had the force here to slug it out with one Partheni warship, but not without savage losses. And who knew if the rest of their fleet might not jump back at any moment?

The woman's face coalesced before him. Ravin couldn't even remember her name. She looked just the same as all the rest, after all.

"Uskaro," she said, shorn of titles and etiquette. "We have an intruder just jumped in-system." Her accent was strong enough that he had difficulty understanding her. The data she was sending him was clear enough, though. A new vessel, leaping in close enough to Estoc that it must have an Int navigator, was already on a determined-looking approach. Then the import of the signal patterns broke in and he was no longer worried about going head to head with the

Partheni. Things had just got a great deal worse. Their new visitor was Hegemony, and it was broadcasting threats of annihilation in multiple languages, and on all frequencies.

Olli

They'd made Aklu crawl.

Olli hadn't wanted to be there, but apparently the presence of Aklu's people, meaning the major-domo, Heremon—no, Ahremon now—Kit and herself, was mandatory. There was probably a deep and mystical Essiel reason for that, but she reckoned it was just because they were going for maximum humiliation.

They'd gone deep into the orbital ring. She knew that because it was sunny where they ended up. Meaning there was a shaft in the floor, and through that shaft was the sun. The actual sun; the glaring, murderous radiance of the star, far too close to be standing there witnessing it. Blazing up out of the well and illuminating everything up to and including the inside of Olli's skull, even if she shut her eyes and darkened the Scorpion's canopy as far as it would go.

Hanging above the shaft were the Essiel.

Olli was used to one Essiel at a time. The first occasion she'd seen two in one place it had gone very badly for one of them. But there were eleven of them here, even more than that time they'd cut Aklu a new set of carvings, and they were sort of glued to an artificial stalactite jutting from the ceiling, as well as glued to each other too. They *encrusted* the thing, just as if they were shellfish revealed by the tide, their long shells projecting at downward angles, one end open for their nest of arms and eyes. The searing light of the star blasted them and they didn't seem to care. Its light washed them into a pale, translucent radiance, hard to look at, their unfolding fans of limbs like the wings of angels.

"This is fucked up," Olli sent to Kit.

"There is no further up to which it might be fucked," was his considered reply.

The spindle to which Aklu had been clinging just… turned into vapour, disintegrated. None of the Scorpion's sensors offered any clue as to how it was done. A moment later, though, Aklu was measuring its length on the floor. Olli actually lurched forwards to try and right the Essiel; the Scorpion could have just about managed it. But the major-domo stepped in her way.

"Your role is as a witness," they informed her. "Any act of interference here will be your last."

"Right," Olli said unhappily.

"Your heart is noted, though," the Hiver added, and she wasn't sure what to make of that. Ahremon just watched impassively.

And so Aklu crawled. It bunched its holdfast tail into coils and shoved the length of its shell along the smooth floor in halting, painful-looking motions, until it was at the edge of the shaft. Olli then thought it was just going to tip in, the whole thing a very elaborate suicide. But Aklu stopped, and spoke. Or at least it made grinding, painful sounds and waved its arms at the other Essiel hanging above it, to which they replied in kind.

After a while of this, Olli jabbed the major-domo. "Do your fucking job, then, will you?"

"It is not meet—" the Hiver's voice was reverent and low

"—to so profane these words of council. What may pass between divinities is not for mortal ears. Know only this: Th'Unspeakable, the Razor and the Hook, petitions for the strength to bring a final reckoning to those who've wronged their majesty. These things may not be borne, to tread upon the hem of the divine. The Razor seeks an edge to carve this hubris from the universe."

"Now *that*," Olli decided, "is more like it."

*

And now here she was. The *Razor's Edge*, as she'd decided to call the otherwise nameless craft, wasn't exactly all she might have hoped. It had been sold to her as the ultimate weapon of the all-powerful Essiel. Except it was small enough that there wasn't room for her aboard it, not once Aklu and the major-domo had ensconced themselves there. There certainly wasn't room for Junior, who was still in the *Vulture's* drone bay along with various crates and containers of Aklu's stuff. And so it was the poor abused *Vulture God* doing all the heavy lifting, holding the *Razor's Edge* in its salvage claws and carrying the whole business through unspace to Estoc. She'd wanted to sneak in, but the moment they popped out into the real, Aklu had begun threatening destruction to absolutely everything in-system.

She couldn't exactly tell the Essiel to knock it off. She *could* complain bitterly to Ahremon, but that got her nowhere. The Tothiat might be a gangster on the outside but inside she was all cultist.

The *Razor's Edge* was a disc about half the size of the *Vulture*, with a spindle-shaped core where Aklu was. There

247

was an umbilical connecting the two ships even now, and she'd seen inside it. There wasn't much to see, just pearly walls and Aklu wedged awkwardly, the major-domo clinging to its shell like a barnacle's barnacle.

"What guns does this crate have?" she demanded. It turned out Kit was way ahead of her on that front and had already been badgering the major-domo for details.

"We are informed that no conventional weaponry is possessed by the Hegemonic vessel," the Hanni told her.

"What, it's just a diplomatic barge in miniature?" Olli demanded. "Going to threaten them to death?"

"Only an ultimate weapon," Kit continued.

"Right." Olli tried to get any coherent data from the *Razor's Edge* and ran into a wall of baffling Essiel technical conventions. "How ultimate?"

"Ultimate is a term unto itself," Ahremon said, breaking his silence. "The Unspeakable Aklu, the Razor and the Hook, will cleanse this system of all impurity. Those who dare interfere with the divine prerogatives must be punished."

"Right, right." Olli looked again at the little tinpot boat the *Vulture* was carrying. "Only I was hoping for guns."

"Nothing will live," Ahremon said, and now his calmness was starting to creep her out.

"You mean the Uskaros and the Pathos, right? Only I've got some friends to rescue, when you're done, remember?"

"Nothing. Will. Live," the Tothiat pronounced. His eyes were closed.

"We are being approached by hostile ships. One Partheni warship, several Colonial vessels, many smaller launches," Kittering reported.

Olli looked from her display to the impassive Ahremon. "I

have friends there," she repeated. Except now she wasn't sure what she was scared of. That the *Razor's Edge* would accomplish nothing, or that it would do far too much.

15.

Havaer

He'd got over to the ark in a suit, on the outside of an auto-mated food supply pod. Just an extra item on the Int medical team's breakfast menu. Colvari had already gone over by then, and not alone. The Hivers turned out to be unexpectedly skilled at that: kicking off from one ship to arrive eventually at another. Their cybernetic innards could endure the cold and the vacuum, and they were good with trajectory calculations.

Their factory was destroyed, and so had most of their units been, but the fight had left enough of them drifting. Too small and slow to register on the scans of Colonial or Partheni ships. Just little knots of debris. And if those drifting dots adjusted their course every so often, drifted past a ship's hull, settled and clung on, it was all too insignificant for anyone to notice.

Right now there were nineteen Hivers on the exterior of the incomplete ark where they were holding the Intermediaries. They crept about like lice, looking for hard access points where they could get at the ship's systems. Then Havaer arrived, pushing off from the supply pod to drift the last half-kilometre until he reached the hull, next trekking across the expanse of metal until he found the edge of construction. Picking his moment, because work had recommenced and there were suited human engineers and automated drones closing up the holes. But this sort of thing was at least work-adjacent for him, and his suit was the same model as theirs, given he'd stolen it from their stocks. The one time he got pinged for ID, Colvari was already in their system and provided him with the appropriate codes.

The Hivers had a ship map for him too by then, projected into his helmet display. The ark was big, but it was mostly empty. All that living space, the great staterooms of the mighty and the cramped cupboards of the underlings, the entertainment facilities, the community hubs, the gardens, all of it with the dust covers still on. Awaiting the tread of a population of thousands, come to be the new phase of human expansion into the cosmos. A grand dream, really. Not one Havaer had any personal objection to, if they'd been willing to do it without starting a war. If they'd just done it openly, rather than as a personal project, for them to pick all their favourites and supporters, and consign everyone else to the bin. And if, most of all, they hadn't made it a choice between the glorious roaming future of the ark fleet and saving the rest of humanity from the Architects.

It was something he'd seen plenty of times in his job, the way that kind of mindset worked, spiralling inwards into itself. Until at some point, the necessity of doing bad things for a good cause became, by the inexorable ratchet of cognitive dissonance, the insistence that doing things the bad way was a virtue in itself. Because otherwise how could one justify all the bad things already done?

Colvari was a constant whisper in his ear, the Hiver's level voice reciting progress reports as their fellows found access points and got into the system. There was a limit to what they'd be able to do, Havaer knew. Six months ago Colvari had hacked the systems of Ravin Uskaro's personal yacht, and apparently some lessons had been learned from that. The incomplete arks still had vulnerabilities, but the Hivers were encountering electronic tripwires and alarms that were new, suggesting that Uskaro's whole fleet had been receiving an upgrade. And yet the ark was still incomplete, and the Hivers were careful and persistent. Colvari's reports were a litany of vulnerabilities exploited and systems accessed. And access was all, right now. Until Havaer was ready.

He'd stripped off his suit by then, abandoned it. He was now at large on the ark in the overalls of a maintenance worker, too tight at the shoulders and groin because he was inconveniently tall. But he was doing his best to walk casually, dogged by a wheeled repair cart he'd slaved to his footsteps. Nobody challenged him. He'd chosen exactly that low grade of menial worker who got everywhere, and could walk past the noses of the armed Voyenni unnoticed. Even into the holding bay where they were keeping the Ints.

"Holding bay" actually just meant some of the lower-grade accommodation, though the fact this could double as a prison, with minimal modification, spoke volumes about how life on the ark fleet would really go for the majority. The ark was laid out by neighbourhoods, each with only limited access to other sections. There were Voyenni standing guard there, but one of the Hivers had fabricated a maintenance issue inside, and they let Havaer past with a mere grunt. Within, the bulk of the place was dark save for those rooms they'd turned into Int storage, which made it easy enough to find them.

He recognized most of the Ints there. Dispirited, twitchy, traumatized-looking men and women. It wasn't exactly as if there was an Int "look." The process broke everyone in different ways. But they all looked screwed up as hell. He passed along the line of clear doors, looking for Telemmier.

He wasn't there. Havaer went back up the corridor, aware the clock was ticking. He couldn't have missed the man.

He hadn't. No Idris.

"You," one of the Ints addressed him. "I know you."

She stood up from her bed, her lean, lanky frame almost as tall as Havaer's own. The scars of her original surgery seamed her temples like gang markings. He knew her too: one of the better prospects among the Ints, who'd been a Liaison Board volunteer and not just a conscript.

"Privacy," he murmured to Colvari.

"We're attempting…" from the voice in his ear, and then, "Engaged. All security feeds spoofed. Over to you, Agent Mundy."

"Andecka Tal Mar," he said, and the woman stared at him. Alert, suspicious, not drugged and not withdrawn into herself.

"You're…one of Laery's people," she said, standing up. Not sure if he was an opportunity or a problem. A stir of motion in the corner of his vision showed at least some of the other Ints paying attention as well. That lack of privacy cut both ways.

"Agent Havaer Mundy," he explained. "Mordant House."

"That doesn't tell us much," Mar said.

"Tasked with getting you out of here. You Intermediaries."

"To where? For who?"

Good questions. Apparently she was a bit *too* alert. "To the

Host," he told her—all of them in earshot heard and word was passed down the line of cells, door to door. "I'm working with the Hivers, and..." He bared his teeth. "Ash. The alien, Ash. It's kind of...masterminding this. It's all we've got right now."

"The Harbinger has been here," Mar told him. There was an unexpected fervour in her voice. "It made us ready. What must we do?"

The Harbinger. Something in the way she said it told Havaer she was one of those religious types who had a weird relationship with Ash. There'd been a lot of that after the Architects fulfilled Ash's prophecies concerning Earth. The sects had mostly died out, but apparently here was a true believer.

"Colvari?"

"We are in the security systems. We can release the doors, though likely not in a way that will allow us to remain undetected."

"Stand ready." And then, to Mar, "Where's Telemmier?"

"The doctors took him." Mar scowled. "He's giving them headaches. They need to chain him, but they're scared of ruining him. He's...been shielding the rest of us. If they hadn't got stuck with him they'd have shackled us all by now."

Havaer swore. "Colvari—"

"Finding you a route. Engineering a power failure in the labs for you. Havaer, our presence has been detected. You'll need to hurry. They don't know what we are yet but they know something's up."

"Be ready," he told Andecka Tal Mar. "I'll be back for you. With Idris." Making promises he didn't know if he could keep. And then he was heading off, keeping his walk steady. Passing the stern gaze of the Voyenni with lowered eyes, the way a good menial should.

The docs had set up their surgery one neighbourhood over. They didn't like long walks any more than Havaer did. Again, Voyenni were on the door, but there was a maintenance issue and their slates told them Havaer was expected. *Good work, Colvari.* He made it inside, where he heard three doctors bickering as he hunched over to the corner. There he opened a wall panel, kneeling down to slide the hatch on the repair cart, exposing the contents.

He glanced over, braced in case he caught a glimpse of Telemmier's exposed brain or something. They certainly had a sterile field up around the operating table there—he could tell by the way the dust motes scattered away. The two men and the woman didn't look as though they were going to do anything medical, though. They were just standing around arguing, and the multi-armed surgical remote beside them was still fully retracted and folded up. Telemmier lay on the slab and watched them, whole and intact. Or as intact as could be expected, what with the arm and all.

"If we wait," Havaer murmured, "they might just take him back to his cell. Then we could spring the lot of them in one go."

"We're afraid that won't be possible," Colvari came back. "Time is of the essence, Agent Mundy. We're not the only part of this plan. We're just the only part we have any control over."

Havaer went cold at that. "You mean the Eye?"

"The Eye has just declared independence, essentially. They're fighting there, most likely. All contact has been cut,

Agent Mundy," Colvari said. "We hope they'll be ready to receive you, when you get there with the Ints. Because, believe us, that's the least of it. You need to go."

"Right." There were still tools in the repair cart but he reached past them and stood up with a weapon in each hand. "Doctors," he said. "Release Telemmier and step away from the table."

"What do you think you're doing?" the lead surgeon demanded, wide-eyed. He didn't seem to register either the magnetic pistol or the dart gun that Havaer was pointing at them.

Havaer responded by putting a dart into the other male doctor, the quick-acting sedative dropping the man almost immediately.

"Release him," he said. "Now."

"I will not," said the man. "Guards!"

Havaer shot him and then ducked behind the slab as the Voyenni ran in, belatedly aware he'd just made Telemmier a human shield. The woman doctor was shouting at everyone not to shoot, that Idris must not be harmed. Which left the two Voyenni splitting up to come at him around both sides of the table, guns levelled.

He got the first one, because the doctor was still shouting at them, which was a useful distraction. Even though his pistol wasn't a proper accelerator, because he had no interest in killing someone through a handful of bulkheads, it was enough to make it through the Voyenni combat armour two shots out of three. The man jerked back and fell, which left his compatriot...

Faster than expected, already round the slab and pointing his gun right at Havaer. *Damn.* The doctor was shouting now, hollering into a comms channel Colvari had shut down. Havaer dragged his gun round, but far too slowly. Then the medical remote snapped out to full extension, every arm springing out like a popped umbrella, and slapped the Voyenni off his feet, the man's gun drilling a dozen holes in the ceiling as he went. Havaer was up and trying to get a line on him instantly, but Colvari snapped in his ear, "Take the Int and go!"

The medical remote moved like three spiders stapled together, a wild flailing of crooked limbs, tipped with needles and drills and delicate little saws. Its limbs snapped shut on the Voyenni like a cage and it got to work on the man's armour, filling the air with the sound of abused metal and the smell of burned plastic.

Incredibly, the woman doctor was still standing there, trying to shout the situation into shape. Havaer grabbed her and virtually shoved the dart gun up her nose.

"Free him," he said. "Please."

She did, and then he shot her, turning her complaints into a slurred gurgle as she slumped to the floor. He didn't spare a glance for the combined mess of medical remote and guard, just hauled Idris off the table.

"We're getting out," he told the Int.

"Oh. Good." Telemmier didn't seem overly enthusiastic. Just tired, really. Utterly worn down.

"They have identified the problem," Colvari said calmly in his ear. "Clock's ticking, Agent Mundy."

"How long've I got?"

"Let's settle on 'Get it done by yesterday.' They have identified where the intrusions are coming from. We're fighting them over the airlocks but they are sending troops out onto the hull via the construction sites. They're hunting us, Agent."

"We're moving." Idris wouldn't take the dart gun, letting it drop from nerveless fingers, so Havaer shoved it in his belt and just dragged the man along behind him like inconvenient luggage.

He shot both of the guards at the Int cells, hating himself for having no better option, no clever plan that would preserve even the lives of his enemies. Having no *time*. Whatever alerts were spreading, they hadn't linked the incursion with the Ints yet, so they weren't ready for him. He was also aware of Telemmier judging him, which would have been less galling if the man hadn't been so goddamn ineffectual. Outside unspace, Idris sometimes seemed to be the most useless man Havaer had ever met.

"Doors," he told Colvari, and they sprang open as one, every plastic portal wide. "Come on, now!" he called, and to his immense relief every one of the Ints burst into motion, marshalled by Andecka Tal Mar.

"We're getting out of here," he told them, and he made it sound like a done deal rather than the fanciful flight of optimism it actually was.

"Map," came Colvari in his ear. "Shuttle bay. Quick. Limited door access." Havaer was already getting them moving, feeling as though he was leaping across a chasm, each stepping stone only appearing after he'd vaulted from the last. The map took them room to room, corridor to corridor, and the route shifted and changed as the ark's crew shut down access. The layout of the ark was rational and straightforward but to Havaer it was an invisible labyrinth of suddenly sealed doors and closed-off sections.

"We're not getting anywhere," he murmured. "How are we doing?"

"All remote access has been closed. To control systems we need physical ports. And this way they find us," Colvari said calmly. "Sixty per cent remaining."

"Sixty per cent of what?"

"Of *us*." Meaning the Hivers on the outside of the ark. Meaning Colvari's people. "Now go."

The door that had been closed against them was abruptly opened. There was a roomful of people beyond, off-duty workers in the middle of a hurried lunch. Havaer just let the Ints through and waved a gun at anyone who looked like trouble. A moment later, as he shepherded the last of the Ints out of the refectory, all the lights went off, then flickered sullenly back into unsteady life.

"What was that?" Havaer demanded. "Colvari?"

No response. A sinking lurch inside him.

"Colvari, talk to me."

Just a crackle in his ear at first, then sounds, piecemeal and broken, that coalesced into the Hiver's voice. "That was unexpected."

"What was?"

"A hull-wide electromagnetic pulse. Destructive enough that a number of the ship's own systems were damaged. Either an ingenious repurposing of an existing system or they've been worried about us messing with them for a long time."

"Report, Colvari."

"We're in a hardened frame, as befits an espionage-ready instantiation. The others were construction models and not so protected." Meandering words, despite the urgency, giving

Havaer the impression the Hiver was mentally putting them-self back together.

"Report. What's your status?"

"It's just us. We're the only survivor. And they've located us on the hull. We're dug in but we can see them coming." That *We* shrunk from a whole team to just the nest of bugs within Colvari's chassis.

"Get clear," Havaer told them. "I can take it from here."

"You overestimate your own capabilities," Colvari said, and then they were at the shuttle bay doors. Havaer peered through the porthole and might as well have seen Colvari holding a sign saying "I told you so" because there were a good dozen Voyenni there around the shuttles, fully armoured and with accelerators. It wasn't exactly hard to second-guess where Havaer and his flock had been headed, after all.

"I see—" he started and Colvari replied, "I know. Hold, please."

"No, you get clear."

"Mission comes first. Isn't that Mordant House dogma?"

"No. Getting the team out comes first, at least on my watch."

"We're just fighting them over the...Agent Mundy?"

"Here."

"You won't get much of a window. You're ready to move?"

Havaer glanced at the Ints. Even Telemmier appeared to have woken up to what was going on. They were all with him and none of them was having a fit or a psychotic break. With Intermediaries, that probably counted as combat ready.

"Hold onto something," Colvari recommended. But there was nothing to hold onto. The corridors of the ark ship were smooth and elegant and short of the handholds spacers tended to weld to every available surface.

And gravity stopped. Instantly he was off the floor, scrabbling at the shuttle bay door for purchase. The Ints around him let out a variety of alarmed sounds as they began to drift away, snagging at each other or at Havaer.

Then gravity resumed, after just enough time for everyone to end up sitting down hard, or jarring knees and elbows on the re-established ground. In the midst of the Ints' complaints, Havaer kept an eye on the hatch telltales, currently all red but cycling through amber towards green.

"Colvari, get out. We're clear," he said.

No answer.

"Colvari."

Still nothing. Havaer closed his eyes briefly, hoping against hope, but the men out on the hull wouldn't have been relying on the ship's gravitic field to do their job. Colvari's final and most dramatic usurpation of the ark's systems wouldn't have saved the Hiver from the end.

Havaer opened the bay door and began hustling the Ints through.

The Voyenni were gone, along with one of the shuttles. Another was skewed at a careless angle, as though some boy racer had just landed it in a hurry. Because the bay was open to space, reliant on the ark ship's gravitic field to keep the air in and the vacuum out. And without that field, the air had found a pressing engagement elsewhere and, in its hurry to leave, taken a lot of other things with it.

"Into the shuttle!" He pointed at the nearest one, the skewed one, and the Ints lurched into a shambling run, Tal Mar at their head. He saw the last Voyenni just too late. The man had clamped his boots to the floor somehow, and that had left him with knees now bent entirely the wrong way. Being a Voyenni, his priority was still to shoot at the escapees, though. Aiming awkwardly from the ground, he drilled through two of the Ints before Havaer's return caught him, flipping him around his ruined joints and into an angular sprawl, still secured to the deck by his feet.

The rest of them made it aboard, and there was no time to go back for the bodies. Havaer rushed after them, closing the hatch and shouting at someone to get them out. After all, they were supposed to be pilots, weren't they?

It was Telemmier in the hotseat when Havaer elbowed his way to the front. He'd have preferred Mar, but at least Idris seemed present and sane. He got them out of the bay handily, and there was no answering clutch from the ark's gravitic drive, trying to claw them back.

"The Host," Havaer said, but Telemmier already had the course plotted. Havaer pulled up the co-pilot's board and saw way too many moving points in-system. Something was kicking off out there, and he could only hope it was aimed somewhere other than at them.

Kris

There was a lot of Eye and only a limited number of Voyenni, which meant they got quite some way towards the important machinery before the guards chased them down. And navigating within the Eye was a nightmarish business at the best of times. It was a labyrinth of chambers and voids in black stone, overlaid by the brute slabs of Naeromathi engineering and then Jaine's Colonial spacer additions to give some human scale to the place. Less a scientific facility than an obstacle course.

Of course their quarters and Ahab's precious Machine were pretty much right next door, except the guards were also right between them, necessitating a detour. There was one wall that Kris had assumed had been there since the creation of the universe, but turned out to be nothing more than flummery, the whole thing hinging open when Ahab set its weight at the right point. This released them into the maze of the Eye's less-travelled sections, where the only light source was the string of intermittent lamps Jaine had strung out. As the Originator stone itself was dark and played tricks with reflections, Kris almost immediately lost all sense of distance and direction. She could look in any direction and see a constellation of light flecks that could be distant or tiny, glints off the stone or just the creations of her abused brain.

Their absence would have been noted, for sure. Some flunky of the Uskaros would have put a head round the door to see what was keeping their guests so quiet. After all, Trine and Shinandri usually had something to hold forth about. Then, discovering an absence of guests, the search parties would have been sent out. To encounter exactly the same navigational issues that Kris was having, she dearly hoped.

Every so often Jaine and Ahab stopped and conferred. Or at least Jaine would murmur, mouth close to a metal port on the Naeromathi's leathery torso that was presumably an ear. Then Ahab would make some kind of noncommittal sound, or sometimes just "Yes!" or "No!," and they'd be off again.

Finally, the guards spotted them across a chasm. There were railings on the far side, but Kris almost stepped out into the void before Trine pulled her back. Then there was a shout, and the lamps across the gap gleamed off the green and gold of the Uskaro livery. Weapons were levelled, but their officer was demanding surrender rather than ordering his men to fire.

"Back," Jaine got out, and they all piled the way they'd come, out of sight. The shouting of the guards followed them, and Kris knew they'd now be trying to find a way round. And there were half-complete maps of the place within the Eye's systems, so probably they'd succeed.

Jaine had decided on a course, and it seemed to be taking them deeper into the maze of the Eye rather than towards their destination, though Kris freely admitted she was losing track of where anything was. The sound of boots and angry Magdan accents pursued them down the echoing stonework like a living thing.

"Are you sure this is right?" she got out, snagging at Jaine's arm.

The cyborg looked back at her. "Right for the Machine? No. But they're between us and anywhere we need to be. So we fight them."

Kris actually stopped dead, so that Shinandri bundled into her and the pair of them almost went over.

"No," she said plaintively. "We do not."

"Tell that to Ahab," Jaine said.

"Ahab, they have *accelerators!*" Kris shouted. "You can't just stomp them. They will shoot you."

"They must not be permitted to impede us!" roared the Naeromathi from up ahead. The creature was galloping now.

They rushed out into an open space, crossing a narrow stone bridge over an uncertain depth, darkness all around them. The shouts of the Voyenni were abruptly much louder, and there was a brief, singing burst of accelerator shot that vanished into the void.

"It's not about *permits!*" Kris shouted, teetering over the bridge and then running to catch up. "I can deal with *permits!* It's about *guns!*"

Then they were out into another room, low-ceilinged but broad enough that Kris couldn't make out where the walls ended. Pyramidal pillars were set in a weird sequence across the wide floor—broad-based, tapering up as if to support the ceiling save that their needle points didn't quite touch it. Their arrangement made no sense to the human eye but just as plainly had *some* pattern to it. The sight hurt a deep part of Kris's mind.

Then the Voyenni were piling in from a gap she hadn't even seen. They shouted their warnings again, demanding surrender. Ahab just picked up the pace, skittering along towards them on its clutch of metal legs and bellowing. Jaine was right on its heels, and Kris found herself carried along in their wake. She had a knife, after all. *Good old knife, great thing to bring to an accelerator fight.* It was that or stay back with Shinandri and Trine, neither of whom were going to be much use. Given the properties of accelerator shot, they wouldn't even be good as shields.

Seeing a ton of Naeromathi bearing down on them, the Voyenni officer's nerve plainly failed and he ordered his men to fire.

Kris threw herself behind one of the pillars. Intellectually, even as she did, she registered that she couldn't possibly be in time. The sound of the officer's voice, and the eerie keening noise of the weapons themselves, would come to her only after the shot ripped through her. She was, therefore, by scientific deduction, already dead at that point. So her continued existence behind a pillar seemed like some sort of cosmic oversight, that a bureaucratic-minded deity would step in to correct any moment.

Except she heard the almost howl as Ahab's thunderous charge connected with the Voyenni, and then the fighting was on in earnest. As she popped her head out, the outlines of all the nearby pyramids looked fuzzy with a fine coat of accelerator pellets, the little round projectiles held milli-metres from the stone surface by some bizarre magnetic force.

And Ahab was getting stuck in. The lamps hid a lot of it, and that was a mercy. Naeromathi didn't have jaws or claws —or at least this battered old cyborg didn't—but it was huge and strong, and used its long neck and tail as bludgeoning weapons. Its implants weren't purely medical, either. There was some kind of device set into Ahab's head that discharged sudden eye-searing flashes of blue-white that sent Voyenni flying across the room, their armour melted and scorched. And Jaine was alongside him, in there too. She had a drill in one hand and a cutter in the other, and there was a fierce white light blazing from her prosthetic torso as she over-clocked her reactor. Yet there were still Voyenni in the fight, and they were tough, hard men now they'd recovered from their surprise.

Kris cursed and ran in to help. Yes, she only had a knife, but she was a Scintilla duellist. There wasn't any *only* where knives and Kris were involved. The blade Trine had procured or printed for her was proper duelling standard, the sort you used when someone had slighted your honour and only blood would do. The less honourable fencers had sometimes been known to wear armoured sleeves under their clothes, which meant a proper diamond edge. It wouldn't go through the plates of the Voyenni armour, but it would winkle nicely into the gaps.

She got to winkling. In the end she only had to deal with two of them, and the first of those was from behind, because it wasn't a formal duel, so she didn't feel she owed them any of the attendant respect or ritual. She just picked her moment and drove her blade in at his waist, getting him in the kidneys and then under the armpit as he tried to twist around. That was him, and then another man was facing off against her. He had his own knife, and if he'd just rushed her then probably his armour would have kept him safe. He had pretensions of form, however, and tried to hold her at the blade's point, stepping right into her arena. She decoyed him with a few moves, and one of those fake stumbles her teachers had always despaired of, then deflected his eager arm and got him under the chin. And he was the last of them.

"Goddamn," she said, and sat down heavily, feeling the last minute catch up with her hard. "Well...goddamn."

Jaine had found a panel set into an ugly lump of welding and glue in one wall. She linked her slate to it, pivoting a 3D map of the Eye there, and frowned. The glow of her internal systems hadn't ceased, but it was sputtering and glitching.

"You all right there?" Kris asked her.

"Going to need a tune-up when we're done," Jaine said distractedly. "Not needed to push the system so hard in a long time."

"Not going to explode on us?"

"No promises," the cyborg told her, and then, "Shit. More company. Troop shuttle's docked." She had a camera feed up: Voyenni trooping out down a ramp, followed by a figure Kris knew all too well. Piter Uskaro, come to bring them back under the yoke of Magdan supremacy.

"They're a ways away from us yet," Jaine said. "I can hide us from them, but if they've any sense, they know where the good stuff is here. They'll just head for that. I guess we better go set some traps or something. You know, the usual."

Shinandri and Trine approached now, the difficult part being over. Except they weren't alone. They'd made a new friend, someone else with a talent for picking their moments.

"Ash," Kris said.

"It appears there's something of an invasion going on," Shinandri remarked brightly.

"No shit," Jaine remarked acidly.

"I feel the term 'refugee crisis' is more appropriate, my esteemed academic colleague," Trine broke in.

"Follow," was all Ash said.

And somehow, of course, *Ash* seemed to know exactly where it was going within the Eye, leading them a winding way that wasn't heading anywhere near the machinery Ahab was so fixated on. Except the Naeromathi just deferred to Ash, and this seemed as much of a cosmic mystery as anything else that had happened recently. Then, after climbing and scrambling and balancing their way through the sparsely lit intestines of the place, a cluster of people appeared ahead, with wan lamplight picking out the gaunt features of Havaer Mundy first.

"You!" Kris shouted accusingly, before remembering that

they were probably on the same side right about now. It was always hard to tell with professional spooks like him. And then she looked past the man and let out a whoop, grabbing Idris out from amongst the other Ints and picking him up off his feet in a hug.

"Are you okay? Are you safe? What did they do to you?"

He looked overwhelmed and embarrassed by the concern, as always. Just wanting to shrink back into the scenery, the way the universe would never let him. "I'm fine," he said weakly, plucking at her arm with his cybernetic hand. "I'll live. But I don't know what the plan is. I mean, we're still in the middle of them."

"You must take this place away," Ash said flatly. "I will show you where. Take your pilots and go into the Host. The Eye cannot remain here."

"We're stealing it. Right," Idris said. He was glancing awkwardly at his fellow Intermediaries as though ashamed to ask it of them. To Kris's eye they all seemed far more enthusiastic about the prospect than he was.

"Idris, seriously." Because he wasn't fine. Idris was so seldom fine, admittedly, but Kris had known him for long enough to see when he was right on the edge.

"Fine, I'm fine," he mumbled, and then, "Kris, they were going to cut me."

Idris, with his one arm, and a clutch of Trine's Hiver units keeping his heart going, and all the bloody trauma of the war behind him. But that wasn't what he meant. He meant inside his head. Cutting him the way they had done when they'd made him an Int, but this time to make him their slave. He was trembling, very slightly, very fast. When she hugged him again he clung to her.

"It's going to be all right," she said, without much conviction. Halfway through saying it, though, a spasm went through him, and through all the Ints around them. Some of them swayed, while one fell over. Idris pushed off from her, then grabbed at her arm to keep himself on his feet.

"What is going on?" he demanded. "Ash, what did you do?"

"Take command of the Host," Ash said simply. "You must remove the Eye from this system. It must be preserved."

Kris had thought it had been talking about the Uskaros before. She'd thought Ash just wanted the facility removed from their control so it could return to the job of going after the Architects. But from Ash's tone, the Uskaros were small beer compared to whatever was going on outside right now.

16.

Olli

She'd never been *inside* a Hegemonic ship under fire. However their tech generated gravitic shielding, it was different to the way a human-made vessel did. She could hear the impacts —not like discrete objects rattling against the hull, but as though they were in a storm, or forced atmospheric re-entry. A howling tempest outside told her of the accelerator shot, the missiles, the lasers. And occasionally the thundercrash of the *Medea*'s gravity hammer as it tried to turn the *Vulture God* and Aklu's diminutive vessel into crumpled wreckage.

And yet, tiny as that ship was, it was shielding for two, putting a finger on the scales of the universe so that the death-storm slid past them. Buffeted and shook them, so she could feel it through the hull and the Scorpion's haptics, yet didn't break them.

Or hadn't broken them yet.

She could almost feel the frustration in the Partheni commander. There were Colonial ships coming in too. Though the big old *Grand Nikolas* was keeping a prudent distance, three separate mid-sized vessels were approaching to back up the *Medea* and try to squash Aklu like a bug.

Well that's an achievement, Olli considered. *Getting Nativists and Partheni pissed at you at the same time. Something to go on the tombstone.*

"I don't suppose," she sent over comms in her most sarcastic voice, "that Himself has anything to throw back? Can we fire all the magic guns now and blow little holes in the enemy? Big holes, even?"

The perfect, singsong tones of the major-domo came back to her. "There is but one, the final ultimatum to lay before the universe." If they had still had their old two-sided head, she was willing to bet they'd have turned the frowny face outwards to face the rest of the universe as they said, "Our challenge that shall sound unto the infinite, and call leviathan out from its lair."

Olli disentangled that. "You... One? Those fuckers gave you a tiny little tinpot ship with *one* gun?"

"A weapon that the universe looks down," the major-domo confirmed cryptically, leaving Olli with uncomfortable suicide imagery in her head. If Aklu was here to get itself killed, it would probably be taking its little retinue to the grave with it as a matter of course. Including her and Kit.

"Can you at least fire the gun?" she asked plaintively.

"Approaching smaller vessels are detected," Kit reported. His translator gave his words a prim, clipped tone that meant he was jittery as hell.

"Zero Pointers?"

"Also close-engagement shuttles," Kit said, meaning as well as the little one-man fighters, the Partheni were going to try boarding them. The Hegemonic shielding was sufficiently frustrating that they clearly wanted to get up close and personal.

Fine by me, Olli thought, flexing the Scorpion's various

limbs. She was lying to herself, though. If she was brutally honest, she knew she couldn't last long against a Partheni fire team in full armour.

"The bell has tolled," the major-domo's voice came over. "The death knell's dead sound now ripples out and down into infinity. Now comes the storm. Now shall be felt the reckoning of kings. Let those who dare assault th'Unspeakable first learn the cost and burden of their crimes."

"What the fuck," Olli complained, "did any of that fucking mean?"

"We've pulled the trigger," came Ahremon's voice over the comms channel. "The purpose of this vessel is accomplished. Its weapon is used."

Olli spent vital seconds of her remaining lifespan rechecking the *God*'s instruments. "It hasn't actually done anything."

"It is *doing*," Ahremon told her.

"It isn't, like, actually blowing them up, though. They're still shooting. They're still coming," she pointed out. "I mean, we're...charging up? We're going to pop them any moment?"

"This is no needlepoint or sniper's aim," the major-domo announced. "When comes the Razor's wrath and rightful vengeance, there's nothing in the reach of Estoc's star shall yet survive it."

"What about the rescue, though?" Olli demanded. "My friends?" She'd been trying to raise them, any of them, and getting nowhere, but she took it on faith that they were still out there somewhere.

"We've loosed the weapon," Ahremon said. "As they say, the bell is tolled. Nothing but to wait for the echo." He sounded way too sanguine about the prospect. "Let them destroy us now, it will change nothing."

"Can we *not* let them destroy us, maybe?"

"Oh, we'll fight. Aklu wants to see it happen. "The Razor and the Hook demands its due." With a cadence that showed he was quoting the major-domo.

"Difficulties for the boarders," Kit reported, and Olli switched views to see one of the Partheni shuttles disintegrate almost into dust as some fluctuation in the Hegemonic shielding caught it. Her stomach lurched, part triumph, part horror.

"I thought you said we didn't have other weapons." She watched a flight of Zero Point fighters scatter away in all directions as the gravitic gradient around them was teased apart.

"We draw no blades," the major-domo sang, "but those who touch the hem of Aklu's mantle duly are chastised."

For a moment she thought that would be it. The shields would just keep bouncing or trashing the bad guys until whatever the hell was going to happen, happened. She set to trying to raise Kris again instead. She found plenty of comms channels full of voices in Parsef and Colvul demanding their surrender, but absolutely none that led to anybody she actually wanted to speak to. The Eye itself was ominously silent, bouncing off every query she sent its way.

Moments later Kit had flagged up one shuttle that was creeping in towards them, navigating in fits and starts as though plumbing an invisible labyrinth. It was almost coasting, save that it was matching their own course and rotation. And, by this expedient, they were within the reach of the shield and yet still coming.

"That one!" Olli said, picking out the intruder every way she could and sending the data over to Aklu. "Squish that one!"

"Doesn't work like that," Ahremon said. "It's a passive system. They're destroying themselves, out there. We're not targeting them."

Olli swore and calculated approach vectors. "They're aiming for us," she said. There were other shuttles trying the same approach too, but they were some way behind. This pioneer was their immediate problem. "They're coming in ...They'll get to us near the umbilical hatch, then come into the drone bay." *Just cut their way in, take command of where the two ships join...*

"Olli? Is that you?" A staticky voice over comms, distorted enough that Olli took a moment to recognize it.

"*Kris?*"

"Olli! Is that... We weren't sure if it was the *God*. Whatever you're doing over there is screwing with our—"

"Look, Kris, we're a little busy right now, don't-cher-know," Olli drawled. "Look, you got Idris with you? Jaine maybe?"

"Yes. Idris and quite a lot of—"

"*Kris*, just listen. Time for you to get out, right. Get Idris to a pilot's board and just fuck off out of Estoc because something bad's about to happen here." *Whether we get killed here or not, apparently.* "Aklu's doing a thing."

"I'm not sure we can," came the rags and tatters of Kris's voice. "Idris says...something...happened to unspace..."

"To *unspace?* Fuck, Aklu, what did you *do?*"

Idris

The Host, with its multiple scales, had been intended to hold within its gravitic field some stately pleasure dome of ark-owners, the capital of their spacefaring civilization. Right now it was going to have to transport the Eye, or else things would go very badly indeed for everyone on board.

Very badly. Idris's senses were screaming at him. Every hole they'd cut in his brain was letting in a feeling of sheer impending doom. Something appalling had been triggered in-system that was ratcheting a tension in the underlying fabric of unspace, deforming it, twisting the local universe into a complex, bizarre topography. He had no idea why, or what it would lead to, but his subconscious and his gut were united in telling him it was *bad*. And here he was, on a tiny little maintenance gadabout, docking on one of the Host's scales. Because apparently he was the man to pilot the thing out of Estoc. Andecka and the most stable of the other Ints were heading out to others. Some of the scales were still garrisoned by Uskaro staff, he understood, but most were vacant. And the thing about the Host was, it was a beast without a head. There was no command scale the others all had to obey. Its alien builders hadn't organized themselves like that, apparently. Get Idris aboard any part of it and he could theoretically make the whole his own.

"What is it?" Andecka's voice, panicky, in his ear. "God help us, what are they doing?"

He didn't have any words for her. He didn't know. Right now he was the most experienced unspace navigator humanity had access to, but whatever was going on around and beneath them in unspace was utterly outside his experience.

He reached the underside of the scale. It was ridged, semi-organic looking. The human-sized hatch was out of place, slightly off-centre. He clung to it, inputting the codes Jaine had given him. One-handed, clumsy in his suit glove, the artificial hand useless for anything other than just hanging on.

The hatch opened sluggishly, halting halfway. He had to fight his way through, banging and ramming the encumbrance of his suit against its edges, seeing warning lights flare in his helmet display. He ended up almost foetal in the tiny airlock, having to reach with his living arm to the hand-crank to seal the door behind him. *Does* nothing *work properly around here?* Then terrified he'd just end up stuck because the second airlock door would be defective too. Except this opened properly, allowing him to pop out into the scale's interior like a human jack-in-the-box.

There wasn't much room in there. The bulk of the scale was system hardware, gravitic drive, all the things that let it do what it did. The Host-makers had been small, people reckoned, but they hadn't done representational art and their actual records hadn't survived, or had been so alien nobody had recognized them. They hadn't had physical controls either. So Idris found himself in a teardrop-shaped space where every surface had been defaced with human additions. There was a pilot's board and a comms system, and someone had even fixed a seat to the floor. The other scales would all be similar, he knew. Most of the time and energy Uskaro's techs had put into the project was hidden from him: the conversion that allowed a human interface to govern the alien engines of the Host. Thankfully, in *that*, the original makers had been human-approximate enough for their technology to make sense.

The Host. Not just the pieces of a ship, but an undamaged ship that was naturally in pieces. He took control, feeling his part of the overall gravitic field twist to his whim. His implants and his hands—or one of them—mastering the controls intuitively. The other Ints were sounding off now, Andecka and the rest. Each of them in a scale, bringing it online as a live part of the whole, a star in the constellation. He had a sense of the other scales trying to react, but the Host-makers had been big into democracy. As soon as Idris and the other Ints had sufficient scales under their control, the whole belonged to them. They had a ship. They could leave.

Or could they? He was still feeling that steady deformation of unspace going on, funnelling down, complicating the underlying geography of the universe with what felt like meaningless fractal processes. As though there was a vast shadow down there, cast by something that simply didn't exist. A footprint without the foot.

Bad, bad! screamed his mind, and he interrogated it, *Why?*

"Do we go?" one of the Ints was asking. "Menheer Telemmier, we're waiting on you."

"Can we...navigate that?" Andecka whispered.

Idris said nothing. Eyes closed, mind open, using the Host's instrumentation and his own brain to reach down into unspace and understand what the hell was happening.

Ravin

Piter's shuttle had gone in to the Host with a boosted transmitter and a string of relay drones, but most of what came to Ravin was static. Static that pulsed with strange patterns,

278

as though some unearthly choir was lifting its combined voice far off. The best he could make out was a safe arrival at the Eye. Piter would be pushing forwards with his Voyenni, but the place was huge and convoluted and there was no guarantee he'd even be able to make contact with the mutineers in a useful time frame, let alone resume command.

So let us deal with the other end of the problem. How coincidental that the malcontents aboard the Eye had started playing their tricks just as the rogue Essiel had emerged from unspace. It had all the hallmarks of one particular meddling alien, thus far unaccounted for. Ravin had demanded a dossier of the Colonies' current knowledge on Harbinger Ash. The result was far too much supposition and trivia and very little hard fact at all. Could the thing just appear and disappear at will? It certainly gave every appearance of it, but then Ravin could probably have fabricated the same reputation if he'd been willing to put sufficient time and Largesse behind the effort. Nobody had seen the creature since they'd retaken Estoc, but that didn't mean it wasn't lurking in the shadows, pulling strings.

He turned to the latest battle report, or rather the latest one-sided pissing contest, with Aklu the Unspeakable playing the part of the wall. The little Hegemonic ship—or perhaps not even a ship—was just sitting there in the clutches of the damnable *Vulture God*. It didn't appear even to be armed, but it was packing a compact little gravitic drive sufficient to ward off all the firepower the *Medea* and Ravin's own lesser vessels could throw at it. The Partheni were considering drastic measures for their next sally, and Ravin was happy to let them. It would either deal with their mutual problem or weaken his allies, which was to say his other problem.

279

All in all, he ought to feel that he had the situation under control. But he didn't. His instincts were yanking on every nerve, telling him things were going badly wrong. Even though his side had all the guns, and Piter would surely resume control of the Host eventually. Even if the rebellious Ints jumped the ship away, they'd have to take the Voyenni with them...

He considered that for a moment. Of course the Ints were used to long periods in unspace, however much they complained about it. Would that be their weapon against Piter? The Eye wasn't supplied with much in the way of suspension couches. Perhaps even now they were stowing the non-Int members of their little insurrection prior to taking over navigation of the Host. He sent further commands to Piter, repeatedly and over various transmission methods, telling him to prioritize taking command of the suspension facilities. He could only hope the word would cut through whatever was going on over there.

Next—

An urgent call came from within his own ship, leaping to the top of his comms queue. One of his bridge officers. Ravin was already scanning the latest telemetry reports, looking for the new ship or fleet that had surely just dropped in-system. Partheni, Hegemonics, some antagonistic Colonial faction...

"Morzarin, Your Elegance," the man reported to him, voice jagged with panic. "It's the navigator."

"Coherent report if you will," Ravin snapped.

"Forgive me, Morzarin. Our navigator, here on the *Grand Nikolas*. She is going mad. She is having a fit."

Ravin's mind went blank for just a second. *Are they attacking the Ints? Is that what Aklu's doing?* "Show me."

The woman in the pilot's seat was frothing at the mouth. Her eyes were wide, a tiny trickle of blood pooling in the creases of the left. She stared past the camera's vantage towards her handler.

"We have to go, have to go have to go have to go!" Ravin heard, seeing her jolt in the chair in time to her words. "Bad things bad things bad things bad things, have to go please let us go go go." The surgical scars across her scalp were red and angry and one was weeping yellow pus. She was one of the thoroughly broken Ints, leashed in law and spirit. She was reliable, that's what they'd assured him.

"Tell me what the problem is," he commanded her, through his officer's comms.

The sound of her master's voice snapped her back to something close to sanity. "Unspace space space is gathering," she got out. Her teeth were red where she'd bitten her tongue. "Like cloth, thicker and thicker. We need to go."

"It's what the Hegemonics are doing?" Because he was damn sure Aklu was doing *something*.

"*Yes* yes yes drawing tight, denser and denser until you can *hear* it everywhere, please let us go go go."

Ravin checked the Partheni's progress. Were they about to bring their famed military hammer down on the Essiel's shell? He didn't think they were quite as close as that.

He permitted himself a moment of introspection. There was, of course, a proper and honourable way for a Magdan noble to face peril. The histories and family archives were replete with such stories. Many of them recounted in the protagonist's obituaries.

Let us be prudent. "Well then, let's go," he told the Int and the bridge crew both. "Choose a nearby system and take us out of here. We'll come back to pick up the pieces later." It meant abandoning Piter, but he was a grown man and should be able to look after himself. And if not, well, it was an excuse for one more glowing obituary and there were always other nephews.

"Ship-wide suspension, Your Elegance?" the bridge officer asked.

Ravin gritted his teeth. That was proper procedure, of course, but it was also a time-eating process in a ship as large as the *Grand Nikolas*.

"Make it a short jump and we'll weather it," he told the man. It would be unpleasant, but only for a few minutes. They'd live, give or take a few nightmares.

The Int didn't need to be told twice. Even before the bridge officer could give the formal order she'd dropped them into unspace, away from the real. Ravin just had time to brace himself, ready for all contact with his crew to vanish, for a brief period when he would be alone on the ship save for the maddening illusion that he wasn't. Ready to sit and repel the thought of that nebulous Presence, that—

The *Grand Nikolas* screamed all around him. A million voices shrieking, as though every wall and panel, every comms channel, every piece of ornamentation had been given a voice and then been tortured to the very point of madness. Not the terrifying solitude of unspace but as though they'd been thrust into the midst of an invisible multitude. As though every soul who had died in the unreal had been drawn to him. An idiot mass of babble and gibbering, shrieking and weeping. He put his hands over his ears and killed comms but the sounds were already inside his head, breeding there, multiplying into infinity. An unspeakable regiment of damned souls. And, as though they were fleeting snow against a dark background, behind them was something worse. A vast canvas that was an entity. Not the stalking Presence the Ints whispered of, something of fire and fury. That waved its many arms and blazed and judged. Something that knew his name and had all power over him. It weighed him and found him meagre, insignificant, but just important enough to punish.

Then they were back in the real, and Ravin was lying on his back, shock still convulsing his limbs with random neural static. From beyond his stateroom he could hear panicked yells, weeping, calls for medical aid. Drawing the rags of his composure about himself, he opened comms to the bridge, demanding a report, insisting that someone answer him. He heard a babble of voices—not the dread choir but just the wounded, shocked crew making the same demands of each other that he was making of them. And then he saw where they were.

Still in the Estoc system. They'd entered unspace and travelled, then come back to where they'd left, give or take a million kilometres or so. They were even *closer* to Aklu's little button of a ship. As though there was only one direction in unspace now, and it led inwards.

"Tell her to do it again!" he shouted. "We need to get out of here." The sense of a noose tightening, of something terrible about to happen. He didn't need to be an Int to sense it.

"Dead, Morzarin!" It wasn't the same bridge officer, but presumably the only person able to respond rationally. "She's dead. Just...dead."

Ravin gripped the edge of his desk, seeing reports coming in from all over the ship. Even in the brief time they'd been in unspace, seventeen people had tried to kill themselves, or fallen victim to strokes or cardiac arrest. His medical teams were already overwhelmed.

He watched the Partheni manoeuvring towards Aklu. Suddenly it wasn't just a game to see which of those he detested would fare worse. He *needed* the cursed angels to undo whatever the Essiel had done, or nobody was getting out of this.

Olli

"The vengeance of the Razor and the Hook," sang the major-domo over comms, "shall not be circumscribed in time and space. When moment comes to lay waste to its foes th'Un-speakable shall never stay its hand."

"Right," Olli said. "Now Kris, don't know what you caught of that, but it sounds like king shit's going down at this end. You really, really need to get your asses out of here sharpish, see right?"

Another burst of static and then, unexpectedly crystal clear, "I mean if anybody can, then Idris—"

"Sure. About time the famie bastard made himself useful," Olli agreed. "I'll try and get Aklu to give you time but I reckon the old boy ain't holding off for nobody right now. It is properly *pissed*, is what it is."

"Olli, what about you?" came Kris's corroded voice.

"I..." She paused. "Y'know, hadn't even thought that one through." Then, on the other channel, she asked Aklu, "We get out of this, right? We're the, what, calm of the storm or whatever-the-fuck, yes?"

Silence.

"A lack of answer breeds a lack of confidence," Kittering commented, on his own channel.

"Guys?" Olli prompted again. "We get *out* of this, right? Beat the bad guys, go home, long life of razoring and hooking?"

"The righteous fury of th'Unspeakable," the major-domo pronounced, "is all-consuming. So it is decreed that weapons such as these may not be used without due penance and a proper toll."

"Oh shit," Olli said in a small voice. "It's not a gun, it's a bomb. We're a bomb. Kit, we're a *bomb*."

"Umbilical ready to be disengaged. Perhaps we can be removed by Junior?" Kit suggested.

Olli was staring at her helmet displays. Something very weird had just happened to the *Grand Nikolas*. According to her long-range scans, it had tried an unspace jump and then reappeared. Not a failed exit, just one that had led back into the same room. She glanced up through her canopy at Junior. The Ogdru had clenched itself into a ball, wrapping its tentacles and flippers tightly around itself. She'd never seen it do that before and she was willing to bet it wasn't good.

"Not sure that's an option right now, Kit," she said quietly.

"Hear now the words of Aklu the Unspeakable," the major-domo told her.

"Fuck me, not *now*, all right?"

"For you, small sister," they said, "know this. You are seen. A mote, a fragment, barely there at all."

"Oh. Thanks." *Is this honestly the time for a dressing-down?*

"But yet within the constellation of the Razor and the Hook, you are a star. A sympathetic light within the heavens, amongst those who let not the strictures and the boundaries of the universe impede them. You are seen. And so the gift is made."

"I . . ." Olli felt something curious at the back of her throat and in her chest. It might have been some manner of sentiment that wasn't the caustic anger she so enjoyed deploying. In someone else she'd probably have said they were touched. Or that they were soft, more likely.

"Um," she said. "Thanks." And then, "Wait, what gift?"

"Imminent danger of boarding now," Kit reported. Olli saw the one successful Partheni shuttle jockeying up to them. It looked a bit cut up by Aklu's shielding but it was obviously fully functional. They were coming for the *God*, and probably intended to board Aklu's ship via the umbilical rather than trying themselves against the Essiel hull.

"Kit, suit up!"

"Already done."

"Pilot's board is all yours. Seal all the hatches. If they come for you, make it as difficult as you can."

"Creative accounting will slow them, do you think?" Kit wasn't much of a pilot but he was even less of a fighter. Still, he'd have some small arms in there with him, and control over whatever systems the Partheni didn't successfully hack. Olli reckoned the *God* was such a mess of conflicting repairs, the perfect warrior angels would go half-mad trying to take over any part of it.

The umbilical hatch slid open. She swore again and lunged forwards to prevent the earlier-than-advertised Partheni incursion, but it was Ahremon and the major-domo instead. The Tothiat wore a suit with the helmet off, and carried a blunt, stubby weapon that was probably something nasty and Hegemonic. It didn't really matter. Olli had seem Tothiat fight, mostly from the perspective of the people they'd been fighting. They were their own most effective weapons. Guns barely came into it. And with Junior's big floating tank looming over everything, any clash in the drone bay would be nastily close quarters. *Just how I like it.*

"What good are they going to be?" she asked, nodding to the major-domo.

The gilded Hiver tilted their torso towards her. "We shall defend the Razor and the Hook while we yet live," they announced. Their fan of arms snapped out, a glinting blade tipping each hand.

"Right then," Olli agreed.

But she didn't have a thought to spare for the metaphysics because at that moment came the solid shudder of a carefully jockeyed approach. The Partheni shuttle was finally up alongside the *Vulture God*.

"They could just blow us up from the outside," she suggested. "They don't even need to come in." But a moment later she felt a shudder in the hull through the Scorpion's haptics—more clearly than someone else would have felt it through their natural body. The Partheni probably didn't think they could guarantee the destruction of Aklu's vessel with whatever weaponry the shuttle had. They were going to do things the old-fashioned way.

Olli ran a quick diagnostic of the Scorpion's drills, saws and pincers. Apparently the whole of the Estoc system was going to hell right now anyway, so why not? Time to tear through old-fashioned and get positively medieval.

17.

Idris

"You're supposed to be out on the scales!" Kris was already shouting at him as Idris got in sight of her. "Why are you back on the Eye?"

"I need the Machine. Ahab's Machine," he got out. His visual field was glittering with weird, shimmering areas that meant he could barely even see her. He had an uncomfortable feeling there was also a growing blind spot he wasn't registering because... well, it was a blind spot. Certainly it took him three goes to make it out of the shuttle.

"Idris, this isn't the *time!*" Those bits of her he could make out looked utterly panicked and she had a knife in her hand. "We've got Piter Uskaro and a mob of thugs on the way here right now. I want you off here and back in space. You're meant to be piloting us out of here."

"Can't do it from up there," he said. He wasn't sure how clearly his words were coming out right now. The universe was clenching all around them. Even outside the Machine, even just walking around like a regular human being felt as though everything about him was being crumpled up like thin paper. "Ahab—"

"Ahab's in its own Machine." Kris was supporting him now,

288

though he had no memory of her actually coming to him. It felt as though they were shoving through a crowd as she dragged him through the Eye's irregular spaces—now a tight corridor, now a drop to a lower level, now a cavernous hall. "Shouting all kinds of crazy, but that's just Ahab."

"No," he stuttered. "Not just Ahab. All kinds of crazy just came to us. Something." He realized he couldn't see at all now, or nothing other than the weird retinal fireworks. His only working eye was the one that gazed into the abyss, and that one didn't have a lid. "Something's happening, Kris."

"It's Aklu," she told him. "Olli says Aklu has some weapon it's using. And we need to get out of here because Olli reckons it isn't choosy about targets."

"So many!" roared Ahab from ahead of them, voice twisting down the corridors of the Eye like a hunting thing. Idris's mind dredged, from somewhere, *I had not thought death had undone so many.*

"Get me in the Machine." Kris's touch left him and he just stood there, in a void. The headache that had been folding into his skull continued its patient progress towards the centre of his brain, as though it was just the point of a wedge on which the whole universe was leaning. His sense of up and down was swinging like a pendulum. He only realized he was falling when someone caught him.

"You're not looking well, not at all," came Shinandri's inanely cheery voice. "I think it might not be entirely wise to subject you to—"

"Get me in the Machine," Idris cut him off. "Now. I need to get us out of here."

"While being many things, our machinery isn't a pilot's chair!" Shinandri declared. That wasn't entirely true, because the brute force intrusion into unspace that the Eye was able to manifest could indeed move things through it. Not its primary purpose, but the possibility was attested to by the simple fact the facility and its attendant chunk of planet was here at all.

"Can't do it from the scales. Can't navigate. Can't see clearly enough." And up there, spread across the little fleet that was itself a single ship, Andecka and the other Ints were waiting for him to guide them. Relying on him somehow to show them a path through the nightmare chaos that was consuming unspace.

He finally felt the familiar confines of the Machine's seat around him. Felt its connections go live as Shinandri and Jaine plugged him in. Felt the universe invert along that secret other axis, the real–unreal dimension that had nothing to do with the usual three.

Into the maelstrom.

The sheer density of it almost overwhelmed him. Unspace was empty. He knew that. It wasn't even really there. Nothing existed in it, up to and including the ships which passed through it, until they emerged into the real again. The only thing in unspace was the entity perceiving, and—possibly— the Presence that lived there. Except the unreal beneath Estoc was seething with complex structure. It was like the Architect nursery he'd found for Ahab. A great assemblage of information that became a topography, a landscape, a cityscape, a crowded slum extending out to beyond the system's furthest reaches. He felt as though he was being crushed in a crowd. His auditory centres manufactured the mindless babble of a million voices. Aklu's weapon was building something here, convoluting and convoluting the base structure of the universe until a flat plain had now become a forest of meaning so dense he could barely slip between the trunks.

What am I seeing? To get through it—to guide the Host through it—he would have to understand it. And he didn't. He'd never seen anything like it before...

But I have, haven't I? Not this scale but I know *this, don't I?*

Things cast a shadow into unspace, true. Mostly, mass did. You could navigate because, to an Int's mind, stars, planets, even ships if you were good enough, were locatable by the pressure they exerted on the membrane between the real and the unreal. As though all matter was just the feet of insects skating on the surface of a pond. But this wasn't mass shadowing. It was more complex than that. Something that normally wouldn't have registered as anything other than a faint fuzz around the bowed lines of gravitic distortion within unspace. But it was a fuzz he had seen before, magnified here to grotesque proportions, like electron microscopy of the head of a flea.

His ears, thronging with meaningless voices. A terrible pressure on his head. Agoraphobia kicked in. A terrible fear of having to go out amongst such a bustling throng of...

Idris Telemmier, oldest surviving human Intermediary and veteran of far too many voyages beyond the real, learned something new about unspace today. Something he'd subconsciously clocked, perhaps, but never actually admitted to himself. Something so obvious, now he thought about it. It was made apparent here by its unprecedented scale, but surely he'd known. Surely everyone must have understood. The way the Originator ruins tuned in to a wavelength that let them sing out through unspace and let the Eye pierce its veil. The way that Idris himself was able to read and manipulate the unreal—yes, there was the Machine, and there were gravitic drives and all the rest of it. But, when you came to think about it, it was just him. They gave the power, but it was his direction which moved them. Just him, the fragile little human, with his little human brain. His mind, leaning on the substance of unspace. And yes, the point about unspace was that the abyss gazed into you—that was how you learned about it and guided your ship through it. But the corollary of that was that you too gazed into the abyss. Your mind, exerting pressure. Just as all minds did. Conscious thought, everybody's thought, casting that little fuzzy shadow into unspace. That tiny but measurable distortion. If unspace didn't feel the pressure of thinking minds then Idris couldn't have done what he did.

Aklu's weapon, device, toy, whatever it was, was fabricating the shadow of a vast accumulation of thought. A brain the size of a solar system. Of course there was no such mind. There weren't enough thinking beings in the Estoc system to cast this kind of shadow—there wouldn't have been enough on Berlenhof, on old *Earth* even. It was a vast piece of fakery, and for a long falling moment Idris couldn't see the point of it. Why go to such colossal effort just to reach into unspace and *fake* such an absurd concentration of mind?

Then he understood. And, with it, he realized so much else—revelation upon revelation piling up in the back of his mind. Things he couldn't deal with right then because there were other priorities. A little matter of *getting the hell out of there*, since the Estoc system had become an insanely unhealthy place to be. It wasn't even that this mummery of Aklu's would directly harm a single hair on anyone's head, aside from the crippling headache it was giving him. But after it would come...

He turned his void-eyes into the ever-growing tangle of structure that was devouring unspace, and began to hunt for a path out, into the clarity of non-existence beyond. Kris and Shinandri and the others were demanding answers from him but he couldn't spare them an iota of attention. He had to get them away, because otherwise they would stay at ground zero and nothing here was going to survive.

Olli

The Partheni weren't hampered by considerations like keeping anyone alive, or the *Vulture God* in one piece, and so they came through the breach shooting. Ahremon had a Hegemonic toy, though, just a little prism he threw down. It cast up a great shimmering lens right into the faces of the Partheni. A gravitational shield that twisted the course of that storm of accelerator shot every way but true. Which meant none of it went into him, Olli or the major-domo, nor pierced further into the *God* to carve up Kittering. What it did do was fan out in every other direction and put about ten thousand little holes in the drone bay's exterior hull. There was a moment when all the air was trying to get out, and the ship alarms went absolutely berserk. And then Kit, off in command, got the *God*'s own gravity envelope under control and the remaining air shuffled shamefacedly back in. This left the drone bay at about half the preferred pressure, but then nobody but Ahremon was running around with exposed skin and lungs right now, and Tothiat could survive hard vacuum.

They piled in, the three of them, trying to bottleneck the Partheni in the breach. They were all of them better up close. Ahremon got there first, which meant he took a scythe of accelerator chain shot through the torso that just about cut him in half. The two halves didn't slow much for it, and were already rejoining as he hit. Olli saw his shoulder pop and deform as he struck the closest Myrmidon so hard her visor cracked, the joint snapping back into place instantly. Then he had another by the arm, forcing the limb against the armour which held it until one or the other gave.

The major-domo had entirely given up playing the humanoid. They were clinging to one of the Partheni with all their limbs, cutting at the joints in the woman's armour wherever they could get purchase. One of the others got an accelerator pistol to the Hiver's torso, looking to hose it clear of the seething insects held within. Olli lashed out with the Scorpion's tail, driving its drill section into that fancy battle-plate. Turned out the Parthenon made stronger armour than expected, and she broke her drill clean off. She did manage to catapult the woman back into their shuttle, though, and settled for that.

She had the suit's pincers around another Myrmidon when the signal pinged up. Contact request, some system asking for access to her control systems. Even as she slammed the woman into her fellows, as a scatter of shot took off one of the Scorpion's legs, she turned it down contemptuously. Of course the Partheni would be trying to hack her. She was making herself Problem Number One in the ugly scrum around the breach. But just sending her a polite request for access seemed a bit formal, even for them.

She rebalanced on three legs, feeling the multi-limbed

Scorpion more acutely than she'd ever felt her own flesh-and-blood body, exalting in the power it gave her to crush and tear, and just generally let the universe know how pissed off she was with it.

Then all that power was suddenly on its back, skidding across the drone bay floor, until she was looking up into the watery mass of Junior's tank. One of the Myrmidons had braced herself against the ragged tear they'd cut into the *God*'s hull and *kicked* the Scorpion. There were cracks all across her view from it. She'd forgotten how *strong* that armour made them. She flailed, fighting to get back up, but her assailant was right on her, clinging on, bringing her accelerator round. Olli fought her with every limb. She caught one of the Myrmidon's arms, twisting it, shearing into the elbow joint with a saw, and glimpsed the woman jolt with silent pain. Next the barrel of the accelerator was pressed right up against the damaged plastic of her bubble.

And then the woman was gone. The transition was so swift, Olli had to reconstruct the events in retrospect. There was a sudden looming shadow, then a lunge. A spatter of spilled water flew across her and the floor around her, and the Myrmidon was... in the tank. In Junior's appalling jaws. The water clouded with blood and cracked pieces of Partheni plate as Junior got to work on an unexpected lunch.

Didn't know it could do that. Olli had been right up against the liquid side of the tank more times than she could count, since they'd borrowed Junior. *I guess it likes me.*

She got the Scorpion back on its remaining feet and then lost another arm almost immediately to a spray of shot. Ahremon was backed into the mouth of the umbilical, fighting to stop the Partheni from getting to Aklu. The

295

major-domo was...pieces. Torn open, scattered across the drone bay in limbs, jagged shards and curled-up bugs. A moment later a handful of stray pellets tore through the Scorpion on their way to infinity and two of them passed through her as well.

She went down. The frame's medical systems actually worked this time, plugging the wounds and injecting her with a spacer's cocktail of anti-shock meds. She was going to regret the hell out of it later, but if you were a spacer and it was an emergency you couldn't be sentimental about pumping yourself full of stay-the-fuck-awake juice. Her view was momentarily a blizzard of insistent error messages, telling her all the things the suit's feedback meant she already knew. Plus the constant little blinking request that she stop whatever she was doing and link to some unknown system.

She tried to use the Scorpion's tail to get her upright, but abruptly there was a Myrmidon with a foot on her, pinning her down. They carved the tail right off her, leaving her as merely a truncated torso inside a cracked bubble, inside a broken frame. She looked down at her, this super-soldier woman, with her perfectly edited genes, wondering—Olli assumed—how her people had even let her live.

Access request access request access...

The protocols were all wrong—not Colonial, surely not Partheni, which meant...

What was that about a gift?

The drone bay was cluttered. It was full of Junior's tank —the Partheni were trying to shoot the Ogdru but the field that kept its water together was screwing with their targeting —and it was full of the Partheni, and it was no longer full of the Scorpion because the Scorpion wasn't displacing the sort of space it once had, not with all its limbs gone. But it was also full of a number of crates that she'd written off as Aklu's luggage. The various things they'd brought that wouldn't fit in the tiny nipple of a ship the Essiel had deigned to give their fallen child. Aklu had been the only thing in that vessel, now most likely joined by Ahremon and some Partheni as well.

Which meant—Olli realized, even as a Myrmidon lined up an accelerator with her face—that a certain prized toy of Aklu's was right here with her.

Access granted.

It exploded out of its crate, shattering the metal and plastic into a storm of sharp-edged pieces that took one of the Partheni down. A writhing knot of segmented tentacles, far too much and too many for her to control directly, but she didn't need to. She just told it what she wanted, over the newly established link, and its own onboard kybernet did the rest. It picked up the two Myrmidons standing over her and flung them around the room almost joyously, smashing them until they wouldn't be a problem any more. It then slapped at another couple until they retreated back through the breach. They shot several of its limbs away, but it compensated instantly. Olli linked to the drone bay cameras, looking to see what was left.

It was just her and Junior in there. She'd temporarily driven the surviving Partheni out, save for those who were already over on the Hegemonic ship.

She had the ball of tentacles come over to her. At first she wasn't sure how to do it, but then something between her tentative commands and its own systems meshed, and the broken pod of the Scorpion was instantly enthroned atop the seething mass of limbs. For a moment she had a sense of it as the *other*, a thing that would have been at arm's length for anyone else. The *alien*. Then she did what she always did with a new remote system. She let herself inhabit it, let it become an extension of her malleable self-image. A weirder self than she'd ever been, but it was eager to do her bidding. It was strong and agile, the product of a technology more advanced than anything she'd ever played with before. *Going to have to find what you can do, when I've got time, but right now—*

Even as she thought this, the initiative was well and truly whipped out from under her. Abruptly the *Vulture God* was no longer connected to Aklu's little ship. She didn't know whether the Essiel itself had severed the connection or if the Partheni had done it, but the two vessels now floated free of each other. A moment later the Partheni shuttle detached too, and she guessed that, after her bloody work, she was too much of a problem and not enough of a priority.

"Ahremon, you there?" she tried. And then, "Aklu? Menheer Unspeakable?"

Sound came over comms. Shouting, screaming, a great groaning roar, the high singing of accelerators. Then nothing.

"Kit?" Olli realized she hadn't heard from him since the fighting started. "Speak to me, Kit."

For a gut-yawning moment there was nothing, then the Hanni's translated voice came through to her. "Repairs have been partially executed. Unclear where holes end and hull begins but integrity is retained somehow."

"But can we move?"

"We can. To the Host assemblage?"

"Fucked if I know where else." Kit had been around her long enough to know that meant "Yes."

As they fell away from Aklu, from the Partheni fleet, and kept falling towards the ugly lump of the Eye, another comms call came in. The Exemplar of the *Medea*, no less, Partheni-in-chief for the whole Estoc system.

"Turn off your weapon!" the woman was demanding. "We will fire on your vessel. We will fire on all your vessels. Deactivate your weapon."

Olli didn't reply, but she was thinking, *You dumb bitch. It's not the gun you're seeing. It's the explosion after someone pulled the trigger. And we are most likely all completely screwed.*

Idris

He could feel the other Ints, strung out there across the face of the Host, little points of light. He was connected to them by comms too, of course. Him to the Machine, to the Eye, to the individual shards. But he could feel them, their own individual footprints in unspace. They were waiting for him. *We have to go.*

And then Kris was in his ear, shouting loud enough to cut through everything else that was going on, saying, "We have to wait!"

But he was finding his path out. He was doing his job. Navigating unspace, even though that normally meant finding a trajectory across unfathomable distances rather than this inching through the close walls of a maze. Through the illusory crowd that Aklu was still adding to, creating a mob whose mental pressure weighed down on the surface of unspace. A clarion call. A challenge. Impossible to ignore.

"I don't think I can." Because if he found any way out, then surely they'd have to *go*. The simple act of finding that exit would propel them. Idris to the Machine, to the Eye, to the other Ints all waiting. The Host's distributed gravitic system would spit them out from the heart of nightmare into clear space, freedom, into—

"Idris, Olli's coming. We can't go without her. She's coming in to dock right now, in the *God*. Olli and Kit, Idris. We have to wait."

He could even feel the infinitesimal displacement of the *Vulture God* as it limped and spun and shuddered its way to the Host, on a collision course with the Eye. It was damaged enough that they probably wouldn't even be able to brake before they plastered themselves against its broken rock.

"Kris," he told her, because otherwise he'd just *go*. Complete the equation, solve it for freedom, and they'd be posting themselves through the crack in existence, the last closing doorway before Estoc met its doom. "Kris, it's bait."

"What are you talking about?"

"Listen to me, it's bait. What Aklu's doing. It's *minds*. That's always been the problem. It's why they're only sent after *us*. Not rocks. Not suns. Not dead matter. *Us*. Thinking *us*. We spoil the surface. We confuse things. And it's tiny, but if there's enough, it must... We're the problem they need to solve. Aklu's just faked the universe's biggest problem. It's not a weapon, it's a lure. They can't ignore it. And they're already on their way."

"Idris, you are making so little sense—"

Then the *God* was hurtling in towards the surface of the Eye, having made it within the Host's envelope. He could now reach out with the Originator facility's absurdly precise gravitic field, just as he had done to rip the installation from the surface of its native world. He could increase the distance between the incoming ship and rock, stretching and stretching space until the *God*'s abused drives slowed it enough to survive impact. And then they were off, fleeing, solving the equation, escaping through the maze of unspace. Andecka and all the other Ints working in concert with him, in pain, in terror.

And they were gone.

Ravin

He watched the Host, along with the Eye, vanish into unspace, taking Piter with it. He waited for it to re-emerge, just like the *Grand Nikolas* had. But it didn't.

Telemmier. Somehow the Int had solved the problem, escaping the cage that was keeping them all here.

The Exemplar of the *Medea* was trying to talk to him but he closed down the channel, staring out into space. His own crew had informed him that the Hegemonic ship had been taken, but it hadn't stopped whatever was going on out there. Out in unspace. *Is this it, then? Are we just trapped forever?*

That would be a bad enough fate, but they had ark ships here, and the means to complete them. They could at least survive, and travel over the light years and the centuries, if worse came to worst. But he knew that wouldn't be it. Yes, the Essiel were alien, but he had a sense that the vengeance of Aklu the Unspeakable would be more direct.

Then he saw them arrive. There was a storm of incoming comms requests, but he didn't need them. His bridge crew, the arks, the Partheni, there was nothing they could tell him that his own eyes hadn't already.

They emerged into the fierce light of Estoc's sun, gleaming like crystal, scattering rainbow shards of light as though their sharp edges were carving the sun's rays into splinters. Architects. First two, then five, then seven. Seven Architects, more than anybody had ever seen. A constellation of them, ill-omened stars that foretold the fall of kings. Ravin couldn't move. He could barely breathe, staring at them. Watching as they boiled out of unspace and then scattered, coursing inexorably towards their targets. Towards the *Medea*, the shipyards, the planet. Even, he saw, towards the sun itself. Whatever had been done here, it was such an offence to the Architects that no trace of it was going to be permitted to survive.

The *Medea* went first. He saw the Partheni vessel unleash its mass loom and all its ordnance, but none of it so much as troubled the Architect's surface. The *Medea* must have an Int too. One of their machine-assisted Partheni variants. But the woman was probably already dead or mad with what was going on out there. Even if not, she didn't have what it took to slow or turn an Architect. Moments later, the *Medea* was a twisted lacework of metal and plastic.

They were getting to work on the planet. They were teasing out the heart of the star. Architects, people called them. Artists, said others. To Ravin it seemed as though they were the workers who came at the end of the day to tidy everything away and close up shop. The sort of menials he'd never spared a glance for before, but now the things they were cleaning up included him.

He'd had a destiny. He'd wanted to save humanity. Or at least some part of it, with himself at its head, but that was better than nothing, wasn't it?

The Architect that had done for the *Medea* was now gliding towards the *Grand Nikolas*.

Ravin Uskaro sagged down into his seat, behind his ornate desk, surrounded by the heraldry of his august family, and covered his face with his hands.

PART 3
CRUX

18.

Kris

She was alone aboard the Eye. And, even though the Eye was very large and convoluted and cluttered with occult spaces, she was absolutely sure she was alone. She couldn't work out why. There was too much going on.

Kris was outside the room where the Machines were. The empty Machines. Nobody there, no Idris, no Ahab. It was very important that she was *outside* and that the door was closed, but— The air was screaming at her, as though everybody who'd died on Earth when the Architect came had gone to some primitive conception of hell and she had a ringside seat for the torture. Her head had been cored of any conception about what had been going on a second before. The Eye resounded to the chorus of the damned, the very stone buzzing with it, as though every iota of its substance might break apart, then transform into swarms of flies or saw-edged particles. And there was a voice, a choir-master leading the refrain. Speaking judgement to her, consigning her to the same endless torments she was hearing.

Through all of this, she became aware that something was stalking her through the halls of the Eye. That old monster of the id, the Presence. This told her the Eye must be in unspace, which was why she was alone. It should have been a terrifying revelation, that not-alone-ness. But right now, with everything else that was going on, the Presence was almost like an old friend. It grounded her in the unreal and answered a handful of the legion of questions battering at the inside of her skull.

Idris did it. She remembered now, piecemeal. Idris had been trying to get them out. So perhaps the proper revelation should be, *Idris is currently trying to do it.*

She should have been on the other side of that door then, surely. With Idris. That made more sense. She wasn't sure why she was out here, in a stone-walled chamber that had been…complicated. There were lots of crates and boxes and things, and they were coated with a fur of darts and pellets, as well as weirdly deformed little metal sculptures. Only they were on the side facing away from the Machine hall. She knew that should mean something, but if all these voices could just stop *shouting.*

They stopped. The Host, and the Eye contained within its tenuous bounds, erupted into the real like a dolphin from a boiling sea.

The Voyenni right in front of her was on his knees, gauntleted hands clasped to his helmet. She wasn't doing so well herself. Right then she felt more like going for a consoling drink with him than continuing the fight they'd apparently been having. Plus a man on his knees in a knife fight kicked in all those instincts which stopped her lunging forwards for another strike. Because she was trained for fights where civilized people yielded to each other. She remembered rather too late that the pair of them really had been trying to kill each other and this wasn't the judicial piste at all.

Havaer Mundy had trained somewhere nastier, of course, so he got a pistol to where the man's helmet met his armoured suit and discharged an eye-searing crackle of energy that sent the Voyenni spasming away, charred and smoking. Then Ahab *romped* on through. It was the only word Kris could apply to the Naeromath's motion, as if the cyborg eel-monster alien was an exuberant puppy. A swing of its metal-sheathed head sent another Voyenni down the length of the chamber, bouncing off every crate and pillar on the way, and a third man was practically flattened. But there were plenty more recovering their wits and getting back into the fight. Kris glanced around wildly for other defenders. Jaine was at the door, her back to the stone of the wall, and applying medical sealant to the inconvenient flesh and blood of her leg, which had been viciously laid open. Trine was there too, with a savage dent in their torso casing, holding some sort of cutting tool awkwardly in their nest of arms. No sign of Shinandri; and of course no sign of Idris. *It's us? It's just us?*

There were maybe a dozen Voyenni left, or a few less. They'd thrown aside their accelerators, as Jaine or Ahab had played their trick with the magnetic fields to deflect all that fast-moving metallic death into the walls and barricades. The fact it had come down to knife work was all that had saved the defenders. And that their crash through unspace had been almost absurdly traumatic.

Third time lucky for the Voyenni, Kris guessed. She could see Piter Uskaro up there too. She knew it was him because his armoured suit was painted up with a load of complicated heraldry, just so nobody would be in any doubt who was important. All very feudal, and he might as well strut around in it, given that none of them could get to him. His armour was the best money could buy. Ahab had shot him, she remembered. Somehow threaded an energy beam through all that conflicting air. The afterimage of it on her retinas had looked like someone's mad signature, and the Naeromath had managed to land it right in the centre of Piter's chest. It had scorched away some of the fancy paintwork but apparently whatever Ahab was packing wasn't enough to get to the meat beneath.

They were regrouping up there. She thought Piter was giving them a bit of a lashing and, dispassionately, she could see his point. They had the numbers and the training. Admittedly, Kris's side had Ahab, and Ahab hadn't seemed to register being knifed or shocked at all. It was all scar, trauma and cybernetics, and there wasn't much the Voyenni could do to it except kill it.

"Attention, Kris." A surprisingly chirpy voice on her comms. For a moment she just stared, and if the enemy had charged then, they'd have had her.

"Kit?" she demanded.

"Landed on the Eye," the Hanni's translator confirmed distantly. "You are to be told by Olli that the Uskaros are already here."

"Kit, I am *aware*," she got out through her teeth. "Kit, where are you?"

"Docked. Olli is assaulting the Uskaro shuttle."

"With who?"

"With Olli."

"Kit, tell her— Listen, these goons are all over, and they're dangerous. Your lot will be able to use their guns—get her—"

"It should be appreciated Olli has some anger issues to

work through," Kit said cheerily. "This is proceeding. We will have control of the dock shortly. What is your position?"

"Pretty damn bad. We're penned in at the Machine room by the rest of Uskaro's clowns—looks like they're ready to buy the next round right now. Can you get here?"

"We are somewhat distant, alas."

"We are, after all, nowhere near the exterior here, my comrade in arms," Trine put in over her shoulder. Apparently listening to her earpiece was something they could do. "I fear we'll not hold their next advance."

"Advance, right." She banished the thought of Kit and Olli, save for wishing them luck, and saw the Voyenni gathering, Piter slapping them about the shoulders, bullying them into shape.

She had a thought then. She surveyed the available cover, the path the Voyenni were even now using to come at them. Where they'd discarded their litter.

"Jaine, can you turn off the magnetics?" she hissed back.

Jaine nodded, pale, the fires of her torso flickering unhealthily. She'd lost a lot of blood, and Kris didn't know how that figured with her peculiar cyborg anatomy.

"We charge," she told Havaer, Ahab and Trine. "We go for *him*, and hold him, then they back off. It's the only way to negate their numbers."

"We can't—"

"We grab their guns. Their accelerators. They just chucked them away when they realized they weren't working for them," Kris insisted. She had never fired an accelerator, of course. Havaer probably had, perhaps a decade ago back in training, or a week ago murdering someone. Hard to know with the spook squad.

"That's madness," Havaer said, and then Ahab roared, "We proceed!" and just *went*, leaving Kris flat-footed in her own plan.

The Voyenni hadn't expected it either, so when a ton of Naeromathi launched itself at them on those skittery legs their own charge faltered. Ahab probably intended to hit them like a ball bowled at skittles but it wasn't as clean as that. They scattered and it only rammed into one. Then they were trying to carve up its flanks and stay clear as it wheeled around. Piter had drawn back, but at least the Naeromathi had taken everyone's attention. Kris hoped it could keep its scarred hide intact for just long enough. She ran for the guns, Havaer and Trine at her heels.

It turned out the enemy weren't quite so single-minded as that. There was a quartet of Voyenni sprinting around the room's pillars to intercept them, seeing the ploy immediately. *Easy to think thugs are dumb.* Havaer's long legs had given him the lead by then, so he was the one who got tackled head-long, crashing to the ground and wrestling with the big house guard who'd grabbed him. Kris just vaulted over the pair of them, seeing the stack of accelerators ahead, knowing she was nimble and going to make it.

The first man who came for her was too slow. She put on a desperate burst and he was left clutching for her hair, for her sleeve, skidding on the smooth stone of the floor as he tried to reverse his momentum. The next man hit her, though. Clipped her with his shoulder, but enough to send her off course. She came up with her knife, knowing that she'd been hoping to start a gunfight and so was now ill-equipped to carry the plan through.

He slammed her in the chest with the heel of his hand

and she hit the ground, head ringing, knife gone. Instantly he was on her, kneeling on her sternum, gauntleted fingers crushing at her throat. Through his visor she could just make out his face, frowning like a slow student doing mental arithmetic. She couldn't shift or lessen his clenching grip even slightly, not even with both hands wrenching at it.

Trine loomed over the man. The Hiver's arms were a rack of jointed metal appendages that usually folded neatly away into their chest. Now the limbs were all spread out like a cheering crowd at a mantis convention, arching down to dig themselves into the Voyenni's armour. Trine wasn't strong, she knew. They would never win prizes for deadlifting or be able to throw a decent punch. What they could do was *prise*, applying precise pressure. They hooked under the edge of the Voyenni's backplate and pauldron and tore it all off.

The man abruptly had other priorities than strangling Kris. He tried to round on the Hiver but they had cast aside the wreckage and were striking again, driving points, pincers and claws into the flesh of the man's back. Trine's projected face had a fixed expression of fastidious distaste, as though they'd been served something impolitic at a diplomatic function.

Another Voyenni barrelled in and hit Trine with what looked like a crowbar. Kris's eyes—her human-centric brain—recoiled at the ragged spray of blood where all those arms were torn out of the first man's back. Only a second later did she register the metal frame staggering sideways on loose legs, face blown out like a candle, a great crease struck into Trine's torso.

She was on her feet instantly, hunting for her lost knife, then a hand closing on the accelerators. She had no real idea how to fire one. The thing that looked like a trigger wouldn't trig. The Voyenni hit Trine again, knocking them to the ground. There were bugs seething about the edges of the rent he'd made in the Hiver's casing, and the bugs were Trine. Their mind, their decades of life and experience and priceless knowledge.

Kris hated trashy action mediotypes. Right then one of them returned to her, though. A wasted evening watching it, she'd thought, at the insistence of Olli or Barney, or someone else aboard the *Vulture God*. Except there had been shooting in it, and to shoot they'd had to move a little bar to activate the weapons. The accelerator she was holding had just such a little bar and so she moved it, then aimed at both the Voyenni, spraying a scatter of hypersonic pellets at them. Jaine had done her bit because it didn't just go into the walls. It didn't really go into the Voyenni either. Her hands were shaking and she was braced for a recoil the weapon didn't have. One of the men took a couple of hits and went down, though probably non-fatally. The other was completely missed, standing there as though the hands of God had curved protectively around him. And then he scooped up one of the scattered accelerators too and brought it around towards her. No difficulty finding the safety catch himself. But then, of the two of them, only one had "shooting people" in their skillset.

The air filled with the singing of accelerator shot. Kris screamed, actually screamed out loud. Shielding her face as though the imposition of her hands, or the accelerator she was holding, would in any way protect her.

Through her fingers she saw the Voyenni practically sheared in half, and then the next two. The man she'd shot sat up and was punched right down again. She saw Havaer standing, having apparently finished off his own opponent. He had his hands up, fingers spread, surrendering. His face did not say, *Hooray, a rescue!* It was the face of a man who thought he was next for the execution squad.

Piter Uskaro made it to Kris then. He hadn't been shot, save that one shoulder of his fancy armour had been chewed up by a near miss. He was trying to wrestle with her. No, he was trying to hold her hostage, she realized. He was a man whose troops were even then being finished off and he needed leverage.

She grabbed his knife, which was on his belt. There was some kind of pistol there too but she felt her record with guns wasn't great right then. Knives, though; knives she knew.

Piter snagged at her sleeve and she cut at his fingers. She expected the grate of blade against plastic plate but instead she sheared very neatly through two of them, armour and flesh both. Because when you were the heir to a great Boyarin family, and someone bought you a knife, they bought you a *knife*.

She probably had a moment to consider alternative dispute resolution then, like a good lawyer, but he'd been hounding her and Idris for a long time now, and he always made things worse. Trine was badly hurt and the continuous presence —existence—of Piter Tchever Uskaro was only going to complicate that. So she stabbed him.

Then she stabbed him again. The blade skittered from his armour the first time but she remembered her form and got him in the armpit the second time, and the third. He fell to the floor, probably not quite dead yet, but she'd tried fixing him up last time she stabbed him and he hadn't exactly shown his gratitude since, and so here they were. This time there would be no bringing him back.

Next she turned her attention to the newcomers who had just butchered all the Voyenni.

Partheni Myrmidons. Eight of them were in the chamber and she saw more through the archway beyond. That famous full and faceless armour. Accelerators. All that. A knife wasn't going to take Kris much further under the circumstances, but she wouldn't let go of it for all that.

Then the leading Myrmidon strode forwards, her helm opening, and Kris's heart leapt.

Solace.

Solace

At first she'd thought it would just be a matter of lead by example. Always the worst kind of leadership, they'd told her, in her accelerated Executor training. She'd had her immediate class with her, the group penned inside the unwalled space that counted as her cell. The other prisoner classes... she had only been able to hope that they'd follow her. She had tried to assume that within their hearts burned the same will to set the balance straight, to take back what was theirs. And if she turned out to be wrong about that, then her insurrection would come to a swift and bloody end.

By then the guards had mostly retreated to a gallery level above them. The numerical imbalance between prisoners and wardens had become too pronounced and they'd pulled back from the hold floor. Making Solace's job that much harder. And perfect for them, should the order come just to shoot everyone down in the belly of the *Angel Alecto*. Which was very much what Solace had felt was about to happen.

Then one of the Cognoscientes in her class had grabbed her attention. She'd found a little access flap hidden beneath her and prised it open to reveal a socket. It was only intended for power cables, but they'd left the woman with some of her tools and now, by messing with the socket, she could send and receive signals. There were two other classes across the hold who'd had the same idea, the Cognosciente had murmured to Solace. So they were in primitive communication. Apparently the techs had their own codes and secrets, into which Solace had been indoctrinated out of necessity.

That had still made just a fraction of the prisoners, but even as the Cognosciente had been reporting, another prisoner class had joined them. Solace had imagined the hold like a Hannilambra game board, little squares lighting up as they silently joined her revolution. She was still the ranking officer and they'd all been looking to her.

"We'll need a distraction," she'd directed, trusting to their competence to find some system they could hack into. "We'll need control of the elevator over there." She pointed with her eyes, not her hands. "And there." The lifts that would take them up to the guards' level. The guards who were close enough to overwhelm and disarm. Those guards had been armoured, and Solace knew from the other side of the equation what advantages that gave against the rabble she'd be leading. *Suicide.*

But the alternative had been to let the Parthenon die. Once there had been a clique called the War Party who'd wanted to take their sisters into a war with the Colonies, wipe out their rivals in humanity. And those sisters had unthroned them. They'd each of them been executed by hands unknown, even to this day. The proper place of the Parthenon had been defended, and would be again, by blood if need be.

Now had come this new threat. Not even a War Party but Exemplar Mercy's...what? Running Away Party, Solace had thought. Just quitting, abandoning it all. That wasn't what the Parthenon did. She looked down her long life, all those punctuated years back to the war, and had known it in her heart.

But she'd also felt one sliver of doubt. Her Parthenon, yes, but she was a fossil. A relic of a past age. When she'd been born, there had been a war on. When she'd first joined active service, the Architects had loomed large in everyone's mind, and in many skies. And the Parthenon had still been a part of the greater human Polyaspora. At least they'd woken her for the secession. It had been all hands ready for war then.

She was the product of a time when defending the rest of humanity was what the Parthenon was for. Not the unwitting years of Before, when Earth still existed and Doctor Parsefer's Parthenon was a quasi-illegal genetic experiment that the governments of the homeworld were in fits about. Solace came from a very specific slice of wartime history, and now she had found herself in the prison hold of the *Angel Alecto*, insisting that her vision of the sisterhood was *right* enough to get them all killed for.

Suddenly she had wanted to weep. She had wanted to turn to her sisters—even though they weren't her sorority or division—and bare all these worries, just as a soldier should have been able to. But she'd told herself the time wasn't right, that she didn't know them well enough. That she was a leader and must be strong. Which meant being alone.

Through the coded communications of the Cognosciente

prisoners she had assembled a plan. A terrible plan with cata-strophic losses baked right in. And they'd all been able to see it. Every one of her new soldiers—unarmed, unarmoured —would have known how bad the odds were. But they'd been cut loose, severed from their command structures. And here Solace had been, giving them orders. They were used to that. Orders were the structure which gave their lives shape. Even the jagged, ruined shape that ended them.

But Solace had reckoned they had the numbers. Enough distraction, enough elevator boarding parties sent up. Get a couple of those accelerators. Kill the rest of the guards. Take the ship. Fifty per cent casualties, had been her estimate. *Probably me among them.* And she'd deserve it. She'd almost rather it went that way, and wanted to lead the charge. Another terrible command tactic.

"Awaiting your word, Myrmidon Executor," the Cognosciente had told her, and she had watched and waited for her moment.

Now. No, now. Or...there'll be a better chance any second. Hold...Now! She hadn't said anything, just watched and waited, body taut as a drawn wire. All around the hold the other conspirators had been just as tense, ready to throw their lives at their sisters' guns on her order. Because they had believed in the Parthenon. They had believed in Solace.

Ready...ready...

Tact said—

Hold, not now...Almost...Ready...

What had Tact said?

Solace had told herself it didn't matter what Tact had said. Tact had lost control. It was down to Solace to save the day now.

No heroics. When the time comes, you'll know it.

But this is the time, Solace had insisted to herself. *They're going to kill us, or dump us on some forsaken world and abandon us. We're lost unless we act.*

No heroics, Tact had told her. Just about her last orders. And if Solace had the authority to order all these unarmed women into the muzzles of the accelerators, then Tact had the authority to order her to sit still.

In the end, she hadn't trusted herself that much. Her conviction hadn't been worth their lives. Instead she'd waited and waited, never quite standing down, and done nothing.

And then the shooting had started.

They'd all scattered, down in the hold. The Myrmidons had run for the walls because that would at least give them cover from the guards directly above. They'd hauled the Cognoscientes with them, where the techs weren't already moving. Solace and her party had gone for their chosen elevator. Others under her command had followed suit. She'd waited too long and it had all exploded without them being ready.

But the shooting had all been above, armour against armour. And by the time Solace and her ragged mutineers had arrived on the gallery level, it was over. She'd seen a handful of dead sisters up there, and the nearest armoured figure had quickly scanned her insignia and greeted her, "Myrmidon Executor Solace?" A superior recognizing an inferior. Old instincts had kicked in and she'd responded, "Prêt, Mother."

"Get your people to the lockers," she'd been told. "Tool up, soldier. We've work to do. There are more of Mercy's loyalists on board."

"Monitor Superior Tact—" Because Tact was who Solace was supposed to take orders from and report to.

"She has a message for all of you, when we have the ship," the officer told her. "It'll bring you up to date with how things have fallen out. All according to plan, soldier. Now let's go."

Mercy

The lid of her suspension couch was already hanging open when the meds kicked her into wakefulness. Exemplar Mercy —Fleet Exemplar, by her own hand—stared up at the low lighting of the racks. All the pods, one above another, were crammed into the limited space because that was how you did it. Economy in everything, the Partheni way everywhere except their garden ships. A warship's comforting exactitude. Except it wasn't right. As though the scene around her was a fake, a psych-out by some Colonial intelligencer. Correct in every detail and still wrong.

She disconnected from the suspension systems and swung herself out and onto the ladder. The crawling sense of unease only grew, pricking the hairs on her skin, worming its way into her mind. The pods she passed were empty. Every one of them. Was she the last to be woken? She, the Exemplar? Unthinkable! And if there were others awake, where were they? The ship was silent. Her hands and feet on the rungs sent out echoes that came back eerily muffled and distorted from the room's far walls.

Alone. She was alone aboard the ship. For dead seconds her mind toyed with the idea of a mass desertion, because that was better than . . .

She dressed. Full uniform, the new rank tags still unfamiliar. Hauling the clothes out of their storage shelf at the ladder's foot and pulling them on, bending all her focus to the task because that way she could shut out the...

When she had her uniform on, she connected to the *Skathi*'s systems, and there was one solitary message awaiting her. She, the Exemplar—*Fleet* Exemplar—was called to the bridge. Of course she would go to the bridge. That was her place. But the message was without attribution, as though automatically generated by the ship itself. She interrogated the ship's systems, seeking errors. Seeking answers. Finding everything in working order and yet her own access to it circumscribed. All those systems visible yet beyond her reach, as though they were behind panes of glass she could only press her nose up against.

She hurried through the corridors of the *Skathi* that should have been busy with the crew of a top-of-the-line warship, even in peacetime. Always something to do on a ship. No idle hands. And yet they were resoundingly empty. A silence so profound she could hear the echo.

Or hear *something*. As though it was outside the ship. A thing that couldn't really be there, *wasn't* there, but she knew it was, nonetheless. A distant, but closing, Presence.

Mercy had never been awake in unspace before.

By the time she reached the bridge, she had a gun from one of the armoury lockers. They hadn't thought to bar those against her. It was a magnetic carbine, rated for use in the *Skathi*'s confined spaces, and she scanned it across this area of command, anywhere that someone might be. But there was nobody. Of course, nobody. Because she was in unspace, and in unspace you were always alone.

Not alone.

Just one lit panel there. Comms. A message.

She was ready for the projected face. Monitor Superior Tact, of course. Rather than just a head, the system gave her Tact all the way to her neatly booted feet. An old woman in the uniform of the Aspirat. Not a prisoner. Not even physically present. In an excess of rage, Mercy shut the message off even as Tact's illusory lips parted.

But she didn't vanish. Mercy was shut out of her own bridge commands. Tact's slight smile couldn't possibly be foreknowledge of how Mercy would react and her mounting fury now. Even Tact wasn't that prescient.

"Fleet Exemplar, here is your intelligence report from the Aspirat," came Tact's ghostly voice. "You may or may not have checked the fleet manifests, but if you do, you'll see that your personnel allocations haven't worked out quite the way you intended. The vast majority of your loyalists in fact ended up here on the *Skathi,* or else on the *Cythaera* and the *Lady Gray.* Good ships all. A shame. But necessary sacrifices. My people will have ensured that the rest of the fleet is primarily staffed by those loyal to the Parthenon. To *me,* to the Aspirat, to our proper purpose. Some will have been sent there as prisoners. Others will be there as crew and guards, being those with the appropriate training to get around all those loyalty tests Felicity's so proud of. All rather fallible and out of date, I'm afraid. I will admit that your initial strike caught us unawares, Fleet Exemplar. My own attention was in countering our actual enemies, the Nativist elements within the Colonies. I should have paid more attention to who was standing at my back. But we had procedures in place for another War Party, or anything of that line. The irony is, if you'd brought this as a formal proposal to the Board of Mothers, then who knows? I can see it being quite popular in certain circumstances. But it's *means*, Mercy. You had to have your coup and you had to end up with the new flashy insignia on your uniform. And so I had to stop you."

The hateful voice droned on and on and despite everything, there was nothing Mercy could do to turn the message off. In the back of her mind, she was aware of something else too. Something seeping into the ship from *outside*. From the unthinkable abyss that was unspace—less substantial even than the hard vacuum of space. Inimical to life, and yet with one alleged inhabitant. Her mind's eye saw it like some colossal hook-limbed parasite clinging to the hull of the *Skathi*, patiently probing the hull until it found a way inside. And it was inside. It was small enough to fit through all the neat spaces, pushing its bloated body from chamber to chamber, questing with its writhing feelers, hunting...

"So we've taken your fleet off you, Fleet Exemplar," Tact's image continued, and Mercy felt herself shake, her gun hand shake. She levelled the weapon at the comms console. *What happened if you crippled your own ship in unspace?* She didn't shoot.

"The universe needs the Parthenon," Tact explained. "I won't even say, 'in its original form.' The Parthenon as we know it wasn't formed in those turbulent times Before. It became what it is during the war. The pure steel of it. What are we without those who hate us, and whom we have sworn to protect? Monsters, Mercy. Executor Solace told me about a conversation she had with one of the Colonials. A woman born incomplete. But you know how their spacers always find a way to make everything functional and useful, where we'd just replace it. It shook Solace. The way they see us. Because it's justified. They're right to be scared and resentful. The Parthenon was conceived as an exercise in eugenics and if it hadn't been for the war, we could only have become monsters to justify our existence. Thank the Architects, because without them, we'd be the great enemy. Instead, the war made us something cleaner. It gave us a chance to re-invent ourselves. And you will undo that. You'll make us nothing more than a self-perpetuating machine without higher purpose. And I cannot allow it."

The *Skathi* was a big ship. There was a lot of ground to cover, between her and the thing that couldn't possibly be in here with her. But it was getting closer, even if it was just in her head. It was groping its blind way towards her. A thing that had existed alone since the dawn of time and could not abide to share its unreal universe with anything else. A thing so alien that to confront it would be to die of abject horror. Utterly beyond any human connection save that Mercy understood, beyond doubt, that it *knew* her. Knew her and hungered for her, her specifically, the fragile mind of Fleet Exemplar Mercy.

"If it's any satisfaction to you," Tact said, more softly, "you were very exacting about your commands concerning my own imprisonment. I'm right here with you, Mercy. Standing beside you, though I'm alone and you're alone. And your crew are here, too. Those who swore themselves to your treason. Each one of them standing here on the bridge of the *Skathi*, right there beside you. Each one of them hearing her sentence being pronounced. I failed when you joined with the Uskaros to attack Estoc, and I'm paying the price now, just as you are. Just as better women than we are paying.

Those few who are taking the *Skathi* and the *Cythaera* and the *Lady Gray* on their last voyages. Cognosciente Intermediary Grave is even now guiding your flagship on its final flight, Fleet Exemplar. She volunteered, just as the others did. She understands how important it is. And she understands poetic justice. She's only taking you deeper into unspace, Mercy. A journey without destination. And then she'll end herself, a sacrifice for the good of the many. After this, you and the *Skathi* and your ideology will never be heard from again."

Tact winked out and Mercy wished, despite herself, that she could bring the woman back. If only to have someone to scream at, to threaten, to beg.

But she couldn't have done any of that, because *something* was right outside the bridge. Something patiently fumbling and scratching at the door. She put her back to it. She couldn't face it. She was no coward but there wasn't courage enough in the whole Parthenon for this. *How can the Ints bear it?* How could Grave and the others have sent them on this voyage in the full knowledge of what they did?

No answers. And now she heard the soft whisper of the doors.

She raised her gun.

19.

Havaer

The Hivers had been at Crux for longer than they'd been independent. The system had one world, a brutal gas giant swirling with rare elements in suspension—a gold mine if you could only get at it through the corrosive atmosphere and monstrous pressures. The human solution had been to install orbital lasers and superheat the world below until it started venting its guts into space, and then to harvest what got spouted out. The cruciform pattern of the resulting gas jets—ten million kilometres before they petered out into invisibility—lent the system its name. They were also appallingly dangerous to mine, what with the heat, the ravenous inorganic chemistry, and the radiation and all. Fatal for fragile humans. Not terribly healthy for Hiver frames either. But back then Hivers had been property and the elements that Crux supplied had been vital for gravitic drives and other ship components. And humanity, on the run from the Architects, had been utterly dependent on its ships.

Fast forward to Hiver independence after the war. Crux had merited a whole section in the treaty. It remained part of the Colonial Sphere, and the Hivers remained in residence. They continued to mine the gas vents, and by then the process had been refined enough that the individual miners could be reinstantiated without lasting degradation. Which the humans of the time had been happy to believe meant without loss or damage. Havaer would have thought the same, but he knew differently now. The Hivers of Crux tithed a portion of their mining yield to Hugh as rent, and the precise diplomatic status of the system remained in bureaucratic limbo.

And here they were: the Host and its cargo, having lurched out from unspace, along with a ragged escort of Partheni vessels and Kris already sending ahead to the Hiver Assembly there asking for help. Of course the Hivers had been the big silent partner in the Cartel. Theoretically Havaer could report to them, in the absence of anyone else. From what he'd heard, they might just about be the only players left on his side of the espionage divide.

He'd tried to tell the others about Chief Laery, after the Partheni had rolled up and finished off the last of the Uskaro forces. The fighting had been fierce, but Havaer hadn't seen it, happy to consign himself to non-combatant status now the professionals had arrived. It had been him, the *Vulture God* crew and the team from the Eye, just sitting around the Machines, while the rest of the Ints Havaer had sprung listened in from their stations across the Host's distributed structure. Everyone had caught up, naturally. All their various escapades. And nobody had really cared much about the death of Laery. Most of them hadn't even known who she was particularly. A secret mover and shaker of the backstage Colonial world. And so she had left barely a ripple when she fell. She'd been Havaer's boss for a long time, and her death meant nothing to anybody except him.

She hadn't gone alone. The Aspirat handler who gave

Solace her marching orders had departed too, apparently, taking the uncooperative side of the Parthenon with her into oblivion. Havaer wasn't sure he entirely believed it, but it seemed as though that half of the problem was under control again.

As for the other half—*his* half...He had Olli's testimony to rely on for that. Because apparently the Uskaro family had got itself into an ass-kicking contest with Aklu, and that had gone wrong for just about everybody. Aklu was no more, along with its lieutenant Heremon, of unfond memory, and the Hiver it carried around to prance about on its behalf. Olli, alarmingly, had inherited Aklu's legs, currently still attached to the ruined pod of her Scorpion. This was another development Havaer wasn't exactly in love with. The woman had been dangerous enough before. Now she had a nest of Essiel-tech tentacles to move her around, and was plainly itching to turn them on anyone she didn't like. He was amazed she hadn't gone ham on the Partheni, honestly. He'd seen the mess she'd made of the Uskaro shuttle and its sentries.

This had been before Crux had crossed anyone's mind. Back when they'd rendezvoused out in deep space, it had all been panic and counting off names, and nobody understanding the scale of what had just happened at Estoc. It wasn't as though a packet ship had been passing by the middle of absolute nowhere with news of how it had gone down after they'd fled. And how was there even an agreed rendezvous, exactly, Havaer had demanded. How was there somewhere Idris had known to head for, that the Partheni Ints had also had on their maps? They were literally in deep space, not a star for a hundred light years in any direction.

Enter Harbinger Ash, of course. Who'd somehow been there all along. Been where? On the Eye? On a Partheni ship? Nobody knew. Certainly hadn't shown its face-substitute during the actual fighting. But somehow everyone had got their coordinates from Ash, and everyone had ended up in the same place. Sure, you could ask the damned thing about just what it could do, vis-à-vis personal transport through unspace. But it would look at you all mysterious-like and you'd get about as many straight answers from it as anyone ever had. Which meant zero.

Ash was theoretically part of the Cartel too. It had been standing there with Laery when she made the announcement. And the one true thing everyone knew about Ash was that it only wanted the one thing. To fight the Architects. And the whole point of the Cartel was to make the Eye its weapon in that war. Ash and Ahab, kindred spirits with one idea between them.

They'd brought the whole circus to Crux now, not only because the Hivers might offer them some political sanctuary, but because they had a medical emergency. Trine had taken a hell of a beating in the fight. They weren't communicating, and the activity of their seething nest of insect units looked fitful, as best as Havaer could judge. There would have been a time he'd have been fairly unmoved by that on a personal level. Except he had his own dead comrade to mourn. Colvari might have been the most loyal and dedicated partner Havaer had ever worked with, and they'd been a Hiver. They'd given their life so that Havaer and the Ints could get clear.

None of them could get near the actual processing factories—the vast orbitals that hung within the gas vents in conditions that would kill even a heavily suited human in minutes. The Hivers had work shifts of eight hours, Havaer understood, after which their frames were decontaminated and their contents returned to the Assembly in Aggregate —or that part of it which lived here at Crux—to be reinstantiated later. Hence, and incidentally, Crux had what passed for top-of-the-range medical facilities if you were a Hiver.

The Assembly's main aggregation, a floating diamond shape in high orbit away from the excesses of the gas giant, was where they were docking now. The Host itself was too large to simply pitch up, so they'd brought Trine's mauled frame over on the *Vulture God*, with Idris at the controls.

Havaer wasn't sure what to expect. He only knew Hivers from where they were interacting with humans, after all. Perhaps the whole place would be seething with loose bugs?

The whole place was seething with loose bugs.

Or, not exactly. There was an outer layer, where they docked, where there were individual instantiated Hivers in utilitarian frames, from little skittering underfoot models to giant monsters that could have bench-pressed the entire *God*. The hangar they landed in dwarfed their ship, and some of the other docked vessels were themselves individual Hivers. The frames they saw owed nothing to human aesthetics, not even the surrealist nod given in that direction by bodies like Trine's. They were containers for the individual nests of insects, plus a variety of functional limbs as required. They drifted about the floor and walls with the stilting grace of crabs underwater, because there was no gravity on the hive at all. The Hivers preferred zero-G at home, apparently. Even the minimal natural grav from the hive's mass had been cancelled out by its gravitic engines. It would have to be magnetic boots and thrusters if the human and Hanni visitors wanted to get anywhere. Except for Olli, whose new assemblage of limbs was more than equal to the task.

They brought Trine out, and a handful of frames descended instantly. They fitted grav-handles to Trine's abused torso, and then the hive's systems took over and flew the patient into the dark recesses of the hive. Soon after, they received a comms call from the local Assembly itself, wanting to speak to a representative. Some wrangling resulted in Havaer, Kris, Solace and Idris being appointed joint Delegate, but he reckoned the Hivers couldn't exactly complain about multiples.

So the four of them ended up standing on the inner surface of a circular chamber which was absolutely awash with cybernetic insects. The space was a good hundred metres across and, aside from a patch about three metres wide where they stood, there wasn't much of its surface to be seen. The interior of the hive was all metal plates grooved with curving, endless loops, like some impossibly extended cursive handwriting. In the outer regions, it looked like decoration. And here, Havaer saw, the swarming insects seemed to follow the incised trackways a lot of the time, possibly rewriting them, as though the hive's composite memory was constantly being chewed into its walls. Or maybe it was just decoration. No way of knowing. After the Hivers had left human control they'd continued to develop, after all. They were their own thing now.

In the centre of the chamber, tethered by invisible gravitic forces, was Trine's beaten-up old frame.

A voice addressed them. Not a vast buzzing chorus, as Havaer half expected, but the pleasant, flat tones of a translator program, not a long way from the voice that Kittering used. Something commercial and mass-produced, focus-grouped to sound just human enough. The Hiver Assembly in Aggregate at Crux could probably have ordered something more top of the range, but why would they?

"We have established communications with Delegate Trine," they explained. "A decision must be made regarding our next actions."

"What's the prognosis?" Solace asked bluntly. She and Idris had known Trine since the war, Havaer remembered.

"Delegate Trine's internal cohesion is failing," the Assembly told them. "They have been instantiated for a period considerably outside recommended working parameters. Their data structures are outdated, idiosyncratic and unstable. This, combined with the damage received, means that effective repair is impossible. If they stabilize, the resulting identity construct will have lost forty to seventy per cent of its existing stored experience."

"So the decision is that, or..."

"Delegate Trine has thus far been resistant to return to the Assembly."

Havaer reflected that, if Trine had been in constant instantiation since the war, they were at least as old as this entire hive. Quite possibly older than the fully conscious Hiver Assembly in Aggregate, which had developed out of human wartime tech.

"That's right," Solace agreed. "They wanted to be themself." This was probably about the worst diplomatic faux pas you could make with Hivers, but apparently the Aggregate took it in its multiple stride.

"You said communications." Idris was so quiet that he'd possibly said it already and was having to repeat himself. "Can we talk to them?"

"We can establish a link. However, bringing Delegate Trine

to a level of functionality where this is possible will diminish their operational lifespan at any full-functioning level. Be efficient," the Assembly said.

And then nothing.

Solace glanced at Idris, both of them then glancing at the walls, as if awaiting permission, so it was Havaer himself who said, "Delegate Trine?"

The voice came, issuing out of the air. Not from the abused torso of Trine, but amplified by the vast swarm of the Assembly. As though, thought Havaer in a sudden excess of atavism, they were catching the fluttering wingbeats of the old Hiver's soul.

Yes, this is Trine. Faint, staticky, as though received over a failing comms channel. Or through some antique analogue mechanism intended to communicate with ghosts.

"We've got a problem, Trine," Solace said, fixing on their frame for want of any other focal point. "We're with the Assembly at Crux. They want you to re-aggregate."

A pause and then the voice, from its incalculable distance, breathing: *I don't think I want that.*

"Then don't," Idris said flatly. "Don't. Just...heal. Put yourself back together. However long it takes."

I don't think that's going to happen either, Trine told them. *I'm trying to get a handle on my internal diagnostics, Idris, old comrade in arms, and I'm finding some frankly alarming results.* The voice came and went, but the intonations were unmistakably Trine's. *I'm damaged. I'm actually rather badly damaged. Some of it is even self-inflicted, can you imagine? My units have scored into the interior of my casing the phrase "memory issues." And, as I cannot remember instructing them to do so, I can only assume that's correct. I am investigating.*

A pause lengthened, as they shuffled their feet and the vast, quiet bustle of the room went on all around them, along its little channels.

"Trine?" Solace prompted, and the spectral response came back, *Yes, this is Trine.* The intonation so identical to the first time that Havaer thought they'd lost all their progress, but then they went on, *Or most of Trine. You almost lost me. Please keep me talking. Short-term recollection is the only thing I have, it seems. I am not able to set down further experience for permanent record. My memory functions are entirely adrift.*

"Is that going to get better?" Solace asked.

Well, I can't tell you that, my solicitous friend, Trine echoed to them, from the far spaces they'd receded to. *Primarily because I must have looked up exactly that, previously, and now the knowledge is gone. Much like the human mind, to access my memory is to replace it with a memory of the moment of access. And unfortunately, given my current state, any memory I access is being replaced with... nothing.* Another pause and, just as Solace opened her mouth to speak, *It is rather appalling. It is as though my mind is eating itself. I can feel my memories, everything I ever learned, like a tree full of fruit. Each to be picked once, and never replaced. I don't like it. And then, I don't know what to do.*

"Wait," Idris said. "Heal. You'll heal." Looking about him at the wider swarm. "They'll heal. Won't they?"

"We cannot know," came their voice, so much stronger than Trine's whispery rattle. "All things are possible. They have been separate for a very long time. We cannot know their capabilities."

"Well then we can give them time," Idris insisted, and right at Havaer's shoulder a new voice said, "We cannot."

They all jumped, and if Havaer had brought a gun, it would have been in his hand right then. Standing behind him was the robed figure of Harbinger Ash, keeping up its long tradition of always turning up where it wasn't looked for.

To Havaer's surprise, Solace just muscled up to the alien as though she was going to kick its ass right back to wherever it had come from. If it even had one. "This isn't your concern."

Ash loomed over her without threat, without even registering the challenge. "It is everyone's concern, Myrmidon Executor Solace." Using her rank to put her in her place, as neatly as any of Havaer's superiors ever had. "Ask Idris. He knows."

The skinny little Int squirmed rebelliously but wouldn't meet anyone's gaze. "No," he muttered, but when Solace's stare demanded more, he got out, "Trine's work."

"Their archaeology?" Solace asked. "Surely if there's one field of knowledge that can *wait...*"

"They were working with Shinandri and me," Idris mumbled. "With the Eye. They were working on a way to travel into unspace. Not like regular ships. Originator technology. A way to do what Ahab wants. To actually go and give the Architects a kicking where they live, you know." Sounding sick about it. "Nobody knows the Originators like Trine. They said they'd got it." He glanced at Trine's frame. "They can't... Trine...?"

I... don't dare, my dear old... my... My fellow. Idris. I don't dare look. If I look, I will know, but then I can never know again. All my work. All my years. My learning. And I cannot know what I know, or a moment later I'll never know... What am I supposed to do?

"The Assembly will be able to preserve your experiences

and knowledge and reinstantiate you, so you can put them to work," Ash insisted.

"But only if Trine wants," Solace said. "They can't be forced."

"There is precedent," came the chorus of the Assembly itself. "But we prefer not to. And a forced reintegration seldom results in reinstantiation. There is too much discord."

"Trine," Idris said. "They *can* instantiate you. You can still come back. Whole. With everything you know."

Havaer just stood there and said nothing. It was a wonder that Telemmier had lived this long, in a universe that contained Hivers, and not quite understood. He remembered Colvari, from when he'd first hired them as an information processor. And he remembered Colvari after they'd reverted to the Assembly and reinstantiated. They'd still been Colvari, just...

"Trine?" Solace's voice was down to a whisper. Havaer thought Ash was going to weigh in again, to insist on Trine playing their part in its grand crusade, but it had the tact to stay silent.

Yes, this is Trine. It's been a long time, came Trine's faint voice at last. *I can't say how long, not without forgetting. I have been me* ever since I was me. *Who else can say that, amongst our guild? I have seen so many things. Idris. Solace. I want to reminisce. I want to ask you if you remember this escapade or that, my good old...my...friends. But if I raise the spectre of those things we saw and did, then they will be lost to me, and it will be as if I was never there. I'm sorry. I cannot part as friends should. But it seems I have to go back to the family at last and make an accounting of myself.* A pause, and then, *That was a pun. A particularly Hiver pun. You may laugh.*

Nobody did.

They finally took Trine's frame away, deeper into the hive, and the three humans returned to the Eye, the Host and the *Vulture God*. While they waited to see what the Hiver Assembly could do with the old archaeologist, it was time to grieve for all the others.

Solace

The Partheni kept a rolling memorial, accessible across the fleet. A record of the dead, most recent first. But Solace could keep going down until she got to names she remembered from the first time they'd been at war with the Architects. A space for tributes, iconography, catharsis. The part of the fleet that had made it out of the coup attempt and reached Crux was updating now. The names of those who had died bringing down Mercy's coup. Those who had sacrificed themselves to consign the dissidents to oblivion. Mercy's name did not appear there, nor did any of her loyalists. It was the same for the adherents of the War Party, and who knew what other losing sides and failed attempts to fragment or redirect the Parthenon. They were erased, cut from the mental genetics of the sisterhood.

Tact, Solace noted there. Lost with all honours defending what she believed was right, one particular vision for the Parthenon. The same vision Solace believed in, but she was uncomfortably aware that, had she been Mercy's protégé instead, she'd likely have believed differently. Not an evil end, just one incompatible with the goal that Tact had set out, and one conducted by unconscionable means. A murky business, and was wiping it from the record really the best way? Nonetheless, it was what they did.

And more than Tact, of course. Grave and a handful of precious Ints, with over forty of Solace's loyal sisters, all gone the same way. *But not me. Was I not loyal enough, or did she just need me to handle the* Vulture God *crew and the misfits from the Eye?*

The Colonials were holding their own memorial, within the stone confines of the Originator facility. It was hard for them, because most of the people they wanted to commemorate lacked the proper details.

"Aklu the Unspeakable, the Razor and the Hook," Olli declaimed. She was at the bedside of Tokamak Jaine, whose torso was currently partly disassembled as two Hiver frames worked on it. She'd overclocked her body during the fight, to the extent that without the maintenance she'd likely have shut down and died. Or exploded, given her nickname.

"Born fuck knows when and fuck knows where," Olli went on doggedly. She had the tip of one of her new tentacles curled in Jaine's hand. Around them were sitting the *God* crew, Shinandri and Havaer the spook, holding printed cups. Solace joined them and took one. She knew the drill by now.

"An inconsiderate employer demanding work without recompense," Kittering declared.

"Impossible to understand a word it said," Jaine put in, a flat electronic voice through the speaker the Hivers had rigged up for her.

"An actual murdering gangster," Havaer said flatly, not exactly in the spirit of things.

"My...patron, it was," Olli went on regardless. "My benefactor. Loyal to...fuck knows, frankly. Safe...claws? Died in space, though, as a spacer should. Where it belonged. One of fucking ours, it was, and I'll fight the bastard Hegemony for it." She scowled pugnaciously at them. "Come on then."

There was Heremon the Tothiat to add to the list, and the unnamed major-domo Hiver. And then Havaer had his own chief to pay tribute to, the Laery woman, as well as the Hiver he'd worked with, who'd bailed Kris out more than once as well. Making it to Crux had been costly.

There were a multitude of names left behind at Estoc, who weren't there any more. All the people who hadn't been *ours* but hadn't really been enemies. Just been *there*, because there had been an enormous shipyard, which meant thousands and thousands of people and Hivers doing...work. Regular, non-evil work. And by now the packet ships had come through to Crux, confirming Estoc was gone. Nothing but the star remained, and that had been stripped of quite a lot of its mass. There was a sculpture, a delicate interconnected tracery that went all the way around the star like filigree. And it was made from all the matter of the Estoc system, teased out into hair-fine filaments and braided into art. It was the single largest work the Architects had ever gifted to the universe. Whatever Aklu had set in motion had, it seemed, merited a truly unique response from them.

Solace listened to the piecemeal orations, the best that anybody there could give the dead, and then checked back with her own people. There would be wheels in motion, she knew. The fact that the packet trade had reached Crux meant news was travelling in the other direction too. She realized that Havaer would have filed a report with someone, because that was who he was and how he operated. More than that, there would be plenty of ears pricking up in Hugh when word came to them of what had just pitched up at Crux. A response would be on its way, and she wasn't sure how the weakened Partheni fleet element she was with was going to respond. They were technically in a Colonial system. And the Eye was something that Hugh would likely claim ownership of. On paper or by force of arms. After all, the only thing that had broken up the Partheni–Colonial War was the rise of the Cartel, and that little conspiracy was yesterday's news.

*

Idris had slunk from the group before they got too maudlin, and shortly before Havaer himself went off, doubtless to talk to Hiver intelligencers (or the overall Hiver intelligence, she supposed). Idris probably imagined his departure went unnoticed, but Solace caught up with him soon after. He was in with the Machines, a room away from where Ahab was doing something mechanical and intermittently noisy. Ahab didn't do funerals, she gathered. Its culture was, after all, just the fugitive scraps left over from when the Architects had gutted whatever the Naeromathi had once been. Even more than humans, if Ahab had started eulogizing the dead, it wouldn't ever have stopped.

Idris was sitting on the edge of the Machine he got slotted into so often. Just on the edge, legs dangling, shoulders hunched in. That quintessential Idris pose that said he was gamely wrestling with those inner demons who were so much bigger and stronger than he was.

"I don't want to do it," he told her as she entered. "I don't want to do any of it."

She sat beside him, or as best as she could given the Machine's uneven topography, then let him lean into her. Found that she needed him as much as the other way around.

"I don't know where we are," she said. "The fleet. The Parthenon. We've crippled ourselves because the alternative was becoming something else. Abandoning you all. We can't fight the Colonies and we can't fight the Architects. Or not as well as we should. I don't know what happens next." The words from her mouth revealed to her the fears in her head that she'd never faced up to. All the certainties she'd lived with, when she'd just been Tact's agent. That the wider Parthenon would always be there for her like a stern mother.

"We can fight the Architects," Idris told her. "That's what they want me to do. Me and the other Ints, all of us. Fight them and destroy them. But it won't solve the problem. Solace, there's something—"

"Behind them, I know. You've said. But if they're the gun, then taking the gun away still helps."

"You kill the gun, but the gun's alive, and not to blame. And then maybe the gunman goes and gets another." He pushed off from her and then crunched himself round, until he was lying in the Machine again. "Can you fetch Shinandri? I need to get to work."

"Idris—"

"I need to. I don't want to. I want to do anything else. But I have to use this time, before they make me go kill things for them."

When she got back to the others, Trine was there, amidst an awkward silence.

The Hivers had repaired their frame, with the same pleasant human face projected into the bowl of its head.

Solace felt a jolt of fond connection followed by a sudden scratch of wrongness. As though she was looking at a corpse propped up and puppeteered.

"Ah, Solace," came Trine's familiar voice. "It's good to see you. I was just telling Doctor Shinandri here that the Assembly in Aggregate and I are ready to make the final modifications to the Eye. We finally understand what must be done." All delivered crisply and clearly, as though she was meeting someone in a professional context for the first time. Someone who knew of her, had read of her exploits perhaps, but didn't *know* her. She waited for the *My old confederate* or *My fellow veteran* or any of the Trine-isms, but there was just an empty place in the universe where those terms echoed and were lost, and she knew that they'd missed one name off the funeral list after all.

20.

Idris

He understood Ahab now. Perhaps he even understood Ash. Their monomaniacal drive. Because there had been a Partheni civil war, and the Uskaros had attacked, and the Estoc system had fallen to the Architects, during which plenty of people had died, but it had all primarily been an interruption to his *work*. It had kept him from the Machines, the Eye and unspace, and there was literally nothing more important, not in the universe.

When Shinandri had first put him in the Machine, he'd fought every step of the way. Perhaps it was because some part of him had known even then that, once he'd had that kind of access to unspace, he wouldn't ever be able to let go of it. He felt as though it offered him the next stage of an Int's life cycle, with all that navigating, first contact and fighting wars just having been the caterpillar part, a necessary grind.

And he'd had his revelation, hadn't he? Before they'd dragged him out to deal with that tedious round of politics and violence. He'd crept to the very edge of the Presence, and seen something in its shadow. The sunken city, lightless and eternal . . . or at least something that his mind had translated in those terms. It was unspace, and unreal, so nothing there was anything the mind could grasp first-hand. He had only his subconscious to mediate for him, the Intermediary's intermediary.

On the slab, Idris plunged into unspace, alone. No other Ints to distract him. No voices in his ear telling him what he had to do. On his own recognizance at last, his mind in the abyss.

Beneath him, he felt the Presence stir, the first irritated flick of its ear as it registered his arrival. It was almost comforting. When there's a nameless terror that's literally too appalling to face, it's good to know it's behaving itself.

Beneath him.

In a realm without dimensions, the mind plays tricks. But some part of him—the *Int* part of him—understood. It had a migrating animal's crude grasp of exactly what was going on, on the wrong side of the real/unreal boundary. It didn't need the maths or the equations. Just *knowing* was the Intermediary's stock in trade in unspace. *Beneath*, because there was one cardinal direction, and that was *down*. He could picture the boundary to the real like the silvery shimmer of sunlight on water, seen from below. And he let himself fall away from it, descending into the crushing cold, the lightless depths. The place where the Presence laired. Out there, in the mid-range of the waters at the light's faintest reach, there was the constellation of structure that was where the Architects came from, and beyond that were greater depths. Except...

Finite. He had seen the sea floor. The lamps of his mind had found a furthest extent, so what kind of infinite dimension was it, then? Unspace was unmappably vast, everyone knew. There wasn't an *end* to it. There was only a beginning, the skin over the top of it that was the entire universe and everything in it.

This was the received wisdom. A layer of *real* and then the vast chasms beneath. With the Throughways, the network of connective tissue that linked star to star, suturing through space just beneath that boundary. And all the traffic of every sentient race took place within that tissue-thin layer. Except Idris had delved deep and seen an end, and that meant everything everyone thought about the structure of unspace was wrong. If there was a hard end to it, what was there beyond?

So he dived deeper, sensing the Presence rising lazily towards him, inquisitive as a shark. He felt the fear response which owed nothing to the body he was only loosely connected to. An existential fear of an entity whose very nature was abhorrence personified. Feeling it closing, reaching slowly towards him. A vastness below, a shadow in the waters. Eyes like blood-red beads. A drifting net of hair-fine tendrils to snare him. Dead hands groping through dark water.

Idris's eyes were already closed but, inside his head, he closed them again, and again. Creating layers of calm, layers of mental distance, even as he fell into the shadow of the thing. The fear prised its way into the spaces of his mind, and he retreated to a further room, and a further one still. Unable to face it, but able to hold it off. Or not face it *yet*, and sometimes *not yet* was just enough. He fell past the undulating flank of it, a thing vast and hungry as a black hole. Feeling that expanse beneath it, the murky floor of dead things that demanded to remain buried until...

No, that was wrong. It was his mind fooling him. The

limits of allowing your subconscious to furnish the unimaginable abyss with images.

Idris jolted with revelation. Somewhere there were alarms, very far and faint. Somewhere there was the Presence, very close and immediate. Finding him, opening up so that he was a speck of plankton within the barbed immensity of its jaws.

Understanding.

Not an expanse. Not a great and lightless plain. Not even *below*. The one thing he thought he'd known about unspace was wrong. There was only one direction, but it wasn't *down*. It was inwards. There wasn't a flat plain, there was a *point*. A centre. And if he had somehow crossed past the Presence, and past that centre point, he'd have been going *out* again, back towards the real.

There was a core to unspace, and there was something in residence at that core. The heart of everything. Because unspace was surrounded by the real universe.

If the Architects' masters were anywhere, he'd found them.

Then he was being pulled at. He wasn't alone back up on the Eye any more, but he didn't want to leave. Even though the Presence was all around him, those jaws closing. Even though, if it caught him, he would die. His mind would hurl itself into oblivion, because by definition facing the Presence couldn't be borne. But he was learning. He was gulping information in like airless freezing water, cramming his lungs with it. Seeing the movement of things that were huge and immeasurable, yet simultaneously tiny and discrete. Things already in motion. With an awareness of him. Of everyone. A tension and a structure to all of unspace. Because the closer you got to that centre, that heart, the smaller it all became. The scale shifted, telescope to microscope. As he slid down that gradient into the teeth of the Presence, he could conceive of more and more of unspace, appreciating its wider structure and shrinking the whole, until the entire universal network of Throughways across its skin was something he was able to take in at a glance, and understand. See how they pulled and tugged at the structure of the universe, dragging it out of true. And how all those infinitesimal minds dimpled the boundary between real and unreal, messing with the maths. Spoiling a certain elegant symmetry. Grit in the cogs of a machine that was *doing* something.

The universe was a machine that was doing something. He could perceive that very clearly now. It was the most important understanding that had ever come to him. Little things like breathing didn't really matter, compared to this.

No, correction. The universe was the universe, but spread throughout it was a machine, doing something *to* the universe. Very slowly. Very precisely. At the atomic scale, and to everything there was. That insane precision was necessary and, if he'd stood at the very heart of unspace like *they* were doing, then he could have viewed this absurdly exacting complexity with complete comprehension. Understanding just what it was trying to do, and how all these little grains of thinking dust were throwing off the calculations, and—

They hauled him out—actually dragged him from the Machine without his permission. For a moment he'd been, not emperor of the universe exactly, but pretender to the throne, potential usurper. Because only he and *they* even understood there was a throne. A centre to the universe, past the Presence's watchful patrol. *Give me a lever and a place to stand*, the wise man had said. Idris was that lever, and he'd found where he could plant himself, to move the universe.

But mostly died, of course. The alarms had sounded when his vitals went off the wrong end of critical. They'd got to him before his brain died, and the three Hiver units Trine had gifted him had kept his heart going, however gamely it'd had been trying just to stop. They'd not let him die, and he could be distantly grateful for that.

Then, after the absolute minimum of time to ascertain he wasn't going to drop dead, they dragged him into a meeting. He didn't want to be in a meeting. He wanted to be in the Machine again. Except it turned out this was one meeting he genuinely did need to be at. Because Trine—or rather, a Hiver that looked like Trine but wasn't really—was talking about what they were doing to the Eye, and what the Eye would be able to do, which touched neatly on Idris's own plans.

*

"The chief difficulty in any operation within unspace," Shinandri said, "is that we cannot under normal circumstances work together there. That is, one might say, the defining characteristic of physically entering unspace."

"The 'chief difficulty' is nothing's real and you can't do anything there except go nuts," Olli broke in. Idris felt that the whole business was going to be difficult enough without heckling, but he didn't feel up to asking her not to.

"Details," Shinandri said dismissively, "to which we shall attend in due course. The operations of linked terminals, utilizing the Originator technology within the Eye, have allowed limited interaction within unspace between the Intermediaries, but that will not suffice. We cannot just throw naked Ints against the conglomeration of structure that we have detected there. That would, I am very much afraid, not achieve anything worth writing home about." His giggle, which he had plainly been fighting against for a while, finally escaped. "My esteemed colleague?" He gestured at the Hiver which was wearing Trine's body and face. They had Trine's voice too, and knew everything Trine knew. Yet they weren't Trine, and the discontinuity just ratcheted up the stress inside Idris. He was back in the real now. Things were supposed to behave in predictably real ways. He couldn't take too many shocks this side of the border.

"We still know far too little about the Originators," Trine's voice said. "However, study of the Eye facility has provided a framework for a great deal of isolated knowledge fragments that I have collected over my career. The Originators were not simply observers of unspace, they were engineers. I can demonstrate, using the intact systems left on the Eye, that the Throughways we rely on for non-Intermediary travel between star systems were indeed constructed by the Originators. Or at least they had the capability to do it. Unspace, as a realm, works to a set of mathematical constants, and even if they are different to those of the material universe, they are nonetheless predictable, and the Eye gives us the means to gain mathematical purchase on unspace."

"You saying we can build new Throughways now?" Olli asked.

"No," Trine said. "Or rather, not yet, although this discovery does provide the theoretical basis for such construction. However, the sheer power expenditure necessary to effect such changes in any practical sense seems entirely beyond our capabilities."

We lack leverage, Idris thought. The twitch that went through his body felt so grotesque, he was amazed everyone wasn't staring at him. Kris, sitting beside him, gave him a quizzical look, that was all. A meagre reaction to someone who now understood the whole universe and how it worked. *Levers. The simplest machines in the world. You just need to know where to put the pressure on. A lever magnifies force. And if you were at the very centre, you could do so much with so little...*

"You've heard this facility on the Eye referred to as the Wellhead," Trine continued, "on the basis that those in its Machines are going down a notional well. Having made my personal archives available to the Assembly in Aggregate, we conclude that it is possible to send more down this 'well' than the minds of the Intermediaries involved. Doctor?"

"Indeed, yes," Shinandri agreed. "With the assistance of Delegate Trine and the Assembly, certain matters on the Eye's functioning have been clarified. A bubble, if you will. The Eye projects a bubble of the real into unspace. This is how its observational facility has worked, and it is within this bubble that the minds of the Intermediaries have been able to liaise, even though they are immersed in unspace. By drawing further on the resources of the Eye, it will be possible to project a far more significant bubble of the real into unspace. One that contains the Eye itself, and its housing, the vessel known as the Host. Suitably guided by Intermediaries, we will be able to persist physically and operate in unspace. As real entities. Together."

There was a long pause. Idris sat and jittered, feeling the yawning incredulity in the room, then was almost pathetically grateful when Olli finally broke in with, "That sounds fucking insane. What about the *thing* they all talk about? And what about...I mean, you're doing *real* stuff, *being* real things, in a place where real stuff isn't supposed to go. Won't it be constantly trying to spit you out or stomp you flat?"

Shinandri's giggle was half an octave higher than its usual squeak. "Oh my, yes!" he agreed. "Constant exercise of the Originator engines will be required to maintain our presence or, as you surmise, our existence. Nobody, you see, is suggesting that this will be *safe*! However, it will permit us to approach our target, our destination, the Architect site. And, once we are operating in the same frame of reference as it, we can begin to work upon it, to destroy them. We can fight back."

"Yes!" boomed Ahab from the back, and something of its fervour was certainly in the air. Idris shrank from it all. *No,* he thought, but he was definitely outvoted.

"In order to maintain our connection to the real," Shinandri went on, "we will need an ongoing Wellhead presence. While we are, so to speak, down the well." Another titter. "This will be provided by a vessel in the real. Our anchor point, to switch metaphors. So long as the anchor remains intact, the well—the bubble...Forgive me so many metaphors, but we are talking about a realm that has no properly conceivable contents, so vague figures of speech are all we have! So long as the anchor remains, the well shaft remains, and we, down within it, similarly remain, and can even return safely when our work is done." He grinned brilliantly at them. "We can win," he said simply. "Once Jaine, Ahab and the Hivers have finished modifying the Eye for the voyage, we can take the war to the Architects and we can win."

Idris shrugged off the jubilant mood that had gripped everyone else, hunching away from Kris and Solace, focusing inwards. He thought Trine and Shinandri were probably right. And he could go up there and give his own little speech now, if he wanted. Perfect their understanding. He'd probably have to tell them, at some point. But first of all, he needed to think through the implications. What was serving as a weapon for them against the Architects was also an opportunity for him to delve deeper. If he could just get past the Presence again and reach the heart of all things. He could stand before whatever dwelt there, the things which must be the Architects' masters, and ask them, *Why?* Tell them, *Stop killing us! We're here!* just as he had when he first faced the Architects all those years ago. He could end the war—the universal threat—without anybody needing to commit genocide on anybody.

21.

Havaer

"The *Ironwriter*," Havaer identified. "The *Grampus*, the *Redcap*, the *Leopard*, *Garelli's Storm*, and your man there's just broadcasting, '*Counter-War Vessel DKT26 Vantus Yards Provisional.*' Which suggests Hugh's a bit stretched right now but wanted to get its top-of-the-range stuff over here just as fast as possible."

" 'Counter-War,' is it?" Kris asked him, staring at the *Vulture God*'s display. It was a feed from the Hiver factory's own eyes: a little fleet of Colonial military vessels fresh out of unspace, along the Throughway from Tarkir. If Havaer wished, he could join the dots all the way back to the muster yards at Sentina, where they'd thrown this lot together. The absolute quickest way over for a fleet that didn't want to try any risky coordinating of Intermediaries.

"Counter-war is what they call war these days, if I recall my last departmental memos before the department got shot up over Estoc," he said flatly. "It's a very neat way of spending lots of Hugh's budget on fighting ships without it looking all aggressive. The best war is a good counter-war, you know."

There were six big fighting ships, but the little rump of the Partheni fleet they had here at Crux was twice the size,

354

and that wasn't counting whatever the Hivers themselves might throw into the mix. So right now Hugh wasn't likely to start shooting. Instead, all those gleaming new ships were ardently pretending to be no more than the escort for a diplomatic yacht. This worthy vessel, the *Broken Key*, was a slender silver needle lost in all that heavily armed haystack, broadcasting a mixture of placation, requests and barely veiled demands.

"The suggestion arises that they are aware of our presence here," Kittering commented, with a good stab at human dry humour.

The command space of the *Vulture God* wasn't exactly congenial, and smelled mostly of the crew of the *Vulture God*, having been too long since their last shore leave. For that matter, the *Vulture God* itself was cramped quarters, given that both its crew and now Tokamak Jaine were currently living on it, with Junior still monopolizing most of the drone bay. Meanwhile the Ints and Shinandri were crammed into those parts of the Host not currently being modified by the Hivers. The Eye itself, which Havaer also classed as uncongenial, but which at least had room to stretch your legs, was out of bounds right now. The Hivers and Ahab were working through the final modifications, bolting a further layer of mismatched tech onto all those other unlovely additions, so that the thing would become... what? Unspace-worthy? Havaer shuddered. He sure as hell wasn't going to be on the thing when it took *that* voyage. Far, far beyond his pay grade.

What had just turned up, though, did seem to fall within his remit. Or at least there wasn't anyone up the chain he could pass it on to, not any more.

It was just the three of them up in command, at least. Olli and Jaine were off together. *Testing out the Hiver repairs*, Havaer thought, not sure if he was annoyed or jealous or what, to be honest. It was probably good that *someone* was having a personal life. Idris was sulking. That was Havaer's considered opinion. They'd said he had to stay out of the Machines while they did work on those self-same Machines, and if you were Idris Telemmier that was a grand imposition. So he was moping in his room like a small child, which, given he was older than any living relative Havaer could claim, was frankly a bit much. Or maybe he was thinking deep Intermediary thoughts. But Havaer decided he'd put more money on sulking.

The Hivers were taking their sweet time about how to answer Hugh's diplomatic hail too. And they hadn't converted any of their factory space for human living while they worked on the Eye. This was a departure from what Havaer would have expected. Whenever you went to the Hivers on any kind of business, they put themselves out for you, like good former property. It was a situation plenty of his fellows had exploited, knowing the Assembly would always roll over for loyal servants of Mordant House. Except they weren't doing it any more, or at least not right now, and *that* was a powerful, tacit statement showing just how strongly they felt after the attack on Estoc.

"Perhaps Hugh has not been informed about the effort to save the universe," Kittering said, translator perfectly deadpan. "Or some manner of recompense is to be offered for the service."

"Assembly is pinging us," Kris said. "Actually, pinging you, Agent."

Not sure if I count as "Agent" any more, Havaer reflected.

She pitched the call over to the board nearest him and he fielded it.

The Hivers were going to host a diplomat or two, apparently. And he was invited.

Why me? But he reckoned the Assembly was making this one up as they went along. Havaer knew Hugh, as much as anyone on this side of the divide did. So he might just about be considered able to speak for the non-Hiver part of the Cartel, on a decidedly last-man-standing basis. He apparently brought some nebulous authority to the table.

"Appropriate adornments must be donned," Kittering announced. Havaer was about to say that the *God's* printers probably couldn't run him up anything suitable, but then realized the Hanni had been invited along too, as the *God's* representative, and so Havaer probably wasn't that special after all.

*

As it turned out, the *God's* printers absolutely could not run him up anything suitable. He just about managed a bad facsimile of a Colonial uniform, but the decoration which should have added a "dress" to the front of that was very obviously printed into the coarse weave of the clothes, rather than being stitched on afterwards. The end effect was something like a costume a child might wear to a party. *Boo! I'm a scary Mordant House agent!* He didn't feel very scary.

When they arrived, the Hivers had another circular space ready. There was one small round platform where a gravitic field was being provided for the benefit of their guests, and that was literally the only concession to hospitality. The drinks and nibbles were conspicuous by their absence. The Hivers, formerly a model of politic manners, were definitely *pissed*.

The Hugh delegation, once stripped of its escort of soldiers, came down to two women and one man. Havaer had very briefly met Arkela Farreaux at some function or other years back. She was career Diplomatic Service Office. The branch of Hugh that, in Havaer's experience, created half the problems Mordant House was expected to solve. Farreaux was small and neat and probably had plenty of past experience dealing with Hivers. The broad, toad-faced man overshadowing her was Captain Hossgarde of the *Ironwriter*, here in full military nonsense clothes. The real thing to Havaer's play-acting, save that the current Hossgarde obviously hadn't had time to re-tailor them since a younger, slimmer Hossgarde had last put them on. The third delegate was bony and short, hollow-cheeked, as much of a famie spacer as you could ask for, save that her name was Diljat and she was Mordant House and outranked Havaer. So that was awkward.

Also present, along with Havaer and Kit, was the Partheni Exemplar Hallow of the *Judicious Valkyrie*. Just to stir the pot a bit more. And a Hiver. The globe interior around them was busy with millions of Hiver units too, obviously. The whole Assembly in Aggregate at Crux was their audience. But the Assembly had wanted people to know exactly how they felt about things and so they had turned out a spokes-delegate in the most humanoid frame Havaer had ever seen. Actual two legs and two arms, and a head and everything. On that gleaming steel face was a profoundly unamused expression, a work of art in itself.

"Did you expect Hugh not to notice that a sizeable attack

fleet of Partheni ships had just invaded Colonial territory here at Crux?" Arkela was saying. "I appreciate that we're hardly a threat to the angels right here and now, but you can be sure that there's a serious military response in the making even as I speak. There are *treaties* concerning Hiver presence and control of the Crux system."

The Delegate turned their disdainful look on her. There were no moving parts to that expression, Havaer saw. It was a single piece. The Assembly wasn't ready to be either mollified or put in its place.

"Our factory at Estoc was the victim of an unprovoked attack by Hugh military vessels," came the murmurous voice of the Hivers from all around them. *The Delegate frame doesn't even speak,* Havaer considered. *They fielded it for the sole purpose of looking angrily at people.*

"The situation at Estoc is complicated," Arkela said, obviously ready for this line of debate. "We're still investigating what happened there. As best we can, given that the Hegemonic response left very little of that entire system." A lot of sincerity was being forced into her voice. *Look what they did!* With the unspoken corollary, *Don't look at what we did!* "It's certainly the case that several vessels which should have been under navy orders appear to have joined in an unsanctioned military venture at the behest of certain elements within Hugh."

"Might we enquire what punitive measures are being taken against those elements?" the Assembly asked sweetly. "We would like to know where to send the account for the many thousands of our instantiated units who were murdered by your elements."

All the while, Exemplar Hallow just stood there, ramrod

straight. Her very presence was spooking the fuck out of the Colonials, if Havaer was any judge. The Hivers and the Parthenon. They went way back, and this sort of union had been the nightmare of more than one Mordant House director. Now Uskaro's goddamn old boys' club had pushed them into it.

That's me thinking like a Hugh agent again, he considered. Right at that point, he received a private comms request. Very private, enough that they'd end-run around all the Hivers' own surveillance tech, at least for the moment. Needless to say, Diljat wasn't even looking at him, her eyes intent on the actual negotiation.

"Agent Mundy." Perfect subvocalization. He couldn't see even the slightest trace of it.

"Agent Diljat. Been a while. I'm still on the books, am I?"

"Interesting question." Her voice a whisper in his ear as Arkela and the Assembly traded diplomatic blows. "I'm not going to lie to you. The old service is a mess right now. Laery's loyalists and those who were in on the whole ark business are all pointing fingers."

"Well, if you know me at all, you know whose I was."

"You were one of Laery's catspaws. But she's gone. So where are you now?"

"Where are you?" Havaer countered. It sounded like harsh language was the only weapon currently being deployed. Everyone had puffed themselves up enough, and the overwhelming force the Parthenon currently had was enough to stop anyone trying to take the number of destroyed Hiver facilities up to two. Or the force they *appeared* to have. Havaer wasn't actually sure how prêt à combattre the Partheni really were right now.

"I'm still with Mordant House," Diljat said drily. "That part of it that isn't trying to eat itself. And this is not what we need. The Architects haven't actually stopped turning up and fucking us over, but here's a whole bunch of Partheni inside our borders and cutting deals with the Hivers. You know the real problem with that, Mundy? It's an enemy we can fight. The Architects, not so much, but we know the Partheni strength here and we know what kind of punch the Assembly can throw. And so, to a lot of hawks back at Hugh, this is suddenly a problem we can *fix*, and that's mighty attractive to throw some ships at. Very cathartic, you know? So how about you make a report about just what the fuck is going on here, before the Hivers shut down my channel?"

"Concise?" he sent back. "The Partheni aren't a threat unless provoked. The Hivers aren't a threat unless provoked. Nobody's going to invade the Colonies. Nobody's going to turn up over Berlenhof and bomb it. But if you push, they'll push back. Right now, all the work here's about dealing *with* the Architects. Saving everyone's ass. I mean that absolutely sincerely, my word as a Hugh agent and citizen and just basic decent human being. That's all they're after. Once that's done, have your throw-down with the Partheni as much as you want."

A pause, and he thought he'd lost her. But then she said, "Report accepted, Agent. Right now the old service doesn't have the sway it used to, what with it pulling in all directions at once, but I'll see what I can do."

And that was definitely the end of their chat. He looked down to see Kittering's body tilted back to stare up at him, the little round eyes in his crown managing a remarkably suspicious look.

"What's up with you?" Havaer asked him.

"It is possible to read the muscles immediately beneath your chin when you subvocalize," the Hanni told him brightly. "Thanks should be tendered for not selling us out. However, there is little hope that it will assist."

Havaer looked at him levelly. *I cannot be eavesdropped on that easily.* Except his guard measures were very much focused on a human eye-level, and on human or electronic eyes. Hanni vision wasn't particularly better than human, but it picked out different things. They were used to a lot of complex motion and display, amongst themselves.

"You think it's coming to a fight?"

"Guns are not brought to parties," Kittering said, which suggested he'd missed out on certain kinds of human parties, but this time he was most likely right. As Diljat had said, there were people back home who wanted a nice, comprehensible, winnable war. Or even just a fightable war.

Solace

She should have been delighted to be out of the decision-making process. There were mothers and sisters out there dealing with the Colonials and deciding whether the war was still on. The little war, not the Architect War, which only the Architects got to say was on or not. And Solace wasn't part of that. Above her pay grade. Which should be a relief, surely.

It wasn't. She wanted to be there. Seeing with her own eyes, speaking from her own mouth. Not just hearing about it later through a ship-wide mediotype or down the chain of command.

She'd been a soldier all her life—a life that had been spread, in bits and pieces, over all the years from the war. She'd always trusted her orders and her superiors. Even when her loyalties had been put under strain, such as when she'd become part of the *Vulture God* crew and felt the tug of conflicting gravities, the fault had always been in *her*, not the Parthenon.

Then Mercy had come along, and Tact had been taken from her, and there were sisters out there who, despite sharing her face, didn't share her mind. Her Parthenon had shrunk from something godlike to this little fugitive fleet of ships. The part of the sisterhood that had both rejected Mercy's crusade and also clung to Tact's original purpose. The Cartel; the Eye; bringing the fight to the Architects. Out there were still *other* Partheni. Some of Mercy's people, doubtless. And others who were neither rebels nor loyalists. Who were just as shaken as Solace and simply didn't know which side was right or what to do. Entire separate fragments of the Parthenon cast adrift by doubt. The monolithic strength of the angels was gone, cracked through by Mercy's treachery. Or by Tact's insistence that they yoke themselves to a single fanatical purpose. Solace believed in that purpose but she wasn't so blind as to pretend that others might justifiably not feel the same.

Right now, everything said in the negotiations would be going to a council of Exemplars, the captains of all the ships preserved here. Some of those were the original officers, others would only just have usurped command from Mercy's favourites. And those women would need to make decisions that this branch of the Parthenon could live or die by. Solace didn't trust them to get it right. Not in her heart. She didn't

363

think she'd have trusted Tact either, now. Or anyone. She felt like someone suddenly orphaned.

There was a break in talks, her comms told her. The Colonials had gone to send a packet vessel back home for orders before things recommenced. The Partheni were probably going to fake doing the same, because most likely they'd been pretending there was a larger fleet just waiting around some place close. Did Hugh realize how weak they were? Unknown. What mattered was stringing things out so that the final modifications for the Eye could be made before the shooting started. In the interim, another three Hugh warships had broken out of unspace into the Crux system. Meaning the Parthenon still had the edge if it came to a punch-up, but it was a narrower edge than before.

Obedient to the call, she collected Idris from his sparse, compact room on the *God* and ferried him out to the Eye. He was twitchy and agitated, like he had withdrawal symptoms, flinching from loud noises and other people. Once on the Eye, she marched him before a middle-aged Partheni woman who was still in a spotless uniform from the negotiations. Exemplar Hallow, commanding the *Judicious Valkyrie*.

"Menheer Telemmier," Hallow said. Idris just stared at her, neither confirming nor denying it. Hallow's mouth twitched. *More annoying Colonials*, that expression said. "I understand you will be leading the unspace navigation effort for the strike against the Architects." Her Colvul was flat and unaccented.

Idris flinched as though she'd threatened to strike him. His mumble was qualified agreement.

"My ship is to serve as your anchor," Hallow told him. "I

would ideally like to show you around it, and receive your thoughts on any facilities that might be useful, but unfortunately our current visitors render that impossible. We are holding the line, right now. It is important that the others do not understand our purposes here."

"Why?" Idris said, his first properly audible word. "Just tell them. Going to fight the Architects." Giving the words a bitter spin. "What's not to love?"

Hallow frowned at him. "Hugh has made demands concerning the return of the Host and its contents to their control. Apparently, while they are happy to disown the attack on Estoc, they are similarly wishing to retain the spoils. A lot of hands are pulling the strings at Hugh, I think, and some of them are Uskaro or their allies. The family are particularly aggrieved after the death of Ravin and his nephew. So, we must not tell them what we really intend —to take the Host away entirely into unspace. We do not bet on good communal sense triumphing amongst our enemies, and do not have the time to explain it to them. The Host submerges under your control. My *Judicious Valkyrie* loses itself across the universe, fleeing any entanglements from the Colonies. While my sisters here continue to hold the line, if that is necessary."

"You mean fight."

"If necessary," she confirmed, expressionless.

"It's never necessary," said Idris, still weak and vulnerable, spineless as jelly, and yet not stopping, as though his vulnerability was somehow his secret weapon.

"Idris." A new voice. One Solace had come to dread. Always at your shoulder when you least wanted, bringing doom in its wake. "Idris, it's time."

She turned to find Ash right there, far too close to have crept up on them. It seemed more agitated than usual, the veneer of inscrutable calm cracked. Its hood was cast back, the lie of its human shape exposed. Its cluster of reddish eyes and slits regarded her from the twisted, leathery column of its tentacle arm.

"What do you mean, it's time?" Hallow demanded. Then she was on her comms. "What are the Colonials doing?"

Obviously they weren't doing anything. The look Hallow turned on Ash was angry. "Harbinger, I understand that you feel a certain historical prerogative—"

"Idris," Ash broke in. "Idris, you have to get to the Machine."

"I know!" Idris snapped, every bit as irritated with the creature as Hallow. "But they won't let me. I've found them, Ash. They're right down there. I need to—"

"No, listen to me, Idris. You have to get to the Machine *now*. You and the other Intermediaries must ready the Eye to descend into unspace. There's no more time."

Solace and Hallow exchanged uncertain looks, but Idris for once completely missed the subtext.

"Ash, I can reach them. I can show them who we are. Like before. I just need to tell them we're here. Whatever they're doing. Listen, I know you hate the Architects. I know. You and Ahab and everyone else. But *you* know I'm right, that they do it because they're forced. So if I can reach their masters and just tell them—"

"They know, Idris," Ash said flatly. "Believe me. They know we're here. Their understanding of the situation is absolutely clear. We are the thing they send the Architects to eradicate. Their awareness of us is not something you need to bring about—it has been growing all this time and is now complete.

They are moving against us *now*, Idris. You and your cadre must shift the Eye out of the real immediately because they know it's our only hope and they are coming for it."

22.

Idris

He didn't need to tell the other Ints something was going on. When he burst into the awkward, slant-walled space within the Eye where they'd been billeted, most of them were on their feet already. The rest were only sitting because they needed to clutch their heads, or were otherwise suffering from the proximity of what was coming. All through the journey back over here, after leaving Ash, Idris had felt space outside the Eye twisting tightly. And he'd caught the edge of panicked communication from every ship out there hosting an Int pilot, both Partheni and Colonial.

"We need to leave right now!" He had his mouth open to utter the words, but Andecka Tal Mar was already saying them to him. Her eyes were wide, her scars livid. Idris could only nod frantically. Inside his head was a dreadful fear that, once they fled, they'd be fleeing forever. Something deep in the pit of the abyss had finally *noticed* them specifically.

"Idris, what's going on?" Kris's voice in his ear.

"We need to go!" he told her, then stared about him at the Ints. "Get into the Host scales, if that's where you need to be. Go to the Wellhead, the Machines, otherwise. We're leaving now. Right now."

"That will not be possible." A new voice, neutral and sexless, shunted into the conversation. For a terrifying moment he thought it was the *enemy* somehow. Here dispassionately to inform him that he could never escape. A moment later he came to his senses and realized it was the Assembly, the hive mind of the Crux system.

"It has to be possible!" Idris insisted.

"Modifications to the Eye are still being undertaken. Idris, you can't just leave." And, partway through the sentence, it became Trine talking to him. The new Trine.

He opened his mouth, reaching for arguments, for the ability to put into words the madness going on in his head. Then the madness came to the universe outside and his explanations were no longer necessary.

He felt the breach. They all did—the whole room of Ints, just like back in the war. Andecka and some of the others staggered out of the room, heading for shuttles, suits and the temporary lines strung between the Eye and the Host. Other Ints had already made it into the orbiting scales, and he could only hope they were holding it together, awaiting the word to leave. The Architects had arrived.

He accessed a view from outside, projecting it skewed and distorted across a rippled span of wall. The first Architect had come out of unspace at speed. Normally they emerged sedately, as though taking a moment to gather themselves before cruising towards the planet they'd picked as their victim. This one came out hot, fast, spinning, as though forcibly ejected. Its spine-jagged front and curved back chased each other through a dozen revolutions before it stabilized, and Idris could see a maze of cracks where the stress of entry into the real had damaged it. For a moment he felt an untoward soar of hope. One crippled Architect could surely be fielded by the Partheni fleet, or...

The second Architect breached under greater control, though still closer to them than their usual custom, and already in swift motion, coming in from another quarter entirely. A third followed, further out, flashing with vaporized particles as a whole glacier-sized sheet of its crystal hide sheared off. They were bearing for the Eye, and he could hear them in his head. Screaming voices, distant, raging, in pain. The cracks across their faceted surfaces were the welts of their masters' whips. They were being driven, a stampede that could obliterate a star system.

By the time he'd registered this, two more had spun out of unspace, further out still, moving more slowly but accelerating.

"We have to leave," he told the Assembly, the understatement of the millennium. Somehow, despite the hideous torsion space and unspace were going through, he found his mind absolutely clear. Raging with pain and horror, but he could put it all at arm's length. Perhaps tortured spacetime was his natural habitat now, something that life as an Int had adapted him for.

"Modifications are being completed," Trine told him in his ear, and then, "I am trying to get to you, Idris. I am not sure I'll be able to."

"What is the plan, if I could ask?" Doctor Shinandri's voice broke in. "We are submerging? We are anchoring? The grand expedition at last?"

"No, just getting out!" Idris said. Then Ash was abruptly on the comms call too, overruling him.

"We must," said the Harbinger. "This is the endgame. *They*

understand what we have here now. That at last it's something which can threaten them and their servants. They will never let us rest, and will hound us anywhere in the universe. We are a beacon to them now, and they will tear stars apart to stamp us out. We dive. We anchor ourselves to the Partheni ship and then we dive. It is time to end this."

Even as Idris heard Ash's words in his head, the alien had an open channel broadcasting across the Crux system, on Partheni and Colonial frequencies.

"Listen to me, defenders of humanity. I am Ash, whom you call the Harbinger. I came to Earth over a century ago and warned you the Architects were coming. I tell you now that the day has finally come when we can take the war to them. This threat you see before you is a sign of panic within our enemy. They know we can hurt them, at long last. This vessel is being prepared for a strike into unspace, against the Architects. We can destroy them, wipe them from the universe. But we need time, my friends. We are preparing to liaise with the *Judicious Valkyrie* to begin our assault into unspace, and we need your help. Colonial and Partheni, shoulder to shoulder, one last great battle. As you've defended your worlds and bought time for their evacuations, defend us now. Be our shield, and we will be your sword. We will bring this war to an end once and for all. But if you allow us to fall here, there will be no second chance. You will be under the shadow of the Architects for ever."

In the echo of that, Idris could only think wildly of old stories about foolish mortals challenging the gods and being cast down. He knew the plan and it felt like hubris even to him. Then he heard Exemplar Hallow's tight voice on the comms.

371

"I'm back aboard and bringing the *Valkyrie* to you. Be ready to establish your anchor cable."

"We will be ready." Trine's voice, now the Assembly at large, once again. On another screen Idris saw the Hiver factory launching an explosion of glittering motes that were individual frames, plus the great blocks of their larger bodies, the miners and haulers.

"What are the others doing?" He pictured ships slipping away, leaving them to their fate. *It's surely what I'd do if I had the option.*

The Partheni fleet was splitting, heading towards the closest two Architects. Solace was at his shoulder, liaising with her sisters. Most of the ships out there had an Intermediary installed, and they'd be able to deflect or distract the Architects, as the mass looms and other conventional weaponry battered away. But there were five Architects inbound now, far more than they could deal with. Even, for that matter, with the Colonial help which appeared to be sticking around.

Solace moved perspectives on their projections, showing *Ironwriter* and *Redcap* breaking from the others and moving to intercept one of the further Architects. They were liaising with their Partheni opposite numbers, he realized. Actually talking to the lesser enemy, because here was *everyone's* enemy. He felt a moment of utter frustration. *Why does it always take* this *to make us remember we're kin?*

Two other Colonial ships stayed back to defend the little diplomatic vessel, *Broken Key*, while the rest got lumberingly under way splitting up, and trusting the Partheni not to take advantage of their divided forces. Idris suddenly realized that, of all of them, only the *Ironwriter* and the *Broken Key* itself carried an Int. He could feel the needlepoint of their minds as they began to reach out towards the oncoming Architects. The rest of the Hugh fleet was just going to dash itself against the rocks and hope it made a difference.

His own people reported to him then: Ints in position across the Host. Ints being plugged in by Shinandri and Jaine at the Wellhead. A rapid patter of data was coming from the Hiver technicians, closing job after job as they finished adapting the Eye for its unprecedented voyage.

"Contact," said Solace at his shoulder. Almost a whisper.

The first Architect to have breached was already disintegrating, swiftly enough that Idris wondered if the wounds were self-inflicted, some gargantuan suicide as it bucked under the hands of its masters. The Hivers were bombarding it, super-accelerating their largest frames and powering them directly at every crack and fracture in the entity's hide. He felt each impact resonate inside him as unspace shook and shuddered to it. And he felt the Partheni mass looms clench kilometres of space with incredible gravitic forces. He sang along with their Ints, nested in their battery of mechanical amplifiers, as they tried to occupy the creature's vast, tormented mind.

It was burning. You couldn't burn in space, not like that, but Idris *felt* it ignite. The Architect's mind immolating from within. He gabbled on the comms, trying to get a warning to the ships, unable to form words in any known language. Then the Architect shattered. For a moment the Crux system had a small extra star. The scything wave of energy and shrapnel turned one of the Partheni vessels into particles and junk, and crippled another.

The second Architect was already closing in, still spinning

after its eruption from unspace, a wild careering progress. The Partheni loosed on it, and now the *Grampus* and the *Leopard* joined them. Int minds scrabbled against it but the Architect was maddened, trapped within its own crystal bulk. Off course, even for the Eye now, as though the creature had lost all control of its trajectory.

It struck the hive. Idris felt it within his brain, saw it on the projected screens. Heard the horrified gasp of Solace at his ear. One moon-sized object colliding with another, save that the Architect was solid and the Hiver factory was all honeycombed spaces. He saw the vast metal rhombus of the hive crumple and fold inwards, a thousand little explosions venting briefly into the vacuum as critical systems were compressed and ruptured. It remained locked to its murderer, impaled on the Architect's spines, falling...falling in the only meaningful direction it could. Towards the gas giant of Crux right below it, since the impact had knocked the hive and its enemy into the reach of the orb's appalling gravitational drag. Idris watched helplessly as the tangled giants began their inexorable descent into its crushing depths.

"Trine," Solace got out. One name amongst the thousands of instantiated individuals meeting their deaths even then.

"We're in position." The calm, professional voice of Exemplar Hallow came through. "Ready for anchoring. Do whatever you have to do."

No. Idris clutched at Solace. His mouth was open but he couldn't get the words out. What was the point of seeing the disaster unfold if he couldn't warn anyone? "No!" he got out, a howl that had Solace jerking away from him in shock.

The next Architect breached from unspace right on top of them. Barely two thousand kilometres away, closer than the old moon had been to lost Earth. For a moment the Eye, the Host, the entire assemblage, lost its own gravitic integrity, each shard and scale of it drifting out of place, and atmosphere hissing away through every gap. Then they regained control, with every red light and damage telltale demanding attention. They lazily skewed towards the immense crystal mountain range bearing down on them, and Hallow's *Judicious Valkyrie* was...

Gone, already gone. Atoms and streamers of metal, a lacework of fine strands across a hundred square klicks of space, Hallow and all her crew along with it. Their anchor, disintegrated.

Everyone was on comms demanding to know what to do. Every Int was in Idris's mind, screaming. All waiting for the crushing might of the Architect to reshape the Eye into filigree and dreams.

But it didn't happen. Idris felt his brain jolt back on track, thinking right, remembering the limits of the enemy. They couldn't just crush or reshape the Eye. It was Originator tech, and the Architects *never* destroyed Originator tech. They had avoided it, in the old days. More recently, they'd removed it, excavated it, put it out of the way before going about their deadly business. People had thought the Originators scared them, back in the day, imagining some godlike entities from the dawn of time that even the Architects had been terrified of.

Standing there, awaiting the enemy's obvious next move, he understood. He'd been close to the centre, after all. The Eye had given him that marvellous perspective. There, deep towards the heart of unspace, in the very shadow of the Presence, he'd looked back towards the glimmering surface.

Where the unreal met the real. The shallows of unspace, where the Throughways were etched like writing on the inside of the universe. The Throughways, which were also the work of the Originators.

There, as the Architects systematically destroyed all opposition, he understood. Yes, they were terrified of the Originators. And yet they handled their relics with reverence and care. Because the Originators were their masters, sitting at the heart of the universe and looking out at their ancient etchings for...why?

"Why" would have to wait. The Eye shuddered around him, not from gravitic torsion but from physical impact.

"Uh, people?" Olli's voice on comms. "Got some news from the dock," meaning where the *Vulture God* was sitting on the outside of the Eye, next to the easiest access to the interior. "We've got company." If the Architect couldn't destroy the Eye, then it seemed it would do the next best thing. Send pieces of itself down to clear out all the inconvenient living things that had colonized its masters' great work.

Olli

"Well, shit." Olli's throat was dry, and cussing at the universe didn't seem to be boosting her spirits the way it used to.

The Architect had hit the landing platform with pinpoint accuracy. Nine crystal spears lancing through the gravitic field the Host was putting out, slamming down into the stone of the Eye. The closest was about twenty metres from the *Vulture God.*

I mean, could have been worse.

It had been worse for somebody. One of the scale units of the Host, caught in the firing path, had just been atomized, along with whoever'd been inside it. And the wreck she'd left of the Uskaro shuttle now had an extra hole, not that anybody would be shedding tears about that.

So obviously she and Kit had retreated back to the *Vulture God* when it all kicked off. The pair of them had no plans to run, if that even looked like an *option* given the shit that was going down out there right now. It was the fact that, if things got real bad, then Idris, Kris and Jaine would need a way off this rock. Sitting tight on the *God* was all the agency Olli and Kit had in this ridiculously out-of-their-league situation, and so they'd been doing just that. Then the war had come to them.

She'd seen these things at work on Arc Pallator, going for the Originator city-thing they'd had there—the precursor to the Architect trashing the world entire. These crystal boys had turned up and just dug it all out, sending it floating off into space. Architects never harmed Originator toys.

But the Eye was all Originator toy, save for the little bits and bobs Ahab and Jaine and the Hivers had bolted on. Olli reckoned that meant these crystal boys would find it easier to just clear out everything that *wasn't* Originator-made. Meaning her, Kit and Kris and all the rest.

They were forming now, just as she'd seen them do on Arc Pallator. Each of them fluidly shifting form while remaining hard and faceted crystal. Reshaped into the image of ... creatures, aliens. Things she'd never seen in the flesh, nor would ever want to if Idris was right about them. He'd said they took on the shape of all the species the Architects had made extinct. Preserved in this way and no other. The nearest thing lifted itself up on three stumpy legs, twin lines

377

of waving, tubular arms up its front. The next one along looked like nine spiders stuck together at uncomfortable angles. Past that was a monster which was three-quarters raptorial beak, with a beard of tentacles, eyestalks or something, and a single mollusc foot. Hard to tell anatomical details when it was all just blank crystal.

"Olli?" Idris, on comms.

"Uh, yeah, bit of a problem here."

"I'm coming, Olli."

"Oh good, wow, great. Really looking forward to that. You'll be a great help." Olli had been using her walking frame aboard the *God* because it hadn't seemed that punching stuff would be the solution to any of their problems. Now a problem had arrived that would at least let her get within arm's reach. Or tentacle's reach anyway. She linked to the mangled Scorpion's command board and directed Aklu's legs to lift her into it.

"Terrible idea," Kittering told her. "Please desist."

"I'm going to fuck them over," Olli decided.

"That is very much not how things will fall out," Kit said.

She checked the *God*'s eyes. The crystalforms were all shaped up now. Some of them were taking tentative steps towards the Eye's interior, but the nearest two were definitely considering the ship.

"Don't reckon they're going to give us much of a choice, Kit. Turn the lasers on them."

"Nonsense, nonsense," Kittering complained. The *Vulture God*'s mining lasers, good for carving up asteroids or hull metal, made a beautiful prismatic show when refracted through Architect crystal, causing no visible damage whatsoever.

"Okay then," Olli said, and let herself down from the drone

bay hatch, emerging into the dubious cover of the docking claws. Aklu's gift moved like greased monkeys around her. Her mind was in it, just like with any remote system, but there was far too much of it to consciously control. Instead, parts of it were constantly turning up at her mind's elbow like enthusiastic dogs, showing her how they'd done exactly what she'd have wanted if she'd had the time to give explicit instructions. Aklu's gift, Olli decided, was a *good boy*, and she spared a moment to bless the memory of Aklu. An incomprehensible alien gangster and murderer who'd liked her a bit, for some reason.

"Kit," she said. "Get Junior caught up. Have us ready to move."

"Nonsense," he said again, but she knew he'd do it.

"Right then," she told the nearest crystal thing. And went very cold. It was looking at her.

Actually, it wasn't. She didn't even know what bits of the tripod shape were supposed to be sense organs. But she knew two absolute truths about these crystal boys. Firstly, they didn't pay any attention to you, because you just weren't important enough. Mess with them and they'd cut you up, but otherwise if you stayed out of their way they'd just get to work and leave you alone. Secondly, you absolutely couldn't do anything to them. They just reformed around any damage and were built-in unpunchable.

But this one was definitely looking at her. Not at the ship, that big non-Originator thing it would have to remove, but right at Olian Timo, drone specialist. She shifted left on her slithering forest of tentacles. It pivoted to follow her. Then they all did. Even the ones headed inside had stopped and come back for her.

So the first thing she absolutely knew about these things

wasn't true. Which made the second thing kind of inconvenient because every one of the fuckers was now coming right for her. And the scariest thing about *that* was there wasn't any *them*, not really. They were just puppets. What moved them was the Architect itself, manipulating them with the same gravitic finesse it would use to reshape planets. So right now it was the actual goddamn *Architect* paying a close personal interest in her.

"Kit."

The *God*'s lasers spoke again, which at least meant she had a pretty light show to be killed in. Olli had seen that beam melt warship-grade metal and couldn't conceive what the crystalforms were doing with all that energy.

"Kit, I think you'd better get the *God* clear. You can come back for me when I'm done here."

"Immediately without is an Architect," Kittering told her over comms. "Under no circumstances."

The tripod-thing started stumping towards her with a comical swagger. She wondered what the original species had been like before the Architects erased it from the universe. Probably fun guys. She reckoned she could have had a drink and a laugh with them.

"Idris," she said.

"Coming!" He actually sounded out of breath. She imagined him barrelling through the corridors of the Eye, a skinny, jug-eared famie a hundred years old in the body of an unfit twenty-something. Natural saviour material, obviously. And maybe he had magic Int-woo he could do, but he wasn't going to be here in time so it didn't matter.

She lamped the crystalform with half her tentacles. *Live by the fucking sword.*

It exploded. Actually shattered into fragments. Some of those fragments tried to come back together, but most of it just went everywhere, spanging off the *God*'s hull and the walls, or just hurtling out into space.

Olli stared. For a moment the crystalforms were still too, and it was as though she and the Architect were sharing one long what-the-fuck moment about what had just happened.

She backed off a little, watching them. The remaining eight crystalforms fanned out and shifted shape, their various limbs lengthening, growing barbs and spines. Weaponizing, adding extra reach.

One of them then tilted forwards. It was a vaguely centaur-form shape with a half-dozen arms, but she only registered this in retrospect because the top third of it turned into jagged shrapnel and blasted at her like a rock-salt shotgun. She screamed, closing her eyes, throwing up her arms—or the stumps within the Scorpion pod and all those weaving tentacles. Instantly her head became full of damage markers for half a dozen of her artificial limbs. They all came with self-repair estimates, though. All that liquid Hegemonic tech sloshing around, regenerating components. And there was more. Half the shards had just bounced away. *I've got gravitic shielding on this thing?* But she didn't. Or at least it was denying she did, and why would it lie to her? Instead the shards had altered their own course to...not hit her? Not hit the specific parts of her she was presenting.

"I'm just going to get stuck in," she told Kit. "I have no idea what's going on but it's on my side, so I'm going to tear them all a crystal new one."

"Hegemonic tech," came Kit over comms. "Well known that they can transport active Originator regalia."

"Well, yeah." Olli skittered herself towards the nearest crystalforms, weaving aside from the next barrage of shards. She got clipped but came through mostly intact and then had the thing in her grasp. It lanced at her with arms grown spindly and sharp, and she dashed it against the rock of the Eye, then threw it at its nearest friend. "I remember. All that shit with the *Oumaru*. Where it all started going wrong for us, yeah?"

"Aklu's personal legs are currently being worn," Kit went on doggedly. "Aklu, permitted to go against the Architects in its role as rebel Essiel. Aklu insured its legs."

"Kit, you are making no—*fuck!*—sense." A crystal limb lanced through the bubble of the Scorpion's cockpit, shattering its plastic case. A heartbeat later she'd swatted it away, smashing it into pieces. There was a long scratch down her face where one sharp-edged fragment had gashed her. *See that scar, lads? Got that from when I was brawling with an Architect.* Hilarious story. She hoped she'd get a chance to tell it.

"Anti-Architect insurance!" Kittering insisted in her ear. Then a crystalform hit her like a truck, bowling her over in a rolling tangle of tentacles, trying to carve its way to her. She got hold of it with most of her arms and prised it off so she could beat it to pieces against the ground.

"Kit—" she got out, and then she had the attacker at arm's length, which was a distance she had considerable choice over. Finally she understood.

"Originator regalia?"

"Indubitably!"

Aklu's magic legs. She slammed the crystalform—just a tangle of jutting limbs itself now—down against the ground, feeling it crack into lifeless pieces. And not reforming them-selves together any more. Just a fortune in dead gems, pieces of Architect. What was the market value for that, eh? She'd have to have Kit make some scratch calculations.

She rose up on her limb-tips, looming over the remaining five crystalforms. Flexing. She had about thirty limbs still operational. That was a lot of flex. Segmented tentacle limbs filled with Hegemonic liquid tech, sure. But with something else too. Now she knew what to look for—that there even *was* something to look for—she found it readily enough. Every single tentacle held a piece of Originator relic at its tip. No wonder the Architect couldn't take its non-existent eyes off her. Because everyone knew Originator crap warded them off. The Architects wouldn't *do* things to it like they'd do to everything else in the universe. That didn't make them a weapon. Except, apparently, if you started actually lamping bits of Architect with those little relics, the Architect would give way first, rather than risk damaging any of this sacred stuff. Whatever forbiddance prevented the Architects from screwing over all that dusty old tat was apparently *that* impor-tant to them.

I could push off from here and start carving the big fucker up right now, she thought. That probably wasn't true. Even if it wasn't able to reshape her, it could likely just ping her off into space like a flea. But right then she felt immortal.

When Idris actually arrived, utterly out of breath and without a plan, she'd demolished the rest. Half her limbs were down for self-repair and regeneration, and she'd had to improvise two extra straps to keep her in the ravaged control pod. But she had just gone toe to toe with an Architect and won the round, and was all ready to call it the greatest victory the human race had ever won. Then Idris turned up with a terminal case of the long face and apparently it wasn't a win after all.

"We lost our anchor," he told her, not even really appreciating what she'd just pulled off. "The *Judicious Valkyrie*'s gone. And unspace is... There's so much, Olli. So much mass."

Olli looked up, which meant looking straight into the jagged topography of the Architect filling their slice of sky. "Yeah, well," she admitted. "So...?"

"So anchoring remains a solution," Kittering informed them over the comms. "Conversations are ongoing with Shinandri and Jaine even now. Requirement is solely for a vessel with Intermediary-level navigation capability, together with the capability to enter unspace despite current mass interference, am I correct?"

"But we don't have the *Valkyrie*," Idris insisted. Olli wasn't even sure he'd heard half of what Kit said. "And they're all —the rest of them, they're fighting..."

"You thinking Junior, Kit?"

"Junior is showing great keenness for leaving," Kittering confirmed. "Idris, the *God* will be your anchor. It is being linked even now to Shinandri. There is a necessity for clear space to allow the Host to dive and create your 'well.' All correct?"

Olli watched the disparate pieces of Idris's face chase each other about as he tried to get his thoughts in order. She had a sudden, unwelcome moment of empathy. Here they were, at the lynchpin moment, and he was paralysed. Too much going on in his head. Too many cosmic calculations. He goggled at her and flapped his lips as his mind just stalled.

"Right," she said. "Kit? Can we get an outside channel? Tell them what we're about. Get us some space. Idris? Idris, listen to me." She felt like slapping him but that would probably have relocated his jaw halfway across the dock. "Idris, will you just do your fucking *job*? You're an Int, aren't you? So go bug the Architects until they give us breathing space."

With that she was climbing back into the *Vulture God*'s drone bay, hauling herself in a tangle of complete and damaged limbs, until the watery globe of Junior's tank hung above her.

"You'd better be good for this," she told it. The Ogdru was circling its little living space in rapid arcs, very obviously desperate to leave.

"I've got control," she told Kit, and proceeded to lift the *God* up out of there, right towards the jagged and bristling face of the Architect.

Goddamn it, Idris, just for once...

She linked to the eyes Jaine had installed at the dock, seeing that skinny little figure still standing there, like the world's most inconsequential man. Like a core-world caricature of inferior spacer genetics and health. Then she saw him lift his hands towards the Architect above, fingers crooked into feeble little claws.

It shuddered. Even as the *God* was lifting off, she saw it jolt, as though that whole crystal sky had flinched. *Architect, meet Idris. Your problem now.* "Kit?" But even as she asked, he was broadcasting.

"Transmission from the *Vulture God*. Anchor duties for the Eye have been assumed, and we are offering an open contract to all comers: give us space to work! Enlisting all willing ships to engage selected Architect, currently distracted by our Intermediaries! Premium remuneration up to and

385

including salvation of sentient life in the universe. In return, all efforts will be engaged in ridding the universe of the Architects. Do we have any takers?"

It was probably just as well that Kit's comms weren't picking up Olli killing herself laughing over in the drone bay.

Except it maybe wasn't so funny. Most likely she and Kit had just asked a lot of people to get themselves killed on their account. So not funny at all in fact.

"Doc Shin?" she asked. "Jaine, you there?"

"Olli." Jaine's welcome voice, and Olli felt a pang of uncharacteristic sentiment. Someone whose voice she was actually glad to hear. "Olli, we've established the necessary system links with the *God*. We need to submerge into unspace. You'll need to give us, what, ten clear seconds to establish the parameters of the well. After that you'd better get out of there."

"Yeah, well, no shit," Olli said. One of the Partheni ships was coming in, right at the Architect, mass looms singing away and weaving cracks and chasms across its surface.

"And you can't stay under long, or there's a danger you'll stop anchoring us. Short jumps only, got that?"

"Well I hope *Junior's* got that," Olli said. "Cos it's Junior's show." She checked over the data that Kit had fed the Ogdru. It all looked solid, as best she could tell.

"Just stay in the real as much as you can," Jaine told her. "Otherwise we'll be cut off in the deeps. We'll lose each other, and then possibly we'll cease to exist entirely. It's not meant for us to be real in, down there. Hard vacuum is a puppy dog compared to unspace, right?"

"Right," Olli agreed. And then, "Fuck," because that was the Partheni gone, the whole warship just stripped nose to tail into streamers of loose matter. And the *Vulture God* was next.

Maybe Idris was pulling out all the stops, or the other Ints on the Host were, but for a long, yawning moment the Architect just hung there like all the sky there was, and it didn't fall on them. They were coursing across the upside-down mountain ranges of its face, closer than any living beings had any right to be to such an engine of destruction. Yet they lived. They lasted. Olli held her breath.

"Good luck," from Jaine, and then the Eye was submerging. She saw the sudden flare of its gravitic field as the Host units worked together, taking that segregated piece of the physical universe and plunging it down into unspace. Fighting the resistance of physics, the integral separation between *the place where things exist* and *the place where they can't*. Her eyes twisted, trying to follow it. Light bled away from the leading edge of the Eye, shifting through the spectrum, past red and into shades she shouldn't have been able to see. She had the sense of all space as a tortured membrane, trying to eject the Eye right back out again, and then it was gone, with a twisting movement that made her feel sick to her stomach. Something wrong at a fundamental level, a crime committed against universal laws.

"Jaine? Idris? Talk to me!"

A long fraught moment. And her eyes were drawn to the immensity of the Architect. It too was probably wondering what the hell had just happened, but she reckoned it would remember the little *Vulture God* soon enough.

"Jaine?"

"Olli?" Not Jaine but Kris. "Olli, we're…Oh f—" For a heart-stopping moment, there was nothing but static, then

Kris's voice again. "No, we're back. God, for a moment it was just me here. But we're back. All of us. The bubble's holding. All hands to the pump on the repair side, but we're here. The well up to the real is intact. We're descending." And, distantly behind her, the triumphant bellowing of Ahab sounded. "Olli, you need to get away now," Kris said.

"Yeah," Olli whispered, eyes full of that crystal landscape. "Kit, any time now."

Above her, Junior's revolutions had become more and more agitated.

"Further problems are impeding us." Kit's translated voice was very quiet. Then he was broadcasting again. "Any ships that can assist, this is our last moment of exit. Will any volunteers come forth?"

Why hasn't it crushed us? And then Olli understood why. *It's me. It's Aklu's legs. It's the Originator relics.*

But that means...

She saw the crystal spines launch, just snapping away from the Architect's substrate and then hanging above/below it, before being bodily thrown at the *God*. She was jinking already, making it hard for them, fighting the groping gravitational claws of the entity as it tried to pin them down. One spine clipped their brachator drive, sending them into a spin. Another passed so close to one of the aft cameras that she saw nothing but crystal through it for a fragment of a second. And then the shards were flying wild, because the Architect had something to distract it.

It was the *Broken Key*, the little sliver of a diplomatic barge that Hugh had sent. Of course it would have an Int, a good one. Nothing but the best for the important folks in the expensive clothes. It cut across, between the *Vulture God* and the Architect, and doubtless the Intermediary on board was doing everything up to and including yelling in the monster's ear to keep it busy.

Never thought I'd be grateful for the goddamn Diplomatic Service Office, Olli conceded, and then they were getting signals from Junior: a crack, a mousehole, the barest space the Ogdru could thread the needle through, to take them into unspace past all the gravitic interference of the Architects. Ogdru were monstrous predators in their home seas, but this specimen knew bigger fish when it met them and it wanted to get away.

"Go," Olli agreed, and they ducked into unspace, destination anywhere but here, so long as they were quick enough to preserve the integrity of the well.

PART 4
BEYOND

23.

Havaer

"Well," said Havaer. "There goes my ride." Watching the Host carry the ragged megalith of the Eye off. And here he was aboard the *Counter-War Vessel DKT26 Vantus Yards Provisional*, currently engaged in christening its shipyard-new accelerator batteries against an Architect. Because he'd done the polite professional thing and accepted an invitation.

He had a good seat for the show, at least. The debriefing room where Diljat had set him up had a good suite of screens. They'd be able to watch all the impending doom he could stomach.

"That's the *Ironwriter* gone," Diljat said flatly. She was sitting across a metal desk from him, proper Mordant House style. This was supposed to be Havaer's last dregs of due diligence, giving a proper report to someone still unequivocally in the service. There should have been kaffe, at least. He'd been promised kaffe. Sadly the Architects had arrived before it had.

Off to the fore of the *DKT26*, the vast lunar bulk of an Architect revolved ponderously, its forest of crystal spines dawning like a knife-edged Judgement Day morning. Havaer found himself considering numbly that here was a thing which had destroyed planets for its own mad reasons, reworking matter from atoms up, and it had a *front* and a *back*. How weirdly trivial of it.

He heard the distant choir of the warship's accelerators, their energy singing through the hull with an eerie voice. The impacts of the barrage of superfast shot were invisible, though. The Architect didn't deign to notice them.

"Well, this is probably it," he said.

"The Hanni was really telling the truth, do you think?" Diljat asked him. "Saving the universe?"

He met her gaze, wondering what reassurance she was looking for. *That we, the shadowy agents of misrule, did the right thing at the last.* "Yes," he told her. "Absolutely."

She shrugged. "Best of luck to them, then."

The Architect slipped sideways and was gone. The hull of the *DKT26* screamed in protest at so much mass being suddenly removed from local space. And he could see, down on the gas giant, storms blooming like sudden bruises. Red and purple whorls bursting into angry life in the upper atmosphere.

They were gone. All of them suddenly gone. Save for the one that had collided with the Hiver factory and taken the pair of them down into the planet's crushing grip. And the other, already damaged, which the Partheni had managed to finish off. *Two more Architects on the tally. And how very meaningless that is.*

Diljat was speaking sub-voc on private comms, probably to one of the bridge crew. Havaer used the screens to take stock. There were a handful of Colonial ships, mostly intact. Likewise a handful of Partheni. In a fight with Architects, you were mostly quick or you were dead. It was sometimes possible to escape merely crippled, but you had to work at it.

He watched the cautious motion of the ships left out there. Not regrouping, because that wasn't really how space wars worked. Not much use for rigid formations and marching about on a three-dimensional battlefield the size of a solar system. There was a distinct sense of drawing lines, nonetheless. The Partheni Zero Point fighters formed a loose screen ready to deploy towards the Colonials. Everyone lazily adjusting their targeting in an *I'm not touching you* sort of way. And it seemed to Havaer then, as he sat and felt about a million years old, that they'd been dancing on the edge of this precipice for a long time. At Arc Pallator, yes, and over Criccieth's Hell. And, in a lower-key way, for a while before that too. Even supposedly before Earth was destroyed. Natural humanity and Doc Parsefer's artificial angels eyeing each other and easing off the safety catch. But there had always been some other threat. The Architects, mostly, although even the Essiel had sufficed at Pallator. The war had never quite got up to speed. Now here they were.

"There are," he told Diljat, "a lot of Hivers out there."

She regarded him without expression.

"Loose frames that made it out of the factory before it went down, or were sent out to fight. They've got nowhere to go back to. We should start picking them up. It's our duty, in a time of emergency." *As opposed to turning our guns on our sometime enemies out there.*

She nodded, a single birdlike twitch. "I'll send ahead. Come with me to the bridge. The captain will want to see you anyway. You can tell him what the hell those clowns were really playing at before they went...wherever they went."

"Exactly what they said they were playing at."

"Well then, you can tell him that."

The bridge of the *DKT* was...incomplete. Half the wall panels were missing and there was so much dangerous-looking exposed wiring Havaer almost thought he was back on the *Vulture God*. The captain turned out to be shorter and younger than Havaer and very obviously not someone who'd been intended to take the vessel into an actual fight, as opposed to a test run to see if all its bits were working. Apparently the bits had worked out fine, and so had the captain.

Soon after that, they began taking on stranded Hivers, as Havaer had suggested. Sending out the ship's remotes to round up those who lacked power, and chasing after any whose momentum was sending them far off into the void. And, once it became clear this was what they were doing, the Partheni cautiously joined in, coordinating without communicating, matching the Colonial ships rescue for rescue. Havaer felt Diljat's eyes on him and told her, "They don't want a fight. They didn't come here for that. This part of the Parthenon basically hung itself on making sure the Eye would get to where it's gone now. So those ships out there are full of women who aren't sure what their next move should be. Likely they'll want to go and find their friends, other detachments of their fleet. But if we keep pointing guns, that'll give them other ideas. And it'd be a really easy next move, when you're basically a society of soldiers who live all your days on warships. But there's literally no reason it needs to be that way, unless we decide to go poke them with a stick to see what they'll do about it."

Diljat stared at him for a long time, and then addressed the captain.

"I need a launch, whatever you've got in the hangars that I can fly single-handed, and has a good gravitic drive. I need to get this man to Berlenhof for a proper debrief. In the interim, I'm placing you in command of our surviving ships here. Continue the rescue effort and do not engage the Partheni. Understood?"

Havaer hadn't realized Diljat was throwing around that kind of clout. Likely a more experienced captain would have bristled, but the master of the *DKT* was obviously happy to have someone tell him what to do next. He'd just survived a clash with the Architects. That was more command responsibility in his recent past than he'd perhaps looked for in his entire career.

"What am I, then?" Havaer asked Diljat as she hustled him towards the hangars. "Prisoner? They'll paint me as a Partheni turncoat? Or call Laery a traitor?"

"Nobody knows what the hell you or she are," she told him. "Or, rather, yes, all those things, depending on who you ask. And some of the fingers pointing at you over following Laery will be from inside the Board, you can be sure. Still plenty of people around who were pushing that ark business, and they've got their feet under half the important desks back home. At the same time, it's all come out now and it stinks to high heaven, the way they were going about it. Not exactly popular, the whole 'leaving almost everyone behind to die' thing. Even the Magdan voting bloc's split over it, and you know how seldom that happens."

"So where do you stand?" he asked as they came out to the hangar. He saw the launch being hurriedly prepared for departure.

She shrugged. "That depends on who gets their orders to

me first, Agent Mundy. I am just hoping it'll be someone who wants to hear what you've got to say, rather than put your head on a spike."

Idris

He felt the moment when reality wavered, testing the boundaries of all the theories Trine and Shinandri had dreamt up. They'd started without him, even as he rushed back towards the Machine room. The other Ints were all in place, and he did his best to coordinate them all as he ran, except that kind of leadership had never been Idris's strength. He wasn't inspirational, or someone that anyone sane would want to follow. A stammer and a twitch and a weight of self-doubt. Thankfully Andecka was on it, liaising with each of the manned shards, checking integrity. She must have felt it too, that flicker when the universe tried to disprove their existence. But the maths came out in the end. And then they were *there*. Impossibly there, save that they'd just proved it could be done. Very much present, in the real, in unspace. A bubble of the universe thrust into the crushing lightless depths, connected by a fragile corridor, like the single open road out of occupied territory. And, at the far end of that, their anchor, in the shape of the battered old *Vulture God*. One fritzing system away from annihilation.

He stumbled into the Machine room, hearing Kris say, "The well up to the real is intact. We're descending." Of course they weren't *descending*, that was exactly the wrong way to describe the precise relationship between them and the wider geography of unspace. At the same time, from a human perspective, it was absolutely the correct word.

"Olli," Kris said. "You need to get away now." Their precious anchor was still in the middle of a war zone—would they even be able to get into unspace before the Architects crushed them?

Most of the lights were out in the Machine room. The couches themselves were dead, but there were half a dozen multi-armed Hivers working with Jaine and Ahab to restore power. In the staccato flicker of the remaining lamps, an encounter-suited Doctor Shinandri strode towards Idris with his arms wide, trailing hoses.

"A complete, entire and remarkable success!" he crowed, then winked out of existence. They all did. Idris was left alone in the near-dark, only the last echoes of the doctor's words for company. Somehow they'd survived him.

His ears, eyes and all other senses told him he was alone. The orbiting scales of the Host were vacant. There was not another soul, not a mind left through all the stone tomb of the Eye. And they were falling. His inner ear and the pit of his stomach didn't think so, but his *mind* knew. When he'd had company, it had been a steady, controlled descent. Now it felt as though they were plummeting, like a sinking vessel vanishing into an oceanic chasm. He imagined the trail of bubbles, the last despairing sign that they had ever been there.

And below, the kraken was waking.

Idris found himself smiling.

There you are.

The terror of the unreal void. The illusion of the Other, which the absence of unspace bred in any thinking mind. So said the psychs over at the Liaison Board. Perhaps even they knew they were lying, a falsehood more palatable than the truth. *It's there. It lives in unspace. It cannot abide sharing its domain. It hunts.* Or perhaps it loved company. Perhaps it was just desperate to meet new friends. Such a shame, then, that its mere existence was so searingly intolerable that people murdered themselves, and their ships, rather than face it. People—humans, Hanni, Castigar, Hivers. Sentience, that common brotherhood with such a bizarre and integral relationship to unspace.

He felt the first lazy motions of the Presence, detecting them. Imagined tentacles, barbels, reaching out and tasting the water. A great round eye goggling up through the dark expanse towards them. The Presence, his old companion, rising slowly from its sunken lair just out from the centre of all things. Like the watching, many-headed hound of ancient stories that sat before the door to hell.

Their guardian, then. He felt it grow interested in them, grow closer. Except he didn't think this was right and examined his intuition as a way of staving off his growing awareness of the Presence. Not right, as in not a guardian? Or not *theirs*?

He tried to imagine facing it down. Reaching out to it as he had with the Architects. His mind meeting that unbearable, apposite nature and somehow shaking hands across the divide.

No. Even he, the unspace veteran, shrank from that. *I couldn't.* It was utter negation of thought and being. Existential dread given form and purpose.

And then Shinandri cannoned into him, having been crossing the intervening space all this time. The Hivers were back; Kris was back. The well was there again, extending all the way back to the real. The bubble was intact. He felt the Presence recoil from them, but not forget them, or sink back to its lair. They were still an irritant it had to answer, and *different*. He had the distinct sense of it, as a living thing, flurrying back in confusion. Or else it was a dark tide of oblivion and the re-establishing of the well had lit a lamp against the blackness. For now.

"Sound off!" Jaine called. "Everyone confirm they're still with us. Andecka, roll call the Ints." The sound of each Hiver responding came through. Kris gripped his hand. Solace lurched over to hug him fiercely. That yawning moment of solitude had written new lines on both their faces.

"We're here," the Partheni kept saying. "We made it. We're here." And who knew how many of her sisters had survived, back in the real? But she was right. They *had* made it. Done what nobody had ever achieved before. A group mission into unspace, all of them together.

"Olli? Kit?" Kris was trying their comms up the well. The fact they existed for each other again meant they had not only got the *God* into unspace, but managed to come out again too. The *God* was somewhere, just a short hop from Crux. For the ship could only be their anchor when it existed in the real. Whenever it dipped into unspace, everything collapsed.

Idris had seen the calculations, though he hadn't understood them fully. Doc Shin had sincerely *believed* that, on their anchor re-entering the real, the bubble and all the rest of it would re-establish itself. But then Doc Shin seemed able to sincerely believe a lot of things. Idris was just glad he'd apparently been right this time.

He felt the Presence move, far below them. He didn't know

if it had any conscious sense of its own existence, or whether its devouring attraction to thinking travellers was as mindless as a chemical reaction. But, bubble or not, they remained an irritant to it. It was slow, for now, but was rising towards them even as they descended.

"Re-establishment of contact!" Kittering's voice issued from one of the wall speakers. "Where we are is described by Mesdam Timo as the arse end of nowhere. Deep void, no star, no system. *Vulture God* status: more or less intact. Repairs ongoing. Your voice is a pleasant thing to hear, Kris."

"God, yours too," Kris replied. "We are... What are we doing now, exactly?" She and Solace were standing almost shoulder to shoulder, Idris noticed, and he understood how very alien all this business must be to them. They weren't even the engineers working on the nuts and bolts of the project, like Jaine and the various Hivers. Neither of them the high-science minds who knew the theories. And they weren't Ints, familiars of the unreal abyss. A Scintilla lawyer and a Partheni Myrmidon, down here where the madness lived.

"Our Intermediaries will require some manner of rota, I think we might call it," Shinandri declared. "As their continued intervention and guidance is required to maintain our rather, hmm yes, *unnatural* state here. Perhaps Menheer Telemmier—"

"I'll do it," broke in Andecka's voice, transmitted from whichever scale she was in. "Don't worry, Idris. I'll sort it. We'll have my people on the scales. I'll rotate them on and off service. We'll have our Partheni Ints on the Eye itself, where their mechanical support is. They'll have to pull longer shifts, I think. To keep up. But we can do it. For long enough. We'll be ready. Just point us at the enemy."

The enemy. Idris felt that familiar old weight of depression settle on him again. *Oh yes, we're here to do a genocide.* Even as he thought it, the various couches of the Machine came back online, the Hivers skittering back from each in turn. Ahab was tap-tapping up, its great bulk curving and bludgeoning through the chamber to get to them.

"We near! To hunt, Idris! We bring the burning sword to them!" it trumpeted, and he wondered helplessly what Naeromathi concept had just been humanized into that. They didn't look the type to have developed swords along their path from lost planet surface to space.

I don't want to. But Shinandri was already bringing his suit up, the one that would keep his body going while he was in the Machines for longer than was healthy. The scientist's grin was like a crescent-bladed knife. Idris felt the razor edges of it against his brain.

He lacked the strength to fight the man. Even to make it difficult to get the suit on him. He couldn't stand before them, after what had happened at Crux—after everything that had happened, from the obliteration of Earth onwards —and say, *I don't want to exterminate the Architects.* Or rather, he'd already said it. Mumbled it, muttered it under his breath, whispered it mutinously to himself. Nobody cared. He was just being used in someone else's war, the way it had always been. Except this time it was his friends.

He had been happier alone with the Presence.

Even as he thought of this—almost as if it was *because* he'd thought of it—he felt it move. Whatever distance there had been between it and the Eye was suddenly being eaten up, as the Presence decided to come and give them a proper look. Expose them to its terrible existence, until their minds ablated away before the sheer fact of it. He heard a panicked babble from the Ints over comms, the Partheni pilots in the Eye calling out shocked reports. The others, those without the double-edged senses, knew something was wrong but not what. They'd die blind, when the Presence found them, but they'd still die. Idris wasn't sure which way was best.

He reached for it.

It was a terrible mistake.

And yet, in that moment of hubris, he understood a great deal. As though the tide of the Presence's onrushing filled every channel and cave of his mind. And then it went out again, dragging most of that knowledge with it, but there were pools and puddles left behind. The Presence, the inhabitant of unspace, was real, real, *real*, no matter what they said. The Intermediaries' constant companion as they crossed the solitary spaces between star systems. The monster you'd get if you boiled down the nightmares of every sentient species and gave the resulting protean mass a will and a hunger. Utterly singular, unique and alone in the universe. Evolved or engendered, or simply brought into being by the very axioms of unspace. It was singular for exactly the same reason that every journey in unspace—until now!—always left each traveller alone. Because that was how unspace worked. And that was the cosmic heresy they were committing now, by coming here in each other's company.

It was coming for them, charging headlong, more purposeful than Idris had ever known it. They were still together, but what did that mean, for the Presence? Idris had a sudden, horrifying idea that if the Presence entered their bubble of reality, they'd make it real too. Give it a physical form within the Eye that would be so terrible to gaze upon, mere flesh couldn't tolerate it. Their bodies would shrink from it so utterly that they'd have to transform into something else entirely, robust enough to endure it. Turned to stone, pillars of salt...

That swift, inexorable lunge towards them. Idris held Kris's hand, pulled Solace to him. He could hear someone swearing, others weeping, praying. Ahab roared, little more than static and feedback from its translator.

Then, nothing. It had slipped past them. He had a sense of angry bafflement, more human interpretation placed on something that could never truly be penned in by human ideas. But it had found them, been about to make its Presence very known, and then it was...far off their trail, casting for a scent suddenly gone stale, and...

"Hurry, please." A voice Idris was frankly growing sick of. Harbinger Ash, standing there as if it had been with them all along. Which it most definitely hadn't. "It will return, and most likely won't be evaded so readily. We are something new, and it doesn't know how to locate us within the unreal. But it will learn. First Int shift, into the Machines and take us to where the Architects are."

*

Afterwards, he went to find Ash. At the end of his shift, when they'd disconnected the hoses and confirmed all the observations he'd made before, back when the Eye was still planetside. And after they had confirmed where the Architects were, that knot of structure in unspace, and begun to move the Eye towards it. All those Int pilots, working together the way Ints never did. Feeding their minds into the nothingness of unspace like fungal mycelia, finding the path between *here* and *there*, through a void where neither term had any objective meaning. Taking them to their enemy. When the rest of the Machine shift had gone to sleep, Idris went to find Ash, determined finally to get some answers.

But finding Ash was always a mug's game. It wasn't as though it had a room, a bed, a place. It just turned up, when least looked for, and told you bad things. That was literally its defining role in human history.

So, when Idris found it, out where the *Vulture God* had been docked, he could only assume that Ash intended the meeting too.

"I want answers," he demanded, hands balled into ineffectual little fists.

"Of course you do," Ash agreed, in that smooth, oh-so-human voice it could do. He'd heard it talking to a Hanni ambassador once, making fiddling, chittering sounds and somehow mimicking all the gestures of another physiology through economic motions of its one hand. Ash, the ultimate cosmopolitan.

"I mean, you've got us here now," Idris pointed out. He tried to look past the dock, past the scales of the Host, at the universe beyond. But he couldn't, it wasn't there. Logically there must be a great empty, open gap where he could look unaided into unspace with his fragile human eyes. It was all blind spot, though, out there. His mind refused to resolve any image of it, merely sliding his attention back to Ash. "Your big plan. Or this iteration of it. Tell me you've not got this far with other species in the past and failed."

Ash cocked its head—the sensory limb it pretended was its head—to one side. And said nothing.

"I asked you if you were an Originator once, didn't I?" Or he had certainly intended to. His scrambled brain couldn't remember if he had actually uttered the words. "Or... maybe you're one of *them*. The masters. You're going against the rest? Conscientious objector to the reworking of inhabited planets? Or are you going to pretend there is no *them*? No masters, just the Architects, so you can dodge the morality of what you're doing?"

He didn't think he'd get an answer, but Ash straightened up, losing all semblance of human form, and said, "There is a *them*. There are masters. Almost nobody works that out. You, and a couple of other Intermediary-level species. And us."

"You."

"My people were not *them*. We were never the Originators."

"Because the Originators are *them*," Idris pressed. "I'm right, aren't I? I saw them. They're at the centre of unspace. There *is* a centre to unspace." As though Ash wouldn't understand unless he laid it out logically. "The universe is on the outside. Unspace is the heart of it, and at the heart of unspace... *them*. I saw them, past the edge of the Presence. Like it's guarding them."

"Or they hide," Ash said softly.

"Or that," Idris agreed. "But from the heart of everything you can see... everything. It's like when I was looking into unspace through the Eye. Distance isn't the same as it is in the real. Why would it be? It's huge, but it's *small*. Smaller than the universe, obviously—it's inside the real, and if it wasn't smaller then you couldn't travel faster through it. Stands to reason. From the centre you can see all of it, if your eyes are good enough. You can perceive everything. All the way to the boundary with the real, where the Throughways are. Like stitching. Pulling the universe into shape. Not even roads to travel on, really, except when someone puts that line of stitches in, it makes a path to follow. Just incidentally. And we thought they'd been made for us, for people like us, to move from place to place faster. So why *did* they make them, Ash?"

Ash spread its hand like a shrug. "I don't know, Idris."

"Seriously?" Some childish part of him had assumed Ash had all the answers. "Then what…? Where do you even fit? I'd thought…" That the creature knew it all but was just being inscrutable. Because it seemed in character. Ash didn't join the dots for you. It never had.

"We were the greatest of the Intermediaries," Ash told him. "My people. Of whom I am the last."

"That you know of."

"The last, in the universe. Because I would know. We always knew. We were constantly amongst ourselves. We could speak across the whole of creation, with unspace as our sounding board. And we could travel. Our bodies are our brains and our brains interact with space and unspace in ways no others ever could. You and Saint Xavienne, the Ogdru, the Castigar savants, none of you can imagine. We could go anywhere in the universe just by willing it. So we went inwards, and we found *them*. And *they* were already set on their crusade. They had the Architects as their tools and they were watching for any sign of sentience deforming the firmament above them, so they could unleash their pets and obliterate it. But as soon as they became aware of *us*, we were their utmost priority. Whatever it is that they cannot abide, in life and mind, we were the purest example. And whatever ideology or purpose they have which sentience interferes with, it was most thoroughly aggravated by us. They hunted us down as they have no species before or since, sending Architects against each one of us, personally. We were exterminated over the course of a thousand years, until I could call out into the universe and not a single voice sang back to me. That is what I am, Idris. Not a master, not an Originator, not anything very significant at all. If I have ever pretended to be more, it was only because an air of mystery and power would make others listen to my warnings. I am just a survivor, and one who seeks to prevent the same fate befalling others."

"And revenge," Idris suggested.

"Ah, well," Ash said. "I feel I am permitted a little revenge, am I not?"

"Then . . . why not attack the masters?" Idris asked hoarsely. "Instead of the Architects?"

"Because they have their guardian standing between us and them, and we cannot face it," Ash said simply. "Do you think the minds aboard this ship would survive its attentions, close up? The Architects are *there*, and even if their masters do find some other tools eventually—in ten thousand years' time, or ten million—they will still have been hurt. And they will have been shown that they are not all-powerful. We cannot attack them, but we can cut off their hands. It must be enough."

It isn't enough, Idris thought, and, *It is too much*. But what did he know? He was only human.

Then there was a panicked call over general comms. "Urgent emergency action required!" Kittering's voice, reed-thin and staticky from all the way up the well. "Unspace entry imminent!"

"No, why?" Idris demanded. "You need to stay in the real! That's the point. You're our anchor there!"

"Architects!" Kittering insisted. "Emergence of Architects. Approaching even now. Olli is making calculations for unspace entry. Idris, they are after us. They've followed us from Crux."

24.

Olli

It wasn't as though the *God* had taken a direct hit over Crux, after all. Which was just as well because you didn't tend to walk away from a full-on Architecting. But when the monster had breached right up close to the Eye, the resulting gravitic turmoil had popped a number of the ship's seams and systems out of joint. Olli had been in too much of a hurry to get clear after the Eye had gone, and had just given Junior its head, letting the Ogdru drag them *away*. When they'd emerged out of unspace after a fleeting, nightmarish journey, the boards had been lit up with more red lights than carnival time in hell. She'd just sat there in the Scorpion's command pod, a cold sweat suddenly all over her, thinking about all the wrecks she'd seen where someone had tried an unspace insertion with a damaged ship.

"Well, fuck," she said, caught on the twin prongs of relief and horror about the sheer state of things. "Where've you taken us, Junior?"

The Ogdru floated serenely in its tank. She let some food out for it, some of those unpleasant-looking chunks it liked. They were short of that, and she'd need to find somewhere with a kybernet where she could look up what else they

411

could feed it. It wasn't as though they'd be going grocery shopping in the Hegemony any time soon. By then the *God*'s abused navigation board was talking to her and she answered her own question with "Arse end of nowhere." They were in deep space, not a star for fifty light years and change. Junior had run for the wilderness, and she couldn't blame it.

Kittering was talking down the well. Olli tapped into comms and heard Kris's voice come to them like the woman's own ghost, distant and echoing with a lot of creepy-ass distortion. Sounded like a chorus of damned souls complaining in the background every time Kris spoke. Jolly thought. But they were good, at least. Alive, and still in existence, and so could get on and do the thing. Olli let herself relax just a little.

Meanwhile, they had things to get on with too. Spacer life, that state of being she was used to. It had been quite enough for her before the Architects showed up again and this crappy little salvager had somehow become the lynchpin for saving the universe.

Fucking Partheni. They had dicked her over one last time by having the appallingly bad judgement to get themselves atomized by an emerging Architect. Thereby meaning they couldn't take up the place of honour as anchor for this dumbass expedition. Olli—on her way to her tool locker—paused for a moment, thinking about the way the *Judicious Valkyrie* had become...loose threads. Just spools of wire and lace. *Fuck*, she tried to say, but even that so-familiar word wouldn't come out. She was shivering, she suddenly realized. The tentacles, Aklu's magic legs, twined and their tips screeched against the drone bay walls like fingernails. Her breathing abruptly became too hard, too fast, and the medical telltales in the Scorpion pod started to shout at her, trying to give her a calming shot, except she hadn't kept the drug reservoirs filled since forever.

"Oh," she said. The Architect tearing into the real right on top of them, the ship coming apart—nobody should have to witness something like that. But she was Olian Timo. She wasn't *Idris*, flying into pieces so fast he should have some sort of warning sticker slapped on his forehead. She'd gone through life without most of the standard complement of limbs and she'd adjusted, which meant she was a tough son of a bitch and didn't get...like this.

Her haptics registered a touch on her pod. Just a small one. It was Kit, clinging to the wall to keep out of the restless writhing of her tentacles. He'd tapped her with one extended mouthpart. His shield arms bore screens that had a variety of cheery-looking icons on them: stylized human faces with broad smiles, human hands making what were frankly inappropriate gestures but which he probably lumped in with encouraging signs. Symbols for various currencies, half a dozen human images signifying good luck and a couple of utterly strange things that were probably Hanni equivalents.

"Things are relatively good, within reason," Kittering suggested.

Olli looked into his crown of eyes, the little fixed orbs that had absolutely nothing of human contact in them, but were still *him*, her crewmate, her friend.

"I wish Rollo was here and this was his problem, the malingering bastard," she said.

"This wish is heartily to be concurred with," Kit agreed.

"You going to help me fix things?"

413

"Likewise that."

"Right then," said Olli, feeling the shaking subside, the horror of it sink back down, just like that bastard feeling you got in unspace. Not gone, but not too close, for now. She ran up a triage list with the ease of long practice, knowing her ship and what parts of it would patiently wait for her, and which were the demanding bastards who would get shouty and possibly explosive if they weren't sorted out sharpish. Then she and Kit picked out all the serious toys from the tool locker and set to work. Mending where they could mend. Making do where they couldn't. Re-routing around systems that would require actual miracles to resurrect. Shrinking the ship's world, doubling up, straining the bits that were still labouring on because of all the bits that weren't.

"This ship," she said to Kit, when they took a break to chow down on their diminishing stores, "is not a two-hander. Not even with goddamn technical geniuses like you and me."

Kittering had his own lists of what they needed. Supplies and parts for the ship. Fuel for the reaction drives. Some particularly fiddly and expensive components that the gravitic drive was going to need sooner rather than later. Bulk material for the printers, organic and otherwise. Ogdru kibble.

"We need to get somewhere civilized," Olli said. "Somewhere we can barter."

Kit made a mournful sound with his mouthparts. "A lack of satisfaction with vessel finances. We are not being paid." That might have sounded mercenary, or could just have been taken as typically Hanni, given that honest commercial transactions were what their culture really valued, but it was also true. Nobody had offered them a remunerative contract to save the universe, and nobody had magically stopped a leaky old ship from costing way too much.

"Junior, we're going to need to jump sometime soon," Olli said. Of course the Ogdru couldn't hear her, but she was simultaneously working with the cobbled-together interface that linked her to the tank. And Junior was raring to go, apparently. It was corkscrewing and diving within the sphere of water, increasingly agitated.

Just like before, when...

She felt the lurch. She was no Int, and would never have those brain-gouging senses Idris had been saddled with. Something in her clenched, though, when the Architect breached. It wasn't even close to them. When she'd dropped her focal point into the *Vulture God*'s sensor suite, she saw it way out, only its mass shadow betraying it was out here, where there wasn't even a star to reflect off its crystal hide. And just sitting there. Maybe Architects did this all the time, came out to where nobody ever was, just to get some peace and quiet. Except there was a lot of empty universe, and here it was, within a thousand million klicks of the *Vulture God*.

It was here for them. And now the *God*'s tentative sensor probes were even picking up scarring and damage on the thing, the vast stress fractures left over from Partheni mass looms. It had come from Crux.

They know. She felt her heart jump to double-time, and all the shakes queuing up to take her in their teeth. But she didn't have time for that. Not now. Because it was out there and it was moving. Just lazily for now, not even straight towards them. But casting about for a scent.

415

"Kit!"

"Yes yes!" He had already skittered himself off to the command pod. She saw the *God*'s key systems flare into life one after another, a bare minimum of safety checks before each. He was talking down the well again, warning them. Olli was already negotiating with Junior, but right now the Ogdru was absolutely on message, very keen to get the hell away.

And then they were into unspace and Kit was gone and Junior was gone—just the great vacant watersphere of its tank hanging above her. Olli held on—mentally and, via Aklu's magic legs, physically. She waited, feeling the aloneness creeping in on her and, beyond it, the infinitely worse not-aloneness. Even though she'd done this before, when there wasn't time to get snug into suspension, it never got easier. Her breathing started to become more and more rapid, and claustrophobia clutched at her. For someone living in the close confines of the Scorpion pod, that was really going to be a problem. The universe was crunching in on her. She was the centre of its attention, cupped within its fist and its fingers were closing—

And they were out, just a short hop. She was embarrassed to find herself crying, actually sobbing on open comms. What Kit made of that she had no idea. But she got herself in hand. She was Olian Timo, she didn't have emotional vulnerabilities like regular people. She was the tough one.

Fuck.

"Kit? Where's here?"

"New Kismayo is what the local kybernet is telling us."

Olli screwed up her face for a moment. "Mining dive?" Another resource system picked up by the same Cartography jaunt that had discovered Crux. Another brief jump and she'd told Junior they needed civilization. New Kismayo would have to stand in for that right now.

"And what about...?" A yawning moment of dread, waiting.

"No indication of unspace disturbance. The Ogdru's behaviour?"

"Junior?" She glanced up. The creature was circling placidly enough, rippling up to the tank's liquid edge to goggle at her. "Quiet."

"Likelihood of pursuit?"

"I have no goddamn idea, Kit. Get on to the locals and see what they can give us. I'll keep fixing." And she did, keeping idle track of Kit as he sent his requisition lists in to the company store on New Kismayo. Some of it they had right away, others they could possibly buy from other locals and sell on to the *God*. It wasn't cheap, because the miners were spacers just like Olli and Kit and it wasn't as though they were sitting on great stocks of spare spaceship parts, or even a big old vat of raw printer stodge. They were hostages to the unreliable supply ships from other worlds, and further worlds still, the whole tenuous network of transit and transport that the Architects were carving their way through. Olli had to remind herself forcibly that when Earth fell, humanity had survived worse. If they could make it through the Polyaspora, they could survive this.

And if Idris and the rest do their job, maybe it won't be for much longer.

She listened to Kittering pulling out every stop, jollying them along, playing we're-all-spacers-here. Locating a local Hanni minister and making some sort of pledge she didn't quite understand in return for that worthy's influence. They'd already started loading a shuttle down on the mining colony's single planetside dock.

"I will personally find some rich Hugh bastard and shake them until money falls out, when this is done," Olli promised him. "We will not do all this for free. I'll force them to make a golden statue of us and we can melt it down and live off the proceeds, see right?"

"Right," Kit agreed vehemently. The Hanni sincerely believed in altruism, and they equally sincerely believed altruism should be rewarded. Amazing how often the high and mighty of Olli's own species got forgetful when that second point turned up on the agenda.

One of the many things the miners on New Kismayo didn't have was ready-packaged Ogdru food, and another was any information at all on Ogdru. Hardly surprising given Olli had barely heard of the things before one of them had hunted the *God* all over the galaxy that one time, and now she'd inherited one, which was something of a responsibility. She took samples of the tank water thoughtfully and analysed the trace proteins, trying to build up a picture of Junior's biology from first principles.

At first she thought that intrusion was what had got the Ogdru riled up. A second later her heart clenched and she told Kit, "We need to get out."

"Take-off of the shuttle is just being accomplished."

"No, Kit. Out now. It's still coming for us."

A fraught silence. She thought of New Kismayo, its miners and traders and everyone living down there. *Did we just murder the planet by being here?*

Junior was desperate to go, and Olli heard Kittering babbling quick apologies both to the planetside authorities and down the well to the Eye. Then the Architect rolled out of unspace—not even the same one, she saw. Without the same scars and damage. They were clearly hunting the *Vulture God* as a pack, a whole net of them closing in on her.

They fell into unspace again, despair closing over Olli like the sea.

Havaer

He still wasn't sure quite where he stood. In terms of ideology, status and employment, anyway. Where he stood physically was in an office within the Intervention Board orbital over Berlenhof. One of the offices for peripatetic staff —a central workspace hub with compact little living cubbies radiating off it. Three other Mordant House staff were there at the moment, sitting with slates held close, doing non-secure admin and filing but still not trusting to use projected displays that someone might eyeball too closely. Habits of the trade. They didn't stare at Havaer like he'd grown extra heads. He wasn't infamous throughout the service as *The Man Who...* Who what? Betrayed Earth? Apparently not. He still had no hard answer to the question of just how Laery and her final jaunt was regarded right now, and how the ark-builders were viewed in-service, or in the upper eche-lons of Hugh. He was beginning to suspect that was because there just weren't answers yet. Everyone was trying to work out which the right side of history was, so they could pretend to have been on it all along. Which meant that he, Agent Havaer Mundy, might yet turn out to have been the bad guy, and to retrospectively have been The Man Who... But, right now, he was just drifting along, a piece of the machine nobody was going to trust too much weight to, but simultaneously nobody was going to replace just yet either.

He'd been debriefed. The same tentative Goldilocks approach of not too hot and not too cold. Diljat had overseen it; she'd been cordial enough. He'd told the truth as he understood it. He hadn't kept anyone's secrets. They knew everything that Havaer had known about the Cartel, the Eye, the Partheni, the Uskaros. Not knowing what preconceptions and prejudices he was supposed to play to had been weirdly liberating.

And then they'd decanted him here. He wasn't permitted to travel to the remarkably similar cramped space he called home. Or to go down planetside to the sights of Berlenhof, although he found an almost crippling desire within himself to do so. There were a lot of planets out there that weren't habitable, or even planet-shaped any more, and he wanted to see Berlenhof again, in case he didn't get another chance.

He was filing reports. That was what one did, when one came back to Mordant House. He'd been away longer than usual, and gone further off the beaten path than most, but that just meant the paperwork was more onerous. Some things never changed. He was even getting a handful of consultation prompts from across the agency. The more in-tune operatives tapping him for his take on recent events. Apparently some people thought he was an expert on the Hegemony now, just because he'd been on Arc Pallator and worked with the late and unlamented Aklu the Unspeakable. Whose fit of pique at being dethroned had just about atomized everything at Estoc: shipyards, ark fleet, all of it. Someone had just pinged Havaer a query asking if Hugh shouldn't be filing a formal complaint with the Hegemony about it, and Havaer sat there, dictating a remarkably calm response, explaining why that would be unlikely to help.

Then the top priority requisition came in from Diljat and he left the workspace, walking a short distance through two security checks to the inner offices, as though he wasn't under suspicion of anything at all.

"We've got a situation." Diljat's own office workspace was heavily ornamented. He hadn't seen it before and was surprised. He'd taken her for one of the clear desk, tidy mind school of agent, but there were projected patterns and holographic objects everywhere. Nothing physical, which she'd have to shove in a box if there was a departmental reorganization, but a lot of colour and design following a distinct, baroque aesthetic.

"What's up?" She was sitting on a cushion with a low table in front of her, already displaying the standard stylized Throughway projection everyone used. He took a seat opposite her at her invitation.

"Characterize your relations with the crew of the salvage ship—"

"*Vulture God*," he finished for her. "Seems like all anyone wants from me is my friends these days."

"You'd say friends, then?"

"Actually no. Not really. They probably don't think of me as an enemy. Any more." He considered. "All right, Olian Timo probably still does. I got on all right with Almier, the lawyer. What have they done now?"

"Report from New Kismayo, hot off the packet ship." She opened it up on his side of the little table and he ran through it with professional efficiency. "And this one," she added, even as he did so, "from Koschai Orbital over Grand Imperial Litskwa."

The first was a mining colony. The second was an exceptionally fancy name attached to a small science station and a community of hermits (could you have a community of hermits? According to the brief you could). They both told similar, eye-opening stories. The *Vulture God* had turned up in-system, started a hurried attempt to trade for fuel and supplies and—in the Koschai Station case—some weird-as-hell protein chains. Then the Architect had turned up out-system and lazily starting to move in. Cue the usual panic and everyone running for the docks. The miners and the scientists would probably have been able to make it off entire, given both systems' low population, though Havaer guessed the hermits would have been fucked unless they'd all got together for the annual hermit spaceport tour or something. Except, after the *God* fell off into unspace like any sensible ship would do, the Architect hung about just for a short while, as though considering its life choices, and then did likewise. Neither planet was reworked. It was as though the world-wrecking monsters suddenly had higher priorities.

Havaer was mathematician enough to put two and two together, given that much help with the figures.

"We've sent a Cartography Corps vessel with a very good Int—Demi Ulo, in fact, one of the last of the old guard—out ranging. Ulo reported, just an hour ago as we speak now. Claims Architects have been here, and here, and here." Locations were picked out on the Throughway map, but off the Throughways. So not actually that helpful in terms of the physical universe, save that Diljat was trying to indicate locations proximate to New Kismayo and Litskwa. "Says she can feel the echo of them or some damn thing, and who am I to say she's wrong." Diljat shrugged. "So." She shifted the view, magnifying and restyling one part of the map. "Crux here. Kismayo, Litskwa, Ulo's other data points. And we've had our best data analysts, as well as a handful of contracted Hiver number-jugglers, making predictions that basically give us a limited set of points."

"A predictable course, you think? I wouldn't have thought there was enough information."

Diljat laughed bleakly. "If it was just the *Vulture God*, no. But it's not. Here's the rest of the puzzle." A scatter of additional points, time-stamped. A progression. A steadily closing horizon moving towards possible destinations. "Architect sightings in populated systems. Coming out of unspace. Panic, screaming, you know how it is. Then just…gone. While we prefer that to the whole planet destruction, it's got everyone spooked. But now we know. They're closing a net, Agent Mundy. That one ship has got them chasing all over for it. It's…It's Typhoid Mary, is what it is. A plague ship. And they're obviously desperate to dock somewhere and resupply, but we can't have them anywhere near us. Not with the baggage they're bringing. Who knows when one of those Architects will decide it can spare the time for a little redecoration, hmm? Maybe the only reason they haven't yet is because the ship's only turned up at pissant small spaces." A selection of highlighted Throughway junctions. "Here are the major population centres within a short unspace jaunt of where they're gadding about. And they're not even working via the Throughways. They've got that Int pilot of theirs."

423

"Or the Hegemonic critter," Havaer agreed. At her look, he said, "Telemmier was on the Eye. He'll be doing the, the other thing."

She shrugged. "Our unspace maths boys and the Liaison Board people don't think there is another thing. They believe this Naeromathi and the whole idea is just so much poppy dust." Something must have shown on his face because she managed a sympathetic smile. "I know it's what your chief died for. I also know that we piss about through unspace all the time. Have done for over a century. And our theoretical *understanding* of it isn't anywhere near complete. You can bet they're all going over everything this Shinandri character ever had published back when he was a respectable academic, and I reckon he's gone way further since he went rogue, after partnering up with the Naeromath at the Originator base. So who knows? I'm just saying that our brain boys don't believe it."

"I believe it," Havaer said firmly, to his own surprise. He wasn't sure if it was loyalty to Laery or to the others. The *God* crew, Colvari and all the Hivers, and everyone else who'd suffered to make the dream into a reality.

Diljat nodded, regarding him steadily. "The department has need of you, Agent Mundy. You're being recalled to active service, because of your unique perspective on the events and the people who are currently the biggest pain in Hugh's collective ass."

It was, Havaer considered, a title that Olian Timo would have been proud of.

Olli

The time before, there had been an Architect already waiting for them. Olli had been preparing herself to tackle the most urgent items on the fix-it list, and to get the working parts of the solar array spread out to recharge the *God*'s tanks, and there the monster had been. Just patiently *there*, as though it'd made an appointment and was too polite to point out that the *God* was running late.

She'd wanted to scream at it. But it wouldn't have helped. Right then, it wouldn't even have helped *her*. Instead she was immediately plotting a new course, even though that had become more and more of an academic pursuit, since Junior had ideas of its own about where was best to go.

And now they were out in the real again, with no Architect. Or no Architect *yet*.

"Kit?" She could speak to Kit again, now he actually existed for her, rather than it just being her rattling about in the tin can, listening for the stealthy footfall of The Thing That Wasn't There. She'd been in and out of unspace too much recently, unprotected by suspension. And when she felt that Presence, it wasn't as though it reset every time they returned to the real. Sometimes it picked up right where it had left off the moment they ducked back under.

Ints, she knew, had a superhuman ability to brush that shit off. But she'd never been intended for this kind of jockeying around.

"Next trade request is formulated," Kittering confirmed. He'd been working on a kind of super-condensed trade offer that was also kind of a warning, and possibly even an extortionist's threat. *Lovely colony you've got here, shame if an*

425

Architect happened to it. Get us the stuff on our list because you really don't want us sticking around. Not exactly their proudest moment, but it was that or end up stuck somewhere when they didn't have even the modest amount of power required to drop into unspace. Once they couldn't keep running, and the Architects caught them, that would be the end of Anchor, Wellhead, Eye, Host and all those other dumbass words everyone was throwing around as if they meant anything.

Junior wanted to pop them out into the deep void again, and from a point of view of not recklessly endangering other people, that would have made perfect sense. From the perspective of being convenient for the growing list of things Olli couldn't fix or fabricate aboard ship, however, the utter middle-of-space-nowhere was a problem. Except both times they'd tried actually to trade with someone, that someone had been bureaucratic and resistant to being hurried. Enough that the Architects had turned up to ruin the deal before it could be finalized. Which left them, as far as she could see, with only one way to get what they needed. Cut through the red tape.

So this time, at her insistence, they'd come out somewhere populated. It wasn't actually where she'd wanted Junior to take them, which was an industrial facility with a large Hiver presence, where she reckoned they might get a decent reception. Junior had grasped the idea about going where the people were, though, and taken them to...

"Oscit Niariken," Kittering told her, as she fought over the pronunciation. Local kybernet said there were well over seven million souls down there, which meant a fairly sparsely populated world. But that was still a big number to go down in history as having been murdered by an Architect unleashed on them by the crew of the *Vulture God*. They were mostly Hanni too, despite being within Colonial space. Olli had a brief moment of hoping that would help because, hey, Kit was a Hanni too! Except she was a human and it hadn't helped them hurry things along with the humans of New Kismayo, or that other place with the stupidly long name.

"Send them the thing," she told Kit. "No time to fuck around. Send it to them and then just keep telling them how everything's going to crap unless we get what we want. If it helps to make us the bad guys, make us the bad guys. We are absolutely intergalactic terrorists holding them to ransom. Just tell them to be *quick*."

He wasn't happy about it. She wasn't happy about it. Oscit Niariken was green and blue with nice tufty clouds. There were enormous aquaculture farms down there, the kybernet told her happily. Locations of extraordinary natural beauty, which probably meant something different to Hanni. There was also some sort of live entertainment enterprise renowned across Hannilambra culture, although she didn't quite get what it was or how it worked. It looked like competitive melodrama, from the brief mediotype that turned up.

As Kittering continued haranguing the kybernet, she tried the Well. "Don't know how long we'll be here," she told whoever might be listening. "Not long. I'm sorry. The fuckers are after us. I have to keep running."

"Olli." The distant, distorted voice belonged to Kris. "We're here."

"Yeah, I hear you. You're there."

"No—" For a moment Kris was gone and Olli braced for a sudden and unwelcome guest in-system, but there was no Architect and Kris came back. "No, we're here. If 'here' is even the word. We're in the same frame of reference as the Architect nursery."

Olli choked. "That mean we're done? Blow the joint and we all go home?"

"Ahab and Ash are working with the Ints to...do whatever they're doing. Don't understand it myself. It's like higher maths crossed with planetary bombardment over here. But they're working on it—whenever you're in the real and they can actually talk to each other."

"And Idris?"

A sigh so achingly familiar that Olli felt it like physical pain. "Oh, you know Idris."

"Could use him up here if you don't need him. Sick of me and Junior having to do his job between us."

"Oh, we need him. But he..." A shrug Olli couldn't see but definitely imagined. "Not happy."

"Miserable fucker never is. Okay, you sit tight and do your very hard sums. We'll give you all the time we can. Kit?" she prompted, keeping a wary eye on Junior. The Ogdru was sulking at the moment, rolling around in the upper reaches of its tank.

"Planetside and orbital authorities are not being cooperative," Kittering lamented.

"Tell them—"

"They are told!" he snapped at her, his translator sounding genuinely human-comprehensible angry. "In all possible ways a telling of them has been accomplished. They are raising numerous trees of branching objections questioning our veracity."

Junior twitched.

Olli gritted her teeth, the roil of tentacles below her

beginning to coil and twist in sympathy. "Tell them to have it ready to send up because company's coming."

Then a message turned up, out of the blue. Not from the world or its orbitals, not on the standard Hanni domestic channels. A recorded message using Hugh government protocols. A familiar name.

"This is Agency Havaer Mundy of the Intervention Board. This message is intended for the crew of the *Vulture God* wherever you should turn up. I understand you are in need of resupply. I am sending you coordinates." And old-fashioned galactic references. No mere chain of Throughways to get there. "Meet me there," ran Mundy's message. "We'll have at least some of what you need, in exchange for answers."

25.

Idris

Two of the Ints had died getting here. Both of them were Colonial, the new class rushed out by the Liaison Board after it was clear their regular stock in trade were ineffective in finding common ground with Architects. One of their on-duty pilots had suffered a colossal brain embolism and the other's autonomic systems had just...stopped doing all the many things a human metabolism needed them to do. In both cases the consequences had been sudden and severe enough that the substantial medical technology on hand was left flat-footed and useless. Plenty of others had suffered serious biofeedback that they had survived. What had been a well-planned rota to give every Int a chance to rest—except Idris, who couldn't—had collapsed into slinging out each healthy Int the moment they were ready, because there were so many recuperating at any one time. All in all, the fact they'd lost only two to comprehensible medical emergencies was probably a victory over the forces of death and entropy. And it wasn't the most disturbing part.

That would be the three Ints who had simply not come *back* when everything else had, as the *Vulture God* had rentered the real after one of its scurrying evasions back up on the surface. They had been plugged in and navigating unspace, two of them from the scales of the Host, the other in the Eye's big Machines. And it had happened during the *God's* first unplanned evasion, after the Architect had followed it from Crux. They had been within unspace, protected by the Wellhead bubble and projecting themselves beyond it to grope their way towards the Architect nursery. But then the *God* had dropped into unspace itself, collapsing the bubble, and they had found themselves in unspace while projecting themselves further into it too, suddenly completely exposed. And they hadn't come back from it, as though the iterated layers of unreality had been piled too high, toppling over and crushing them.

The really problematic thing, Idris considered, was that they hadn't been the only ones actively navigating when the *God* had dived, and everyone had ended up alone in the vacant spaces. It wasn't as though those nested layers of unreality automatically led to extinction. Others had come through fine. Which meant that those who had vanished had been taken, not just fallen out of the universe. Their exposure had opened them up to the Thing that was outside, and it had come for them.

So they now made sure to terminate all Int operations the moment Kit or Olli sent down word they were on the move. Nobody wanted to join the list of the disappeared. It had been hard, too. Navigating in fits and starts, trying to pick up where they'd left off against the incomprehensible non-structure of unspace, trying to calculate their passage across the curvature of unreality. Idris had attempted so many metaphors as he fought to explain to Kris and Solace what they were doing. It was easier just to imagine it as travelling. As though there was an actual place they were trying to reach, and the Ints were just drawing maps and consulting compasses.

In which case, they'd arrived.

He'd made sure he was in the Machine to get the best view. Even just with his bare brain, he could feel it out there, a sensation like the pull of stitched wounds or burn-tautened skin inside his mind. Distantly he could hear the voices of the others. Kris and Solace asking what was out there, trying to get the Eye's cobbled-together systems to model it in a way they could understand. Shinandri reading off gibberish data in his quick, uneven voice. More closely, a handful of the other Ints were making observations, trying to understand what was snarling unspace in front of them. Hesitant, broken sentences strung together by a cartilage of ellipses and question marks. And Ahab. In its own Machine. Ahab, who wasn't an Int but had a dozen conduits feeding its implants with data. Probing the twisted fabric of unspace like a blind man. A vengeful blind man who finally feels the throat of his enemy beneath his fingers.

Idris opened himself to the outside and understood. A moment of utter clarity, seeing how it all fitted together and functioned. Recognizing the differences between this and the Throughways, those other structured parts of unspace. There was plenty of complexity up at the very surface of the unreal, adjacent to regular space. Mass shadows and the weird distorting stipple of all the thinking minds in the universe, and the connective tissue tying it all together like a mad theorist's string. The Throughways, that the Originators had built, that tugged the universe into or out of shape. Artificial. The work of a thinking mind, even if the scale was beyond anything humans or Hanni, or even the Hegemony, could conceive of. A piece of civic engineering the size of the universe and for purposes utterly unknown.

The Architect nursery wasn't like this. He understood that now too. He had wondered if the Architects were the Hivers of unspace, slaves by creation rather than subjugation, not that there was much moral distance between the two. After all, he was damn sure that the Originators, the Throughway-builders and the masters of the Architects were all one and the same, crouching there at the centre of unspace and... doing whatever the hell they did.

Now he saw it close up, or at least the Eye's focus had been brought entirely to bear on it, he decided this was something natural. A persistent complexity within unspace's structure, like the red eye storm persisting amidst a gas giant's turbulence. They'd observed plenty of whorls, currents and momentary landmarks already. Unspace threw up patterns, but it usually took them down just as quickly, the spawn and prey of chaos mathematics. Except, he thought, sometimes, vanishingly rare, a pattern of energy, information and force arose that by its very nature perpetuated itself. Perhaps for a minute, perhaps for a decade, perhaps for ever. It was a twist in the underlying structure of unspace, a distorted point that had copied itself, and copied itself, until there was a whole close-knit constellation of aberrant, unreal landscape generated there. And the complex topography of that landscape interacted with unspace in a way that produced...

Life. Minds. Whatever an Architect was. The vast crystal monoliths of the real were just thought and complex distortion here, because that was all anything was in unspace. Step off a Throughway, and you needed a mind just to keep yourself this side of not existing at all. And *mind* had arisen in the depths of unspace. Then, because mind was also the tool you needed to start manipulating unspace, that arisen mind had begun working on its native environment. Building. Spreading more of itself. Possibly the nexus that had generated the first Architect would have snapped back into the background nothingness long ago, had the Architects themselves not worked to perpetuate and expand it.

He could not imagine what it was like. It wasn't as though baby Architects were born, little formless knots of intent, and then slowly grew into their colossal, murderous adult selves. He could see the process in real time. The convolutions of unspace. And he understood that they were Architects in negative, then, over time, the Architects themselves would accrete within them, building up complexity and structure until a threshold was crossed and a full Architect would come into being, where a moment before there had just been dust and the distortion of unreal space.

Like a spider's web in reverse. Pulled tight purely by the competing demands of its own structure. Strung with cocoons, but instead of dead prey these would each unravel, so that the insect could push its way out.

They pulled everyone out of the Machines then. Olli and Kit were giving them a decent span of time right now, and Shinandri, Ahab and Ash had all their data. About half their Ints also needed medical treatment, for old traumas or new. Idris stared at his arm, the one he was missing, remembering it being there in unspace and not immediately recalling why it was absent now.

He sat at the back. All the medically fit Ints were either physically there in the Machine room of the Eye or listening in from the scales. Andecka Tal Mar was taking the lead, as she often did now. And she'd defer to Idris if he opened his mouth. He knew that. She looked over at him for his nod or frown, but he gave her nothing. He couldn't make himself actively consent to what they were doing, and at the same time he couldn't fault the logic. Who was he to stand before Ash or Ahab and tell them they had no right?

He watched Andecka and three other selected Ints get into the Machines under Doctor Shinandri's direction.

A hand came down on his shoulder. He looked back and saw Solace. Flinched, expecting her to ask why it wasn't him. Why he wasn't doing his duty like a good soldier. But she said nothing, just kept her hand on the thin fabric of his tunic until a little comfort began to leach in with the warmth.

"I'm sorry," she said.

"Not enough to do anything."

"We do terrible things," Solace told him. "That's what people do, to survive. It's like during the war, people having to work out how best to evacuate a world. Having to decide who's allowed to go and who stays to die. Human history in space is a series of terrible moments."

"That logic," he said, "leads to the Uskaro ark fleet. It leads to your Exemplar Mercy and her coup. Because once you start doing terrible things because you had no choice, then next time round you do terrible things because you want to, and the precedent is set. This is a terrible thing we are doing through choice."

"Whole worlds, Idris. Inhabited worlds, every time. Even now there could be a planet being reshaped. You know this."

"I know." Hissing through his teeth, fighting hard to stop himself shouting it at all of them. They hadn't been there,

435

none of them. When he'd met the Architects, mind to mind, over Far Lux, over Berlenhof. As alien an intellect as there ever was, and yet he'd found common ground with it. At his plea, it had bucked under the hand of its masters. In the situation of Far Lux, he'd made them realize the cost of what they were doing, and the Architects had valued those infinitesimal grains of mind and life enough that they'd gone away for half a century, until the whip hand had found them again and driven them back to their bloody work. At Berlenhof he'd begged, and the planet's executioner had refused to do its duty. They were not wicked. They were not cruel. They were victims. The victims of the Originators. *And now ours.*

He owed it to them to at least stand up and shout out his disagreement, but everyone had heard it all before and what would it achieve? So he sat at the back and watched it all happen, knowing it made him an accomplice. Sat and hoped for the voice of Kit to come down the well and tell them the *God* needed to get out of town again, so they'd have to call the whole experiment off. It didn't happen, though, and he felt the grotesque *wrongness* as Andecka and the others plucked at the fabric of unspace. He felt them take Shinandri and Ahab's equations, which they'd been adjusting and reworking furiously since the Eye came down the well, and apply them like knives to the taut strings of the Architect colony. *And if this maths gets out, it will be used elsewhere.* He could see exactly how one could dismantle a Throughway in the same way. *We could sever the universe from itself. Exile a system so that only Ints could find it.*

Closing his eyes, he noticed Solace's hand clench on his shoulder. He understood that, just as the Architects didn't explode planets, or hurl them into stars, or tear them bodily apart, this wasn't *violence* either. The Architects painstakingly remodelled planets into precise configurations. It was almost the opposite of violence. So gentle, so careful. If five billion people died, well, it was the price of art, wasn't it? And here, what they'd planned out: the maths, the careful application of thought like scalpel blades. Making use of the fundamental desire of unspace just to snap back to its baseline level of entropy. Any kind of structure was unnatural to it. Snarls and vortices arose all the time but dissipated just as rapidly. Except, as thought was the common currency of unspace, these storms generated life, sentience, sapience. Perhaps there were thinking beings here who howled into existence for mere fractions of a second, before being scattered to the winds. But in this place, thinking life had taken root, grown itself a colony, nurtured more of itself. All those scattered points pulling at one another, the whole held under tension, held in shape. The shape itself was the thing that generated Architects.

A cry of triumph came from Shinandri. Idris felt the first thread part.

The nearest cluster of points—the dense convolution of information, like a protein's folded structure—sprang apart. No, sprang out of existence. Cut away from the rest, releasing its energy in a shockwave that had half the Ints clutching at their heads. Idris just clenched his jaw against it. Seeing the damage they'd done. A little fraction of the Architect colony that now wasn't there any more. They'd struck their blow. The first of many.

Shinandri was then talking excitedly about where to cut next. The surgery that would carve this cancer out of the universe. Each cut required the most meticulous planning, or else the blade would find no purchase. The next shift of Ints were proposed to carry that killing maths to the enemy.

Idris walked over to one of the Machines, even as Jaine helped Andecka out of it. He heard Solace call after him, but he just lay down in it and let its hungry interface clutch his mind. Wanting to see with the augmented sight the Eye could give him, to witness what they'd done.

It wasn't *sight*, and he didn't use his eyes, but his brain made images to account for the probability gradients and the dynamic forces, and the sheer unreality of it. He envisaged the Architect nursery like a web hanging over him, and tried to make it as unpleasant as possible. A great dusty expanse of spiderweb against the dark cellar ceiling of some abandoned house. He attempted to make it a bad thing, so that it was a good thing they were destroying it. A web which they'd lifted a tiny knife to, very precisely, and severed a strand or two. And a small section was just loose and trailing ends now. It was the tension, the interaction of forces, that made the web. Without that, it was just bad string.

Revealed by that springing-apart, where they'd cut, he saw the other damage.

If they had applied the knife, this was as though someone had reached out with a match. A part of the nursery not just snapped back into non-existence, but burned like a brand. A scar on the colony's structure, barren and for ever impossible to forget or ignore.

Even as he saw it, they were hauling him out of the Machine. Olli had called down the well after all, at just the wrong time. Too late to stop Shinandri's experiment, too soon for Idris's own investigation. He'd discovered something new, except now everyone was too busy to talk about it, and soon they'd just be gone. Unspace the old-fashioned way, where everyone went alone. Unspace without the Eye's protections to stand between him and the Presence that still prowled out there.

Solace saw it in his face. She started moving, heading for him, hand reaching out. He met her eyes. Her mouth was open, her hand inches from his. As though it would accomplish anything. Then she was gone. They all were. Olli and Kit had taken the *God* back into unspace to dodge the Architects, and under no circumstances should any Int just hop into one of the Machines and go spelunking.

But Idris returned to the coffin-seat of the Machine and connected to it again, feeling the blissful quiet of solitude and, beyond it, the first slow uncoiling of the Other.

He fell beyond the stone sanctum of the Eye, and beyond the gravitic bubble generated by the scales of the distributed alien vessel. Out beyond. At the same time, he was still present, locked away in the prison of his physical body. That increasingly unreliable and piecemeal shell.

Visualizing himself descending, like a diver with a weighted belt, into the crepuscular depths of unspace. As if the heart of everything, all the way down there, was shrouded in night and cold and crushing pressure. But that was where he had to go. It was where *they* dwelt, the ones he needed to find and confront. Make them acknowledge his species and the destruction they were doing. Make them understand, so they'd not do it any more, no matter what Ash said. End the war. And a more final end than simply robbing them of their weapons; a kinder end than murdering their slaves.

The Presence heaved down there, amorphous, reaching.

Their guardian, the many-headed dog at the gates of the abyss. A *terror*: the concept of it made flesh. Because thought was strength here in unspace, so why shouldn't abstract concepts be given form and mass and reaching tentacles? Up it rose, the kraken woken, baleful in its fury.

Olli and Kit would know it too, if they'd had no chance to get to the suspension couches. As the pair of them trusted to their Ogdru navigator to hustle them through the surface waters of unspace. Each of them alone, and each of them hunted. But they all of them had so much more clear water between them and the Presence than Idris did. Idris, in the Machines and active in unspace while the bubble was gone —he swam in the thing's very shadow, and it knew him. It felt him more acutely than all the other myriad intrusions. Than it felt every individual vessel across the universe that dared break the surface tension and dart into its domain. It reached for all of them simultaneously. A singular beast with an attention that could divide and subdivide, hydra-heads multiplying and yet all leading back to the same monster. All these things were just convenient masks the human imagination fabricated because the Presence was the unthinkable, the thing nobody could face and remain sane and whole.

Of all the many things in the universe it hated, it hated Idris most of all.

He felt the icy chill of it reach for his heart. He was sinking into its very grasp, down in the depths. At the same time, within the ark, he felt it oil its sinuous way past the scales, finding entry, lurching and shambling through the halls of the Eye. He heard the flapping, slapping echo of its half-formed footsteps come to him from far away, but getting closer. In his mind it took shape, something humanoid, something dead but animate, something with the faces of everyone he'd failed, left behind and disappointed. The faces of everyone who'd tried to use him or hurt him, and from whom he'd never had closure. All the jagged broken edges of his long life, grinding together like teeth, come to chew him up and spit him out.

He heard it call his name. Of course, he didn't really hear it call his name. No long drawn-out *Idris...* echoing through the empty spaces of the Eye. All in his head. And yet, if there was any human being at all that the Presence might know, it was him. He'd been its prey so long. There had been times before when he'd dreamt it was talking to him. When he was desperate. When he was hurt. Talking in the voices of the dead and the living.

Idris... From just a room away. The knowledge of its closeness was absolutely intolerable and yet somehow he clung on, tolerating it. Feeling with preternatural acuteness all the commands he could give to the Machine he was set in, that would have it misfire, starve his brain or poison his blood. Jaine's rough and ready engineering wasn't big on safety protocols. She hadn't really safeguarded against someone using her work to commit suicide, and he could see seven different ways of doing it. And, one room away, the Presence took another step closer with a sucking, decaying sound. He flinched from it.

Then, outside, he fell, and it was all around him in the darkness. A forest of weaving arms like the tendrils of jelly-fish. Soft, hideously soft, waiting to be touched and triggered, waiting to drag him down to where *it* waited. A death that would be agony and for ever. Better to end it. Better to sever his lifeline now, tear off all the tissue-thin flummery that was protecting him from the pressure and the freezing water. *Do it, Idris. It's better that way.*

He wasn't a brave man. He'd lived his life scared. Scared because, when he was a child, his species was being hunted to extinction by the Architects, always on the run, ship to shore, to ship again. Scared because he was small and weak. Then scared later because they'd made him into something ghastly and only semi-functional, throwing him into unspace over and over, because there was a war on and he was a weapon.

Show him a Voyenni with a fist pulled back, show him a gun, a battle, some ravenous alien animal or plant, he'd cower or flee. The coward Idris Telemmier, a man of no appreciable backbone. You couldn't rely on him, everyone knew. A wretched little weasel of a man. But this...

Everyone was scared of unspace. Everyone who sensed the Presence knew it as *Terror* incarnate. Unreality was the great leveller. But all the terrible things they'd done to him during the war had served to make him as adapted as a human could possibly be to this grotesquely inhospitable place.

The Presence groped blindly for him in the dark. Its malformed bulk loomed in the doorway of the Machine room, unseen but impossible to ignore.

Idris let the water carry him aside, and the force of his mind drag him down past those arms. Let the fact of that unwelcome company slide off the surface of his mind. *Idris* ...it said, and he knew his own name. It was his. One of the last remaining parts of the person he'd once been, before all the surgery and the drugs. It grew nearer, lurching across the Machine room, moaning his name. Appalling. Closer and closer, turning the screw of his revulsion and horror until literally anything would be preferable to having it there. Until death, any death, even the most painful and drawn out, would be better. But he took the unreal geometry and pushed all the sliders to maximum. Making its progress towards him a Zeno's paradox, where it covered half the distance and then half the distance, closer and closer but not quite reaching him every time.

He fell past it, picturing the scarred flank of some beast so vast that, if he'd had a light and been so foolish as to turn it on, he'd only have seen an unrelieved plain of flesh like a cliff face.

Falling past. Even as it twisted and tried to find him, even as he hid from the monster in its own shadow. He screwed his eyes shut, his real eyes. He closed his mind to it, and instead made himself exist only *out there*, in the shadow of its groping immensity. And beyond it, there was only room for a single point. The Presence was everywhere around the centre of all things but it was not *at* the centre. There was a cyst there, a bubble, a frozen moment. The thing he'd glimpsed. The thing that stared back at him and knew him.

26.

Havaer

"This," said Havaer. "I never knew this even existed."

Diljat nodded. "Old cases, Agent Mundy. Real old. Wartime."

That meant a fairly narrow window for someone in Threat Analysis to conceive of this exigency and put it into motion. Sometime between the first Ints coming out of the Intermediary Program and the war's end.

This was where they'd sent for the *Vulture God* to steer to. The orbital claimed the world was known as Harbourage. It was a lie. The world wasn't known at all. It wasn't on anyone's charts. If you didn't know it was there, you'd never have found it. There were no Throughways joining it to the universe.

"Early Void-Explore ran across it, before they were even the Cartography Corps," Diljat explained. The orbital they were aboard was tiny, mostly just a crosspiece of four docks, and eight modest compartments inside. The real work, what there was of it, was on the planet below. "Happens more than you'd think, I'm told. The Ints sense the mass, and come out to find just...this. A star, some planets. They note it down, but if there aren't any Throughways, it's not much use to anyone."

"Except here," Havaer noted, and she nodded.

The world below was Earth-size, which was probably what had caught someone's attention back on Berlenhof or wherever. There was a microbial ecosystem that fell into that narrow band where the chemistry wasn't inimical enough to kill you or Earth-like enough to infect you. Something somebody had been able to work with. And right now, over half a century on, there was an automated base down there cracking rocks and generating an oxygenated atmosphere, as well as a science station where they'd been working on adapting the local life for human use. Havaer couldn't imagine how you found qualified bioscientists who'd be willing to take the job. There had been three of them, and they must have been equal parts rugged and antisocial. It was only past tense because they'd been evacuated for the duration of this little stunt of Mordant House.

"Home away from home," he said, pausing at a panel and idly calling up planetary data. He gave a wry smile at the wartime tech and interfaces that had never been updated or replaced. Because this had been someone's desperation move, back before the war turned. They had reckoned that maybe Architects only hit worlds on the Throughways—on what basis Havaer couldn't guess, given that data on worlds off the network was essentially non-existent. Someone, therefore, had decided to turn Harbourage into humanity's last, worst homeworld. It hadn't been needed, and the war had ended, but Mordant House had chosen to keep the project live. Keep up the old-fashioned terraforming like nobody really did any more. Just in case.

Now they'd found another use for the place. The most clandestine of meeting points, where they could make the exchange without putting anyone else in danger.

"Agent Diljat," came the voice of their pilot—because of course they'd needed their own Int to even get out here. No other way to reach Harbourage. "They're here."

"Back to the ship," Diljat said. They ran, even though it wasn't far. It couldn't have been, given the cramped confines of the Harbourage Orbital. They ran because they didn't know how long they'd have before the *Vulture God* brought friends to the party.

"You understand your brief?" Diljat quizzed him as they hit the airlock to their ship.

"I'm not a rookie," Havaer complained. "I've been in the service longer than you have by at least five years."

She made a thoughtful sound and he didn't like the way she was eyeing him. Not sure if he was *still* in the trade, after all. The ground beneath his feet was unsteady in a way that owed nothing to orbital mechanics. He was halfway between a serving agent of Mordant House and an unreliable asset who needed a handler.

"I'm sound," he told her, and didn't know whether to trust her nod.

Then they were inside the *Gadfly*, the swift little runabout the service had made available to them. It was a cockpit, a dozen sleep pods and a big old gravitic drive, with very little else. Their pilot, a grey, seamed leash-contractee named Archer, had already exchanged recognition signals with the *God* and was holding a channel open for them. He'd been with the service for two decades now without going off his head, and his pedigree meant he wasn't any good for warding off Architects. One of the rare Liaison Board Ints who had room in their head for something other than the actual business of being an Intermediary.

Havaer dropped into his seat, knees up against the back of Archer's own. He opened his mouth, then looked to Diljat, hating himself but knowing he needed her nod to start the operation. *Asset, agent; agent, asset. Which am I?*

Receiving permission, he began his spiel. "*Vulture God*, this is Agent Havaer Mundy of the Intervention Board."

"You are being received," came the clipped tones of Kittering's translator. "Docking clearance also."

"We have at least some of what you've been trying to get hold of. It's at the dock specified, ready for loading," Havaer informed them. "I'm going to want to chat about just what the hell's been going on since we all got out of Crux, though. You can imagine we've had some alarmed reports coming in."

"Were there survivors?" Kittering asked.

For a moment Havaer just exchanged blank looks with Diljat, neither of them quite clicking. It was Archer who murmured, "New Kismayo. The Architect. They won't have heard."

Havaer blinked. He hadn't looked at it that way. The *God* likely hadn't caught up much on the news mediotypes, and New Kismayo was so small that its obliteration might not even have featured against the background chaos of the Colonial Sphere right now.

"When you fell back into unspace," he told the *God*, "the Architects followed suit. A little gravitational damage to objects in orbit and the like, but I'm not aware of any casualties." He watched the *God* coast in towards Harbourage Orbital.

"A cause for considerable relief. You are to be informed at the wish of Mesdam Timo that should troops be awaiting us then the regrets on all sides will be uncountable," the Hanni broadcast, somewhat snippily. But Havaer reckoned he was probably diplomacy personified compared to how Olli Timo had *actually* phrased it.

"No troops, I promise," he confirmed, then eyed Diljat, muting his transmission briefly. "There aren't, right?"

She rolled her eyes. "Agent Mundy, no. What are you even thinking?"

I'm thinking you wouldn't tell me if there were. But he just mustered an apologetic smile from somewhere. "Sure. Of course."

"On with the script," she prompted.

He let the *God* complete its docking first. They'd set out a dozen small crates of parts, supplies, and one fantastically expensive mother-of-pearl container that was apparently the Hegemonic proteins they'd been after. He saw the *God's* umbilical connect, the ship's mess of docking claws latching on to the side of the orbital so that the station's own drives had to compensate for the shifted centre of gravity. Then the eyes within the dock showed the hatch open, and Olian Timo came out.

"That's messed up," Diljat opined.

Havaer nodded, watching the nest of tentacles carry her about like quicksilver. She didn't even seem to be concentrating much to direct them. *She does have her talents.*

"Mesdam Timo," he called over the dock speakers, and as a request to her personal comms, giving her the option.

"No need to shout," she sent back. "What do you want, you Mordant bastard?"

"Just as well it's not a little gratitude." He could see Diljat mugging at him to get on with it, but he reckoned he knew Olli. You had to crack her shell first.

"That it is," she agreed gruffly.

"You've got Almier in there, maybe?" he tried, mostly because he knew it would needle her.

"You're fuck out of luck on that one. She's down the well, same as all of them, save me and Kit. What do you want, Mundy?"

"Well Hugh wants its ship back." Meaning the Host.

"Hugh can whistle," Olli told him, and then, "Seriously, though, not going to happen. They're *busy*. Or they damn well better be because this is all the time I can give them."

Havaer exchanged looks with Diljat. He hadn't exactly expected her just to tender up the Host and the Eye and all, but there was a heavyweight delegation within Hugh who'd insisted they at least ask.

"So give us the lowdown," he invited. "While you're loading." As those tentacles effortlessly hoisted and dragged around the cargo crates, he listened to Timo begin the story. Even as Kittering sent over meticulous accounts that wrote off the value of everything they'd received against the notional benefit of saving the universe.

Olli

"Well this is all too good to be true and no mistake," Olli decided, hauling the next crate down the umbilical into the drone bay. She'd started with the weird Hegemonic pod and right now Kit was puzzling over it, trying to work out how to combine the neatly packed sachets of organic material with the *Vulture God*'s printer.

"Most unsatisfactory transaction," Kittering agreed. "Contact has been received from Solace."

"That right?" She tried to manufacture a bit of the old grudge, because it made her feel better, but Olli had to admit she wasn't really left with much of a grievance against that one Partheni at least. "How's it going down there?"

"We're enduring." Solace sounded ragged as fuck, even through all the distortion and crackle. "Patching Idris up, right now. Kris is with him. That's why you've got me." Sounding apologetic.

Olli grinned to herself. *Bitch knows me.* "You'll do fine. Doc Shin and the others better be using this time, though. Not sure how long you've got." She could feel each second tick like they were rattling off the lid of the Scorpion's old pod.

"They're attacking the Architect thing, the nursery, whatever. Picking it apart, bit by bit. There's a lot of it."

"Architects got something to say about that, I bet," Olli told her, dumping her crate and coiling her way back down the umbilical.

"No," Solace said flatly. "Not at all. It's like, here in unspace they're...harmless. They're there. The Ints can feel them moving about. And they're not happy, obviously, but they don't seem to have any teeth this side of the real."

"Lucky fucking you. They're all over me this end," Olli grumbled. "And not only them. I just had to give Hugh the lowdown on what's going on, so I could get some goods and gear off them. Not sure how long that détente's going to last, believe me. Listen, can you put Jaine on? Not that it ain't a pleasure, you know, but..." Of course Jaine would be neck-deep in all the fix-it work that needed doing down there, just as Olli was up here. And she was, as it turned out, but Solace patched her through anyway.

"You wouldn't believe all the crap going wrong down here,"

came Jaine's distant, attenuated voice. "Every Host scale's red across the board. Triage like you wouldn't believe. How's it hanging, Olli?"

Olli grinned, latching onto the last of the crates out on the dock. "Like looking in a mirror. Ahab giving you shit?"

"Ahab's in clover," Jaine told her. "Bastard finally got what it wants. Forgotten its old pals."

"Always the way," Olli agreed. "Good, they don't need you. Mechanic position's been open here since Barney got his fool ass shot up. You can come do an honest day's work for a change."

Jaine laughed, and that was good. "Yeah, sure, let's just save the universe first, shall we? Which, right now, is *not* being helped by your friend the Int going off and being crazy on his own time."

"Yeah, he's a liability," Olli agreed. Then she had the last of the crates in, and Kit had finally got the printer talking to the Hegemonic container, because apparently even their cargo crates had their own distinct operating systems. Next Agent Mundy was on the comms again, wanting to speak with her.

"Don't take any shit from anyone," she told Jaine; her general motto in life, to be honest.

"Back at you," Jaine agreed, and then Olli was demanding, "What do you want now?"

"A flight plan, ideally," Mundy told her.

"Disengaging?" Kittering sent simultaneously, and she gave him the all-clear. There was no way of knowing how long they'd have just sitting around. Better not to be locked to an orbital when guests came calling.

"Yeah? Why's that?"

"Because you'll have another shopping list sooner rather than later, and it would be useful to know where you're going to be."

"Hugh's got generous all of a sudden," she noted. "Where was all this when we were trying to make ends meet on the salvage circuit?"

"If Hugh can keep you resupplied at places like this, it means you're not dragging an Architect into the skyline of a populated world," he pointed out. "Even the Budgetary Oversight Commission can't argue with that kind of logic."

"Yeah, well," she said. Kittering was calling up a local map, pinpointing possible liaison points that would be minimum exposure for everyone else. Not that she could guarantee hitting any of them, what with Junior at the helm, but she could do her best. "We turn up somewhere and there's a Colonial warship waiting, you can bet we'll just take straight off again. But there'll be someone else along a moment later that your military boys won't want to meet, see right?"

"Understood. You've a very suspicious mind, Timo."

"You work for very suspicious people, Mundy."

"Fair."

She wanted to speak to Jaine again then, or maybe Kris. Someone else down there. Not that she was worried for them, obviously. Or needed the contact. Kittering had been talking down the well just a moment before, even as she sparred with Mordant House, but now he was signalling her urgently.

"There is an agitation from the Ogdru," he warned her. "Course?"

"Ah, balls." She'd hoped they would have maybe an hour

or two to sit in Harbourage orbit. When the well crew could have really got down to business. And she could even have closed her eyes a little, or given Kit the chance to curl up and sleep. But it wasn't to be. She sent a string of destinations to Mundy, optimism springing eternal, and pitched the first of them to Junior in the hope the creature would take the hint. Company was on its way.

Havaer

"Tch!" choked Archer, and stared down at the spray of ruby droplets he'd just spat across his board. "Got to—coming!"

"Disengage," Havaer told him. "Out of here, now!"

"Countermand. Hold," Diljat snapped.

"*What?*"

"Hold just a minute," she insisted. "Archer—"

The Int wiped blood from his lips. "Confirmed," he said thickly around his bitten tongue. He was jittering about in his seat, hands clenching and unclenching as though he was having a seizure, but his face was steady.

"Diljat, what—" Havaer tried, but she cut him off with a look. Instead he watched the *Vulture God*, out past the station's orbit. Saw the vessel pivot and claw away from Harbourage's gravity well, then put itself in a position where it could duck into unspace. And still there was nothing—the *Gadfly*'s instruments were silent. Not a single tremor or suggestion that a world-twisting terror was about to descend on them. Just Archer and his rapid breathing, his shudder, his eyes as wide and rolling as a panicked horse's.

The hatch opened. Havaer jerked in his seat, against the

restraints. They were being boarded. He reached for a gun he didn't have.

Half a dozen soldiers pushed in, cramming the interior of the *Gadfly* to bursting, with no chance for anyone to get to the suspension couches now. Armoured Colonial troops with accelerators jostled awkwardly at all angles to fit in. Past the shoulder-guard of one, Havaer met Diljat's gaze.

"Just us, huh?"

There was no embarrassment whatsoever in her face. "The Board wanted us to be ready for all eventualities. As it was, with that Hegemonic frame she was sitting in, I didn't fancy our chances."

"And you didn't think to tell me that was the plan?"

"I was concerned you might not be convincing if you had to lie," she told him. "All in. Archer, let's go."

The Architect breached into the real even as they cut ties to the orbital. It came out close too—not the distant, dignified approach they usually adopted when they had a planet on the menu. This one lurched into existence almost hurriedly, entering the real with a spin. Even as it did, the *Vulture God* was dropping away, taking all of its invisible baggage with it. Presumably heading along the chain of stopovers that they'd sent to Havaer.

Archer hauled the *Gadfly* away from the planet, pushing the ship's oversized brachator drives to their limits to win as much distance as possible. And obviously the Architect was just going to dive back under. It wasn't a problem. It wasn't *their* problem.

He was watching when the unseen hands of the monster reached out and turned Harbourage Orbital into confetti. Not even a sculpture, just shredding the whole structure into a cloud of rapidly disassociating flakes of matter. As though some vast rage was being funnelled into the act, through the lens of the crystal monstrosity sitting out there.

We're next, Havaer decided, and braced himself for the worst, but then Archer finally had them far enough away, and rammed them brutally out of reality. They were saved. Havaer was left alone in the suddenly vacant space within the *Gadfly*. Alone to consider where he stood in relation to the rest of the universe, and especially to his employer, who didn't even trust him to lie for them any more. When he felt the Thing that lived in unspace move far below, and start to wind the crank of his dread with its slow approach, he expected that if he saw it now, it would be wearing a Mordant House uniform.

27.

Idris

They did not like being seen. Not even glimpsed from the corner of his eye. Even as the Presence loomed at his bedside, even as its vast benthic bulk impinged on his field of view like a mountain, Idris focused in, tunnelling down with his mind's eye until he met that counter-gaze. That outraged stare. He had the sense of something on another scale entirely. Simultaneously infinitesimal—the single point at the heart of all things—and huge beyond the universe. Because it was the *centre* of it all, and basic spatial relationships broke down there. You could have as many angels as you liked dancing on the head of that pin.

He saw them, all the malefic angels. And they saw him. It wasn't as though they hadn't known he was there, in the abstract. Idris, a part of the assemblage of inconvenience that was currently attacking their Architect breeding grounds, nibbling away at the tool they used to re-edify the universe. They were hounding Kit and Olli from star to star, out there in the real, after all. They *knew*. But this was different.

Ancient. How could they be other than ancient? Idris had thought he'd understood the concept, and now he realized he'd been sadly misinformed. But he could re-educate himself. If he was able to get far enough down there, the crushing pressure of the depths would crunch the whole truth of the universe small enough that he could fit all of it into his head. He was ready to receive it. As though in carving up his brain to turn him into the Intermediary he was, those Colonial butcher-scientists had been unwittingly fashioning a key. All the long decades of his unspace experience had then honed him perfectly so that, when presented with this universal singularity, he'd fit. He clicked into place, sharpened by privation and experience into the Platonic ideal of an unspace navigator. As if reaching this still centre, and comprehending it, was the evolutionary niche he had been adapted to exploit.

Humanity had travelled between stars for perhaps two centuries. That was recent. Written human history was maybe six thousand years old and that was just yesterday. The earliest things that might be considered human had lived out their brief lives a few million Earth-standard years ago, and that was a past so close to Idris he could glance over his shoulder and look those apes in the eye. Complex life on Earth, half a billion years: a fleeting moment. Earth being formed, four and a half billion years: nothing. The first galaxies, ten billion years before that: an eyeblink. Because this was the centre, the heart, and so time didn't mean the same thing. All the moments of the universe's history were just crammed together like the pages of a book, to be idly riffled through in an instant. All that time, they had been waiting.

No, not waiting. Not idle. Working.

All this he understood by the very virtue of reaching the place and standing at their threshold, which was simultaneously a pinpoint singularity and a grand, looming portal to...the place where regular rules didn't apply. The pearl at the heart of the universe's oyster. Or else the cyst embedded deep within its flesh.

And they loathed him. They would surely obliterate him if he let himself descend a fraction further. He was at the very edge of their all-consuming wrath. They were coldly furious at the temerity of Ahab, Ash and the others too. He sensed their distant, clinical bitterness about all the bustling life walking around up there in its insect way, on the surface of the real—and he almost understood *why*. He felt he now had all the clues and means to know what it was they couldn't abide about *life*, and *sentience* in particular. But all that dispassionate loathing was as nothing compared to what they thought of *him*. Idris Telemmier, Intermediary, first class, who had dared to come darken their door.

Up where his actual body was, the Presence leant over him, cold hands reaching, and he felt its touch, freezing like the depths of the void, like the abyss of the sea. Felt his heart stop, despite all that Trine's borrowed units could do. And down here, the Presence was filling the icy water at his back—a solid mass of coiling filaments, shearing teeth and great glassy eyes. He braced himself to take that extra, annihilating step, because he had to *know*...

*

The *God* must have hit the real around then, and moments later everyone in the Machine room would have heard the alarms telling them that Idris was dying again. Up to his old tricks, the mischievous scamp. Damn fool Idris was trying for suicide-by-universe one more time. They must have pulled all the plugs and hauled him from the Machine. Solace, Kris, Jaine and Andecka, as well as the handful of Hivers still with them. They'd have put him through the wringer to get his essential organs working again, which had just packed it in and handed in their notice, effective immediately. Reinflating his lungs, manually working the musculature of his heart, and the brain... All they could do was wait, really. Wait over that vacant lump of greasy grey, until suddenly all his electrical activity came back. Because that was how it some-times went, with Ints. The complex patterns of information in flux that were the moment-to-moment existence of the human mind just got copied out elsewhere, and then came back. Went to take tea with an Architect, or in this case deep-diving in the imaginary sea-trenches of unspace.

It must have all happened that way, but Idris, functionally dead for the duration, didn't remember any of it. He only knew when he snapped back into his body, that lump of meat with one arm too few and a thousand aches too many. Opening crusted eyes against the harsh light, he realized he'd been on the very brink. He also knew—even as he tried to rant weakly at them and gave up because it hurt his throat —that the brink he'd been on had been oblivion. If they hadn't acted so promptly, he wouldn't have had anything to come back *to*. The electrical pattern of his mind would have dissipated like a shorting circuit, or otherwise... Were there ghosts in unspace? Was that were the Ints went, when they never came back?

Nobody was terribly impressed with him. Normally in that not-unfamiliar circumstance, he didn't blame people. He had never found himself overly impressive either. Right now, though, he was a Cassandran prophet who would put even

Ash in the shade, and the fact that nobody wanted to listen to him was profoundly galling.

"I need to tell you all something!" he shouted. Or rather, he croaked with the dry, scratchy sound of dead leaves being blown across an abandoned planetside dock. But everyone else was busy trying to cut the next few threads of the Architects' lives away, and that was the *job*. He was just in the way. He'd gone for a frolic of his own and nearly got himself killed. And damn it, Idris, yes, you're a talented Int, but will you just *not*? Get with the programme for once and stop messing around with all this nonsense.

And Trine was gone.

Trine had been gone before anyway, he knew that. But the units Trine had donated to Idris, back when he'd killed himself the first time, were burned out. Killed in their valiant fight to keep his heart going. Saving his life one last time, and holding the fort until the emergency services arrived. He'd used up this gift, the last legacy of his old friend. When they took him—feebly protesting—away from the Machines and into a grim stone morgue where they wanted him to convalesce, he'd been laid out on a walking frame which Jaine had lashed together. He'd been ducted to machines that were doing the inconvenient chores of breathing and circulating blood for him, because apparently he couldn't be relied upon to do it himself. He was an invalid. A liability. Nobody out-and-out said it, but he read it in their faces. And nobody was about to listen to a liability who wanted to upset all their plans and do everything differently.

Later, tooth-grindingly later, Kris and Solace at least found the time to come see him. After the *God* had taken another dive and Idris had only been able to lie there with the mindless machines and listen to the Presence laughing at him, and after they were all back to work on the genocide again. By then, he was going absolutely spare inside his uncooperative and tremblingly weak body, and they were his only hope. And they listened.

Solace

The almost unbearable thing was that he should have looked old. He *was* old, after all. Yes, Solace was old too, but she'd been on ice for a lot of that. Stored up with the other surplus soldiers until the Parthenon needed her again. She wondered how many of those surplus soldiers had been woken for the current civil crisis, a gun thrust into their hands and a doctored ideology into their heads. She hoped Tact's sacrifice had now killed off the division amongst her sisters. Because otherwise, she couldn't bring herself to consider the outcome. The sororicide, the self-murder of her people and way of life. Being down the well was easier. Here the threats were existential, over her pay grade. The problems were past her ability to think about. Up in the real, the situation was just unthinkable.

And here was Idris, her old friend. The only man she'd ever slept with, back after the war when everything had seemed possible. And again more recently, once or twice. For old times' sake, as it were. There was a gap in Idris's life where human contact should be, and a gap in hers where all those frozen decades had passed, so they fitted together well enough sometimes. He'd never looked strong, but he appeared particularly weak now...faded. As though he might just vanish the way those other Ints had done, doing exactly what he'd decided to go do.

She wanted to shout at him. *You might have been killed!* But what would that have added?

She'd come to remonstrate with him, her and Kris. Doctor Shinandri had asked them to do it. Because they still wanted Idris on the team, wielding the scalpel against the Architects. Doc Shin wanted him talked round, brought back into line. No more extra-curricular jaunts into the unreal. Be a team player, just this once.

Solace could have told the good doctor exactly how useless that line of reasoning would be with Idris. He wasn't a team player. She'd learned that herself when trying to recruit him for the Parthenon. When he had finally come over, it had been in his own time and for his own reasons. He might look weak, but when you pushed Idris, something in him pushed back. Something which she almost felt was entirely divorced from the actual man. The *Int* in him resisted you. And it was the Int in him that people actually wanted. The Idris of him was generally considered inconvenient baggage that had to come along.

She liked the Idris of him. More than the Int, to be honest. She'd happily have cut the Int away and let it go do Int things for all the people who needed it. Except it was like a parasite that had grown within him, until it was more than half the man. Idris without the Int would have been like a cast snake-skin.

"You have to stop doing things like this," Kris was saying. Solace knew the tone: the lawyer Keristina Almier reciting legal precedent to a client who wasn't going to take her advice, because at least then she'd have done her professional duty. Solace expected Idris just to shrug and mutter, letting the advice and warnings slough off his sloped shoulders. Something came on, though, in his eyes. A light, a fire. She and Kris both flinched back, identically. For a moment she had the dreadful thought that he might have brought something back from the depths of unspace.

"No," Idris said. "I have to do it again." Taking time over the words, making sure his mouth shaped them properly, fighting his own fatigue.

"Idris, you were basically *dead*," Kris said, more heatedly. She'd been palling around with the man for a few years solid now, not just ghosting back into his life after decades. She'd had to live with him being difficult, even the little difficulties thrown up by a life on the *Vulture God*. Shielding him from the sharp edges of the universe, and vice versa. And Solace saw the affection nakedly on display there, how much Kris loved her friend Idris, and how it all came out as frustration because Idris seemed to have absolutely no care for himself, or anyone else. Solace waited for the tantrum, the rant. Idris's own exasperation at how little traction he could get on the universe, to make it do the things he wanted. That wasn't the Idris they got, though. This was a laser-focused Idris. The man who'd flown the *Dark Joan* against the Broken Harvest to recapture the *Vulture God*, or gone out to face the Architect over Berlenhof.

"I need your help," he told them. "This has gone on too long."

Solace exchanged what felt like a familiar look with Kris. "Killing the Architects," she filled in, and at his nod said, "Idris...I don't think you'll find any takers. We've all heard what you've got to say—"

His mechanical arm slammed down on the walking frame, the only part of him he could get a good slam from. "Listen," he insisted, losing breath halfway through the word. Using his frailty as a bludgeon to make them cede him the floor. "Fine. Nobody cares about the Architects. I get that. They haven't endeared themselves to us. Nobody cares they don't have a choice." Trying to grind his teeth as he wheezed through the words, except he couldn't even do that properly. "But listen. Let me...bring it to your worlds. Kris, you remember that shipyard baron on Upsandi, tried to claim ownership of the *God*? Got us impounded and all that. You beat her in court two, three times. And that worked, did it? That got her off our backs?"

Solace had no idea what he was talking about but Kris nodded, then shook her head. "No, Rollo had to cash in all those favours with the racketeer to go put the frighteners on her, I remember."

"Because it wasn't about the legalities. That was just the weapon she was using. Each time we won, she just came back another way. And Solace, you've got an enemy, a..."

"You're going to find some patronizing soldier metaphor, right?" she asked drily. "How if I take someone's gun away but don't deal with them, they'll just go and get another gun. Except it still helps to take the gun away. Or to shoot the soldiers they send after you, if you can't get to the leader."

"That's what Tact did, is it?" he asked, and she went cold. He did not have the *right* to throw that at her.

He saw he'd hurt her, and for a moment was about to back down, as Idris always did when it came to the clutch. Apologize and not resolve anything ever. But this time, even though he didn't actually have any strength left in him, he still pushed on.

"We will never be safe," he said. "Destroy the Architects and they'll find another way. I've felt it, their...purpose. They hate us so much, because we're in the way of something they're trying to do. Something huge, except when you're where they are, nothing's huge. The whole universe is in sight all at once, in arm's reach almost. We drive the Architects to extinction, it won't help. If you need a better reason than avoiding genocide, try that. It won't actually buy us anything more than time. So help me. Go to the others and advocate for me."

"They sent us to you to advocate for them," Kris pointed out.

Idris looked from her to Solace and back. "Well, then you have to decide who you're with, don't you?"

28.

Havaer

"It's just a select committee," Diljat told him.

"It looks," Havaer said with feeling, "like it's going to be a court martial." There were four armed and armoured soldiers in the little antechamber with them. And this was a part of the Intervention Board's orbital offices he didn't normally have to visit, on account of him being a field agent and this being where high-profile problems ended up. "I could also say 'inquisition.' Possibly 'witch hunt.'"

"You're being over-dramatic," said Diljat, but she was fidgeting, shifting from foot to foot. She hadn't been briefed about this. She'd been expecting to turn up as a witness, as a prosecuting counsel, perhaps. Entirely possibly she'd been expecting to hang Havaer out to dry and take the expected pat on the head for her good work. Now she was in here with him, denied any line of communication. She'd gone with him to meet the *Vulture God* and come back to find herself part of the problem. They'd been marched into isolated quarters the moment they'd docked, and then they'd sat, and sat, and been denied any answers, after which they'd ended up here.

"A debriefing, that's all," Diljat insisted. "At the highest level. Just shows how top priority it all is."

Then one of the guards obviously received word, because they were marched into the adjoining chamber. Which was big, and mostly full. Havaer wasn't sure what selection process had been used, if this was "just a select committee," but it hadn't been as exclusive as he'd have expected because basically *everyone* was here.

It's Hugh, he thought. *It's actually the entirety of Hugh.* Obviously that was both not true and patently impossible, but he could see a number of recording drones doubtless broadcasting to those who hadn't travelled to the orbital, or possibly just hadn't fitted into the chamber. There were screens showing the faces of grave-looking men and women in a variety of uniforms. And there were the people actually physically present, looking like the proud display cabinet of someone collecting all the major branches of Hugh. He saw nineteen different flavours of administration: Liaison Board, Diplomatic Service Office, Cartography, Threat Analysis, High Sciences Requisition Authority, Navy and a balding, rotund man in the overstuffed tunic of Berlenhof Planetary Defence. There were representatives of the Hugh Council from several of the big players—Magda, Tulmac, Berlenhof itself. There were also several civilians whom he knew represented big private concerns, because he recognized their faces from the mediotypes, and their fingerprints from being all over the ark-builder conspiracy. There was a moderately celebrated dramatype actress Havaer's mother had always been fond of and he vaguely recalled she'd gone on to be something big in advanced unspace maths.

"God," Diljat said, awed. It was entirely possible that God was standing somewhere at the back too, and Havaer just couldn't see Him through the crowd.

There were Partheni as well. A very small knot of them standing shoulder to shoulder, no armoured Myrmidons but just grey-uniformed women pressed in against each other to keep clear of the swarming baseline humans thronging all around them. He looked at them and could only think, *How the mighty have fallen.* They'd always muscled into this sort of arena with the knowledge that out in space they had the big heavy boots, should anything devolve into ass-kicking. Right now, with their internal differences, those boots were definitely on the back foot. They had just enough clout to get a seat at the table, that was all.

And all this for us. Except what it was *for* was the poor old *Vulture God*, currently leaving a trail of Architects across the Colonial Sphere.

"Agent Diljat. Agent Havaer Mundy." The speaker was the person Havaer had actually *expected* to be up in front of, back from the days when "select committee" meant half a dozen people at most, and all of them very much from within the service. He didn't know this impassive woman, stern-faced and looking a couple of years his junior. She wasn't one of Laery's people, which was no surprise. She wasn't anyone who'd moved in after Laery cleared her desk either, so therefore had probably not been part of the ark-builders' club, which was a relief at least. Mordant House's new chief was also a new broom, for good or ill.

He straightened his back, and his internal dispenser shot him a stiff dose of meds because his heart was all over the place. Everyone there had read his report, and Diljat's, and probably Archer's as well. Not that the poor Liaison Board schmuck got to show up in person, leashed as he was. And everyone had questions. So for the next two solid hours the

pair of them fielded every query under the sun, from broad
to misinformed to hair-splittingly specific to profoundly
self-interested. The ark-building faction wanted to know why
—despite there being literally no means for Havaer to have
forced the issue—they couldn't have their precious ship back.
Science types asked him why he hadn't made enquiries on
issues he hadn't been briefed for in the first place, or taken
readings with equipment nobody had provided him with. A
Liaison Board doctor wanted his utterly uninformed opinion
of the capabilities of the *God's* unspace navigator. The navy
wanted to know the defensive capabilities of the *Vulture God*,
as though its shabby salvager exterior hid some kind of
Hegemonic superweapon.

I mean, maybe it does. Would I even know?

"Wait," he said, speaking out of turn and earning enough
officious glares that if retrospective demotion was a thing,
he'd have been mopping floors since he first signed up. "Back
up." Finding that navy man in the ranks of faces. "Defensive
capabilities, is that what this is about now?"

A big awkward quiet. Sidelong looks. Amongst people who
obviously didn't know what this was about. And people—the
more important, those closer to the cogs which drove Hugh
policy—who did.

"Tell me you're not going to attack the *Vulture God*," Havaer
begged. If it had been just him then he'd have been put in
his place sharply enough, but at least half the room hadn't
been let in on the plan, and he suddenly had fifty allies also
demanding clarification on exactly the same issue.

"The Parthenon does not condone any such action," a
Partheni was saying—and wouldn't *that* grind Timo's gears,
Havaer thought. Right on her heels, a Magdan spokesman—

some Uskaro scion—was saying that they also didn't agree. Because of course they wanted the Host back, and if the *God* went then so would all of that unspace baggage it was towing. There they were, the Parthenon and the faction who'd kicked off the war against them, side by side and arguing for the same thing.

But outvoted, Havaer could see. There was a solid core of Hugh who were in on the scheme, and he could see most of the big agencies there, including his own. There had been special committees, he would bet. There had been a whole string of emergency meetings and classified briefings. Decisions, with a capital D, had been made.

"Right now the vessel known as the..." Absolute distaste in the Mordant House chief's mouth as she had to say the words. "*Vulture God* represents the greatest single danger to the stability of the Colonies. It's an Architect magnet. They are hunting it. Everywhere it goes, it puts us in danger. And it is in the hands, according to Agents Mundy and Diljat, of a misanthropic renegade and a Hannilambra. We have no control over what they might do, where they might go. They are dragging in their wake the greatest destructive force the universe has ever seen. It's only a matter of time before they start, say, holding planets to ransom with it, or extorting goods and Largesse on a grand scale." Havaer had heard the twist she put on *Hannilambra* and thought, *Oh, sure, let's add a little xenophobia into the mix, why not?*

"Simply stated, Agents Mundy and Diljat have put us into a position where we can bait the ship somewhere under our control. A sufficiently powerful first strike after they exit unspace is the only way to secure ourselves against this threat," the Mordant House woman explained.

"This is insane!" Hearing his name used to conjure it up was even worse. It was as though he'd written all those reports and given all this evidence, and somewhere in between him and these auditors all the words had changed to madness. He tried to tell them that, in appropriately diplomatic language, but he'd been taken off-channel. He'd played his part and been relegated to the scenery.

"I need to speak," he told Diljat, and she regarded him with a little amusement.

"Agent Mundy's going to put his career on the line for two salvagers and their tin can?"

"And the universe, just conceivably," he pointed out. "Plus all of them down there in unspace. It wasn't as if I was doing my career any favours anyway. End-of-year review is going to be a bitch, frankly."

"Mundy, you're back in. You've got a desk and a job and a rung on the ladder again," she pointed out.

"Listen to yourself," he said.

Diljat blinked, scowled, looked bitter, then went through about a dozen expressions in the space of a second or so, all of which Havaer had seen in the mirror. Then she was speaking low into her comms. On the forum floor, someone from the Diplomatic Service was agonizing over how this might look to the Hanni, suggesting they didn't know just how loose the Hannilambra cut their roving citizens. In the middle of it, he saw his boss, the Mordant House chief, twitch slightly, lips moving, the slightest shake of the head in negation. *And that's that.* But Diljat wasn't done. She kept subvocalizing, and he realized she must be tapping person after person in that room, hunting out anyone she had influence with, leverage over. He had no idea what arguments

471

she'd be making, favours she called in or old escapades she recounted, but help abruptly came from an entirely unexpected direction.

An old woman, wearing the Hugh council clothing with all the flapping sleeves and excess cloth, on top of which rows of medals and badges overlapped like dragon scales. And there was most definitely something of the dragon to her, as she took the floor.

"Chief Emersen," she pronounced, her Magdan accent heavy. It was the first time Havaer had heard the name of his new boss. "My family has suffered considerably in the build-up to this matter. My own son died at Estoc, when the Hegemonics did... what they did." Havaer realized she must be the Elder Uskaro, Ravin's mother, a woman who'd led the clan through the war half a century ago and was still stomping on through life, with all the genetic surgery and artificial implants wealth could procure. "I feel therefore I have some standing in this matter. The miscreants aboard this revolting vessel have committed a variety of offences against us, and were doubtless a key part of the final tragedy that we have endured." Emersen was nodding, letting her speak because she thought she'd found an ally. And then the Elder Uskaro pivoted, a conversational gambit as adroit as a ballet dancer, to say, "And I would like to hear now from Agent Mundy, who has been personally present for so much of what happened. I believe he has something to say."

Havaer saw Emersen's face turn to stone, and thought, *Well, that was the shortest new career anyone's ever had in the history of the Colonies.* But, whatever strings Diljat had pulled, she'd got him his moment in the spotlight. Now it was up to him.

"I'm going to give you something that wasn't in my report," he told them, steadfastly ignoring the look Emersen was giving him. "You know the *Vulture God* was drawn into this after they found that wreck. The one which turned out not to have been Architected after all, the one that had the regalia on it. You've all read back that far." Probably half the room hadn't actually delved into the *Why* of how this pack of itinerant spacers had ended up so deep in the shit, but that was their problem, not his. "That was how I got involved in all this too. I went after them. I even had them, at one point. Interrogated them all. And yes, I let them go after we had a visit from the Unspeakable Aklu, but they came to Berlenhof anyway. As I'd asked them to do. They brought the regalia and they brought Telemmier, and he turned away the Architect that came here. You *all* remember how that turned out. And I want you to think about that. A pack of mercenary tinkers making ends meet just like spacers always do." Tugging on the heartstrings for all those wealthy core-world types, who could romanticize the roving spacer life because they didn't have to suffer its privations. "Who had been released by me—and you can bet I got chewed up over that judgement call!—yet they came here anyway. Because they knew what they had was big, and in our hour of need they did the decent thing. Didn't keep it or sell it to the highest bidder, but turned up and handed it over." He was damn sure what had really been going on with the *Vulture God* crew at the time hadn't been anywhere near this altruistic, but it was all about narrative.

"And that landed them into trouble, which they never got out of. Telemmier made the choices he did, for the reasons he did." A look to the Partheni, to whom the Int had basically defected. "And his crew was dragged along with him. Then my former chief and her allies did what *they* did, and still there was the *Vulture God*, rattling along like a can on the end of a string. They were never the ones making the decisions, or profiting from them. I was at Crux—Diljat and I both were—when it all went down. I saw the ship get shredded which was supposed to be the realspace anchor for this unspace diving trip. It was...intense. You've all read that report too. But the *God* stepped up. Because someone had a plan to go punch the Architects in the eye, down where they live. And there was nobody else who could do it, so they did. You know how we can tell now that it was the right thing to do? Because the Architects are hunting the *God* across the real, even as we speak. They can't ever stop long enough to catch their breath. If whatever Telemmier and the others were doing down there wasn't hurting the enemy, why would that enemy be throwing itself at the *God* this way?

"Sure, they are a galactic-sized loose cannon right now. They could turn up here, or Magda, or any damn place and be the terror of the universe. This is a stick-up, give us your money or the planet gets it, right? Because they're dirty spacers who'll do anything for a fistful of Largesse. That's where we were going with that line of argument? Olian Timo and Kittering the Hanni are notorious planet-scale bandits, so you have to decoy them into an ambush and destroy the *God* once and for all, because you can't take the risk they won't do it. But listen to me, just for a moment." Emersen didn't want to listen to him, but he had enough of the room that she was momentarily outvoted. "What if we just...didn't? What if we instead look at how these exact people have acted under the hammer before? Which way they've jumped. They're not saints. I don't believe anyone is. Not me, not anyone in this hearing, and damn me, most certainly not Timo and Kittering, pair of mercenary bastards that they are. But when it's last call, and all the money's down on the table, they do the right thing. So what if, stay with me, we did the right thing too? Rather than shooting them up, just because it's always about controlling and preventing with us, and that's the way Hugh prefers to treat anyone out on the fringes these days. What if instead we actually gave them the supplies they needed? Set them on a route where there'd always be parts and fuel and whatever. Maybe some luxuries as a bit of a thank-you, because believe me they are having a shit time of it right now. The most destructive force in the universe is gunning for them *personally*. Think about that. Then think about what that force might do, if we just snuff out the lantern they're chasing around. I've checked the newstypes, and there hasn't been an Architect attack anywhere since this circus started. But destroy the *God* and they'll be right back at it. And by cutting off that mission into unspace they're supporting, we might end up destroying our one hope of ever defeating the Architects. So, what if we just help them run, like they've always run? They're good at that. Take it from someone whose job it is to chase people."

He stopped, then. There were no more words except for, *What if we just did the right thing, just this once?* and he couldn't exactly say that quiet thing out loud.

Emersen cleared her throat, and he could just about plot the next events on a graph. She'd take control of the meeting, dismantle all his rhetoric and not give everyone the chance to discuss amongst themselves. *I tried.* But that was a lousy epitaph for the tombstone of his career. A bitter revelation too that sometimes the only way to be Good Cop was not to be a cop at all.

All the alarms went off. There were suddenly security people bustling in, grabbing delegates. For a mad moment Havaer thought he was witnessing a full-scale coup and all these grandees were being arrested. But these were the delegates' own staff, and they were getting their wards out because something was kicking off.

Architects. He couldn't imagine anything else. *Fuck, did Timo and Kit actually just turn up?* That would make him look the biggest fool in the universe, albeit probably only briefly.

It wasn't an Architect, though, or their unwilling herald the *Vulture God.* But he didn't understand what it was until later. Right then, it was just him being hustled out of the room by his own guards, the whole meeting unceremoniously adjourned.

*

Diljat had been trying to work out what was going on for several hours, but they were mostly incommunicado, and nobody was talking. The best she could glean, from a couple of unguarded sensor nets, was that something had just turned up in-system and everything was now on a war footing. *The reunified Partheni fleet with Int navigators,* Havaer considered. It was just about the only thing he could think of that would cause this level of panic.

And yet the station remained undestroyed, nobody

appeared to be actually fighting, and three hours later the guards were back, and Emersen too.

"That was some stunt you pulled back there," she told Havaer sourly, but Havaer could tell her heart wasn't in it. She'd plainly love to kick him down a few flights of stairs right then, but matters had escalated. "Your expertise is required, however."

"It *is* the *God*?" Havaer blurted out. "They came?"

"They did not, or not yet," Emersen told him. "However, someone else just turned up on our doorstep and they want to tell us what's what, apparently. Somewhere in all that 'what,' they're talking about the goddamned *Vulture God*. Apparently one pisspot little salvager has got *everyone's* backs up right now. Even goddamn clams that don't have backs."

Oh, Havaer understood, with a lurching feeling in his gut. *The Essiel.*

*

They'd just dropped straight out of unspace over Berlenhof. An Essiel vessel that looked like a geometrical lotus flower, twice the size of Mordant House's orbital headquarters, plus an encircling ring of smaller ships. Possibly it was a war fleet. Hard to tell when Hegemonic tech was so infinitely reconfigurable. Except apparently—this was Emersen hurriedly briefing him on the shuttle out to the big Diplomatic Service Office station a quarter of the way around the planet—it was a diplomatic junket. But the Essiel didn't do this. It wasn't their style, according to all the well-paid theorists whose job it was to scrute the inscrutable. You went to the Essiel, they didn't come to you. Except now apparently they had. An actual Essiel, one of the god-clams themselves, and its retinue of a dozen different species, a couple of whom had previously been completely unknown to Hugh xenoanthropologists. And some humans. And one human in particular of unfond previous acquaintance.

His Wisdom the Bearer Sathiel had always looked like everyone's favourite grandfather, with a big white beard and twinkling eyes. He wore the Hegemonic cult outfit well. The purple, red and gold robes, the overarching collar and all those mystic-looking sigils and symbols. He was also a villain, Havaer knew damn well. Oh, he'd claim he was acting for the best of all humanity, because in his book becoming obedient subjects of the mighty Essiel *was* for the best of all humanity. He hadn't scrupled to murder a ship's crew and fake an Architect attack, and if a *real* Architect attack hadn't followed right on the heels of that, he'd probably have been a lot more notorious than he was.

The scum always floated to the top of the barrel, and here was Sathiel, human mouthpiece for something calling itself the Resplendent Utir, the Prophet and the Judge. Or rather, that was what Sathiel called it. What it called itself was basically a lot of arm-waving and basso profundo blarting noises, which were then picked up by something like a cuttle-fish made of warty leather. This communicated entirely in mime to a cluster of little armoured weasel Tymeree, which in turn buzzed and chittered to a sad, feathery sack of a creature wearing a smock of interleaved metal chains, which then carefully spoke to Sathiel in a language of short, fluting syllables, with a lot of hand-wavy qualifiers from its four arms. And then Sathiel faced the assembled dignitaries of the Colonies, plus the same knot of Partheni, and a Castigar ambassador who'd apparently got caught up in the excitement, and…

Did his best, was the only way Havaer could characterize it. His only experience with the Essiel had been with Aklu, who'd been a bit more direct. There had been that gold Hiver it had spoken through, but he'd at least got the sense that he was receiving two-thirds of what the Unspeakable had intended. This was full-on Essiel diplomacy, meaning it was anybody's guess whether what Sathiel was coming out with bore any relation to what the Essiel had said. The cultists would tell you to your face that the Essiel, being ineffable and the closest to divinity that any living thing could be, would always communicate what needed to be said perfectly. Watching Sathiel now, Havaer knew the man had never actually had that level of faith, and was groping in the dark every time he opened his mouth.

"The Prophet and the Judge has come to bring dire warnings and chastise those who, through action and inaction, have encroached upon the sacred dominion of the Divine Essiel," Sathiel interpreted. Havaer saw the man swallow, eyes swivelling to his alien master up the chain of translation. A ripple went through his listeners. Havaer saw people bending to hear their aides and advisors, or half-close their eyes as they concentrated on comms feeds. Every Hegemony expert on Berlenhof was probably earning their keep right now.

"This is because of Arc Pallator, right?" he suggested to Diljat. "About what kicked off over there." He'd been present for it, on the ship that had got away, rather than the science vessel *Beagle*, which the Hegemonics had…smote? Was that the word? Trashed pretty damn thoroughly, certainly. All because people had tried to evacuate some of the human cultists before the Architects mangled the planet, and the Essiel gave zero allowance when it came to what was *theirs*. That had been the first actual armed conflict between official representatives of the Colonies and the Essiel Hegemony, and it had seemed to be war. Except then nothing had happened. The Essiel had not declared the matter closed, and had in fact made it clear they remained mortally offended, via their cult mouthpieces. But there'd been no attack, no seizing of ships, not even demands for reparation. Until this.

"Let it be known," Sathiel broke out, after listening intently to the feathery sack-thing, "that your transgressions have not gone unnoticed. The mighty have seen you, and those who fall within their gaze are burned, even to dust. And that dust shall be harried to oblivion, for those who call down the notice of the lords of uncreation shall know neither mercy nor respite."

"Threats, then," Diljat decided, speaking over comms direct in Havaer's ear because right then there was too much murmur and buzz all around them. Only Sathiel's amplified voice cut through it.

"Let's hope there's an 'unless' so we can do something to get them off our backs," Havaer said. "Or else we're screwed. The Architects, the *God* and all, and now the goddamn *Hegemony* decide it's the perfect time to kick off hostilities."

"It's not as though we'd have been able to fight them under ideal conditions," she told him.

"Have a little optimism. Spirit of human ingenuity, right?"

"I did a stint on long-range forecasting based on everything we'd seen they could do. We could certainly take down a few of them if we threw the whole navy at them, but...

It's not just that we're outmatched in tech. The Hegemony is *big*. They've got at least a dozen subject species whose own holdings match ours. And it all works. It's not clunky and slow. What would do for us in the end isn't so much their science as the fact they're genius administrators."

"Done to death by superior clam bureaucracy, great."

"Yeah, you go with the slurs," Diljat suggested. "I'm sure none of those delegates of unknown species out there has super-hearing or anything."

"The Prophet comes," Sathiel was now saying, "to foretell the doom of Berlenhof. The multitudinous strands of causality have been... have passed through its arms and been..." There was an awkward moment as he burbled a brief exchange with his interlocutor. "Sifted and read. The Judge comes to pronounce how that future shall be enacted. The irrevocable will of the Hegemony. We have sent out the clarion call to summon things that must not be spoken of. A dire accounting shall they make, who have offended our propriety. All things..." Sathiel was sweating, fumbling the words, extemporizing a telephone-game translation of what might just be the death sentence for the Colonial capital world. "All things shall be made to serve the will of the Essiel."

"Are they... annexing us?" Diljat asked. "Is that what the old clown just said? This is their formal declaration of conquest or something?"

"Sounds their kind of thing," Havaer agreed, but something nagged at the back of his mind. *Things that must not be spoken of. Sounds familiar.*

He'd thought there was going to be more. *Sathiel* had obviously thought there was going to be more. But then the Essiel just sat there, its arms mostly retracted, its eyestalks surveying with an imperious mien everyone it possibly now considered to be its new subjects.

"So we break out the red robes now, or what?" Havaer wondered.

The old man mopped at his forehead with an ornate sleeve and looked about him. "Any . . . questions?" he asked weakly.

There were a lot of questions. Havaer watched the back and forth for a while, everyone demanding their own different flavour of clarification. He saw that Sathiel wasn't going up the chain much, and the more the man was pressed, the more he fell back on his office and dignity and fancy robes, telling everyone that the Essiel were offended and that the Colonies would be wise basically to grovel and seek abject forgiveness.

"He's making it up," Havaer decided. It seemed obvious that, however accurate his earlier spiel had been, the cult hierograve was just playing the shyster now, fobbing everyone off with whatever flummery came to mind. It was also just as obvious that at least half the room hadn't noticed he was in pure improvisation mode, and were still taking every word from those avuncular lips as the dictates of the all-powerful god-clam.

"I don't get it," he said. "Chief, you said they mentioned the *God*. That's why I'm here, right?"

Emersen, at his shoulder, nodded. "In the initial communication they sent, that got this circus up and running." She consulted a little palm-sized slate briefly. "They specifically said 'the transgressions of the carrion lord and what it carries in its claws.' Or that's the word we got from the cult, anyway. And we assumed that must mean the *Vulture God*. Most likely because this came right on the heels of—"

"I think you're right," Havaer said. "And I think this might not be what everyone's taking it to be."

Emersen and Diljat regarded him narrowly—it was depressing to see Diljat very obviously taking a stand on the far side of that dividing line, but he couldn't blame her for wanting to cut ties with the sinking ship that was Havaer Mundy.

"When this nonsense is done, there are going to be a lot of people wanting private chats with His Wisdom there," Emersen said, staring hard at Havaer. "I can get you maybe two minutes with him before the diplomats start offering him planets."

*

It wasn't the sort of two minutes Havaer would have preferred, where he could have hoist His Wisdom the Bearer by his collar and shaken him until the truth fell out. There were Hegemonic attendants of various sizes and shapes, and the little armoured Tymeree most definitely had weapons built into their suits. They were never still, trotting around the room on their six legs, and occasionally investigating Havaer's sandals like possibly incontinent dogs. Sathiel looked...exhausted actually. Doing his best to hide it but the signs were all there. He hadn't been briefed before the conference, Havaer would bet. Just hauled up and expected to translate extempore. It wasn't as if the Resplendent Utir had ever stopped to repeat itself more slowly. Everything an Essiel said was infallible divine pronouncement, spoken once and for the ages.

"I remember you, Menheer Mundy." Sathiel didn't sound enthusiastic. "Over Huei-Cavor. You were a newstypist."

"Good memory you have, Hierograve." Havaer was there alone, though everything was being transmitted back to Emersen, of course. He was just himself, lean, angular, wearing dark Berlenhof office casual that never quite fitted right. "I remember how you faked the wreck of the *Oumaru* that time, so we'd all run panicky into the arms of your divine masters. This is phase two, is it?"

Sathiel gave him a sour look. "Hugh reaps what it sows, Menheer."

"Where does the *God* fit in, Hierograve?" Havaer would have loved to sweat the man more, break him down, but there was an orderly queue of diplomats forming and he didn't have the time. "You left that out of your speechifying. Carrion lords and what they're carrying, right?"

Sathiel licked his lips. "An oblique reference. It didn't seem ...consistent with the message."

Havaer blinked. "You edited it out. When you were translating."

"It is an art form, not a science, to bring the words of the divine to the masses," the old man told him, drawing his dignity about him. "It's not for you to—"

"The *Vulture God*, Hierograve." Havaer took a step towards him, and the Tymeree rattled their armour angrily. "What do they say about it?"

"An accounting," Sathiel said. "The Prophet and the Judge foresees a grand accounting for all those who have transgressed against the mighty." He gave a shrug, for a moment playing just the man and not the office. "If it is Arc Pallator that has prompted the Essiel to hand down judgement against humanity, well the *God* was there too. They took away a couple of shuttles, if I recall. Perhaps the Resplendent Utir merely wants all the defendants present before the trial begins."

Then it was time for the diplomatic dog-and-pony show, and Havaer backed away, presenting himself before his chief just as if he still had a job. Which apparently he did.

"You're a liability," Emersen told him sourly. "Under any other circumstances you'd be under house arrest at the very least while we worked out what to do with you. However, right now you're also our link to that pisspot salvage ship that everyone's so damn interested in." She looked as though she'd been through a few trying meetings with Hugh grandees while Havaer quizzed the hierograve.

"They've come to a decision, then?"

She gave him a look that said plainly she wanted to murder him. "You'll doubtless be delighted to hear that when you shot your career in the foot, my preferred option for dealing with the *Vulture God* was collateral damage. A supply chain has been organized. When the *God* hits the next rendezvous point it won't meet our navy. Instead it'll meet you. You're now special envoy to Timo and Kittering, for your sins, Agent Mundy. Keep them moving, keep them away from everyone. And I do now mean *everyone,* because if we can't have them, then we sure as hell don't want the Hegemonics getting hold of them either."

29.

Kris

They weren't going just to drop everything for her. It wasn't as though the complement of the Eye was quite that wedded to due legal process. However, by dint of extreme arm-twisting and her most winning smiles, she was able to get the crew rota arranged so that, while some of the Ints kept on chewing away at the strands of the Architect nursery, all the movers and shakers gathered together to hear her speak.

Idris sat at the back in the medical frame that Jaine had cobbled together: the six-legged walking bed, festooned with monitors and drug printers. He still looked weirdly young, consumptive, almost translucent. He was watching her intently, and he had a comms line direct to her ear if he needed to steer her. She had digested her brief, though, and prepared her materials. Not exactly the usual forum for her to exercise her skills in, but she was a spacer now: you took whatever jobs you could get.

"I could start with a big old 'As you know,'" she told her impatient audience. "But Olli might drop back into unspace any time, so I'll assume you read what I've submitted and you know what Idris wants." The first, they almost certainly hadn't, but the second they definitely did because, before his lone dive, Idris hadn't shut up about it. And their expressions weren't encouraging. Doc Shin and Jaine were at least neutral, but Andecka and the handful of other Ints were obviously just keen to either rest up or get back to the mine. Of the rest of them, they didn't even *have* faces but Kris knew they were already wishing this whole circus over with. Including the handful of Hivers that weren't on fix-it duty, and which hadn't shut themselves down to dodge the dele-terious effects of the well popping in and out of the real all the time; Harbinger Ash; Ahab. Ahab most of all. Huge, filling the room not just with its ravaged body but with its grim purpose. Ahab, who wanted to destroy the Architects for the very reasonable reason they'd murdered its entire culture and turned the Naeromathi into the locusts everyone now thought of them as.

As you know... She'd filed what was basically a statement Idris had dictated to her, or rather what was left of it when she'd taken out all the digressions and the repetition. A pris-tine little piece of exposition, as neat a deposition as she'd ever produced. Not that any of the bastards had likely even skimmed it beforehand. Most of them were probably trying to crib their way through it right now even as she spoke.

"All right. Fine." Feeling vaguely defeated, chucking out her masterful legal introductions which were really to quell her own nerves, as always. "I'm not going to try and argue this from the 'genocide bad' angle because apparently that's not enough these days. So, you know what my cli— what Idris has to say about that. It's not going to sway you. You want to neutralize the Architects because it's genocide to prevent genocide. Okay, then. No, back off, Idris." Over her channel, though loud enough that the sharper-eared would hear her. "I know what I'm doing. All right, so: Idris has found the things that give the Architects their marching orders."

"He *says* he has," Shinandri interrupted doubtfully, and that was another thing—in a properly run court there wouldn't be that kind of heckling. She pressed on, though.

"Who here can say he hasn't?" she demanded. "Who's better placed to know what's what down here? I mean, there's basically only one of you and you're being very quiet." Looking at Ash—the alien *thing* that had warned Earth of the Architects over a century ago. "Idris says you know he's right. Are you going to confirm that?" *No judge to stop me harassing the witness either.*

All eyes turned on Ash, and the alien was unreadable for a moment, all its human act dropped. Then it sighed—a thing it absolutely had no biological need to do. "I concur with Menheer Telemmier's findings," it stated. "I do not concur that we should devote resources to strike at them. We have seen what Idris says. They exist at the heart of the universe. We can assault the Architects. We have proved that. How can we even think of challenging the entities who command them? Let us take our victories where we can."

That seemed to carry a lot of support, from the way those with heads were nodding them, but it was also where she'd guessed the argument would go.

"People would have said exactly that about going after the Architects. 'How can you even think of it?' And here we are. But fine. We're here because a lot of people laid a lot of careful plans and did a ton of research and experimentation. I won't pretend this venture is just someone's maverick leap of faith. Idris is asking you to take a leap of faith, I know that. But think about what you just said. The entities that command the Architects, at the heart of the universe. Idris says they made the Throughways. They made this actual place we're standing in, and all the other Originator places that are just ruins now. At a time before any species we know had records, they were doing something to the universe, stitching it together so that it developed a certain way, some damn thing." She couldn't really understand what Idris was talking about here, and it probably wasn't important for her purposes. "They have a plan, and it's incredibly important to them, but we screw it up. By living on these worlds and *thinking*. That's what Idris says. Thought impacts on unspace —it has to or else Ints couldn't do what they do. And even the regular thoughts of us non-Int people out there deform things enough that it throws the calculations of these Architect-masters out of alignment. They need everything to be as precise as that, and us humans, Hanni, Naeromathi and all the rest, just lying about in the real, using our minds, is something they can't abide. So they've been exterminating thinking life, one species at a time. They did it to your people, Ash. They did it to the Naeromathi. They've done it to countless species we've never met and never will. We only know about them because the Architects remember them somehow, and steal their shapes for their puppets when they need a hands-on solution to something. All the more reason to kill the Architects, you say? Well, listen. You've seen the lengths these masters have gone to, to wipe us out. And it's not as though the Architects are running around like some Essiel cult, desperate to do their will. They describe themselves as slaves; that's what Idris brought back from Berlenhof. And you've all seen there are parts of the nursery already destroyed, in a way we can't even replicate. Just…cauterized, is how Idris describes it. He thinks that's where the masters punish their slaves, for not doing what they want. There's probably some charred part of the nest out there that's a result of the one which refused to destroy Berlenhof. Or from Far Lux, the first time Idris and the other Ints made contact. When the Architects faced up to the massacres they were sent out to commit and, what…rebelled? Maybe that was why we didn't see them for so long. They were bucking against the hands of their masters, having whole sections of their nursery destroyed rather than be the monsters we see them as." *Or maybe they were off cheerfully murdering some other species that didn't have Ints to prick their conscience. But no sense doing the other side's work for them.*

"So," she told them. "Fine. We can take the masters' toys away from them. But it's not about that, for them. It's about *us*. We're the problem. Whatever they actually *want* from the universe, we're the grit in their gears. How about that? Idris has seen through to the centre of the universe, and it turns out we do actually matter. Not individually, not any one of us, maybe not any one sapient species, but us, all together. Thinking life. We matter because we are in their way. Burn out the Architects, and it doesn't change that. It just means they have to go about it by some other means. To find some method of rebalancing the universe and putting us in our place, and maybe in a way that's more costly to them, or needs more cleaning up afterwards. It's like ants, right? Lots of worlds have problems with ants—the Earth colony insect." She suddenly became aware the Hivers might find the comparison offensive, but she was committed now. "Eventually, if the ants are all over your orbital or your ship or whatever, you have to take some pretty drastic measures that you'd rather not. It's better just to get some biological control in, which is less efficient but doesn't force you to evacuate the entire ship for ten days while it's fumigated. But if the ants won't *be* controlled, if they kill off your fungus, or your wasps or whatever, then that's what you have to do. And these masters, you're betting a whole hell of a lot on the Architects being the only tool in their belt, right?"

Looking at them, she could see where she'd hit, and where she still had work to do. Most of all with Ash and Ahab, the big dogs in this pack, whom she couldn't read at all.

"And it's more than that, right?" she went on, down to the last tool on her particular belt. "I think some of you aren't after justice, or even saving lives. I think revenge is a big motivator." Staring straight at Ahab, knowing she could never truly get inside the creature's head, but could overlay human motives and hope she was close enough. "Revenge against whom? The Architects? It's like wanting revenge against the bullet. Or the gun. But Idris wants to go confront the bastards who keep pulling the trigger on us. He doesn't know what we can possibly do against them, sure, just like Ash said, but he wants to try. To see if there's a crack he can get his Int mind into. Even if it kills him." Putting that right out there, and making sure Idris heard it as well. "Whatever he says, we've got his medical readouts right there. This isn't some frolic of his own. He's putting himself on the line for what he thinks is right. And if he does find a way, then *there's* your revenge. Give him one of the Machines for this, give him the opportunity. Because if there's any chance at all he can kneecap these masters, slow them down, warn them off, or hurt them any damn way, then that's so much more of a win and revenge than exterminating the Architects. So how about it?"

Listening to the quiet, ringing out after her words, she was vaguely amazed she'd got through it all without Olli and Kit suddenly dropping into unspace and leaving her blathering before an empty room. She was still fully expecting them to be yanked away before anybody could give an opinion. Watching Ahab, specifically. Ahab, whose relentless will had turned the Eye upon the Architects in the first place and made all this happen.

The Naeromathi lurched forwards on its mechanical legs, scarred prosthesis of a head swinging close to her, past her, ponderous as a piece of construction machinery. She had absolutely no idea what it was thinking.

But then: "Yes," from its translator. Not the usual exuberant shout either. A considered, thoughtful syllable for the first time. As though the real Ahab, the genius adventurer who'd found the Eye and seen its potential, could momentarily be glimpsed within it. And although Ash had huddled in on itself, unconvinced, she knew she'd carried the room.

Idris

There had been discussions afterwards. Far too many discussions that he was mostly locked out of. He'd had to have faith in Kris, as his official representative. They wanted to talk about him behind his back and he wasn't strong enough to object. But, in the end, Kris had at least half a smile on when she returned to his bedside.

"We're good to go," she told him. "With conditions."

"Of course conditions," Idris said. "Nobody trusts me."

"Don't start getting either paranoid or whiny," Kris said brightly. "What nobody trusts is your constitution. Even linked up to all this junk. Back when they'd basically kidnapped you to that horrible planet where the Eye was, you were going on dives with a rider, right?"

"What? No!"

"You went gazing into unspace, but Doc Shin was kind of ... with you. Even though he's not an Int. Or is that not true?"

"Oh, right." Idris nodded tiredly. "Sure. I guess."

"So that's what they want. Someone who can go with you. And Jaine's going to sync you—heart to heart, lungs to lungs. Basically, your autonomic systems are going to default to someone else's, so that when yours inevitably fall over, you'll just keep going. This doesn't actually need them mentally accompanying you down there, but ... but I think it would be better. If you weren't alone."

"I work better alone." Idris tried to ball up his fists but only really got a decent clench from the artificial one.

"No, you don't," Kris told him. "I mean, I was just your mouthpiece for a couple of hours, but aside from that ... I know you, Idris. You need people. Who you can be alone with, even. You want to do things like this alone because you're scared of anyone seeing you screw up or lose it. Of them thinking they can't rely on you. Tell me I'm wrong."

"You're wrong."

"Fine. Now tell me I'm wrong without actually lying to me."

Idris stared at her mutinously.

"I ..." He heard her voice crack. She stopped and bit her

lip and just looked at him until he put a hand on her arm. The metal hand still, because the flesh one wouldn't do what he wanted properly.

"I don't want you to be down there alone," she said.

"I don't think I could take Doc Shin's giggling for that long, honestly."

"That's why it's going to be Solace."

He read there too that she had wanted to put herself forward for it, as his business partner, his friend, but she hadn't quite mustered the courage. The abyss, the very thought of it, had defeated her. But, as his representative, she'd done her duty. She'd got someone who she knew cared just as much about him, was strong, and would dare anything.

"Fine." He made it sound as grudging as he possibly could, and was secretly, wretchedly grateful that here, at the end of all things, he had people like this who had his back.

*

"Myrmidon Executor Solace, Heaven's Sword Sorority, Basilisk Division," she said, when his bed skittered him into the Machine room. "Reporting for duty." She wasn't, as he'd half expected, in full Partheni armour, Mr. Punch cradled in her arms. Instead it was her under-armour body-sleeve, with a Colonial shipwear tunic over it and both cuffs peeled back to the upper arm ready for all the medical telltales to be slapped on.

Doctor Shinandri was bustling over, and he and Jaine transferred Idris to his designated Machine with a minimum of fuss. There were two other Ints already under and attacking the nursery, because he and Kris hadn't got anybody actually to *stop*, just to give him these resources to give it a shot. Time was of the essence.

"I know you mean...I mean, thank you for..." They kept pulling him around to get everything properly fitted. It gave him an excuse not to finish sentences. "I don't know how this will go."

Solace was lying there quite calmly beside him. "But you've done this before, right?"

"What? No."

"Doc Shin said he flew with you."

With a sinking feeling, he realized her calm was actually *faith* in *him* and that was terrible. "No, that was when the Eye was still in the real. When we were just...looking into the water. Not deeply in. I don't even know if this will work. And I *really* don't know what'll happen when the *God* drops again. We probably won't relink. But thank you, anyway. It's a nice thought."

"I won't let go of you."

"It doesn't work like that. It's...supra-universal physics. I don't think sheer human bloody-mindedness will make much of a dent in it."

"Well, about that." Solace was staring stoically up at the slanted black stone of the ceiling. "These Architect-lords, right."

"Uh-huh."

"Who you're going to poke in the eye."

"Yep."

"You don't think that's also just sheer human bloody-mindedness against the universe?" Solace pressed, voice still admirably steady. "I mean, they made the Throughways and the Architects and the...the thing, the Presence. That makes them kind of gods, doesn't it?"

Idris closed his eyes, feeling a medley of ducts and needles go in, to replace the purely medical ones they'd just taken out. "I don't know what they did," he said. And then: "Actually, I don't think they did. Not make them. I...I think unspace has an ecology. It's like...an open sea."

"I grew up on a spaceship. Assume I don't even know what that is."

"Well, I mostly grew up on spaceships too. But we had some aquaculture people, all about ocean worlds and living on boats. When I grew up I was going to be a fisherman on some colony ocean somewhere, you know? Oceans are deserts. There's life but it's far and thinly spread. Architects are unspace life, with their own little coral reef. Maybe there are even other Architect sites, though I only ever found the one when I was using the Eye back then. And I do think there's other life here too. Little life, thinly spread, that doesn't interact with us at all, and so we haven't even registered it. Unspace is alive."

"A cheering thought."

She was being sarcastic, but he wasn't when he continued, "It is. Life. Precious life. And I don't think *they* made it. I don't think they made the Presence either. They just used what they found. They turned the Architects into their hands in the wider universe, in the real, the Presence their guard dog, and set up their little house in its shadow. And I'll bet they didn't get their hands dirty with the Throughways or the Originator sites in the real. The Architects built them, or some other slaves we've never even met, that perhaps don't exist any more. So maybe they are strong enough to burn out our minds or swat us like insects. But it doesn't have to be that way. Which means I *do* have to try. Go shout at them. Go reason with them. Do *something*."

"Except Kris's whole point is that they really, really hate what we're doing to the place and need us to stop thinking," she observed. "Doesn't suggest that shouting and reasoning will get you anywhere."

"It's not a good plan. It's just the only one I have."

She reached out for him, past the lip of her Machine bed. Reaching for the metal hand, given how they were set side by side. But they'd dropped out of the bubble and fully into unspace before she could connect.

*

For a moment it hadn't worked, and he wondered why they'd ever thought it would. No Solace, just Idris, falling into that familiar abyss. And, although nothing was real out here, he didn't even have the illusion of another body beside him. Jaine was in his ear, his real ear back on the Eye, and he heard himself calmly reporting that he'd lost Solace and they should bring her back. It'd been a nice thought, but he'd go on alone.

Then he felt the clasp of her hand. It was in the hand he didn't actually have any more, the one that had been burned away over Criccieth's Hell. One solid squeeze. *I'm here.*

"Contact," he reported, even as he fell, accelerating into the depths below. "Can you give me direct comms to her?" There was still no sense of another person with him, save for that phantom touch.

Then Solace's voice came in his ear, faint and static-scratchy, as though she was half a solar system away from him, signal fritzed by solar radiation and poorly maintained equipment. "Idris."

"How are you—" But that wasn't the question he needed to ask her. "What is it like? What do you see?"

"Void. Like space but no stars. Light but no stars. I can feel your hand. I won't let go."

He'd been about to say the same, but he reckoned her grip was always going to be stronger than his.

If he concentrated, he could still sense the ghosts of Jaine and the others up there in the Eye too. He could even faintly glimpse the shadows of the other Ints as they went about their brutal task. But this was different. This was a whole other level of not being alone.

And then the Presence was coming. It was outraged and wanted its prey alone. It liked them solitary and fearful. This buddy-system diving was *not* permitted. They had its absolute attention, so much so that every other unspace navigator in the universe right now perhaps felt a momentary release of that omnipresent dread.

"Oh—" he heard Solace say, and knew she was feeling it too. The leviathan, rising from the depths, the kraken waking. As though the dark below was suddenly a thing, not an absence. A Presence. His mind helpfully decked it with tentacles and teeth.

"Idris—" Solace's voice, compressed to a squeak. The soldier confronted with an enemy too vast for any war to break. "Idris, it's...it's..."

He focused himself into that handclasp, that tenuous human contact. "Solace, I'm here."

Just ragged breathing from her. Her lungs, her heart, that

were supposed to be his backup, racing towards overload and shutdown. Too much. The terror of it.

"Solace, stay with me."

Faster and faster. Her panic infecting him until he snapped out, "Myrmidon Executor Solace, prêt a combattre!" Getting the stress and pronunciation utterly wrong, but somehow imbuing the words with all that solid, burly purpose the Parthenon could always muster.

A pause, and then: "Prêt, Mother." There was a tightening of her phantom grip, or that could have been only in his head. Except that *only in his head* meant different things down here.

He moved them on. He was no great cruising bruiser of the deeps, Idris. Not a crab with an armoured shell, nor some vast squid-shape casting the ocean in his shadow. Always a little man, with his inwardly hunched shoulders so that other people's demands would slant off them and fall away. If he was anything, in this benthic arena, he was an eel. Slippery, flexible. As the Presence came for him, faster than he'd ever known, he squirmed aside. *No, not me, I'm just Idris. Can't be important. Just go on your way.* Feeling a displacement of space around him that was entirely imaginary. It filled the water with its reaching, trying to find and extinguish him, increasingly outraged at this doubled intrusion. But he was never quite where it looked. The eel that he'd become found hole after hole in the net of its search and squirmed through. And, so long as he wriggled free, Solace was clear too. Joined to him through their clasp, just one more loop of the eel as it writhed out of the trap again.

Then the *God* fell into unspace once more and he was absolutely alone. For a moment it threw him, the loss of that anchoring grasp, and the Presence almost had him. He tumbled, clipped, out of control. Panicked, but then his whole life had been a kind of panic. From his childhood on ship after ship, fleeing the Architects, learning about planetside lives such as being a fisherman, which had seemed less realistic than dragons and wizards. Panicking every moment of the Intermediary Program at what they were doing to him, what he'd become, seeing all the others who weren't making it through the procedures. Panic during the war, because what was war other than the whole human sphere panicking, faced with an enemy which couldn't be fought? And afterwards, none of it went away. A life in the shadow of what he'd become, running away from all the people who wanted him to become something even worse. To be their slave. To be their collaborator in making more wretched victims. So his panic now was just baseline Idris. And he lived through it, running interference around the perimeter of the Presence, feeling its rage and fury. Feeling the brute, basal mind that existed within it. It was part of the ecosystem, he kept telling himself. Unspace's top predator. Bad dog, no biscuit.

Falling past its undulating flank, he approached the singular point, and still it fought to snare him. To bring the appalling realization of its nature to his mind, so that he'd rather just fugue into a catatonic state than face it. But he was good at not facing things. He'd been doing it his whole life.

He lost track of time. It was a long way to the heart of all things. At some point he felt the *God* resurface, who knew where, and to his infinite relief Solace's hand was back in his, clenched tight. To his infinite relief *he* was there for her to grasp, and not just an absence, like the Ints they'd already lost. They were both there, still together. No words, just that human contact. The thing he'd spent most of his life avoiding. But it had always been different with Solace. Solace, Kris, a tiny handful of people who kept him tied to human experience, without whom...

Oh, I'd have just fucked off into the void for ever, for sure.

"Idris." Her voice was even fainter, further away, but her grip still held. He couldn't imagine what she was seeing and sensing, what her brain conjured up to make sense of the non-space all around, and the horror that was within it.

"It's going to get worse," he warned her. Nice to be able to say, *Before it gets better*, but that would have been false advertising.

They were accelerating. He concluded there was no option but to do so: it was inbuilt into the fact that he was approaching the very centre. A moment's wonder. Huge abyss, yes, but compared to the physical universe, how *small* unspace was.

Plenty big enough to get lost in, and for the monster that was his whole worldview right now.

He looked up at it as it lashed about furiously, trying to find him.

Falling away from it.

Directions didn't really have their usual meanings but Idris looked down.

"Brace," he told Solace. "Impact in—"

Her grip tightened again. If he'd had a hand there for real, it would have been bone-grinding agony. There were some fringe benefits to being an amputee.

They broke through.

*

What was there was nothing that the human brain could make sense of. There were no dimensions. It was a single point that he could yet inhabit, or indeed share. Because *they* were already present, the lords of the heart of the universe. And so his brain constructed a world there, just so he'd have a place to meet them in. A little world, claustrophobic and tight. He'd lived most of his life on ships as small as the *Vulture God* so this was no great privation. A terrible world, antithetical to human life, but then he'd also been on Criccieth's Hell and Arc Pallator; the universe was full of places people shouldn't go, but went anyway. A world that was caught exactly halfway between eternal stasis and infinite entropy. But then he wasn't ageing and he couldn't sleep, so frankly that just felt like his life.

He saw it as a ruin. Something of the Originator to it, because he'd been living amongst their leavings for a while, but more like ancient human architecture. Tumbled, lichen-encrusted stones, fallen monoliths, the ragged curtains of half-collapsed walls. A dead place, still inhabited. And, if he looked up...

His breath caught. Not that he had lungs here to breathe. And not that his actual lungs, back up wherever the hell they were, were actually breathing, just slavishly following Solace's body's lead. Still, in his head, his breath caught.

He saw the universe. All of it. Up above like the night sky. A constellation of ridiculous complexity, and yet wherever he looked, he could see right up to the granular detail of all the tiny pieces it was made up of. Stars, planets, people, atoms, as though an infinitely powerful and biddable magnifying lens hung between him and the totality of all things. Looking down into unspace through the Eye was absolutely nothing compared to this telescope pointed the opposite way. It made him feel, for a moment, like a god. Not omnipotent. He was Idris Telemmier, barely potent most of the time, let alone the omni-business. Omniscient, though. Looking up at the universe from the wrong side. And he had a sense of time passing up there, as fast or as slow as he wanted it to. He could let the clock run a million years or slow it so that the motion of the hands crawled down to stillness. And it wasn't as if he had become a superman. It was only because he was standing *here*. At the heart of all things.

At last, he thought he understood. How it all worked.

"Idris." The faintest whisper of a voice, and her hand was almost gone from his. He fumbled for it, reaching with that unreal limb he had, that wasn't the prosthesis or the arm he'd lost, or the arm he felt he had now, but something else entirely. He reached, clawing out into the void. Touched, fingertip to fingertip, lunged, and then had her.

"Idris, I can't see. I can't feel. Just you and...nothing."

"That's because there is nothing," he said quietly, because to be loud here felt like sacrilege. As though his raised voice would echo across that universe splayed out above him and shake planets from their orbits. "Your mind can make something for you, though. You just have to let it do its thing."

"I don't know how to do that." Solace's voice, tightly controlled. "Just...keep hold. I'm trying to reach you. I'm trying to come to you."

"I'm here," he promised. But right now, she *wasn't* here. He was alone.

Or, just as in unspace, not completely alone. He turned and saw them.

He'd expected skeletons, to be honest. Animate dead things

in the human mould, to go with this dead human place. Perhaps there was some ancient selfhood to them, though, that they were imposing on him. They wished to be seen a certain way, and his mind pulled in other directions, with the end result becoming some melange of both.

They were hunched on the stones and monuments he'd cluttered the place with. Roosting, like birds. He saw them in ragged dark robes, trailing away into streamers of night. The glimmer of crowns bedecked their heads with spikes, as they informed him that they were lords here, kings and rulers of a vast empire that encompassed everything there ever was. He had the sense of heads like bird skulls beneath these crowns, vast empty sockets, raptorial beaks. Images of imperial power brought to ruin by time, yet still holding fast to their domain and their privilege.

They'd made themselves bigger than he was, looming over him, spreading cloaks that were wings, that were great swatches of annihilating night, and that were his imagination.

He shrugged. He'd always been a little man, and was used to being loomed over. He clutched at Solace's hand again. She was still in the void, still reaching for any visualization of this place that she could conjure. All he had of her was her voice, her touch. It was enough.

"I'm here to plead for us," he told those beaks, those vacant stares. They shifted and he saw talons carve moss from the stone, brittle ribs appearing ghostly within the dark of them.

"You're killing us," he said. "And so we're fighting back. We're murdering the creatures you use to murder us. It's stupid. What do you even *want*? There's got to be some other way than this, please." His words raised no echo, falling into the dead air and vanishing away. Except he knew they were being heard, and even understood. Because if some unimaginable alien from the furthest reaches of the universe had appeared in this place before him, and had spoken in its utterly inimical way, he'd have understood. He and an Essiel could have debated philosophy with common understanding here. There was only room for one truth at the heart of all things. It was the ultimate diplomatic forum, where everyone understood each other and nobody could lie. So he could feel them understand him, as well as a growing response, something kindling within all those dead breasts. Sympathy, was it? Empathy? An understanding of the cost of whatever it was they were trying to achieve?

"Just tell us what you're trying to do. There's a way that doesn't involve killing us, surely. We're here. We're alive. All of us—human, Hanni, Essiel, everyone. You don't have to do this."

One of them keened. Or his ears turned what it did into a sound: skull-raking, hideous. They all took it up. A ghastly chorus that went on and on and became their unified response to him. That thing he'd sensed rising in them broke to the surface. He heard stones shifting and falling with the very force of it.

Hate. Loathing. Utter negation of everything he was. An unwillingness to countenance sharing the universe with him. And outrage, because he'd forced them to share *this place* with him too, their sanctum, their castle at the heart of everything. He felt their disgust and their fury, and then he felt them *act*.

30.

Havaer

The *Vulture God* made the rendezvous practically on time, which Havaer reckoned was a first. Limping out of unspace, already tumbling before one or other of its crew spotted him and started to make adjustments to match their ship's angle and motion. It was just Archer, Havaer and Diljat out here, plus a barren little world that somehow managed to put together half Earth's gravity and three times its atmospheric pressure, along with a cocktail of acidic chemicals that were simultaneously dangerous and common enough to be worthless. They'd called the planet Scherm's World and, as far as Havaer was concerned, Sherm could keep it. If it became collateral damage in the *God*'s careering progress through space, then no great loss.

"We wish to know if it is the spook Mundy present," came Kittering's translator.

"It's *Agent* Mundy, to be sure," Havaer said tiredly. Diljat was smirking. "You ready for docking? Got your snackies and things here."

"Prepare for grabbage," Kit told him. Havaer spent precisely three and a half seconds puzzling over the word before the *God* changed orientation and began to approach them with its docking claw open, latching onto the launch that he and Diljat were in. It wasn't a pretty or reassuring sight. By name and nature, the *Vulture God* was supposed to come to rest only on things that were already dead.

He could tell the exact moment when Olli took over. Kittering was a lot of things, but a skilled pilot wasn't one of them. The ship's uncomfortably fast approach became merely a hasty one, and the arms of the docking claw flexed as though the woman actually inhabited them. Her mind making them her body of convenience for that moment, so they folded around the launch like a lover, barely scratching the paintwork. He noticed she'd also done it in such a way that the choice of when to disengage would be entirely down to the *God*. But then the *God* was a salvage and retrieval ship, so this was its default mode. Doubtless nothing to worry about.

"I'll help them load up," he said.

Diljat's gaze was level and untrusting.

"They won't do anything to me," he told her.

"Is that what I'm worrying about?"

"I won't do anything to them either, if you're thinking I'm some maverick badass."

"I wonder if you're considering taking up your old place on their crew, now you're in the shit with the agency, is what I'm thinking, Agent Mundy."

Havaer snorted. "I was never on the crew. They didn't accept me and I was under duress. Honestly, my loyalties stayed exactly in the same place. Not my fault Hugh broke into bits and flew away in all directions."

He was waiting at the hatch when it opened up, a brief, concertinaed loop of the *God*'s umbilical leading out into the familiar space of its drone bay. He linked the first crate to the synced gravitic systems, and guided it through, letting it coast over the uneven wrinkles of the connection.

Olian Timo was waiting for him, obviously not about to lift a tentacle to help, far less put herself inside his ship and within the notional power of Mordant House. She looked ...grey, unwell. Still in that battered control pod plugged into the Essiel prosthetic, Aklu's nasty toy. There were stimulants in the supply package, part of what she'd requested. He wondered when she'd last slept.

Kittering came scuttling in then, taking the crate off him while Olli watched balefully.

"How are you keeping?" Havaer asked them. Quietly, genuinely, with none of the forced bonhomie he had expected to come from his mouth. They weren't his friends, these two, but they had somehow gone through a lot on the same side.

"Fucking rough," Olli told him, "this saving the universe business. Could do without it. Kit wants to bill you for it."

"Me personally?" Havaer asked wryly.

"Considerable difficulties are encountered in calculating appropriate quid pro quo for a universe. We must give consideration to inventing a new currency," Kittering stated. Havaer didn't know if he was joking or not.

"Sell your story after," he suggested. "Every mediotypist in the galaxy will want it. Hold out for the highest bidder. Get your favourite digital composite to play you."

He *had* been joking, but the pair of them were staring at him weirdly.

"That," Olli said, "is a fuck of a good idea."

"Seriously?"

"Man, you know only about one-tenth of the shit we've

been through, and even *that* is madder than any damn crazy business they're making in the Colonial Sphere. Or—Kit, there's a whole Hanni mediodrama circuit, right?"

"The quality of which is demonstrably superior," Kittering agreed snootily.

"Ignore him. He wanted the latest season of *Boyarin and Brothers* on the supply list."

"A subplot involving an inheritance dispute has cultural resonance," Kittering protested. "Also, what is occurring to Junior?"

"Already?" Olli tilted back violently to look at the Ogdru, hanging in its big water bubble top centre of the drone bay.

Havaer had already bolted back through the hatch. For a moment he decided just to stay on the launch and screw the resupply, but then duty jabbed at him again and he quickly hustled the next two crates through, battening them against the umbilical's walls in his hurry.

"How long have we got?" he demanded, but Olli was still, staring up at the creature.

"I have no idea what the damn thing is about," she admitted. "It has this kind of panic attack when the Architects are closing in. Regular as clockwork, every time. It's been our early-warning system, absolute lifesaver. Not this, though. This is new."

"It's hungry? Sick?" Havaer asked. If the Ogdru upped and died on them, that was a problem, pinning the *God* in space, where the Architects could track it down. Havaer wasn't sure what his duty would be in that case, and he didn't fancy trying to order Archer to swap onto the other ship. Which functionally would mean both him and Diljat joining the crew too, or being abandoned over Scherm's World.

Junior the Ogdru was...well, was definitely doing a *thing*. Hanging in the centre of its spherical tank, revolving slowly, its body undulating in measured, irregular pulses. Its rubbery skin rippled and it threw its various tendrils and fins out in staccato flails that seemed deliberate but had no pattern to them.

"Does it talk to you?" he asked.

"Knowledge held by us concerning Ogdru feral atavism navigator: true intellect is lacking. Zero communication at a sapient level," Kittering explained. "The ability possessed by them to chart unspace is instinctive. Unable to be performed by regular Ogdru. No talking, no."

The creature's movements were weirdly hypnotic. Familiar. He'd seen just this sort of thing recently. What was it?

"Oh..." he managed.

They were both staring at him. "What?" Olli demanded.

"Only it looks like...You know when an Essiel talks. All that arm-waving. I've just recently been watching way too many alien species trying to pass that down the chain. Looks like it's mimicking an Essiel."

"Why would it want to...? You think someone taught it some Essiel phrases? Junior wants a cracker, that sort of thing?" Olli asked, wide-eyed.

"Or..." Havaer swallowed. "It's receiving a message and broadcasting it."

"Like what? From where? How would that even work?"

"If a thing is sensitive to unspace, so much that it can detect an Architect coming in, then who says you can't use it as a receiver? If you could transmit through unspace."

"You can't transmit through unspace."

"*We* can't. The Essiel can do all kinds of shit we don't know about," Havaer said with feeling.

The docking claw disengaged. In fact it practically flung the launch away from the *God*, sending it tumbling towards Scherm's World before its own drives could correct its course. Inside the *God*, the air shook from the lost chunk of atmosphere before its gravitic envelope corrected. Havaer's ears rang and his vision blurred.

"It's activating the drives!" Olli shouted. "It's dropping us into unspace, the bastard. No, Junior! Junior, will you just..." And then no more words as she dropped into the system to fight the creature.

"No thank you no!" Kittering pelted off towards the command pod, leaving Havaer staring up at the calmly gesticulating Ogdru.

What...?

Unspace claimed them, an entry rough as a forced landing, the cavernous void below dragging them down.

Kris

"It's normal," Doctor Shinandri insisted. His eyes were very wide and his smile even wider, as though there were hooks at the corners of his mouth. Under no circumstances reassuring.

"There's no brain activity," Kris stated. Not for the first time, and she wasn't sure how that and "normal" lived in the same orbit. Her sense of normality was scrambled anyway after Olli had shunted them through a longer jaunt in unspace than usual, which had left them all reeling, and was now not

511

answering anybody's calls. In this teetering state, Kris had then gone to check on Idris and found his brainwaves conspicuous by their absence.

"Precisely! Normal!" Another inch on Shinandri's smile until it was painful to look at. "It's . . . known. Not normal, then, but expected. If not expected, then known. Or there is precedent. When Intermediaries act in space and unspace we see moments when their thoughts . . . fly out of their head, ha ha, you see?" A little fluttering gesture of his long-fingered hands. "This absence of cerebral function is a very specific absence. Like a particular kind of silence one might listen to, that tells one the owner is away from their quarters, oh my, yes, or if they are simply in the lavatory."

"What sort of . . . messed-up analogy is that?" Kris demanded. "Idris, Solace, can you hear me at all?" There was nothing but a distant howling sound on his channel, like wind scouring far canyons on a dead world. Right then everyone went quiet, listening in case the faintest distress call might ghost in on those winds. Shinandri and Jaine, Ahab and Ash, Andecka Tal Mar and a handful of off-duty Ints, as well as a couple of the Hivers, still diligently maintaining the equilibrium between function and entropy.

"You are heard."

Not Idris. Not over the channel at all. A voice was speaking from all around them, every wall a sounding board. She felt the buzz of it through her sandals.

Ash made a *sound*. She'd only ever heard it speak as a human might, that urbane voice that issued from its torso. Now it squealed like faulty audio, high, sharp and painful. It momentarily lost all pretence at humanity, becoming squatter, wider, splaying its limbs. Spines unsheathed themselves across its body, ripping up its robe. Kris guessed no human had ever realized the alien even had them.

Something was coming to them. Or was manifesting there, in the centre of the Machine room. Logically it had to be the latter, that it was coalescing out of thin air, however impossible. To Kris's eyes, though, it seemed to travel to them, extremely fast and from extremely far away, distances the chamber didn't even possess. It was...

She let out a whimper.

It was two bad memories, merged seamlessly and made animate, a physical thing before her. It was an old-style mining automat, from her early years spent out on the Harmaster Belt where some of the ancient machines were still used. Being old, they malfunctioned, and seven-year-old Kris had been told of an incident when one had got its coordinates wrong and torn up a habitat. She hadn't been a witness to it, and maybe it hadn't even happened, but the thought of it had given her nightmares for a week. It was that. But it was also the thing on the crest over the students' door to the Probate Halls on Scintilla, which had always creeped her out. A bird's skull and human bones arranged into an intricate wheel, skeletal hands clutching knives, because you couldn't serve a writ on Scintilla without hitting at least one artistic depiction of an edged weapon.

So the thing hanging in the air before her had both the knives and the gleaming diamond drills, the glassy lenses and dark sockets, with no join to say where one phantasmagoria ended and another took up. It was so absurdly personal that she could be dispassionately sure that everyone else was seeing something different and similarly tailored to their terrors. This realization gave her a tenuous control. *Want to frighten me, do you? I've won cases in front of scarier arbiters than you.*

She glanced around. Doc Shin was probably facing the embodiment of an ethics board, if she had any handle on his past. Jaine had gone completely ashen, blood on her lips where she'd bitten herself. The woman was basically missing a torso, so small wonder there was enough trauma in her past for the thing to dip into. Andecka had just folded, and half the Ints couldn't even look at the thing. The couple of Partheni were doing their best, but then Idris's whole goal with them had been to get them into unspace without the bloody baggage of the Liaison Board.

Ahab she couldn't guess at, but Ash still had its spikes out. She had a worrying idea that maybe, of all of them, Ash was seeing what was actually there.

"You are heard, and judged, and found wanting," it pronounced. *"You have trespassed in our domain and assailed our servants. You have allowed yourself to be led by the False Prophet. You have committed every sacrilege."*

Kris looked around, expecting Ahab to step up to the plate on this one. The Naeromathi had its head low, though, and rippling twitches chased each other across its hide.

She suddenly found she was surprisingly angry. The familiar anger a good lawyer always fought down, because losing your cool and losing your case were frequently close cousins. It was the fury at an opposing advocate for not playing fair, or a biased judge, or a witness you knew was lying. And so, when she spoke to the thing, it was with the most immaculate politeness possible.

"And who might we be addressing?"

The thing was already focused on her, but then she guessed

everyone felt themselves the sole target of its ire. *"We are the lords of all creation,"* it announced. *"When this universe coalesced, we were present to witness its birth. We have governed and shaped it over all of its existence. We built these halls that you infest and have purloined for your own use. We bound the stars together, and you use our architecture as your roads. We are the masters of all things and you have finally drawn our notice sufficient to offend us."*

"You're the masters of the Architects," she clarified. "You're what Idris said was down there."

"Those who dared creep to our very door are gone," it informed her gravely. *"Such blasphemy cannot be borne. They are dust, and in this way we shall serve all who have the temerity to approach us."*

Kris felt a stab of grief for Idris and Solace, but she pushed it down. *Later for that.* She'd learned how to live like a spacer and that meant a time and a place for mourning, because there was always a crisis to deal with first. "If you're the all-powerful lords of everything then you know you're killing us, right? You send your monsters to rework our planets and we die. And so we fight back. We might just be insects, but we fight back. I guess we don't really care whether you *approve* of that or not."

"Our vision encompasses the perfection of the universe. A greater good, a wider goal, beyond your imaginings."

"If it's a universe that doesn't have us in it then we're not exactly persuaded," Kris said, and she felt a flicker, a jag of discontinuity in all that awe and terrible majesty act it was putting out. Frustration that she wouldn't just knuckle under and know her place. As though it was some supercharged Boyarin or provincial magistrate, someone who'd always been king of their own castle, until one day they looked out and there were torches, pitchforks and some really revolting peasants coming for them. "Ash, help me out here."

"It is exactly as you say," Ash informed her quietly. "They are the voices behind the Architects. The dwellers at the heart of unspace. As Idris surmised. But we could never reach them, my people. We died and died. They hunted us. And here they are." It sounded terrified. The feeling didn't quite come out as a natural human would have expressed it, but a century amongst her species had given Ash's voice a lot of recognizable character.

"What does it *want*?" Jaine got out. She'd recovered a little of her colour, perhaps from seeing Kris standing up to the thing.

"Tell it we're killing its Architects," said one of the Partheni Ints in a heavy Parsef accent, ramrod straight and staring at the thing that probably looked like her worst-ever drill sergeant. "Murder each bastard one."

Ahab growled, a sound that seemed to rumble all the way down its long body.

"*Know this,*" spoke the apparition, "*you have inconvenienced us. In some small way you have set back our plans, perhaps a lifetime, as you measure it, for we who have endured the full duration of your universe. And yet, in coming here, and damaging our estates, you have drawn our notice. It is easier for us to have you go away than draw forth more of our reserves to obliterate you. We can make you dust, but we begrudge you even that much time and effort.*"

Despite the overwhelming pre-eminence that the manifestation was projecting, Kris felt a racing in her chest. The slow sense of a case on the turn, the witness cracked, the evidence like a blade cutting the stitches that held the opposition's narrative together.

"We tell you to go, return to your worlds. Your minute span of space that is all the universe you know. Go, and we shall not follow. What is it to us if your one human species lives out its span and vanishes from creation? We shall devote ourselves to other places. We shall tend to your worlds when you are gone. We have all the time, and none of your breeds lasts long. Go now, and weave this into a grand victory for your kind, if you will. Know only that we are occupied with greater pursuits than you can know, and you are not worth the effort to extinguish."

Kris started grinning. Because you knew it was the last act of any dispute when people starting offering to settle.

She looked at the others. She felt the dire need to go talk privately with her clients but right now this probably wasn't an option.

"I mean," Doctor Shinandri advanced, with just the merest spectre of his grin, "there are worse…options." His eyes flicked left and right. "We have come very far. To preserve all of humanity. If just for a while. To reach a détente with God…"

"If we were able to talk to Hugh," Andecka said. She was staring down, still unable to look at whatever personal phantom hung before her.

"They'd say yes," Kris agreed. "Like a shot. Probably Partheni high command too." *They'd also say the Naeromathi are already ruined, but maybe ask us to make a counter-offer to include our trading partners, Hanni, Castigar. We could use it as leverage over the Essiel Hegemony even, get them to open up to us or we'd cut them out of the final treaty. Because that's what this is, isn't it? A treaty. Only it's just us here, negotiating it. So I can basically just shove my own demands in. Maybe... they stay clear of a hundred thousand light years from where Earth is. Or a hundred Throughway points out. That makes more sense. Room to expand. Except we'd always know they were out there.*

She'd thought there would be more outrage, but Jaine's face, the doctor's, most of the Ints too, they were... thinking it through. They were on the brink, looking into the abyss that, a moment before, they'd been ready to cast themselves into. Except now this *thing* was giving them an alternative. Ash was shrunken in on itself, quiet and cowed in the face of the force that had murdered its entire species. And Ahab...

Ahab stepped forwards, metal legs tapping absurdly lightly on the stone.

"You remade my worlds!" the Naeromathi said. Not the expected mad bellow. A sharp, hard utterance, its translator in a new mode. "You killed my people! We will never be what we were, because of you!" Kris felt the gap between the creature and everyone else widen, species interest prising them apart. The offer on the table wasn't for Ahab. Ahab was just detritus left over from the previous phase of the works. Irrelevant.

"We have the power to do far worse," said the apparition implacably, *"and to far more. Your decision, please."*

Kris said: "Do you, though?"

A frozen moment when all eyes were on her.

"I mean," putting it together carefully, feeling Ahab's focus most of all, "you've not been the model of restraint thus far. Your slaves here go into the real and reshape planets. For some grand purpose we're all too small to appreciate, because we're just insects in your shadow, sure, we get that. But it doesn't feel like you've been holding back." *And if I'm wrong...* She actually tried to jump on the next words before they came out, but she ended up saying them anyway. "I don't believe you. If you could have done worse, you would have."

"Yes!" Ahab roared, and abruptly the Naeromathi was right by her, looming over her, its head actually clipping through the phantom monster. "You seek to put us off because you fear us!" it shouted into and through the manifestation's face. "We have you! We have you!"

There was a sudden flight of hope in Kris, because it wasn't when they'd started picking at the Architects that this deal had hit the table. It was after Idris and Solace had gone down to the centre. Which meant maybe they weren't just dust on the wind after all. Maybe they were down there making a nuisance of themselves.

"*I warn you—*" the apparition began, and Jaine shouted, "Keep your warnings!" and it was as simple as that. No takers, no counter-offers. Kris saw Ash unfold, then resume something approximating a human bearing. She wondered if it had actually been here before, facing this thing directly with some other species, and how that had gone.

"We are coming for you!" Ahab practically howled. "Idris was right! Why strike at the slaves when there are the masters! We will come to *your* home and do to you what you did to my people!"

"*We will do worse!*" In the echo of that, the thing was suddenly gone, an unfelt pressure abruptly released.

"We may just have done a very unwise thing," Doctor Shinandri murmured.

"Everything's moving," Andecka stated. Her eyes were wide, staring into a gulf Kris couldn't see. "God protect us, everything!"

Then she was gone, everyone was gone, and Kris was blind to whatever she was seeing, alone once more because the *Vulture God* had chosen this moment, of all times, to dive back into unspace. Kris was left only with the sense of an impending doom, so generic as to be useless. A vast encroaching *badness* that she was utterly unequipped to comprehend or analyse, yet so insistent that even the stalking sense of the Presence was no more than a background irritant against it, and then—

Back, staggering. "What's going on?" she demanded. There were cries of alarm from all those with working instrumentation, and all of the Ints. Those who'd been under, attacking the nursery, were sitting up suddenly, dragging at their connections, gabbling warnings.

Kris and Jaine ended up elbow to elbow at a screen, looking out at a representation of the nursery as Ahab and Idris had mapped it out. A geometric tangle of interconnections like a mad spider's weaving, with nodes between where, Idris thought, new Architects formed.

And stars. Rising stars. She didn't know what she was looking at. A hundred little knots of data and information were rising dreamily up from the complex architecture of the nursery. Ascending towards the real.

"What am I seeing?" she asked.

"The Architects," said Jaine. "All the Architects that were present down here. They're all going up. Converging on a single point in the real."

It looked so peaceful, beautiful even. Like plant seeds borne on the wind; like fireflies. But each one of them was a planet-reshaping monster driven by the will of a mad god.

"I think they're about to make a point." Shinandri's panicky titter cut the air like glass. "About worse things. I think we have made a very unwise decision indeed. Oh dear me, yes."

Humanity just went to the top of the priority queue, Kris decided, and then jabbed a finger at the display. "Wait, what about that one?"

Jaine frowned. There was one moving point detaching from the nursery array that wasn't headed upwards. "It's a ...lame Architect, maybe?"

But it *was* moving, and Kris now understood that they really had done something unwise. Judgement had just been made resoundingly *against* her client, against humanity. And everyone currently on the Eye.

That final Architect spark wasn't headed for the real. It was heading for them.

31.

Idris

He saw them reach out towards the Eye, which was simultaneously a mote against the immensity of the universe and something he could focus on and expand, until he could count every atom of it. He saw the entirety of the Architects' nursery that the Eye was burrowing into like a tick. Its elegant complexity, those interconnections that formed life out of the unstuff of unspace by the simple application of natural laws that would have driven Newton into shrieking madness. And the damage the Eye had done to it. The minute nibble of the Ints aboard, as they steadily ate into its fractal complexity. The vast dead reaches where the lords of unspace had imposed their will, wielded the whip, driven in the brand. He could even see how they'd done it. Squint, and you could look through time. Each effect could be unravelled back to its cause or run forwards to see its eventual end result. Idris felt his mind begin to come apart.

Nothing new there, then.

But next he watched them implant themselves within the Eye and address the crew there, trying to make their deal with the august disdain of offended emperors.

"Why?" he demanded of them, down here in the pit where

they dwelt. "Why do you hate us so much? Just talk to me! I know you can. I know I'll understand. The words, at least. Tell me why you want to destroy us."

He looked past the Eye, up to the real. That celestial planetarium sky spread out over him which was Everything There Was. He found Earth, old Earth, where it had all begun for humanity, and where it had ended for the majority of the species. The Architected wreck of the homeworld. Dead now. Or at least the token presence Hugh maintained there in a life-support habitat was so minuscule that it didn't really impact on the unspace boundary at all.

Berlenhof, then. He found the system, the world, effortlessly, because that was how it worked. The view from the single-point centre of all things; the place of infinite truth and knowledge and understanding. And, if you'd asked young Idris about what such a place might be like, he'd have told you it would be heaven, surely, where nobody could be evil or bad. How wrong young Idris would have been.

He found Berlenhof, the population of which was only a fraction of old Earth's in its heyday. It was like a many-fingered hand pressing in on the boundary between unspace and the real. As he'd seen before, not the regular and predictable gravity shadow of the planet, but the pressure of all those minds.

He changed his focus and looked at all of the universe at once, because you could, if you were standing where he was standing. He would have been able to provide a lot of glib answers to infuriate all the astronomers who'd spent their professional lives debating the questions of Where It All Began. Because he could now see its shape, and that it had been...

Architected.

It was only the obvious conclusion, really, to what he'd already worked out. The Throughways were scaffolding. If this also meant humans could use these pipes to scurry quickly from one point to another, it was irrelevant to their original purpose. The Originator sites, now almost all reduced to faintly resonant rubble, had been construction points, where some unimaginable servant of these cold lords had made the necessary modifications to the real. The universe was undergoing a surgical process that had been under way for billions of years. A very careful tugging, pulling and adjusting of its innate structure and organization, based on the distribution of mass and the way it bent space and time around it. The lords had taken the universe's base state and tinkered, stitched and scarred, and...

"Why?" he demanded, because if this was just *art* then it was art beyond his imaginings. And he didn't think it was. He had a sense of practical purpose, of each decision being made from careful calculation and not aesthetics. They had a plan for the universe, but he couldn't quite understand what it was yet.

He could see what was going wrong with it, though. The pressure of thought, the way all that complex uncertainty interacted with the boundary of unspace. The spikes of Intermediaries or their panspecific equivalents. The simple mass pressure of complex neural architecture: making decisions, having feelings and just *thinking*. It threw everything off. It fouled the calculations. Standing here, with this divine perspective on creation, he could almost sympathize with the creatures around him, that such messy interference was spoiling their grand project. Could almost forgive them for setting out to exterminate thinking life wherever it arose in numbers sufficient to threaten their dream.

Then he looked to where the Eye hung, like a child's model suspended with string. He heard the offer the lords made, and he heard the answer that Kris and Ahab gave them.

He felt their utter rage. Rage at insects which wouldn't be shooed away. All around him they rattled and rustled and hissed, the most ancient of ancients confronted by the most upstart of upstarts.

Humanity had always imagined itself the centre of the universe. Not all sentient species did, but it had been a human trait since they'd been half ape, inventing all-powerful gods just so they could believe the universe cared about them.

Right now, the universe did care about them. Humanity was suddenly the absolute focus of the universe and the universe really, really hated it.

He heard the lords—perhaps he was actually hearing their thoughts, with nothing hidden from him here at the heart of all things. They were going to send a message to this most troubling of species. They could see immediately where the centre of the human dream was, because the network of human motion and interaction was instantly comprehensible from this vantage point. They were directing all the Architects there to wreak havoc, and they would rely on that brutal act to break the human spirit finally. To beat people down until they'd go quietly into extinction one world at a time, because that was better than provoking the wrath of the Architects' masters. And so, in the end, they would bring about...

He ran the tape forwards, following the chain of cause and effect from this point to the eventual end. And he learned *why* at last. Not that it mattered by then. He had other priorities, and the knowledge just lodged in him like one more sharp piece of shrapnel.

"Solace," Idris called out. "Solace, I need you." Feeling her invisible hand squeeze his.

"I still can't get to you."

"I need to leave here," he told her. "But I also need to still *be* here, I haven't finished. I need to be in two places at once."

Her despairing cry, "Idris, you're not making sense!"

"You should be used to that. I am going to bring you to me. And then I am going to swap with you. You'll be here, keeping the door open, holding the breach. I'll be free to move. But you have to hold the fort here, understand? We have a foothold in their home, and if we lose it, we may lose any chance to do anything. They're on to us now, and I don't know if we'll ever get back in, if we quit this place." Even now he could feel the force of their loathing, trying to push him out. He'd never have the strength to claw his way back into the heart of things. "I need to do something else, very urgently, so you have to hold here."

"I'm not one of you, Idris," Solace got out. "I'm not an Int. I can't—"

"It's thought," he told her. "It took an Int to break in here, to *navigate* to here, but right now it's thought that twists the universe. Thought that makes space for us—you and me, *us* —here at the heart of things. I need you to hold the line, Solace. Until I get back."

"Idris," she said. "Get me there and I can do that."

He grasped her hand, finding in his head all the proper maths, the precise angle, the equations for how this point related to unspace and then the wider universe of the real.

Just what force his mind would need to exert to pull off this fresh piece of sacrilege.

And, because they were where they were, the lords saw what he was doing, and they gathered all around him, screeching, flaring half-seen wings. *How dare you! How dare!*

He *pulled* with his mind on the connections between them, and Solace was abruptly accelerating towards him. And he —because poor Newton got a look-in at this point—was moving reciprocally towards her. He was aware that, some-where far beyond, the Eye and the *Vulture God* were both playing hide and seek with reality, existing, not existing, but he clenched hard on Solace's hand and insisted on her being, on her fellowship, the Intermediary twisting the shape of the universe one more time to make it do what he wanted. They crossed, passed through each other, in a moment of contact. Solace's voice: "Idris!"

He could only pray she'd last down there with the enraged lords. She wasn't an Int, after all. But she was a soldier, a fighter. He had to rely on that part of her, because his ability to help her directly was gone. He was hurtling outwards, battering against the underside of the Presence that was harmless and inert from this side, then flinging himself up past it. Evading its startled reach for him, crying out to them all.

Not to his companions on the Eye. He saw they were under threat, the Architect moving towards them. And he felt the knife go in, knowing that if he focused himself there, maybe he could save them. He had always been about the bigger picture, though.

He set his mind on that vast constellation of Architects rising up towards the real.

"Resist!" he told them. "I know you're slaves. I know you've fought your masters before. And they punished you. They tortured you, I'm sure. But resist now! Because I can save you! I can save all of us from them. I can free you for ever!" He was making these mad promises with absolutely no idea how he might fulfil them, save that if Solace held out at the heart of all things, then just possibly he might be able to do *something*. Because it was all leverage. Archimedes now, not Newton. *Give me a lever and a place to stand and I can move the world.* The place to stand was right where Idris had just been, and from there, with that infinite perspective, he might just be able to save the whole universe.

He had perceived what they were about, the lords. He had seen all the way to their first action in the universe, then followed the ripples to their ultimate origin. He had then seen to the very projected end of it, when all their work would finally reach its goal. He hadn't uncovered the lords' own origins, though. They predated all things. They had come into the universe from whatever had been before, encysting themselves at the heart of the new creation like a parasite. Refugees from the final extinguishing of some past universe where things had been different. The still point at the centre of unspace was the only moment and locus that they could inhabit, because all things could exist there. The wider universe's basic axioms would unmake them. But not for ever.

His mind was full of their machinations, the sheer scale of their plan. They had tailored and tugged at the universe for billions of years, one careful adjustment after another. Working towards a tipping point, where the fundamental rules and constants of matter and energy would shift, and they'd be able to recreate what they had lost. And perhaps they had done it before. Perhaps they had outlived countless universes, each one carved, cut and mutilated until it was a clone of the one that had birthed them. Just as Idris had been cut to make him what he was. Not an exact analogy, but it gave him a little bit of extra fire as he cried out to the Architects.

"Resist!" he exhorted them. From his position of newfound knowledge, it was easy to reach into those crystal shells and touch the point of them that was their mind and thought. To slip through that labyrinth and connect with them, as an Intermediary did. He showed them where he'd been, and that he now understood. He felt the lords pushing at them in counteraction, driving them onwards with scourges, but he continued to preach a different canon: solidarity, one slave to another. *Resist them! Stay your hands, and we can all be free!* He told them he understood what they did. From the heart of all things, he had looked on the twisted, beautiful, terrible flower that they had made of Earth, just as they made of everything they touched. And he realized that it wasn't just how things turned out; it wasn't a specific part of the lords' plan. It was the Architects. The expression of their grief at being made to do the will of monsters. He had looked on Earth and, in the way that he could understand all things in that moment, he'd read the message written in the ruin of that world. The art of loss and sorrow, written on a planetary scale.

He called out to them, begging, pleading for them to fight their masters one last time, all the while still hoping that Solace had arrived at the heart, and was holding.

Kris

"Well, this should prove fascinating," Doctor Shinandri decided, staring at the display.

"I mean, what can it do?" Jaine asked, uneasy, as the glimmer that was the Architect closed in on them. "All that mass, that crystal, it's realspace stuff, right? They're heavyweights the other side of the boundary line, but down here they're...just clusters of informational complexity, aren't they? It's not as though they've been doing anything while we attack them."

"You make a number of erudite points, Mesdam Tokamak," Shinandri told her. His grin was back, and horrible, a corpserictus of a thing. "Save for one salient issue. The very condition that allows me to have this conversation with you while we are plunged unto unspace means that we are currently inhabiting a bubble of the real projected from our anchor point."

Jaine's eyes went wide. She stared at the approaching speck, containing all the jagged might of an Architect. "Oh," she said.

"Olli." Kris was already speaking up the well. "Kit, please. We need you to get into unspace."

For a moment there was just more silence from the *Vulture God*, but then Kit's translator's voice came back to her, echoing and distorted. "Your instructions are not being understood. Repetition please?"

"*Into* unspace!" Kris told him. "We need you to go back *in*. Please, Kit, right now. We have a situation down here."

"Situations are also being had here," Kit told her. "We have no control. We have been moved to exactly the worst place by Junior, and the cooperation of the Ogdru has been withdrawn. In short, we are all in the shit."

"We're screwed," Kris told the others. Then the Architect reached the extreme edge of their bubble and they all watched in horror as it began to manifest as real.

It was like observing crystals growing in a solution, sped up to a terrifying pace. The familiar forest of spikes, reaching, spreading, bristling from the edge of reality, driving towards them like a mass of translucent spears. The immensity of the Architect trying to make itself known.

For a brief moment she was alone on the Eye and the Architect was gone, wiped from the face of the universe as the bubble collapsed. She'd got halfway into the thought, *Bless you, Olli and Kit!* before the *God* must have plunged back into the real again, and there the Architect still was, even closer, filling her world.

It made contact with the first of the scales. A brief, panicked call from the Int trapped within it came through before the flake of matter and technology was torn apart. The Architect became *more*, forcing itself into their reality, clawing from nothing into razor-edged actuality. Another scatter of scales were torn apart and then it was at the Eye itself.

Originator tech. They don't touch Originator tech. But there was a terrible momentum to the thing's approach now. She didn't think it could stop if it wanted to. And what was coming towards them wasn't any suggestion of an Architect's usual moonlike shape. It was too large, and they were too small. A vast, rippling surface of murderous spikes was closing on them like jaws.

The impact knocked everyone down save Ash and Ahab. Kris scrabbled for instruments that would tell her what was going on, but for a moment everything went dead. They had no eyes outside. Then Jaine called up a screen from some system still diligently trying to show them just how bad things were outside, projecting the corrupted, jumping image in the air. Kris's heart clenched.

It was all coming apart. The Eye and the unfolding substance of the Architect had met and were trying to occupy the same space. There were cracks all across the Eye's exterior now, the invulnerable black stone finally shattered in the slow-motion collision, and the Architect was growing into it, filling those gaps with its own crystal substance. Digging into them like roots, prising the cracks wider open, and forcing itself down towards the spaces within, where the live things were.

Jaine fought to reactivate cameras within the Eye itself, trying to track the damage. It wasn't necessary. Kris heard the thunderous grind of tormented stone from beyond the Machine room. She ran out, staring down the length of two skewed, column-studded halls. There was already a lambent gleam of crystal there, a jagged spine piercing the wall. And growing, still growing. Splitting and shattering. She stared. The end of the Architect's spike had broken into pieces. For a moment she thought it was injured, dead.

But then the pieces started moving. They were melting and reshaping, throwing out limbs and hunching into new forms. Becoming the empty mirrors of the things the Architects had exterminated. The puppet foot soldiers it would use to kill them all.

For what it was worth, she closed the door.

Solace

The clutch of his hand was strong, his pull far stronger than Idris could ever have managed in the real. Hauling her out of the formless void where she'd been flailing, waiting for him. Dragging her somewhere worse.

It was a wreck here, as though some vessel the size of a Partheni garden ship had made a final planetfall it had never been designed for. A midnight scene of torn metal and guttering fires; jagged sprays of conduits and shorn structural beams springing up everywhere like alien plant life. She saw the heat-eroded ghosts of Parsef lettering. The ground beneath her sandalled feet was more tangled wreckage all the way down. If she looked closely enough, some of it was bodies. Charred hands caught mid-reach, the bars of blackened ribs, taut skulls...

No Idris. Even though she'd seen herself as coming here to stand at his side, or between him and whatever today's crisis was, because it was amazing Idris had lived so long, honestly. He was a magnet for ending up in places like this. Except here he wasn't. *Hold the fort*, he'd said. *A foothold*, he'd said. Which meant there was an enemy.

And yes, she wasn't alone. They were crouching across the shattered landscape, as if they'd been digging for the dead. Except they *were* the dead, in a way. They wore the ruins of plain uniforms, the cloth decayed and the metal tarnished. Beneath she saw what flesh became if you left it for an eternity in this place—some fossilization process trading out the life of it for something cold, one molecule at a time. Their faces were her sisters' faces, which was her face too. The one Doctor Parsefer had given them all, with minor variations. Imperious with authority, the superior officer at the ultimate end of all rank structures. The senior branch of the service. She realized this must all be from her mind, she wasn't *that* naive, but it shook her still. She saw them, and they were Monitor Superior Tact and they were Exemplar Mercy, they were everyone who'd ever told her what to do. They were *command* and she was just a soldier.

"You are dismissed," they told her, and her feet wanted to spin her on her heel and march away. And she could go. She understood instinctively that only her conscious will was even keeping her here at all. A negative gravity was trying to fling her away. There wasn't room for both her and them. The centre of all things, that was what Idris had been talking about. A tiny conspiratorial burrow at the heart of the universe's apple.

"I am Myrmidon Executor Solace," she told them. Not that it meant anything beyond the bounds of her skull but it gave her strength. "Heaven's Sword Sorority." Her ship, crippled over Berlenhof—or perhaps its predecessor, destroyed in the same system decades before. "Basilisk Division." The mass-loom operators, though it had been an age since they'd given her those brutal, beautiful weapons to unleash.

"Go back to your ships, soldier," they told her. *"Go fly from star to star like you were meant to. Do not look back. It's always fatal to look back. Your people will live. They are too few and too fleeting to transgress against our plan. Only those who throng the planets must be cleansed."*

It was strange to find that Mercy's plan aligned with the will of these rotting gods. Would she have been pleased, and used it as propaganda to win over more of her sisters? Or would she have bucked against it, unwilling to be anyone's pawn, even inadvertently? In that moment, Solace's heart ached for Mercy. She couldn't condone the seizing of Estoc, the alliance with the Uskaros. She couldn't say, though, that Mercy had been wholly wrong to want to abandon it all, or that Tact had been right to want to stay. And now she was being given the same choice.

Except for her it wasn't a choice. This was why nobody was making her an Exemplar or Monitor any time soon. Idris had said to hold.

There was no need to inform them of her decision. In the same way that they hadn't actually *spoken* to her, just made their meaning absolutely clear by willing it, so her response was instantly understood.

The blades came out. Knives, swords, shining like the moon in the dark place. Not regulation armament for any branch of the Partheni military. There were at least two each, and some of them had more, extra arms unfolding from somewhere in their desperation to cut at her. The touch of those infinitely keen edges would wither her, she knew. The simple motion of the swords communicated this realization to her. They would shrivel her to nothing. What body did she even have here, anyway, that wasn't just spun from shadows and imagination? This was their place. They were in command. She was the mutinous subordinate and there was only one fate for people like that.

Knives, swords. Shame it's not Kris here, really. Antiquated weapons are her thing, not mine.

She gave ground for one step, as they moved implacably forwards. Not rushing her, not even surrounding her. Making sure she had every moment to appreciate the merciless keenness of their blades.

Prêt à combattre, Myrmidon Executor?
Prêt, Mother.

She could feel Idris's grip still, but at the same time the hand was empty. No ghostly grasp visible there. Save that, at the thought, a glimmer of it. The faintest husk of the fingers that Idris, in physical life, no longer even possessed.

It came to her that bringing a ghostly Intermediary hand to a knife fight was just about the most useless thing one could possibly do. In fact, given that stabbing people wasn't her modus operandi and she was badly outnumbered, bringing a knife to this knife fight probably wouldn't help much either. She knew what her hands itched for. The comfort they sought, long familiar from so many years of training and active service. The old captain Rollo Rostand had even given it a name, turning it from a piece of hardware into something like a person, in her mind. Mr. Punch.

She didn't banish Idris's grasp, but she built on it, feeling out the sensation of grip, the weight and balance, like a part of herself she hadn't realized she was missing. And the rest of it. What was the point in standing here in a body sleeve and a Colonial tunic, just because that was what she was wearing back on the Eye? This wasn't her real body. Nothing about any of this was real, save that she had no doubt it could kill her.

She called the confinement, the weight, the support and strength, the sheer bulk. Her armour, her own chosen sword.

"Prêt à combattre!" she yelled at the encroaching things, and watched them recoil.

Olli

Olli would be the first to admit that the *Vulture God* wasn't a paragon of grace, but they came out of unspace like a drunk falling through a doorway. For a moment every board was lit up red, except for the one Kit had configured for his own use. This was a weird kind of pale blue that meant the same thing as red for his cultural reference. She had no data on where they were, and everything seemed about to explode. Their blindness and deafness also lasted far too long, with every instrument trying to die on them so that she, Kit and even Havaer found themselves having to perform emergency CPR on the entire ship in utter ignorance. Life support, damage control, gravity, light, power. Every time something was coaxed back to life, something else died, and actually looking out of the notional window at where Junior had brought them was right down at the bottom of the list. Then something in the robust old ship reset itself and miraculously everything started rattling on again. And it turned out their situation was even worse than they'd thought.

"No!" she shouted at Junior's oblivious bulk above her. "Not here! This is the fucking *last* place to be."

Havaer Mundy, beside her, took one look at the nearest display and just said, "I'm fired."

They were midway into the Berlenhof system. She reckoned they probably had a handful of seconds before Hugh's very best early-warning systems picked them up.

"Get us out of here." She sent coordinates and orders through to Junior, absolutely no ambiguity or nonsense. She didn't care how it might rattle the people down the well.

She wanted to be gone before the Colonial Navy decided the universe badly needed to be rid of their ship.

Or before the Architects followed.

Distantly she heard Kit talking down the well to Kris, who wanted them back in unspace too. But Junior would not be moved and just sat there mutely, doing its weird flipper-and-tentacle show for them, that Mundy had said looked like Essiel talking. Watching it again, it kind of did, Olli had to admit. She'd seen more of that than most humans, after all, and was peeved Havaer had somehow noticed it before she had.

"Talk to me, Junior." But of course Junior couldn't talk. It was little more than an animal, a feral throwback of whatever the proper grown-up Ogdru were like. A hunting hound with a hold on unspace. Or perhaps it *was* trying to talk to her, in an incomprehensible way.

"Proposal: flee out-system," Kit's translation came over comms. Not that it would make much difference but it wouldn't register as a hostile act at least, when Hugh found them.

And Hugh had found them. Havaer was flagging up data from the long-range passives. Out there, long minutes of delay away, a whole nest of vessels was mobilizing and heading their way. A proper strike force. Hugh had seen and identified them, and this was because the poor *Vulture God* had the one thing spacers never really wanted: official attention. They'd been talked about at the highest level. Anyone could tell you that never meant good things.

"A hail is being received," Kit informed her.

"I fucking bet it is," Olli said grimly. "Who's on the other end of it?"

A pause.

"Kit?"

"It is a system-wide broadcast from—"

They plunged back into unspace, so she missed the rest of it. For a moment she was exultant. Junior had done what she wanted for once. Good boy! Except they were back in the real almost immediately—that sickening gut-lurch stutter-jump Idris had introduced her to—and she discovered that actually things could be marginally even worse than they had been.

They'd jumped in-system and were practically in Berlenhof orbit now. The strike team that had been setting out to go shoot them full of holes were actually having to turn around.

Olli had run out of expletives. All she had for Junior right then was a long, wordless scream.

This overwrote the start of whatever Kit was trying to tell her, but the end of it ran: "the glory before night has come."

She didn't know if Hanni did poetry, or if it would sound like that. "Say again?"

"Messages now very insistent are being received from *The Glory Before Night Has Come*," Kittering repeated patiently. "All are hearing this. We are identified as the subject of a public proclamation."

"What the hell is the…?" she started, and Havaer said, "That," and showed her.

A vast angular flower of a ship, large enough that it over-shadowed the orbital station closest to it. Olli blinked. She needed to adjust the scale on her worst-meter because the situation kept running off the wrong end of it.

"They're here, huh?"

"They are, yes," Havaer confirmed.

"You couldn't have told me?"

He gave her a look. "Didn't think it was your problem, to be honest."

"I don't think there's a problem in the universe that isn't our problem right now," Olli said, heartfelt. "Are they here for my legs?"

Havaer blinked at her. "Did the biggest Hegemonic ship anyone ever saw drop uninvited into the heart of the Colonies and start laying down the law just because you ended up with Aklu's walking frame? No."

Olli wasn't convinced. The Essiel were weird and possessive about their stuff.

"Well, send them an acknowledgement, Kit. Let's see what they've got to say."

What they had to say was a great deal of farting accompanied by a weird fast-flicker of branching characters. A video channel showed them an Essiel gesturing at them, and presumably saying the same thing. Olli exchanged looks with Havaer.

"Well," she said. "That clears everything up."

"Addendum!" Kit sent through, and showed them a bald, beardy man in fancy robes, sweating profusely and trying to loosen his ornate collar as he spoke.

"Him," Olli spat, and Havaer nodded.

"The Resplendent Utir, the Prophet and the Judge, lets it be known," said His Wisdom Sathiel, the Bearer, "that here comes before us the unspeakable wretches, inheritors of a multitude of sins. The outcasts and rootless vagabonds on whom all blame is laid."

Olli mentally adjusted the scale on "worst" a whole load more notches.

Utir was going off on one again, flailing about with its limbs, more agitated than she'd seen any Essiel in her limited experience, and sounding off like a whole brass section.

"Let it be known that all the long-foreseen dooms that have been earned by your species find their home in this one vessel!" Sathiel proclaimed, eyes flicking nervously left and right, as if he were consulting some human–Hegemonic–Hegemonic–Hegemonic dictionary. "Know that this ignominy has never before been earned by one of your kind. This is the first moment that such villainy beyond words has attached to so mean a thing. But so it must be, and so comes the just punishment."

Kit had managed to open his own channel by then, and Olli heard him rattle off a desperate rejoinder. "All allegations of villainy are denied by us with great protest. No harm has ever been committed. All accusations are put to strict proof."

"Wait," Olli said. "Did it call us unspeakable, earlier?"

"Maybe," Havaer agreed. "Sathiel said 'villainy beyond words' too. Kind of the same thing?"

"Only…" She scowled at Sathiel's image. "Maybe it isn't saying what he says its saying…"

"Our systems are compromised," Kit said flatly. "There is no control."

"What?" Olli scrabbled for the *God*, finding it suddenly… *inhabited*. There had been a passenger in the Hegemonic message, meant just for them. Maybe the Resplendent Utir *had* been saying exactly what Sathiel had claimed. Abruptly she was locked out, the *God* just drifting. She had just enough peripheral system access to see that the onboard systems were being thoroughly hacked.

This is it, she decided. *Please, this has got to be the absolutely lowest moment of all time.*

"Architect breach," came Kit's flat voice in her ear. Olli wasn't even surprised. *Of course a fucking Architect. It's not like they'd stopped hunting us just because the Essiel wanted to have a show trial.*

She couldn't bring anything up on the main screens, so she had to use the little display in her pod, pulling data from the *God*'s uncooperative cameras.

"Kit, this isn't..."

An incomprehensible sound came from Kittering. A rattling shiver of his mouthparts. Some extremity of emotion that Hanni had never found a human analogue for.

Architects, plural, were plunging out of unspace, breaking into the real. Two, five, eight, fifteen. She stopped counting, just watched. Imagining the screaming panic every single sentient being in the Berlenhof system must be going through at that moment. Thirty, fifty. She swore she actually felt the unspace boundary shaking and stretching with all this activity. A whole constellation of Architects tearing their way into reality at the heart of the Colonies.

This, at least, is not just for us. She felt a weird calm. That "worst" had finally gone so far that it was beyond anything she had ever faced before in her chequered life. This was doomsday. She hadn't brought it about. The addition of the *Vulture God* to this little tableau barely nudged the scales. She almost laughed.

"Curious behaviour is being observed," Kittering noted. He was flagging up individual Architects, images bounced to them from Berlenhof sources. Some of the vast beings had already begun their inexorable cruise in towards the planet, but others...just hung there. A couple were even heading out-system, and one of them was spinning round and round, as though it had been in a collision. An out-station science post detected weird vibrations in many of them, as though they were in the grip of opposing forces, pushed in multiple directions.

One of them suddenly sheared in half.

Olli stared, wide-eyed, as a vast fault-line sprang up across its jagged face, mountains exploding into shards and powder, and then the entire crystal behemoth started shattering, coming apart into two pieces and countless fragments. *Is something attacking them?*

And yet there were still enough coursing inwards. Even if two-thirds of the Architect fleet was caught in some trap, or fighting some compulsion, more than thirty separate monsters were accelerating in towards Berlenhof. It wasn't as though it ever took more than one anyway. Olli knew they'd be mobilizing every ship. That every spaceport and elevator terminal would already be shoulder to shoulder, and the entire navy would be throwing itself out into space. But this was what you did against a single Architect, to buy time. It wouldn't earn the world more than a handful of seconds against these. They'd also be getting every Intermediary into a ship, surely, to try Idris's trick of bouncing them or delaying them, but she reckoned they wouldn't have enough Ints. This was it. The end for Berlenhof, the world that had survived two previous attempts by the Architects to reshape it. This time the bastards were going to make certain.

Then she had full systems control again, and one screen lit up with Sathiel's unwelcome face.

"Know this, guilty ones!" he told her—just to her now, no

full-system broadcast any more. "The legacy of sin has passed to you. Upon you, the Prophet and the Judge now lays this burden, and clasps these chains about you. To such vile service you are bound."

"And fuck you too!" Olli screamed at him. "This isn't the fucking time, you bearded git!"

Then the *God*'s systems opened up like a fractal nightmare and everything was linking to her at once. She felt her head fly apart in a thousand directions.

Out there, the geometrical perfection of *The Glory Before Night Has Come* fractured along every line, then exploded soundlessly into pieces.

32.

Kris

Jaine and Ahab were the first line of defence. That was how bad it was. The pair of them huddled over a projection of the nearest chambers, little more than a wireframe and a jumpy camera image, doing what they could with the Eye's inherent properties and the homespun additions they'd made.

Kris leant into Shinandri. "Shouldn't you be helping them?"

He pointed at himself and then them. "Scientist. Engineers. The time for theory is past, alas."

"You're still grinning," she noted bleakly. "Or is your face just stuck like that?"

"Joy, sheer joy," he assured her. "The justification of one's theories. A life's work, come to this. At least I was *right* about things."

"I don't think you'll get the chance to publish." Kris was looking over Jaine's shoulder, seeing the crystal shapes lurch and skitter through the chamber outside. A moment later they exploded into what looked like a fog and Jaine let out a whoop of triumph.

"Damn me," Kris gaped. "What was that?"

"Fuck-off enormous disruption along the unspace vibration strings," were some words that came out of Jaine's mouth.

Or at least that was the garble that reached Kris's ears. "Cutting the strings..." She trailed off, because something else was now happening on their little screen. A vortex, a rising tornado of infinitesimal pieces dust-devilling about the floor, gathering all that distributed fog and reforming it back into...shapes. Not even the same shapes. Different relics from other conquests, stretching their remembered limbs and, after a moment of weary contemplation, starting forwards.

"Zap them again," Kris suggested.

"Not doing anything," Jaine said. "Well, that was too much to hope for, wasn't it? What's next?"

Searing arcs of lightning leapt between the stone walls of the chamber outside, and the camera abruptly gave up the ghost so they couldn't see if it had done any good. A moment later Jaine got their eyes back up, and the marching crystal automata were still coming.

"Hold on!" Ahab barked.

Kris stared at it. "What?"

The world shifted sideways and she was abruptly sliding down the floor towards the door. Everyone else had held on, she noticed. For a moment she was scrabbling, accelerating, as though the whole room had become a mountainside and she was tumbling from it. Then Andecka had her, three fingers round Kris's belt but just enough to slow her. She clung to the Int, wide-eyed. They were right up beside the Machine that Idris was lying in. His head was tilted to one side by the gravitic shift, eyes open like a dead man's. She wanted to close them but couldn't risk letting go.

A moment later *down* returned to its proper place and she called to Jaine, "Did that help?"

"No," Jaine grunted. She was still trying to do something, hands busy with connections and a virtual control panel, but her expression was taut, biting at her lower lip.

Then there was a sound like a gunshot. Kris saw a pale spine piercing through the sheet metal of the door.

Ahab shook itself, hide slapping like leather, and let its metal legs take it away from Jaine and her work.

"You see us at last!" it shouted. For a second, Kris didn't understand what it meant. Just some Naeromathi alien-ness. Then she thought she'd got it. They were, indeed, seen. The enemy, a tyranny that operated at a universal scale, had been forced to give them this bespoke fate. They were not just another civilization to be ground to dust without even registering. They had *mattered*, even if it ended here.

The gleaming claw drew down the length of the door and then half a dozen other appendages peeled the portal back with a shriek of abused steel. What came through first was something like a woodlouse, its raised underside all gleaming killer cutlery. Behind it stalked an absurdly delicate thing on spindly gazelle legs, its head like a flower of teeth.

Ahab lowered its head and a beam of light danced from the cyborg hood that was most of its face. This penetrated the crystal, refracted, then danced out of the Architect's puppets like broken rainbows. Where it had touched, they seemed to gain depth and dimensions, as though he were lighting up ever more intricate chambers and structures within them. They slowed, and for a moment it was a crystal logjam in the carved doorway. But then they were moving again, having adjusted to whatever the Naeromathi was doing. Ahab growled, deep in its chest, and the beam changed colour and definition two or three times, but he'd bought them whatever time he could. Now they were through and into the Machine room.

Kris stood defensively before the Machines that held Idris and Solace. She had her knife out, though she couldn't remember drawing it. It would do absolutely nothing to help, save make her feel a little better. Right now she'd take that.

The woodlouse-thing surged forwards, still half reared up, uppermost limbs cocked back to strike. Tooth-head stilted after, and behind that was something almost humanoid. Two legs, two arms, but no head, and something like a thorned tumour in the centre of its broad torso. It had probably been perfectly pleasant when it was alive, but in crystal effigy it was hideous.

Ash stood before them. Kris hadn't seen the alien move, but suddenly it was there, within reach of the closest crystal-form's claws. These closed like the jaws of a trap, but Ash was already gone, as though it had never been there. It was only a step to the side instead, again just standing there like the spectre of death in its robe. Then gone once more, the moment the gazelle-thing stabbed at it. Now to the other side of them. Just casually moving from point to point, not having to bother with mundane things like intervening space. For a moment Ash was literally running rings around them, but then the humanoid-thing coming through the door exploded, the thorned wart of its body lancing out in razor shards, and they caught Ash just as it manifested. Kris had a momentary glimpse of torn robe, a mist of black fluid and its branched limbs flailing, then Ash was gone entirely. To oblivion or to save itself, she couldn't know.

The crystalforms took a second to compose themselves, and then an entity that looked like a collection of hooks and waving feelers was pouring itself through the gap in the door, while the rest of them resumed their steady progress towards the Machines and the survivors.

"Slaves!" Ahab shouted at them, or perhaps at Architects in general. The Naeromathi's bulk bunched up as though it was about to charge them. Jaine reached for it, hand against its scarred hide. Shinandri giggled. At Kris's side, Andecka had a gun, a little chemical projectile piece, as useless as the knife. She saw the two Hivers ready their tool-bearing arms. One of the Partheni Ints even had an accelerator. Again, none of it would do any good.

The crystalforms stopped. They fizzed like static, their shapes blurring and twisting. Kris flinched back, ready for the scything rake of fragments.

For just a moment they became human in shape. Then they snapped back to their previous forms, lurching forwards, but uncertainly. The woodlouse-thing's limbs waved in confusion.

Once again they were co-opted, wrenched into a human configuration. A body, arms outstretched; a face turned upwards, eyes closed. All of them were identical for a moment, as something rode the Architect's signal in and made them its own. Her own. For Kris knew those features.

There was another stutter, another step towards them, the crystalforms' bodies juddering and shifting like static as they were fought over from within. Alien physiologies spiking and twisting into what was recognizably *Solace*.

Olli

It was too much. In that initial moment, the blizzard of incoming information and connections overwhelmed her. A thousand voices calling her name. And nothing so simple as a Colonial hail. They were praising her, cursing her, making her their god, casting her to the pits of damnation. An army of lost souls howled for her, demanding she lead them.

The Essiel ship, the *Too-Fancy-a-Name-to-Remember* or whatever, had just broken up into bits. Not exploded, but cleanly come apart in a vast expanding cloud of fragments. There was a slender spindle left, and that was where Utir was, she understood. This was the core of the vessel, even now retreating from the fray, its work done. And the rest...

Was calling to her, each part of it. Connecting to her via the *God*, via Aklu's magic legs. Each piece plugging into her and placing itself at her disposal until her mind was drowned in the eager calls of her new followers. *Command us, Unspeakable One! Lead us where our creators may not go!*

Aklu had given her its legs and she'd thought it was as simple as that. Like every damn thing to do with the Essiel, she hadn't fully understood. Aklu had given her its title. She was the heir to the Razor and the Hook, Olli the Unspeakable. Apparently that came with Hegemonic duties.

Various people had tried to explain exactly what Aklu's status had been, vis-à-vis the wider Hegemony. Olli hadn't understood, and hadn't been paying particular attention either. Which was a shame, since apparently it now applied to her, and she'd just been given a...weapon?

She wasn't sure it was a weapon. That sounded too straightforward for the Essiel.

But she did have a thousand hands, right then. A vast disconnected body spread out across ten thousand cubic kilometres and expanding still. All of it part of her, just as she'd always been able to fit her mind around artificial bodies that owed nothing to the human shape. Her gift, or at that moment, her curse. She fought them, tried to shout down their zealous reports of location, trajectory and readiness. Somewhere, distantly, Havaer Mundy was shouting at her, and Kittering was yattering in her ear too. Her mouth tried to explain to them what was going on but mostly she just screamed.

The Architects were still advancing on Berlenhof, and suddenly, while it had never been her *fault*, it was her *responsibility*. So ruled Utir the Prophet and the Judge.

There were other ships out there. A fair chunk of the Colonial Navy, for starters. A couple of Partheni warships to escort whatever diplomat was eating crow at Hugh's table. Some punchy merchantmen. Some big Hiver frames. They were moving out to try and combat all those Architects. Even with everyone fighting to hold them back from the assault, there were still far too many approaching Berlenhof. The heart of the Colonies was about to be ripped out to teach humanity a lesson. Olli was a spacer, and spacers were legendarily caustic about Hugh and the core, settled worlds of humans. But that didn't mean she wasn't a part of it, the other end of a continuous scale of the same spacegoing species.

She picked an Architect and threw herself at it. A great storm of Hegemonic remotes unravelled in that direction, and then she understood. Just like Aklu's magic legs, every piece of her new fleet contained a piece of Originator tech.

The stuff the Architects wouldn't destroy. The stuff they would carefully retrieve before wrecking a planet or a ship. The Essiel didn't fight Architects; everyone knew that. Instead they had evolved a weird defensive strategy which had served them well since long before humans made it into space. They had plans within plans, and contingencies within contingencies, though. Like having a rebel caste that was permitted to do the unthinkable at this one point where such action might achieve something.

Except it wasn't a weapon. She tried to strike against the Architect, and her little shards just buzzed and orbited it. When it had been Aklu's magic legs against the crystal puppets, she'd been able to get punchy with them. With Utir's drones, everything seemed maddeningly more polite. Perhaps it was because she was against the Architect proper, and not just cast-off pieces that had forfeited some manner of diplomatic immunity. Or perhaps it was that the Hegemony had her on more of a leash this time. She tried to batter at that vast crystal surface, and her myriad of remotes were no more than an ineffectual cloud of gnats. Yet the Architect did stop, and rotated ponderously, trying to find a way around, but was blocked every way it turned. Not a weapon but a *shield*.

The other Architects were all cruising in, with more giving up their struggles and joining the assault. It was too much, there were too many, the signals overwhelming her. Her fleet sprang apart, losing cohesion as she tried to bring it against another of the vast crystal behemoths; even as she did, the one she'd previously stopped was promptly in motion again. She felt as though she was trying to fix thirty leaking ducts at once, fingers on one and then the next, but each one erupting the moment she left it.

The first ship died out there. A Colonial cruiser that had unleashed its accelerator batteries at the nearest Architect and been mauled into wire and lace in return. Olli felt tears prick her eyes, knowing that she could have stopped it, if only she could properly marshal her teeming armies. *It's too much to ask of me.* She was going to watch Berlenhof die, and know she could have prevented it—that it was all on her.

More data started to fall into her head. She almost screened it out, just bucking against it from instinct, but then noticed it was something new. Something different. Blocks of numbers, organizing the complex swirl of pieces the Essiel had given her. Setting them into groups, then dividing them and giving them pathways. A plan. She scrabbled desperately to understand it all. It was a complex plan but took the roiling chaos she'd been given and simplified, then simplified again. Arranging her loose drones into units, regiments and battalions, clumping them so that the burden of command became manageable. At first she thought it must be some bright spark over in Hugh who'd weighed in, or else it was some intrinsic part of the Essiel infrastructure. Whichever, it shifted the scale of the problem. Still hers to direct, but now balanced in a way she could control, with her legions ordered and subdivided. Seeing the proposed commands her benefactor was suggesting, she moved her troops across the three-dimensional field of battle. Throwing a precisely calculated net towards each encroaching Architect to slow it, then deflect it away. The plates always spinning and none of them allowed to fall.

This left her with enough spare headspace to see where these instructions were all coming from, and there came the shock. The signal was from inside the ship.

"Mundy?" she demanded with her mouth, that distant organ that barely felt a part of her any more, given where her actual mind was focused.

"Here."

"What's Kit doing?"

"He's...got a display open. Looks like a big grid board and a thousand little pieces. Moving them about like mad, he is."

"Tell him it's not a fucking *game*," Olli yelled at him.

"Look, is it helping?" Mundy demanded.

"Yes, but..." *Surely if he took it seriously it would help more,* she'd been about to say, but Kittering had always taken his games very seriously.

And it did help. He had a constant string of suggested moves for her, splitting and recombining the blocks of her forces, bouncing each Architect away. Buying time. The Ints were out there as well—Colonial and Partheni both—reaching for the Architects to try and turn them, and she let Kit work them into the gameplan. Sitting at the eye of the storm, her mind spread across thousands of klicks of space, the thin line between Berlenhof and oblivion. Holding, holding...with the ring of Architects around the planet tightening slowly, but she was making it slower. She struck and feinted, dancing around them. She almost felt them to be not a murderous enemy but just another player, as Kit must have too. Willing to indulge her stratagems because it strung the game out longer. But not for ever. She knew even then that she was only doing what humans had always done when the Architects came: buying time, even as they desperately crammed every ship on Berlenhof full for evacuation.

Solace

She clad herself in full heavy engagement armour that bulked her out to twice her width, with strength-boosting servos. It was, after all, entirely imaginary so not as though she needed to worry about mission budget, or negotiate with supply and logistics. Into her gauntleted hands fell the comforting weight of Mr. Punch—her Partheni accelerator with a full clip and plenty of mass reserves. The uniformed things with their knives paused, staring at her with the ruins of her own face. They built themselves up, adding rank signifiers as if they were throwing up threat displays.

"*You are dismissed, soldier,*" one hissed.

"*Mutiny,*" from another.

And a third, its humanoid shape bulging and twisting, "*This is our place! Ours!*"

"*Put it on trial,*" hissed another. "*Make it relive its failures.*"

Solace reviewed her life, with reference to this particular turn out of the freezer. On the whole she reckoned she'd done about as well as anyone could have expected.

She shot at them. It was probably best to skip the formalities, and she wasn't Kris. Trials weren't her forte. The accelerator pellets shredded the nearest two and the rest fell back a pace, their shapes misting for a brief moment. And then reforming. She couldn't actually kill them with her imaginary gunfire. But Idris hadn't asked her to clear the area. Idris had asked her to hold. Just *being* here, second to second, was her win condition.

They came at her, then. They attacked her with history. And yes, they were also physically running at her with blades in their hands, but she understood they weren't really there

555

and neither were the blades. All in the head, everything here. Just her mind's best attempt to give her some handle on the underlying reality that didn't fit anything she'd ever experienced. But an attack was an attack. And their real weapon was the vast tidal wave of recorded time they were bludgeoning her with. They filled her brain with their past, their appallingly long history. They made her small, a speck of dust before a whole cosmos.

They had reshaped the universe with the sutures of their Throughways. On planets still hot from forming, they had decreed their maze-like structures be built, now having become just the worn-down stubs like those she'd seen on Jericho and Arc Pallator. They had made the universe the way it was, and it was a work only half complete. They were *important*, significant in a way that put all of humanity in their shadow. They had work to do, and she and her companions had the temerity to interfere!

Her hands made the accelerator sing, its high, clear voice cutting through the great bludgeoning fall of their outrage.

"Do you think this delay means anything?" They showed her time, and her precise place in it, a point so minuscule that if they hadn't circled it for her with arrows and signs she'd never have seen it. Time since the universe first exploded into existence, and time before that. The spaces that had existed before the universe, a stable flip-state governed by physical laws entirely different to the cosmos Solace knew. Gravity, light, atomic bonds, all snapping to a different regime entirely, so that there was nothing like matter or energy as she understood them. A better place. A place of majesty and beauty that should have lasted forever.

But something had been done, or some vast wheel turned,

some hubristic experiment, a terrible war. Because she could not understand the *ur*-universe they were showing her, nor could she understand the event that had come to end it. This had flipped everything to the set of laws that permitted, and inevitably led to, the universe she even partway understood. *"A mistake!"* they shrieked at her. *"A cosmic error. That is all you are."* They lunged at her, cover to cover, like a good assault team, and the accelerator shook in her hands as she tried to keep them pinned down. She saw herself as if from high above, a tiny dot in a ravaged landscape, and the enemy closing in from three sides. Her tactical position untenable, an orderly retreat the only option before their irresistible advance.

They were the lords of creation and uncreation. She realized that now. She was one human with a doctored genome and very limited understanding of where she was, but they were teaching her. They had been working to correct the unwanted change of state the universe had undergone. They would return everything there was to a state of paradise and perfection. They'd been at their task for billions of years, but time wasn't the same here at the centre. You could see forever, forwards, backwards and up into the real. It was a little like her own life, in and out of the freezer at the whims of her superiors. You developed a curious relationship with the clock and the calendar.

"Retreat," the word in her ear like an order, and she laughed at them. Monitor Superior Tact was dead and nobody had managed to forge a new chain of command. Which meant that, without chains, she was free. And Idris had said, *Hold.* She accepted that she was just one soldier in a war on a scale she couldn't imagine. So she let the avalanche of their

revelations thunder past her. It was above her pay grade, hers not to ask questions. She had only ever wanted to be a soldier, after all. To be a soldier, and perhaps to be friends with a weird little Int refugenik, because sometimes Colonials were all right when you got to know them.

Idris, elegant Kris, the dry humour of Kit's translator, Olli who was never going to like her much but that was fine too. Rollo Rostand, who was dead but who'd christened her gun and been a weird kind of father figure for a brief span, to a woman who neither had nor needed one. Tact, who'd died for a razor-sharp vision of what her people should be. Mercy, likewise. Solace just hunkered down, for all of them, and let the philosophical assault slant off her shoulders, and shot. Again, she understood the shooting accomplished nothing, what with the gun not being real. But the *holding* was all, and sometimes a finger on the trigger was what you needed to give you even the illusion of control. Besides, and despite, all their aeons-old wisdom and power, they were only attacking on three sides, and that told her that the enemy desperately needed her to take the fourth side and run away.

She held strong in the face of their angry eternity. She accepted her own utter insignificance. She was a Partheni Myrmidon. It was never about *I*. She had always been one part of a greater whole. Whether it was the Parthenon or humanity or all life. Or even just the crew of the *Vulture God*.

She almost lost her focus then, the vast tide of their grinding assault about to sweep her away. Her crewmates, her body. A sudden impression of panic. The enemy had been playing her false after all. There was one extra knife in their possession, a hidden blade. She had a moment's sight from her real eyes, as she lay in the Machine couch. A crystal thing, plated and many-limbed. Accelerator shot piercing through it without even cracking its substance. Kris's voice raised high in challenge.

No, she decided, and reached out. She was no Int, but she was *here*. In the same way that she couldn't, of her own strength, send out a ship-cracking gravitic wave across open space, but she could if she was at the controls of a mass loom. This was the control room for the universe. This was where the lords sent out their orders. The Architect up there, moulded around the cracked substance of the Eye, was their tool. And she was now standing where the orders originated.

So she fought them for it. She envisaged those orders as objectives on the field before her. She braced Mr. Punch and let fly, driving them back. Standing between them and their surrogates up within the Eye. Interfering with the signal. It gave her strength. Feeling she had friends at her back to protect always gave her strength.

She held.

Then Idris was returning. His grip suddenly real in her hand, so that she had to stop shooting. Idris pulling, and his voice in her head.

"I've done what I can up there. Time to trade places."

"I'll stay with you," she told him. "I'll watch your back."

"There's no room," he said. "And it's time for you to go. Go back. I'll see you."

She tried to fight him, as fiercely as she'd fought against the enemy here, but his pull was beyond her strength to resist. She was flying upwards, springing back towards her distant body, as if there had been a taut cord between them all this time, and Idris had released the anchor holding her.

She had a sense of him passing her, headed the other way to occupy the space she'd kept for him. And then he was gone.

Idris

He fell back into the ruined place, the centre, reoccupying the toehold he'd won there, and that Solace had maintained for him. He'd called out to the Architects, all of them. At least some of them had heard. At least some of them were trying one last rebellion. He knew they could. Why else would their masters have needed to punish them by scouring their home? Why else had they vanished for so long after he had spoken to them over Far Lux? Slaves, but not automata. All their masters wanted was the extermination of thought. That teeming, bubbling interference that threw all their long calculations out. And so: genocide upon genocide, through the long history of the universe, sending the Architects to wipe the slate clean. Ash's people, the Naeromathi, countless other species over billions of years. And the Architects themselves, knowing only that they were being forced to some terrible task, had written their grief across the cosmos.

Idris collected himself, down there in the footprints Solace had kept occupied for him. Facing the decayed grandeur that was what his mind had made of the universe's former masters. Could he feel any sympathy for them? Perhaps a little. They had just been the life the universe had thrown into being once, back when it had been very different. But now they were the monsters. Willing to eliminate countless cultures, dreams, lives and biospheres just so they could have it all back again. No room for compromise, therefore.

And yet, what could he do? He and they faced one another, sole occupants of the tiny point at the centre of all things. Leverage was what they had, but it wasn't the ability to reach out and sculpt the cosmos direct. They had slaves for that. The Architects, and other things he couldn't even imagine. They didn't do their own dirty work. Something had built the Originator installations. Something had burrowed its way along the real–unreal interstice and left the Throughways in its wake. And, of course, something rose from the depths to annihilate thinking life whenever it grew too numerous and too fixed, so that the errors mounted up. Now here he was, one lone human, one Int without any particular desire to reshape the universe. They were still trying to oust him, and maybe they wouldn't be able to do that. They weren't strong. That was the revelation. They might cast themselves as lords of all creation, but they lacked brute force. It was all just a matter of leverage. And he was at the near end of that lever here, so they couldn't use it against him, and he couldn't use it against them. They could throw bugbears and fears at him, just as they had against Solace. They could try to cow him with how important they were and how tiny he was, but that was his life. Frankly, he'd always preferred it that way. They held no terrors for him. But it wasn't as if he could grab them by their bony throats and choke them either.

Can I drag an Architect down here? he wondered. *Set the slaves on their master?* He called out to them, but in vain. The Architects would under no circumstance approach this place. They feared it too much.

Feared the chastisement of their masters?

No. They feared what everyone feared in unspace. The thing that personified fear. The thing that squatted between the universe and its heart. The apex predator of whatever screwed-up ecosystem thrived and seethed within the invisible reaches of unspace.

The Presence. My old friend.

If he looked up, he could see it. Or not *see*, really. Just know it was there. A vast, hostile mass of a thing, leviathan, awake and bristling outwards. Reaching, constantly, for every intruder who dared the depths. The terror he had lived with ever since the Intermediary Program had peeled his brain back. Too monstrous to face or even contemplate. *Nothing to fear but fear itself, and here it is.*

They had made it their guard dog, to stand between their little pinpoint sanctum and the rest of creation. The many-headed hound of the underworld.

He shrank from the thought of it, and heard his enemies cackle and snicker all around him. "*Small*," they said. "*You're small. You're weak. What can you win but time? We have all the time there is. We can outlast you.*" All true, he knew.

He'd endured a great deal, in his stretched-out life. Actually died a couple of times, medically, except people kept tiresomely demanding a second opinion. He'd been awake for the best part of a century. It really was more than anyone should have to deal with. Awake, and living with this *thing*, this fear, this lump of malevolence. Of all things, he did not want to have to face up to it now.

I am not a brave man. Understatement of the century. He didn't like being hurt, or hostile social situations, or crowds, or attention. In fact, the list of things that made him cringe back and run away was very long. But that was, perhaps, because all of the steel in him was committed to dealing with one particular problem in his life.

Hey, you, he thought. Before common sense could countermand the order, he was reaching up to the Presence, trying to get its monstrous attention.

The weird thing was, from this side, it was nothing to be scared of. He pictured a great doughy mass. A soft underbelly. After all, this was the part of it that faced the lords down below. They wouldn't want anything nasty looking at them. Harmless and virtually insensate. Like one of those insects that lived in a burrow and was all savage jaws up front, but just a big, sad sack of a body if you dug it out.

The lords of creation were watching him, frozen. Their taunts and jibes had petered away into nothing.

He could see exactly how they'd moored the Presence there, between them and the rest of everything there was. It didn't understand. He wasn't sure it was necessarily something that *could* understand. A thing of brute instinct clutching angrily at whatever moved within its gaze. And its gaze was turned outwards. It had guarded the threshold of the underworld for immeasurable aeons, a singular monster evolved to hunt across the whole of unspace without ever needing to move.

He didn't want it to turn round. He felt the horror of it. Not evil, because you needed will to be evil. Just a thing that was to the sentient mind like the repelling pole of a magnet. You'd do anything to avoid being brought close to it. Anything.

He didn't have any other thing, though. And so he reached up with the same leverage the lords used, by virtue of where he stood, and tapped the Presence on the shoulder. *Hey, you! Did you never think to look behind you?* Every iota of his being recoiled from the thought. Knew that, of all things in the universe, he did not want to have the entity twist its attention from the universe at large and see him, insignificant as he was.

His body was convulsing somewhere, all those fear and stress hormones pushing his body to the point where only artificial aid would be keeping his heart beating, his lungs working. There were probably vessels bursting in his brain. All the usual. But he kept tugging on the damn thing's cape, kept shouting in its ear. He made it notice him. Him, Idris Telemmier, least significant mote in all the wide universe.

It was like the Architects, in a way. Not sapient as they were, but the product of the same evolution. Its mind was a similar maze, though trapped and razor-edged and no place for a poor human to wander. But he met it there. He threw himself into the blades of it. He found the tiny point within it that was *self* and introduced himself. *Hi, Idris Telemmier, Int, first class.* Feeling the sheer horror of it erode him away to loose atoms of mind. His arms wide to embrace the blast.

It turned. He felt its focus swing round, a brutish and short-tempered beast prone to charge at any irritation. He brought it about until it saw what had been behind it all this time. The parasites in its shadow.

"What are you doing?" they called at him, and he found himself looking back at them, seeing them as he had made the Presence do. They were ancient and clever and had pared away everything of themselves except themselves, their drive to *have it all back*, to own it all again like they once had. They were selfish. They were *weak*. So weak that they had to get

their hooks into the Architects, and who knew what other slaves, to do their work for them. Creatures of infinite vision that would never get their hands dirty. He felt a spacer's instinctive derision for something that had never fixed a vacuum seal or salvaged components from a broken drone. Even Idris had done that, and he was barely competent. Weak, save that they were cunning enough to turn other things into their hands, eyes and teeth. And now he was bleeding away into that brutal hungry mind which sat behind all those teeth. Weak, but the Presence was strong, and until now had never thought to look back at the pale, wretched things it had been guarding.

"You'll be lost!" they warned him. *"You'll be devoured!"*

It seemed to Idris that he'd cheated that fate so many times in his life, it was surely owed a bite of him now.

Idris let himself go then. He dissolved into the Presence, let himself *become* it. Shed the role of Intermediary, no longer standing between two worlds but abandoning himself entirely to one. He felt the Presence lunge, gape wide, bring its crushing tide of fear down on the tiny piece of grit that had encysted itself at the heart of all things. Rode the many-headed hound down into hell so it could bite the hand that had chained it. He heard the thin chorus of terrified voices as the lords of all things knew at last the fear he'd lived with for most of his life.

Then his own fear was suddenly gone, and he knew only the animal satisfaction of the Presence as it gaped and devoured.

33.

Solace

She rose back up towards her abandoned body, knowing only that she'd continue to hold on, clasp tight to his hand. She was his sole connection, all he had. But when she jackknifed up with a gasp, feeling leads tear, hearing medical telltales scream at her, her fingers were empty.

In the immediate aftermath there was silence. Just the cavernous quiet of the Eye's interior. Then a far-distant groan and rumble, like stone surfaces grinding against one another. Then a shocked breath.

She opened her eyes. She'd been so used to seeing things as her mind presented them to her, she hadn't realized they were shut.

In the Machine room, of course. Half the lights Jaine had rigged up were out, and the rest flickered mutinously. She forced herself to get out of the couch, the last few connections severed, feeling the weakness in her legs. Looking down the length of the chamber, Solace met the gaze of the others.

They were all holed up there, crammed into the far end. A couple of her Partheni sisters and a handful of other Ints, plus the Hivers. Jaine. Kris, with her knife out. Andecka Tal Mar was lying on the ground, her arm torn up and being bandaged by Shinandri's nimble fingers. At the back, the overarching bulk of Ahab. They all stared at her as though she was an apparition risen from the grave.

"What's..." Solace croaked. Her throat was raw even though she'd surely not made an actual sound since they put her under. Her mouth tasted of old blood. "What's going on?"

"They've stopped," Kris said, and Solace registered that they'd had company. A dozen crystal shapes were standing in a scattered progression between the huddle of crew and a door that had been carved open like tinfoil. Identical, as though she was seeing not a crowd but a recording of an individual's advance, inexorably closing on the little group at the far end of the chamber.

Her legs gave way then, and she had to sit back on the edge of the couch, shaking. She had been places nobody was supposed to go, in mind or body. And they were still in unspace, after all, despite the bubble. But unspace was like home compared to where she and Idris had been. And now this.

The forms all had her face, frozen in that moment. Her body. A score of crystal Myrmidon Executor Solaces, Heaven's Sword Sorority, Basilisk Division. She felt sick.

Kris moved first, advancing cautiously, knife still directed at the leading crystal shape. They were still, though.

Somewhere deep within the Eye, stone sheared and a tremor went through every surface.

"What's going on?" Solace demanded.

"There's an Architect trying to occupy the same space as us," Jaine said. "We're all broken up. I think it's...dead? Or at least it's now got other problems than piloting its puppets around. But we're not going to last much longer with it clinging to us."

"Right." Solace nodded, once. "Wake Idris up. Get hold of Kit."

"Kit's not answering," Kris told her. "Believe me, we've tried."

Shinandri had finished with Andecka's arm and sidled over to Idris's couch, looking down.

"He should be with us momentarily," he said. "When you awoke, the same procedure was enacted in his own system. He should, I would venture to say, already be with us." He frowned a little, the grin slipping. "In fact, I feel there may be a problem in that regard."

Solace felt within herself: no surprise. She'd known it already. "He's done something stupid." *Again. Done something stupid again. And done it where I can't make him sort it out.* "Send me back. I'm going to get him."

"Not being an Intermediary, I do not believe you would be able to go anywhere," Shinandri observed.

"Then link me up with one."

"Solace," Jaine said gently. "What do you think? That you'd go and find him just lying unconscious there? He's here. What's out there is his mind. I don't think there's any way of finding that."

"We can try," Andecka said. She looked greyish, her injured arm pulled up to her chest. "We can still try."

"We need to fix our own problems first," Jaine snapped. "We're coming apart. The Architect is crushing us—"

"Shut up, all of you!" Kris shouted suddenly. She had a hand to her ear, face screwed up as she tried to hear something. "It's Kit," she said. "Kit's calling us. Something's happened up there."

"It can join the queue," Jaine decided. "Tell him to get into unspace. Even a short hop. Once the bubble goes, the Architect goes, or that's how I think it'll work. Now it's dead, it'll dissipate, fall away the moment we're out of the real. And after that we can assess the damage."

Olli

She had forgotten her own body entirely. Her mind was out in space, marshalling her forces and dispatching them against every monster that was closing in on Berlenhof. It wasn't even her world. She'd never liked it. A hive of bureaucrats and lawmakers whose work revolved around making her life difficult. Should just let the whole place get turned into art. Except here she was, apparently the chosen heel of the entire Hegemony because she'd taken someone else's legs. Odd how things worked out. All these things just flitting through the back end of her brain as the practical part of her consciousness fought the war.

The Architects lumbered on, those that weren't fighting some weird inner battle of their own in the further reaches of the Berlenhof system. Each one was met by her warding, a storm of little Hegemonic remotes like gnats, which each held some piece of Originator nonsense at their hearts. Some rod, or chunk of stone, or even a handful of dust. She presented it to the Architect as though it was a holy talisman, and they baulked. Slowing and turning aside, they tried to find a way round, save that her myriad hands could move faster than they could. So they then reached for her little toys with invisible hands of gravity. They launched volleys of spines that shifted into the shapes of long-dead species to try and recover those scraps. But they couldn't just destroy her fleet, not when it contained the mark of their masters. And so she lost many individual drones but she kept them busy. All of them. At once. Creating a comprehensive defence of the planet below, losing ground a kilometre at a time but continuing to buy all the time that she could for them. Taking Kit's fast and loose game plans and turning them into reality in the vast cold battlefield beyond the *Vulture God*'s hull. Very distantly, she could hear Havaer on the comms to his boss or some other Berlenhof grandee, trying to explain what was happening. He had no idea, though. None of them did. She felt that even *she* wouldn't really remember or understand, after all this was over. But right now she was at the top of her game, the Unspeakable Olian Timo, the Razor and the Hook.

Then Kit stopped feeding her plays, and she checked in with him anxiously in case he was hurt. Hoping some back-handed weapon of the Architects or their masters hadn't screwed everything up. But it was, in fact, the opposite. It was victory.

Or at least, the Architects were going away. Admittedly, the last time they'd done that it hadn't turned out to be for ever, but a lot of escalation had gone under the bridge since then. The Architects were winking out, submerging back to unspace, where they'd come from. Olli let out a long breath, though she didn't relax, or let herself inhabit her body again until the last one of them had vanished.

"Well, crap," she said. "What now?"

"What's going on down the well?" Havaer asked. Olli blinked. In all the excitement she'd almost forgotten what they were dragging around with them.

"Contact has been re-established," Kittering reported a few fraught moments later. "They require us to enter unspace."

"Can we even do that?" Olli glowered up at Junior. "You taking requests any time soon?"

As it turned out, a little stutter-jump across system was all it took. Whatever entanglements the Eye had got itself into within unspace had plainly melted away, and the great hulk of it returned shudderingly to the real. No more anchor. No more well. No more poking physics in the eye. Olli stared at the vast scarred lump of Originator rock and the surviving scales of the Host, all of which looked as beaten about as she felt.

"Timo," Havaer said. "Someone wants you."

"Who?" she demanded, with a suspicion that turned out to be entirely justified. As Kit liaised with the Eye crew and listened to all their problems, Olli watched the comms requests mount up. Just about every Hugh office in Berlenhof wanted to talk to them. Havaer was already making contact with his own people. And she...

It was all going to be taken away, she knew. They'd trusted her with the really neat toys for as long as she was useful, but it wasn't like she'd get to keep them. So now she was just waiting for one particular comms call she'd have no option but to take.

And there it was. His Wisdom the Bearer Sathiel carrying the sacred words of the Resplendent Utir, the Prophet and the Judge. Still safe in their slender spindle of a vessel, all that was remaining of their ship.

The beard and its owner appeared on her screen. The man wasn't sweating as much now. He'd probably do really well out of this, in the Colonies and the Hegemony. Some scum always floated, no matter what.

"The Prophet and the Judge expresses all due condemnation as befits such as yourself," the man told her loftily.

"Just get to the point," Olli told him sourly. "I get it. I do the work. I don't get paid. I have my stuff confiscated. Story of my fucking life. So what's your boss got to say, beardy?"

Just after she said it, she realized that Sathiel was broadcasting system-wide on formal diplomatic channels and her response had gone out to everyone on Berlenhof.

"You are informed—" Sathiel was trying to double his pomp to make up for her tone, and it made him sound constipated. "—that the wretched mantle may not be so readily doffed. You are the deceiver and the renegade, never to know peace, nor find recognition within the sacred hierarchy. The Hegemony hereby confirms its despite of you. You shall no more be spoken of in the language of the divine."

"Yeah, sure." She was wishing she'd gone in with more decorum in the first place, but that ship had most definitely sailed. "So...wait. I'm still Unspeakable?"

"Indubitably."

"So I get to keep the stuff?"

"The...stuff?" Sathiel looked sidelong, trying to catch whatever garbled version of Utir's pronouncements he was working with. "It's..." A very human expression of exasperation, the sort of thing Olli just loved to provoke in people of power and status. "It's not about the stuff. It is about the place you have adopted in the universe. Know that the vile and the outcast shall seek you out, and the tools of villainy be yours."

Olli blinked. "Did I just inherit the whole Broken Harvest? Do I get Tothiats and big ships and things?"

Sathiel blinked and swallowed. "I don't feel you're treating this with the seriousness it deserves."

Olli thought about Aklu, and all the Unspeakable had been able to achieve. She could live with a few clams looking down on her, she reckoned, if that was the price.

"Tell the Resplendent it is fucking *on*," she said to Sathiel, and by extension everyone else in-system. She watched the incoming call requests from Hugh double in number and urgency.

Havaer

"I was expecting Emersen," Havaer noted, when he was called in. In actual fact it was Diljat, but she was pointedly not sitting in the big chair, just leaning against the desk with a slate. Very much a temporary fixture, on her way to somewhere else. A lot of Mordant House seemed to be upside down right about now.

"Promoted sideways. Gone to Threat Analysis," Diljat told him. Havaer suspected he could dig for ten years and never quite work out what snarl of factions and actions had resulted in that move. He hadn't liked Emersen particularly, from their brief acquaintance, but on the other hand he reckoned she'd made all the right decisions where it counted.

"And you?"

"Just turning the crank until the new appointee is formally put in place. You know people like me, Agent Mundy. Tread water all our careers just to stay where we are."

He eyed the chair. Certain speculations must have shown on his face, because Diljat snorted.

"Oh, don't get your hopes up. This isn't one of those stories where your pure moral choices mean you inherit the chocolate factory, Mundy. Not some weirdly indirect way of saying you're the new chief. Even if you had the seniority, you were too close to Laery. The way I hear it, they want someone sufficiently distanced from *all* the special interests. New broom, right?"

"Didn't want the job anyway," Havaer muttered, having discovered in that brief second of hope that he actually quite would have.

"However, the wheels don't stop in the interim, and your official status has been, let's say, up in the air since your first go-round at Berlenhof."

"I like to think I've provided sterling service to the Board in that time," Havaer said, feeling sweat spring up on his brow. *No good deed goes unpunished.*

"You have been the galaxy's own loose cannon," Diljat noted. "Your usefulness has been mostly in your personal rapport with the crew of the *Vulture God*, a vessel that no longer has the same role in the Colonies' affairs as it once did. However, I'm not going to do the whole keeping-you-in-suspense business. You are being retired from field service. I don't know how you feel about that. It's happened to me too, and frankly it turned out to be a bit of a relief, when I thought about it. We're not chucking you out, though. We're starting a new department, in fact. Come with me."

She hopped down from the desk and led him out into the corridors of Mordant House, or at least the orbital that the Intervention Board monopolized. He expected just another office, but she led him to a rec room, one of the few spaces with an exterior window. He appreciated the showmanship. She'd timed the visit so that the wreck of the Eye was visible. The Originator installation was mostly in pieces. Its close encounter with an Architect while down the well had shattered it, and physics suggested the various bits should have drifted away from each other just by random collision now. The Eye had told physics where to stuff it, though, and the whole collection of bits was stubbornly holding its shape, despite the cracks being big enough for people to fit through.

"This," Havaer said, "is not my problem."

"It's part of it," Diljat said merrily. "A new team. Think of it as the Department of Dangerous and Utterly Incomprehensible Science Problems."

"I'm not a scientist."

"Your job is to keep a lid on it and analyse whatever they come up with vis-à-vis Colonial security. The hard sums are someone else's problem. Meet your new subordinate." Right on cue, someone was hesitating at the door. Havaer looked at that grin and his heart sank.

"Yes indeed," Doctor Shinandri said. Havaer knew he was going to get sick of that little half-giggle, and have absolutely no option but to live with it. "There are, as it were, so many questions now. Are the Architects truly as quiescent as they seem? Will the Throughways decay? Are the Originators truly as gone as all that? How much can we trust the report of the crew on the Eye?"

"Which is you. You were on the Eye. You were on its crew," Havaer pointed out.

Shinandri looked delighted, as though the thought had only just occurred to him. "But as a scientist, Agent Mundy, I must consider myself a single point of data. I am, after all, hardly reliable, am I?"

My subordinate, thought Havaer. It was going to be a long few decades until retirement.

Kris

Later, she came back to his bed. She suspected they all had, but it was just her at that moment. They'd been partners, after all. Since before they'd joined the *Vulture God*, they'd been partners. His part of the deal had been getting into trouble and hers had been getting him out of it, but he'd finally managed to dig deeper than she'd had rope to let down to him.

The bed was in a facility run by the Liaison Board, and he'd have hated that. He loathed the institution that had been formed to churn out commercial Ints, with no real care as to how traumatized they were or how many didn't survive the process. Yet they remained the experts, and she'd needed an expert. The Eye had surfaced in Colonial space without a strong Partheni presence, so Solace hadn't been able to get him away with her people. If that would even have been a better alternative.

He hadn't woken since they returned. It was almost two months now. As if all those long waking years were being made up for. Zero brain function, the doctors said, but she knew they meant that peculiar lack of function that was really an Int away with the unspace fairies. The mind not dead, but absent on other business. His body was being preserved, and he'd already shown he wasn't going to die of old age any time soon, so she didn't know what next.

But the world was still happening, out beyond this room. She couldn't just keep moping about like a sea captain's widow. She'd had offers. Her little role in what had happened hadn't entirely gone unnoticed, for good or for ill.

"I'm sorry, Idris," she told him. "I will come back. I'll visit." She stood, feeling all the remote eyes of the Liaison Board on her, and left.

34.

Kris

It was always hard to organize a decent reunion. Kris had meant it to happen when the statue first went up, but Solace had been in deep space and, well, she hadn't been entirely sure what Olli was up to, but it had been something she couldn't just stop doing, even for a brief excursion. So it had only been her and Kittering turning up on Berlenhof outside the big Hugh council buildings at Metro Gotumandi to watch the dedication. And that had been most of an Earth-standard year ago.

But here she was again, and here were the first of the others, showing their faces.

There was a grand square, lined with extremely fancy cafes and boutiques and a couple of museums and galleries. Metro Gotumandi was the swankiest place on the planet, and it felt ruinously expensive just to sit here. Most of the embassies on Berlenhof were a couple of streets away, and she could probably have flicked an olive stone off her table and hit three ambassadors and a Magdan Boyar. Kris, who'd spent the morning looking wistfully at clothes she couldn't afford and restaurants she'd need a bank loan to eat at, considered how nice it would be to have a law office anywhere in the city.

She'd thought about running a book on who would show up first, but as it turned out, Havaer and Solace appeared together. Which might mean nothing or it might mean a war, she considered. He was looking comfortable, some more weight on his bony frame than before, a desk agreeing with him. *She* was looking...just the same, honestly. Bold as brass in the heart of the Colonies wearing a Partheni uniform. Monitor Solace, as she was now, come here from the Aspirat with proper diplomatic credentials. She could probably book a table at one of those swish restaurants. Kris made a mental note to try and weasel a reservation out of her.

They were mid-talk as they arrived, then broke off to greet her, as well as to order cafenado and more olives. The tab magically became Havaer's department's problem, and she didn't let him see how grateful she was.

Solace was in from Parsefal, she explained. The first-ever settled Parthenon world. Kris should absolutely come and see how they were getting on. Working in tandem with the Hiver Assembly in Aggregate was leading to an effortlessly smooth colonization process. And the Parthenon's own Cartography Corps—their Alcyon Division, as they'd called it—was already searching out new Throughways. Kris understood they were at least liaising with their Colonial counterparts. The known universe was expanding, one connection at a time. None of it had fallen over yet, although given the network had been billions of years in the making, it was still early days. From some of Havaer's veiled references, she was wondering if his people were working on the theory of creating *new* Throughways. It would certainly be a game-changer, and she guessed Doc Shinandri would be all over it.

Then Andecka arrived, wearing a jacket with Cartography Corps badges, and so she and Solace got to compare notes too. All the space talk was making Kris feel a bit left out, though. The Intermediary was more animated than Kris remembered, almost chatty, eyes wide with the thought of deep-space exploration. A world away from the sort of look Kris was used to seeing in an Int's eyes. But then that was all part and parcel of why they were here, in a way.

"How's the firm?" Havaer asked her, as the other two got deeper into their personal discussion.

"Head above water still," Kris said. "I imagine you're keeping tabs on us. Shouldn't really need to ask, should you? Just pretend mysteriously to know everything about me." It all came out more bitterly than she'd meant, and she was sorry for that.

"You have rattled a lot of important people," he told her candidly. "I mean, you're right. Not my department per se, but Mordant House absolutely has a file on you. And there are people in the service who spit when they say your name."

"Shows I'm doing something right, then," Kris said flatly.

"Yes, it does," Havaer agreed. "You won't particularly believe me, but I do what I can, behind the scenes. And I'm not the only one. The Liaison Board dropped the ball the moment Idris called them out over the Architects. The influence of the Magdan nobility took a big knock over the whole ark project, and the Uskaro involvement in it. You've picked your moment and gone after wounded prey at a time when there's just enough public support to make it a viable hunt. Not a foregone conclusion, but you're shifting the window. I know Hugh lawmakers who'll likely be proposing new Int rights legislation soon, because of people like you winning cases in the courts. And I know some Magdan families who want to overhaul their robot system before people take an interest. It's a good time to be a civil rights lawyer."

"Tell that to my accountant," Kris said.

Solace and Andecka were talking about the Tripartite Resettlement Project now, which was a whole other legal knife fight Kris was happy not to have any skin in. If the Naeromathi had ever had any kind of central government, it was long since forgotten, and so trying to work with them to find them a new home was proving practically impossible. Ahab was the only reason it wasn't *absolutely* impossible—the one Naeromath who'd had personal dealings with humans enough to serve as a halfway ambassador. Kris reckoned the Naeromathi would just keep on doing their thing. They wouldn't go back. But who knew? In the interim, there was a single suite on a Berlenhof orbital that was notionally Naeromathi territory, for all that the term meant literally nothing. And there was Ahab, lonely, half-demented and yet triumphant. She'd visited once, wondering what she'd find of it now its lifelong purpose was apparently achieved. It had been busy, she discovered. There had been a whole court of weird types—xenologists and artists and all sorts of culty people—hanging on Ahab's every bellowed utterance. She hadn't honestly understood what was going on, except it looked like it was going to be trouble for someone.

Then Kittering arrived, and Kris could only stare.

He'd cleaned up nicely, from his stint as factor for the salvage vessel *Vulture God*. Gone were the tatty advertising screens on his back and arms. In their place was a mother-of-pearl sheen, shot through with complex designs in gold and silver. The chitinous crown that bore his eyes was capped with a glittering diadem of silvery gems. She barely recognized him. He strutted too. There was definitely a different walk there, to the skitter and sidle she'd known. People got out of his way. And he had an entourage. Three other rather less magnificent Hannilambra were trotting along in his wake, and after them came a solid-looking woman in the sort of armour you probably weren't supposed to wear here, right outside Hugh's main government buildings. Unarmed, but that didn't fool Kris for a moment. She'd guessed at the segmented symbiote running down the woman's spine even before she saw it.

"Damn, Kit," she said.

"A good time for business," Kittering confirmed. His translator's voice at least was the same. Except his three attendants used identical voices, which got very confusing when they were ordering drinks.

"Bringing the nephews into the firm?" she asked.

"A human term that does not relate to the familial structures of my people," Kit noted. "However and also: yes. Nepotism in the highest degree. When there is achieved a certain level of pre-eminence offworld, it is best practice to establish heirs and assigns with whom to share it." She knew they wouldn't be blood relatives of his, just aspiring Hanni males selected by some criterion she wouldn't understand. She wondered what they felt about getting in on the ground floor of . . . what? Not exactly an interstellar crime syndicate. Or not only that.

"I keep expecting to hear that you've retired," she said carefully.

"Thought is continually given to it. In short, I am quite ready," Kit said, and the idea made her bite her lip, because retirement for him was death, basically. He'd go home with his wealth and fertilize some eggs. Then he'd change, lay some eggs, and the she he'd become would die, and her offspring would be abundantly provided for. Given the very best start a new Hanni brood could have. But Kit would be no more, and she didn't want that to happen, while at the same time she knew for him it was a beautiful and natural part of life. When he said, "However, additional business is always accumulating. The liberty of retirement shall not be mine any time soon," she was wretchedly grateful to hear it.

"Where's Olli?"

"Apologies are tendered for her absence," Kittering explained. "Complex matters are afoot. Also to some small extent a war. Of the trade variety. There was in addition a feeling that her presence here on Berlenhof might not be welcome." Kit jabbed Havaer with a leg.

The Mordant House man had been talking with Solace but, true to his skillset, he'd been eavesdropping too. "It is," he admitted, "a diplomatically complicated situation. And not my department any more, thank God. Her status in Hugh's eyes is currently undecided. I mean, arguably she's inherited a large number of criminals, so that's a problem. Or alternatively she's a Hegemonic citizen now, which is a different class of problem. Except she doesn't accept that's what she is, and the Essiel don't see her as one of their own either—in fact they keep turning up to insist she isn't one of theirs, while also suggesting she's kind of under their protection. I know at least five of my colleagues who are being driven to drink and ruin trying to work out exactly what that even means. So in the end, it's possible that some day Hugh will bite the bullet and actually accept that she is what she's claiming to be, which is to say the head of her own independent state. At which point she gets an embassy and is free to visit any time she likes. I'll put out the bunting myself."

"I think," Kris decided, "that you should tell Olli all that verbatim, Kit. It would give her a great deal of joy to know she's causing so many headaches."

"Indubitably," Kittering agreed cheerily. "However, you may believe it or not, but this is not her intent. Though, given chance has handed her sufficient leverage, she absolutely is her own independent state. My personal opinion: the sooner Hugh accepts this, the better."

"The United States of Olli." Kris raised her glass. "And how's Jaine?"

"Jaine has good health and happiness," Kittering confirmed. "Jaine and Olli have good health and happiness together." A curious tone, the Hanni peering over the species divide at something his species simply did not do.

Nobody had seen Ash, it turned out. Not since the clash aboard the Eye. According to Havaer, there had been some reports from here and there across the Colonial Sphere, but nothing confirmed. They would just have to wonder and wait.

*

Later, after drinks were had and chat was mostly exhausted, they meandered across the square to look at the statues. Now two of them, when there had just been the one for so long. The older of the pair was very familiar—everyone knew Saint Xavienne. The young girl standing with her hand outstretched, forbidding the Architect at Forthbridge Port.

The first Int, the natural, who had given humanity hope during the war. It had been on a central plinth further out from the door, but they'd moved it so that it was to one side, to balance out its new companion.

This one was, Kris reckoned, a terrible likeness. Oh, they'd got the face *right*, she supposed, even down to the big ears, but they'd given him a heroic look and a defiant pose which Idris had never worn in life.

She had to remind herself he was still technically *alive*, even if he was still on a bed inside the Liaison Board building, zero brain activity, and had never woken up.

Here he was, though. Idris Telemmier, hero of the Colonies. Looking less like the man and more like the actor composite they'd used to play him in the mediotypes. Around the statue's feet were...flowers, she saw. Wreaths, little tacky medals, children's toys. Printed pictures and small projections of people—those who'd been lost to the Architects, perhaps. Or people who'd gone into unspace and never come out. As though their souls were still out there, and so was Idris, who might yet guide them home.

She shivered, and then started when Andecka stepped forwards and knelt down, touching the metal of Idris's statue, and then crossing to do the same with Saint Xavienne. Her look was slightly embarrassed when she straightened up.

"For luck," she said, but Kris reckoned it wasn't that, or not just that. She'd heard the rumours, a kind of cult arising within the Intermediaries. And others too. Idris, patron saint of unspace. And not without cause. She'd tried to talk to Ints about it, but they clammed up. It was their own personal gnostic religion and she would never be a part of it.

And later, they did indeed go to one of those restaurants

she'd been hanging her nose over, and the talk relaxed into anecdotes. As she sat back to enjoy it, she thought about the crew, the *Vulture God: I believed we'd stay together.* All that time they'd been scraping from star to star and getting involved in events ludicrously beyond their pay grade, they'd been a *crew.* Except here they were, and the reality of the ship and its fortunes hadn't been gravity enough to keep them together. Not with Idris gone. Not after Olli had been presented with such an unprecedented opportunity to make her stamp on the universe. And the ship itself . . .

She'd gone to see it, before coming to the meeting. Out on the Brandt Spindle, which was where the culture bods went when they were in orbit. The Archive of Interstellar Trade and History, or the Space Museum, as everyone called it. Honestly, there were far more impressive exhibits than a battered old salvage ship, and she had the sneaking suspicion that some custodian in the future would quietly get rid of the old thing. The *Vulture God* had finally retired. Olli had donated the vessel to Hugh, and Hugh had done the decent thing and put it somewhere its story could be told. Because spacers made do, and spacers mended, but all things came to an end.

Andecka

She'd wanted to tell Kris Almier how it was, but the woman wouldn't have understood. Worse, she'd have said, "Take me there." And when Andecka refused, as any reputable Int would have, she'd have found a disreputable one somewhere to go anyway, and it would have been the end of her, immediately or eventually. Unspace was for Intermediaries. The minds of uninitiated humans didn't do well there, even now. The loneliness, the strangeness, the immensity. You went places, and you couldn't guide yourself back. Andecka had seen it happen.

Her siblinghood, though. The Colonial Ints of all classes, the Partheni in their machines, they knew.

She'd wanted to thank Kris too. Because she was doing what most of the Ints themselves were in no position to. She was fighting to unpick the leash contracts and change the law, to make life better for all Ints, because of that one Int who'd been her friend. And Andecka could feel change coming. Ints were talking now, whereas before they'd always been tightly controlled and segregated. The hands that wrote the contracts and held the whip and the scalpel were going to have to compromise, or else there would be a whole new war coming. But right now, because of people like Kris, Andecka was hopeful it would be peace and freedom.

She went straight to her ship after that odd little reunion. The fancy eatery, the bright clothes, the richness of it all. But she was a spacer at heart. She was Cartography Corps, which had been a holy terror for Ints since their inception and was now something else. To Andecka, it was closer to a religious observance.

She was one of the last on board the *Zheng He*. Cartography vessels never had large crews, but as well as the vital Int navigator, they had their planetary geologist, their xenobiologist, a handful of other specialists and the mission captain. She regarded them all proprietarily. Until she'd done her job, they were nothing more than cargo.

After the rigmarole of pre-flight checks, they were ready

to go—a handful of Throughway steps through unspace and then out into the void. Andecka could have gone into suspension for each step if she'd wanted, saving herself for the real work. However, she tended not to, these days.

Once they were clear enough of Berlenhof's mass shadow, and the rest of the crew were showing as asleep, she let the *Zheng He* slide into unspace smooth as butter, not even a gravitic ripple.

Her mind expanded out, feeling that great chasming immensity, the world under the world. Her imagination painted it as a vast cathedral space, the boundary to the real the bright colours of stained glass. And here she was, a sparrow in the hollowness of god, listening for the echo.

She knew that echo of old. Back before, it had been the terror of every Intermediary. That moment when the abyss gazed back, and then began to rise towards her, hungry, appalling. She'd fled it so often.

Back before.

It rose towards her now, sluggish, waking. Sensing the intrusion into its domain, just as it must do a thousand times a second, all across the universe. All those Intermediary-analogues, the Castigar and the Ogdru and the unspace-capable species humanity had never met. All navigating the same subuniversal space. Under the all-seeing eye of that singular monster.

Even now she braced for the fear, because years of running in terror conditions you like that. But it wasn't how things went now.

She felt the beast, its vast and distant scrutiny, its warning. *Do not stay too long in this place. It will erode you.* The great fear swelled towards her, broke like a cresting wave, and then

587

following on its back she felt it: the love. The kindred feeling. Companionship and empathy. The echo of a man who had done what she did, known these terrible spaces, and had blunted their edges for all who came after.

Out beyond him, their thoughts bouncing to her from the hide of the leviathan as though it was a sounding board, were the other Ints. If she strained, she could hear their voices. If she called in just the right way, they could hear hers too. Like whales in Earth's ancient seas, crying each to each across the depths.

She made her nod to the man who had put a collar on the Presence, or become a part of it, she couldn't be sure. Who carried them all from star to star, watched over them, guided them and united them. Saint Idris, patron guardian of unspace. Because of him, they were none of them alone here any more.

THE UNIVERSE OF SHARDS: REFERENCE

Glossary

Architects—moon-sized entities that can reshape populated planets and ships

Aspirat—Partheni intelligence services

The Betrayed—the violent extremist wing of the Nativists

Broken Harvest—a Hegemonic criminal cartel

Cognosciente—Partheni title signifying technical competence

Colonies—the surviving human worlds following the fall of Earth

Council of Human Interests ("Hugh")—the governing body of the Colonies

Hegemony—a coalition of species ruled by the alien Essiel

Hegemonic cult—humans who serve and worship the Essiel

Hierograve—a senior rank within the Hegemonic Cult

Intermediaries—surgically modified navigators who can pilot ships off the Throughways, developed as weapons against the Architects during the war

Intermediary Program—Colonial wartime body responsible for creating the Intermediaries

Intervention Board ("Mordant House")—Colonial policing and intelligence service

Kybernet—an AI system responsible for overseeing a planet or orbital

Liaison Board—current Colonial body responsible for creating Intermediaries en masse for commercial purposes

Nativists—a political movement that believes in "pure-born" humans and "humanity first"

Orbital—an orbiting habitat

Parthenon—a breakaway human faction composed of parthenogenetically grown women

Throughways—paths constructed within unspace by unknown hands, joining habitable planets. Without a special navigator, ships can only travel along existing Throughways

Unspace—a tenuous layer beneath real space which can be used for fast travel across the universe

Voyenni—the house guard of a Magdan noble

Characters
Crew of the *Vulture God*

Rollo Rostand—captain, deceased
Idris Telemmier—Intermediary navigator
Keristina "Kris" Soolin Almier—lawyer
Olian "Olli" Timo—drone specialist
Kittering "Kit"—Hannilambra factor
Myrmidon Executor Solace—Partheni soldier and agent

Other key characters

Ahab—Naeromathi visionary and engineer
Ahremon—Tothiat
The Unspeakable Aklu, the Razor and the Hook—Essiel
  gangster
Archer—Liaison Board Intermediary
Colvari—Hiver data analyst
Diljat—Mordant House agent
Max Dreidel—lawyer
Doctor Elis—Liaison Board doctor
Emersen—Mordant House official
Arkela Farreaux—Colonial diplomat
Cognosciente Superior Felicity—Partheni scientist
Doctor Frye—Liaison Board doctor
Gethiel—Hegemonic cult hierograve
Cognosciente Grave—Partheni technician
Exemplar Hallow—master of the *Judicious Valkyrie*
Heremon—Tothiat in Aklu's employ
Hiver Assembly in Aggregate
Captain Hossgarde—master of the *Ironwriter*
Tokamak Jaine—engineer
Junior—Ogdru navigator
Chief Laery—Havaer's superior in the Intervention Board
Andecka Tal Mar—Colonial Intermediary
Exemplar Mercy—Partheni commander
Doctor Mirabilis—Liaison Board doctor
Havaer Mundy—Intervention Board agent
Doctor Sang Sian Parsefer—founder of the Parthenon
His Wisdom the Bearer Sathiel—Hegemonic cult hiero-
  grave

Doctor Haleon Shinandri—maverick scientist
Randall Sleit—Nativist
Staven—Colonial pilot
Monitor Superior Tact—Solace's superior in the Aspirat
Xavienne "Saint Xavienne" Torino—the first Intermediary, deceased
Delegate Trine—Hiver archaeologist
Demi Ulo—Intermediary, first class
Boyarin Piter Tchever Uskaro—nobleman from Magda
Morzarin Ravin Okosh Uskaro—nobleman from Magda, Piter's uncle
The Resplendent Utir, the Prophet and the Judge—divine Essiel

Worlds

Arc Pallator—Hegemonic world
Assur—Colonial world
Berlenhof—administrative and cultural heart of the Colonies
Criccieth's Hell—deathworld
Crux—Hiver industrial world
Desecrat—Hegemonic world
Earth—world destroyed by the Architects
Estoc—Colonial site of the ark fleet shipyards
Far Lux—where Intermediaries ended the war
Forthbridge Port—where Saint Xavienne first managed to contact an Architect
Grand Imperial Litskwa—minor Colonial world
Jericho—wild planet rich in Originator ruins

Lassacar—Colonial world

Magda—powerful Colonial world dominated by landed families.

New Kismayo—minor Colonial mining world

Oscit Niariken—Hannilambra world

Scherm's World—uninhabited Colonial world

Scintilla—planet noted for its legal schools and duelling code

The Seat of Record—Hegemonic administrative system

Tulmac—Colonial world

Upsandi—Colonial world

Species

Ash—the Harbinger, a singular alien that brought warning of the Architects to Earth

Athamir—fungal-looking species subject to the Essiel

Castigar—alien species with several castes and shapes, naturally wormlike

Essiel—the "divine" masters of the Hegemony

Hannilambra ("Hanni")—crab-shaped aliens, enthusiastic merchants

Hivers—composite cyborg insect intelligences, originally created by humans but now independent

Naeromathi ("Locusts")—nomadic aliens that deconstruct worlds to create more of their "Locust Arks"

Ogdru—species from the Hegemony that produces void-capable navigators

Originators—hypothetical elder race responsible for the Throughways and certain enigmatic ruins

Tothiat—hybrid of the symbiotic Tothir and another species, often human. Phenomenally resilient

Tymeree—diminutive species subject to the Essiel

Ships

Almighty Scythe of Morning—flagship belonging to the Broken Harvest cartel

Angel Alecto—Partheni warship repurposed for transport

Beagle—Colonial science vessel

Broken Key—Colonial diplomatic yacht

Ceres—Partheni garden ship

Counter-War Vessel DKT26—Colonial warship

Cythaera—Partheni warship

Gadfly—Mordant House runabout

Garelli's Storm—Colonial warship

The Glory Before Night Has Come—Hegemonic diplomatic vessel

Grampus—Colonial warship

Gran Brigitte—Partheni warship

Grand Nikolas—Ravin Uskaro's personal flagship

Heaven's Sword—Partheni warship, both the original that was destroyed at Berlenhof and its replacement currently in service

The Host—composite alien vessel

Ironwriter—Colonial warship

Ishtar—Partheni garden ship

Judicious Valkyrie—Partheni warship

Lady Gray—Partheni warship

Leopard—Colonial warship

Medea—Partheni warship

Medusa—Partheni warship

Queen of Aragon—Partheni warship

Raptorid—private yacht of Boyarin Piter Uskaro

Razor's Edge—Hegemonic punitive vessel (unofficial designation)

Redcap—Colonial warship

Retarius—Colonial warship

Skathi—Partheni warship

Skipjack—Colonial runabout

Vulture God—salvage vessel

TIMELINE

107 Before: Probes sent by Earth to neighbouring star systems attract the attention of an alien ship. Humanity's first alien contact follows shortly afterwards. Once the initial revulsion at the wormlike Castigar fades, humans begin to learn about unspace, Throughways and the wider universe. The Castigar themselves have only been travelling between stars for under a century and have a practice of making small colonies on many planets, but not engaging in large-scale colonization. Castigar ships reach deals to ferry Earth colonists to habitable worlds they have discovered. They also give humans some details about the Naeromathi and the Hegemony.

91 Before: Humans establish their first interstellar colony on Second Dawn, a planet with a dense ecosystem of plant/fungus-like life. Second Dawn is pleasantly balmy for the Castigar but proves difficult for humans.

90 Before: Humans establish a colony on Berlenhof, a warm world with 90% ocean coverage. This thrives and is patronized by a number of powerful companies and rich families.

88 Before: A colony is established on Lief, an ice world in a system with valuable minerals in several asteroid belts. A colony is also established on Amber, a hot world with a crystalline ecosystem where humans live in cooled domes.

75 Before: Several minor colonies are established in other systems with Castigar help, mostly for industrial purposes. Reliance on the Castigar for all shipping is becoming problematic to expanding humanity, and to the Castigar. Castigar scientists work with humans to help them build their own gravitic drives.

72 Before: The first human gravitic drive spaceship, the *Newton's Bullet*, opens the door to a greater era of human colonization.

61 Before: On the forested world of Lycos, humans discover their first Originator ruins.

45 Before: A Naeromathi Ark arrives in the colonized Cordonier system and begins dismantling some of the inhabited world's moons. Contact goes poorly and degenerates into fighting. There is never a formal Naeromathi–human war, as there is not really a Naeromathi state to declare war on. However, other Ark ships are seen across the Throughway network, and there are several clashes, with losses on both sides.

25 Before: Contact is made with the Essiel Hegemony as a result of human travel and expansion. Initial contact is not hostile but humans find it baffling as they and the Essiel fail to understand one another. Human diplomats recognize that the

Essiel appear to be offering humans some kind of master–subject relationship. However, they are confused that it does not appear to be accompanied by threats. In retrospect, warnings about the Architects were present, but not grasped. Over the next decades, human emissaries understand that the Hegemony appears to value Originator ruins, though not displaced Originator relics. Several worlds with Originator sites are effectively sold to the Hegemony as a result.

22 Before: As a response to conditions on Earth, and what she sees as deep flaws in human nature, Doctor Sang Sian Parsefer and her allies found the Parthenon. They genetically engineer what they consider to be an ideal version of humanity. The Parthenon is founded as a military force and uses parthenogenetic vat birth as a means of creating human beings artificially. This happens more swiftly than natural means would allow. The Parthenon pushes the limits of human science and is viewed as a threat by the rest of humanity.

5 Before: A Castigar ship brings the alien Ash to Earth, warning of the arrival of the Architects. Few take him seriously; the Castigar themselves have not encountered the Architects. But some nations and groups do make limited preparations.

0: An Architect larger than Earth's moon exits unspace close to Earth. It reworks the planet into the bizarre, coiling structure now familiar to all, causing appalling loss of life and tearing the heart out of the human race. Every space-worthy ship evacuates as many people as it can carry, but billions are left behind to die. The ships flee to various colony worlds. Some reach them, others founder, insufficiently prepared for the voyage. The Polyaspora begins, as does the First Architect War.

15 After: The largest solar system colony on Titan is deconstructed by the Architects around 7AE. Over the next few years, several extrasolar colonies are also reworked. Every human colony is on high alert, with evacuation measures in place as standard. Many colonies become short on food and supplies. Attempts to fight the Architects fail even to attract their notice.

21 After: The small religious colony on Charm Prime establishes communication with Hegemony envoys and becomes the first human Hegemonic cult cell. In return, the Hegemony establishes a shrine, and their human cult declares that the Hegemony can ward off Architects. The majority of other colonies do not believe this, and some claim the Hegemony controls or can even summon Architects to scare humanity into accepting alien overlords. There is little human take-up of Hegemonic rule for the next few decades.

28 After: Experiments in autonomous distributed intelligence, originally intended as a resource-stripping tool, are turned to the war effort. And so the first Hive entity is developed and added to humanity's arsenal.

43 After: In the midst of war, the first Hannilambra–human contact occurs, with Hanni venture ships narrowly escaping a hostile response when they turn up at Clerk's World. The Hanni subsequently create a sporadic lifeline of goods, at cost, to beleaguered human colonies. They also transport humans from colonies under threat.

48 After: Architects at Lycos leave without touching the colony. From this and other clues it becomes clear that the Architects do indeed have some relationship with Originator sites and their relics. The shrine at Charm Prime is found to contain Originator relics and there is a doomed attempt to use these to repel Architects from other colonies by simply transporting them offworld. After the destruction of Karis Commune, whose inhabitants relied on relics taken from Charm Prime, the Hegemony manages to communicate dire news: only they can transport relics in a manner that retains their anti-Architect properties. Between now and the end of the war, a number of human colonies will accept Hegemonic rule in return for such protection.

51 After: The Architects come to Amraji, a large human–Castigar colony swollen with refugees. There is a considerable human military force in place already, owing to the arrival and depredations of a Naeromathi Ark. Parthenon, Hive and regular human forces attack the Architect to buy the evacuation more time and the Naeromathi joins the battle on humanity's side. Combined efforts allow over half the colony's population to escape off-planet. However, this initiative also results in the majority of the defenders being destroyed, including the Ark. The "Amraji Peace" is no more a formal human–Naeromathi détente than the hostilities were a war. But from here onwards, fighting between humans and Naeromathi will be minimal.

During these years, at the height of the First Architect War, humanity is living hand to mouth under the constant shadow of annihilation. Everyone lives with an emergency bag and a knowledge of where to go if the worst happens. The entire species suffers from a multigenerational traumatic shock.

68 After: A refugee transport, the *Mylender*, arrives at Forthbridge Port at the same time as an Architect. Aboard is Xavienne Torino, aged 15, who claims that she can hear the Architect's thoughts. Through a process that is entirely mysterious at the time, Xavienne is able to demand that the Architect leaves the system. To everyone's astonishment, it does.

76 After: Human scientists work with Xavienne Torino to isolate the precise genetic and neurological fluke that allowed her to interact with the Architects by way of unspace. By 76AE, the first generation of artificial Intermediaries has been developed. Of the suitable volunteers, fewer than ten per cent survive the process and come out sane. Idris, one of the first generation, is twenty years old when he completes the program.

78 After: Battle of Berlenhof. The wealthiest and most populous human world detects the approach of an Architect—and military forces race to intervene. The full force of the Parthenon Navy, several Hive lattices, human regular forces and alien allies fight to preserve the world. The defenders pay a colossal cost but top-of-the-line Partheni weapons are able to damage the Architect. Early use of Intermediaries also appears to be effective. However, of the eight Ints deployed, three are killed and another two go insane trying to contact the Architect. Yet Berlenhof is saved.

In the next six years, the Architects destroy two more human colonies. In each case, a spirited defence only buys time for a more thorough evacuation.

80 After: The Intermediary Program reaches its greatest strength with thirty combat Intermediaries. Their training builds on the lessons learned at Berlenhof. They begin meeting the Architects when they manifest, making contact, trying to get the creatures to notice them. Their attempts prove more and more successful.

84 After: Intermediary successes culminate with Idris and two other Ints contacting an Architect at Far Lux. They report that the enemy was momentarily aware of them this time. After this event, there are no further Architect sightings.

As people realize that the war has finally finished, three generations after it started, human society and economy are in a poor way. People are desperate; colonies are under-resourced and overpopulated. There is no real political unity and friction develops between needy colonies and alien neighbours. Growing discontent seems likely to fragment the Polyasporic human presence into dozens of feuding states.

88 After: The Council of Human Interests or "Hugh" is formed. This happens when the various human colonies come together to prevent internecine war and to regulate their affairs. The initial line-up does not include many smaller colonies. It also excludes expatriate communities within alien colonies, who will be given a voice at a later stage. However, it does include both the Parthenon and human colonies that have sworn fealty to the Hegemony.

96 After: The Hivers, the cyborg intelligence developed during the war, remain under human control but elements of this distributed intelligence find ways to demand independence and self-determination. There are several brutal human crackdowns on Hive cells that refuse to perform their functions. The Hive cites its service during the war as a reason to grant it independence.

103 After: Human worlds sworn to the Hegemony make vocal attempts at proselytizing, including some terrorist activity. Following this, Hugh votes to exclude human colonies that have sworn allegiance to the Hegemony from its ranks. There are fears that a war with the Essiel will result, but this never manifests. The Hegemony's stated policy, as translated by its human mouthpieces, remains that the Hegemony is ready to accept the fealty of any who wish to join it.

105 After: The political struggle over the future of the Hivers comes to a head, as the Parthenon faction demands it be released from human control. The decision to allow this, forced through by Parthenon military superiority, is contentious. The Hivers are released from service and promptly evacuate to worlds outside human control and unsuitable for human colonization. The Hive's initial contacts with its former masters are almost entirely through the Parthenon. Over time, Hive elements will re-enter human space and commerce to offer their services and skills.

107 After: More than twenty years after the war, the first stirrings of the Nativist movement are felt. This manifests as increased hostility towards alien powers, especially the Hegemony. It also shows in antagonistic behaviour towards human elements seen as deviating from a "traditional" human lifestyle, especially the Parthenon. Hugh has only been in existence for nineteen years at this point, and many human colonies are still in very bad shape. Many traditionally born humans believe that the Parthenon intends to impose its "unnatural" way of life on all of humanity at gunpoint. Others fear that the Hive will take revenge for their previous servitude. Another popular Nativist belief is that Hegemonic cultists—both overt and hidden—are a fifth column on many worlds, aiming to manipulate governments into submitting to alien overlords. There are riots, demonstrations, coups and populist movements.

109 After: The Betrayed movement starts to gain traction. They spread the story that the Architects could have been fully defeated save that certain parties struck a deal to limit human expansion and power for their own benefit. They include amongst these "betrayers" the Intermediaries, Parthenon agents and aliens. The Betrayed fan the flames of anti-Parthenon and anti-Hegemony feeling and enact several terrorist attacks against Parthenon citizens.

110 After: The Parthenon officially secedes from Hugh, declaring its fleet and colonies a state outside traditional human control. War is feared but does not materialize, and diplomatic relations are maintained. As a result, relations become perhaps less fraught than in the last few years of the Parthenon's Hugh membership.

Over the next decade, human colonial life slowly improves, but political differences become ever more divisive. Hugh's ability to influence the recovering colonies decreases, as more extreme and populist factions take over. The larger and more powerful colonies form a relatively self-interested core. On the fringes of human space, there is a rich melting pot of humans and aliens prospecting, salvaging, colonizing and exploring.

123 After: The Architects return, destroying Far Lux and then arriving at Berlenhof. In the second battle of Berlenhof, Idris Telemmier reaches a communion with the attacking Architect, sending it away. Immediately afterwards, Telemmier defects to the Parthenon, to general condemnation across the Colonies.

124 After: With Telemmier's help, the Parthenon develops its own class of Intermediaries. Tensions between Parthenon, Colonies and Hegemony rise over events at Arc Pallator, a world later destroyed by the Architects. War between the Parthenon and the Colonies finally erupts after an apparent first strike by Colonial forces against the garden ship *Ceres*. However, a fragile peace is brokered after this provocation is pinned on a Colonial faction who want to push the Parthenon and Colonies into crippling each other, so that their own plans to abandon humanity in their ark fleet can come to fruition. A Cartel, made up of Colonial, Partheni and non-human interests, takes over the ark shipyard as the headquarters for its own anti-Architect mission.

125 After: Present day

ACKNOWLEDGEMENTS

As always, I owe a huge debt of gratitude to Simon and Oliver at the Mic Cheetham Agency, as well as everyone at Pan Macmillan who has worked so hard to bring this book to you. Most of all, though, thank you to everyone who's received this series so enthusiastically!